HEAT OF PASSION

HAROLD ROBBINS

has also written

NEVER LOVE A STRANGER

THE DREAM MERCHANTS

A STONE FOR DANNY FISHER

NEVER LEAVE ME

THE CARPETBAGGERS

79 PARK AVENUE

NEVER ENOUGH

SIN CITY

HEAT OF PASSION

Harold Robbins

ROBERT HALE · LONDON

© 2003 Jann Robbins
First published in Great Britain 2004

ISBN 0 7090 7592 8

Robert Hale Limited
Clerkenwell House
Clerkenwell Green
London EC1R 0HT

This is a work of fiction. All the characters and events portrayed
in this novel are either fictitious or are used fictitiously

2 4 6 8 10 9 7 5 3 1

Typeset in 10½/13½pt Baskerville
by Derek Doyle & Associates in Liverpool.
Printed in Great Britain by
St Edmundsbury Press Ltd, Bury St Edmunds, Suffolk.
Bound by Woolnough Bookbinding Ltd.

'Look!' he repeated, hoarsely, holding the lamp over the open chest. We looked and for a moment could make nothing out, on account of the silvery sheen that dazzled us. When our eyes got used to it, we saw the chest was three parts full of uncut diamonds, most of them of considerable size. Stooping, I picked some up. Yes, there was no mistake about it, there was the unmistakable soapy feel about them.

'We are the richest men in the whole world,' I said.

'Hee! Hee! Hee!' went old Gagool behind us, as she flitted around like a vampire bat. 'There are the bright stones that ye love, white men, as many as ye will; take them, run them through your fingers, *eat* of them, hee! hee! *drink* of them. . . .'

—*King Solomon's Mines*

PART 1

THE
HEART
OF THE
WORLD

1

Win Liberte, Beverly Hills, 1997

The phone next to the bed rang and Jonny stirred beside me, her bare leg cocked over my thigh, her knee warm pressed against my groin. I had the Heart of the World in my hand and I wasn't in any hurry to answer the phone. I knew who was calling. It was the front desk informing me I had a visitor.

I held the walnut-size diamond between my thumb and fingers, letting it catch the morning light from the window. Pieces of stars, that's what diamonds were, the hardest substance on earth with fire a billion years old trapped inside. And no diamond on earth had more fire than the one I was holding – a forty-one-carat blood diamond. Not the 'blood' of conflict diamonds that fueled African civil wars, but a rare fire-red diamond. It was a gem with a history. Murder, lust, greed – the worst of the deadly sins – were part of its pedigree.

There was no other diamond like it in the world.

Vanity and greed, that's what they say the diamond industry is based upon. And that the human race could be relied upon for an endless supply of both. The stone I held in my hand was able to fuel explosive levels of both vices.

My visitor wanted the diamond. She was part of the history. Not the part where kings who possessed it lost their thrones, but war, murder, lust were contributions she made to the diamond's bloody history.

The phone rang again and Jonny pushed her knee harder against my groin, sending a shot of desire through me.

'Answer it,' she said.

'It's your mother.'

'Fuck her.'

I have.

'Send her up,' I told the caller.

Jonny rolled over onto her other side. Her name in Portugal was Juana, but at the Sacred Heart Academy in Beverly Hills, she was known as Jonny. At eighteen, her body was taut, skin tight, golden brown, kissed by the Lisbon sun. Her breasts were small and firm, honey melons with rosy nipples that always looked like they were excited. Young, beautiful, wild. She reminded me of a young lioness cub I saw once in Africa, big enough to rip with teeth and claws but who needed a warm stomach to snuggle up to at night.

I started to get up and Jonny grabbed my cock and pulled me back down.

'Fuck me before she comes up. I want her to smell my cunt on you.'

I pushed her away. 'Jonny, you're too much for me, I need a grown woman who isn't going to wear the point off my pecker.'

I felt sorry for kids her age, kids who are light years away from their parents and anyone else over thirty. Older people have nostalgia for the good old days, but there are no good old days for people nurtured in a culture of sex and drugs. What do they talk about when they meet up with old friends? The times they were getting high together? Getting laid? The first rave party they attended? Raised in an era when *Baywatch* plastic sexiness was confused with sensuality, Jonny's generation was one in which a good-night kiss often started with the guy unzipping his pants, a generation that didn't believe in Santa Claus and whose dreams were all digital.

She came to me last night, in pain from being young. I put her to bed on the couch. In the middle of the night, she snuck in my room and crawled into bed with me, needing a warm stomach to snuggle against. Sometime during the night she slipped under the covers and down between my legs, cuddling my penis, slipping it into her mouth while it was still asleep, letting it wake up and get excited as she sucked on it.

I slipped on a robe and went into the suite's living room. I pulled the door to the hallway corridor open a few inches. I had already opened the drapes and was calling room service for coffee when Simone pushed the door open.

She stood at the doorway for a moment while we looked at each other. She hadn't changed in the three years since I'd last seen her. Neither had I. She still made my blood pound.

11

Unlike Jonny's thin, hard body, Simone's body was fleshy, padded succulently so a man could get something in his teeth. She aroused me infinitely more than her daughter. Simone's body was a fine wine, to be savored and enjoyed for hours. She stirred prurient thoughts in me that Jonny never could. When Jonny's tight body clamped onto my cock with her cunt, it was like being squeezed by a vise. She was exciting, but making love to her mother was provocative and memorable – if you survived the foreplay.

While Juana was an overgrown kitten, her mother was definitely a full-grown lioness, able to hunt and kill on her own. She was a few years older than me, in her late thirties, a time in a woman's life when she's the sexiest and the most desirable, when she's replaced the thin brightness of youth with plush sensuality.

Her Latin blood was hot enough to fuel cars at the Indy 500. She was dangerous, but not in a crazy way. Her crimes were always cool and premeditated. When she wanted something, she took it. And you had to count your fingers afterward if you were holding it when she grabbed because she would take them, too.

'You look good,' she said, stepping in, closing the door behind her. 'Rich, successful, not at all the boy I once seduced.'

'Life has been good. I've got money, health, envy – everything but a good woman. Good ones who will tolerate me are rare.'

'You're probably looking in the wrong places. The gossip magazines call you a Hollywood playboy.'

I laughed. 'I think you have to be a movie star or at least buy a studio before that label sticks.'

'You forgot to say good-bye,' she said, moving by me, toward the open doors to the balcony.

'I was too busy running from the Portuguese Mafia.'

She stepped out onto the balcony. My Bel Air hotel suite looked out onto a tropical garden lush with shaded dark green ferns and sun-loving purple bougainvillea, the kind of stuff that grew well in the Southern California desert climate. The sunlight glowed through her white dress, outlining her body.

'White's a deceptive color for you to wear,' I said.

'I could take the dress off if you prefer.'

She knew me. That's the trouble with being a man – women know we think more with our testosterone than brain juices.

'Last time we tried that you took off everything but a gun.'

She came closer, near enough for me to feel her body heat, to smell the sex in her perfume. Women didn't wear perfume to make them smell sweet, but to stimulate a man's sex drive. Wasn't some guy named Odysseus held captive by a sweet-smelling woman? He wasn't the first or last guy to get bowled over by the scent of a woman.

I knew this woman was trouble – she'd tried to kill me once – but I guess it was like the fascination some people got playing with deadly snakes – the danger just made it more exciting.

'I've missed you, Win,' she said.

'You know where I've been. You stayed in Lisbon.'

'You don't understand loyalty,' she said. 'You were an only child, then an orphan; you've never had anyone to be loyal to. João took me off the streets, away from selling my body for food and drugs when I was younger than Jonny.'

'He's old enough to be your grandfather. And you've fucked everyone around him, from his lawyer to his chauffeur and friends.'

'I have a woman's needs, but I've always been there for him. When he dies, I'll cry at his grave. He knows that.'

'That makes you a regular Mother Theresa. Congratulations – now what do you want?'

'Do you have it? I'd like to see it, see what all the fuss is about.'

I hesitated. I was expecting this, thinking about it since I got the call. I wasn't afraid she would grab it and run. Simone wasn't stupid or amateurish – she'd be more likely to pull a gun out of her bra and shoot me between the eyes. Something else bothered me – the simple truth was that I had a hard time sharing the stone because of plain, old-fashioned greed. Maybe the gem carried a greed virus and infected everyone who touched it. Whatever it was, the fire diamond affected everyone that way. Like a sorcerer's stone, its mysterious magic cast spells.

Ask the people who had killed for it – or died because of it.

I took the Heart of the World out of my robe pocket and gave it to her.

She held it up to the light. 'My God, it's a piece of fire.'

'Fire of the gods, hurled down from a star. It's almost as old as the earth itself. It took a billion years to make and a billion more to find.'

'I've never seen a ruby-red diamond before,' she said.

'They're rare. They have one sitting near the Hope Diamond at the Smithsonian, but it's smaller and not as brilliant as the Heart. There's no other diamond like it.'

'I heard that computer billionaire who bought a Hawaiian island has

13

offered you a fortune for it. Are you going to sell it?'

She was cloaked in innocence, as if we both didn't know she'd come to Los Angeles for the stone. If she was in town, João was here, too. And he would never give up until he had the fire diamond – or one of us was dead.

'I don't know.'

But I did know. I couldn't sell it, any more than I could chop off an arm or leg and put it on the market. It wasn't like money to me, money was meant to be spent; it was something I've done without and can do without again. Diamonds are like sex: you never forget and never stop regretting good sex if you give it up. And this one was like owning the *Mona Lisa*. There was nothing comparable.

'João thought of you as a son, you've hurt him very much.'

'I'm sorry, it must have been the bullets flying by from his thugs that caused me to be ungrateful.'

'You don't understand, you never did. João was trying to protect you. He still wants to do something for you.'

'He can. He can die soon. That would help us both, wouldn't it?'

I took the diamond from her and she came closer. She pulled open my robe and wrapped her cold fingers around my cock. My blood pounded. Her lips brushed mine. My blood ignited and I felt the lead rising in my pencil. I wanted to push her away, but I was weak.

'I missed you,' she whispered.

'Hello, Mother.'

Jonny stood in the bedroom doorway, naked.

Simone's eyes came back to me.

I shrugged. 'She dropped by on her way home from school for cookies and milk.'

Simone and Jonny left, bickering, bitching at each other about times and places and things that meant nothing to me. And without the diamond. But the game had just begun – again. Simone would be back. She knew how to please a man, stroking his cock like it was her best friend. Until she got what she wanted. Then she'd bite it off.

The coffee came. I stood on the balcony and drank the steaming hot liquid, thinking about the past. New York. Lisbon. Africa.

There was something alien to me now about those times and places, like 'past lives' the Buddhists talked about, and there was a surreal quality to my memories.

Christ, if that past-life stuff was true, I must have been an ax murderer in a prior life to deserve what I've been handed in this one.

A woman wearing a tennis outfit came by and gave me the look. But I wasn't in a mood for women in white today.

LIFE'S A BITCH AND THEN YOU DIE, some bumper-strip wit once said. I never thought of life as a struggle, not even when the chips were down and my luck was running south. But I had learned something about myself, something that would sound strange to the people who'd been around me. I had been running scared most of my life. That's why I always went for the gold with everything I'd ever done, why it had always been all or nothing with me – Win wasn't just my name, it was how I lived.

I'd spent my whole life living like there was no tomorrow.

Maybe there wasn't.

PART 2

NEW YORK

2

Win Liberte, Long Island, 1971

When I was a kid, there was this quirky thing about the JFK assassination. People always knew exactly where they had been when they heard the news that Kennedy was killed. My father told me he was bending over a diamond at his office at West Forty-seventh and Fifth Avenue in Manhattan, studying it with a jeweler's loupe, when one of his associates ran into the room and told him Kennedy had been shot. Uncle Bernie claimed he was on the pot reading good news on the racing page – Last Chance had come in the money in the third at Belmont – when his secretary threw open the door and screamed that the president was dead.

I had the easiest recollection of all. On 22 November, 1963, I was in a taxicab on Broadway being born. My mother had taken the cab from the family apartment on the Lower East Side, to tell my father it was time to take her to the hospital. I had bad timing in arriving late, with the meter running, a trait I'd maintained all my life.

The death of Kennedy stuck with me throughout my childhood. It seemed like no other president could live up to him, could instill the confidence that he created in people. I must have heard my father say a hundred times during the Johnson and Nixon administrations, 'If Kennedy was alive . . .'

I've never had an interest in politics, so I don't know if Kennedy was a great president or a Great Hope for people. But like people whose dreams of a great America died with him, dreams died hard for me, too.

When I was eight years old my father took me out of the crowded living room – by now we'd moved to Long Island – and into the small office he kept at home. He was a diamantaire. That's what people in the industry

18

called a diamond dealer, those international close-to-the-chest back-roomers, who buy and sell diamonds in the half-dozen great diamond exchanges of the world.

Most of the diamonds my father traded were roughs – uncut stones from the mines with dirt literally still on them. It was a hard business, one of the toughest in the world, a white-knuckle trade in which a bad call on a big stone could put you out on the ledge of your office building, ten stories up, looking down at the street, wondering what it was going to feel like kissing the pavement at a hundred miles an hour.

My father handled the business well, with quiet strength. He wasn't the type to get excited or angry during negotiations – he was more cerebral than most of the dealers I've seen in action. You could almost see the gears moving in his head when he was evaluating a deal. He told me that his father taught him to watch a buyer's eyes, that when they saw something they really liked, the pupils would get a little bigger. That kind of explains my father, a subtle man who could make a major decision based on an almost infinitesimal change in an eye.

As I followed my father through the living room, the conversations around us were subdued, not the laughter and loud talk you usually got when my parents had people over. My mother was Portuguese, while my father, Victoir, called himself a Gypsy because he was living in America after being born in Warsaw, raised in Marseilles, and married in Lisbon. The name Liberté was one my grandfather adopted in France after leaving the Warsaw ghettos behind, his Jewish–Polish name being a foot long. My own father dropped the accent over the 'e' when he came to America. Assimilating, it was called. But he still pronounced the name 'Lib-er-tay.'

My mother was beautiful, with soft red hair, warm brown eyes, and pearl skin. I inherited her eyes and a red tint to my own brownish hair. I remember her as quiet and delicate. She never raised her voice but she commanded the household with the velvet iron of her will. My father never disagreed with her, at least never in my presence, and I never heard him raise his voice to her.

Kids don't really understand the love their parents have for each other. It wasn't until I grew up and loved a woman myself that I understood how much my mother meant to my father. In those days, I really only understood how much she meant to me.

My father always treated my mother with an old-fashioned gentleness and respect, almost as if she was something more than a wife to him.

Maybe he treated her a little different because he was quite a bit older than she. In many ways, he handled her with the gentleness of a fragile flower that blooms for only a short time. They didn't know she had a heart condition until she became pregnant with me and was told by her doctor never to risk another pregnancy. But she had always been fragile. In his quiet, analytical way, I think he intuitively knew that some day he would lose her.

Inside his home office, my father opened an old safe that had ACME SAFE COMPANY written on the door and removed a cigar box. From the box he took a piece of white paper folded seven times to create a pocket for a gem. He turned on the desk light and had me sit on his knee as he unfolded the paper to reveal a two-carat diamond. It glistened and sparkled, fifty-eight facets turning 'white' light into sparkling brilliance. Diamonds had the power to gather, bend, and throw off brilliant colors. A well-cut, clear diamond is so alive with light and color, it appears to be a blaze of glittering fire. I guess that's why diamonds are called the 'flame of love.' And yeah, if you're the cynical type, maybe they call it that because so many men figure they have something coming in return for dropping a rock on a woman.

'I met your mother in Lisbon in fifty-seven,' my father said. 'She was sitting at a sidewalk café on the Rossio, the main square in the heart of the city. I hadn't been back to the city since the war ended. It had been an exciting place during the war, a time when Portugal was neutral and there were thousands of refugees like me, men and women who had fled the Nazis, jumping off at places like Lisbon, Istanbul, and Tangiers, in the hopes of buying false travel papers that would get them to America.

'Someday I'll show you an old movie called *Casablanca*. It'll give you an idea of what it was like in Lisbon during the war, what a desperate feeling it was to be without money or travel documents in wartime Europe. We expected at any moment that Salazar, the country's strongman, was going to side with the Nazis and turn us over to Himmler's gang of goose-steppers.

'I finally managed to get out of the country, getting into England with forged papers and then to the States. After that, I only went back to Lisbon once, to attend the funeral of an old friend, a man who had helped me during the war when I was broke and hungry, a jeweler who gave me stones on credit so I could make my first deals in Lisbon when I was a refugee with holes in my pockets. Pocket peddlers, they called us, gem sellers without an office or store, carrying our merchandise in our pockets, ready to make a deal in a bar, café, or on a street corner.

'After his funeral, I was wandering around the city, visiting old memories, when I saw her.'

He fingered his jeweler's loupe as he spoke. He always had it with him, no matter where we went. He was like a doctor with his medical bag – he never knew when someone would ask him for an opinion on a gem. Diamantaires made deals at bar mitzvahs, weddings, funerals, and when the ship was sinking.

'Your mother had been to a recital, she was a music student, a violinist, and she had just finished a performance with other students.' He gave me the loupe and a pair of tweezers. 'Look at this diamond, tell me what you see.'

I caught the diamond between the claws of the tweezers and used the loupe to examine it against the background of the white paper. I had done it before. Some kids grew up with a baseball mitt, I had a jeweler's loupe.

'It's flawless,' I said.

'Yes, it's flawless, no cracks, blemishes, nothing to diminish its beauty. It's like looking into a star. That's what I saw the first time I saw your mother. I was walking on the street when Elena looked up, smiling at something a friend had said. I looked into her eyes and I saw her heart and knew that she was the woman I would love for the rest of my life.

'Win, we Jews give our wives a flawless diamond when we marry so that the marriage will be perfect. But my marriage was perfect because the woman I married was a gem without equal.' His eyes became watery and he looked down.

I left my father hunched over the table, staring down at the diamond, looking back to that night in Lisbon when he had first seen my mother. I quietly opened the door and went into the living room. I kept along the wall, not wanting to be hugged or pampered by relatives. There was a priest talking to my mother's Portuguese relatives and a rabbi talking to my father's friends. I saw two of his business acquaintances in a corner examining a diamond. It wasn't considered impolite any more than talking about baseball would have been. It was just a business to us, it was a way of life.

I slipped into the drawing room where my mother lay. When she came home from the hospital, my father had her bed put into the room because she liked the view of the street better than the one from their bedroom in the back of the house. She had refused to stay in the hospital when her heart began to fail.

I stood beside the bed.

She was white, paler than I had ever seen her, so white her red hair looked afire. I took her hand and stared at the diamond on her finger, the ring my father gave her when they were married.

I cried when I touched her cold hand.

3

Manhattan, 1974

'What's your weight, Win?' Uncle Bernie asked me.

Bernie was my father's second cousin, but because he was so much older than me, I always referred to him as my uncle. He was a good guy, kind of loud, a little bottom heavy – he claimed it was because of gravity from sitting all day, rather than what he ate.

We were in my father's offices on West Forty-seventh Street, New York's Diamond District. The House of Liberte and a couple thousand other dealers had their offices on the one block of Forty-seventh Street running from Fifth Avenue to Avenue of the Americas. That's how the diamond industry worked, everyone clustered together, making deals in the hallway, out on the street, walking to the subway, or gnawing on a sandwich.

There was no business like it in the world – it was based upon absolute trust. A dealer's stock in trade was his word. Gems worth a small fortune were passed hand to hand by dealers who hardly knew each other – and the only thing the selling dealer got was a marker saying he'd be paid. But there was also a world of caveat emptor – you buy at your own risk whether it was dealer to dealer or retail. You could buy a diamond on West Forty-seventh Street for half the price of the prestigious stores up Fifth Avenue – Tiffany's, Bvlgari's, Harry Winston's, Cartier. Yeah, and you got what you paid for – you had to count your fingers after shaking on a deal in the Diamond District. There were plenty of dealers who 'bumped' up the gem's rating a notch or two or had 'gem certifications' with as much credibility as those preacher's licenses they sold back in the sixties as tax dodges.

It was also the most unpretentious business on the planet. Dealers dressed down, offices were frugal – sometimes I wondered if there wasn't a contest to see who could look the poorest. Maybe it had something to do with getting robbed and murdered. Men in black suits and fedoras or skull-caps walked from building to building, carrying black briefcases, often empty except for their lunch, but with a million dollars worth of gems in their coat pocket.

The buildings were as unpretentious as the people. My father's offices weren't luxurious; to the contrary, their looks were so dull and plain, they might have been the small office suite of an accountant – except that the front door was steel and the safe was six feet tall. Although there was an occasional sell to a heavyweight retail client, most of the business was wholesale, bringing in diamonds from around the world and marketing them to other middlemen who sold them down the chain until they finally reached a woman's hand in Palm Beach or Palm Springs. The way the world diamond pipeline worked, the rough stones hauled out of the mines in places like Africa and Brazil were sold and cut into gems in Antwerp, Tel Aviv, Bombay, and to a lesser extent in New York. The diamonds often passed through a number of hands before they went across the counter at a retail store and onto the ring finger of a woman.

It was a tough business. Bernie claimed to succeed at it, you needed the ability to talk a dog off a meat wagon.

We'd moved back into the city after my mother died. I came by the office most days after school and often got a lesson from my father or Bernie about the diamond business. My father said he didn't want me raised in a fishbowl because someday I'd have to swim with sharks, so he made me go to a multiracial, multicultural public school, the kind of place where you didn't let the other kids know your old man was in the diamond business because they'd figure out a way to shake you down.

'I don't know, maybe a hundred pounds, maybe a little more.'

'Wrong! You weigh two hundred twenty-five thousand carats. Remember that, my friend, not pounds, but carats.'

'People would think I'm weird if I told them my weight in diamonds.'

'Yada! Yada! Yada! You wouldn't be the first, you know. There was an Indian prince who got his weight in diamonds each year for his birthday . . . or was it gold?'

I left Bernie pondering the question of gold versus diamonds, wonder-

23

ing if the prince went on an eating binge before being weighed, and went into my father's office. His hair had turned prematurely gray after my mother died and his face took on a thin, haggard appearance as he threw off weight, making him look older than his fifty-four years. He'd been in his late thirties when he married my mother. He claimed he had waited so long to marry because he was looking for a perfect gem. He had found it and lost it. Now he seemed to be withering into an old man.

Two years after my mother died he remarried, not out of love but a sense of responsibility. He had a son to raise, was busy with his business, and felt I needed a mother. My stepmother, Rebecca, also had a son five years older than me and light years different. I would come by the Diamond District when commanded by my father, but I liked girls and my wind surfer better than cold stones. Leo's passions were diamonds and money. Some kids wanted to grow up to be a fireman or doctor, Leo wanted to be a sight holder. One of the quirks about the diamond industry was that 'the Syndicate,' the De Beers African diamond cartel, dictated so much of it, worldwide, controlling supply and demand to keep prices up. And they sold diamonds only to a select few, less than two hundred in the world had the privilege of getting an invitation to buy diamonds from the cartel. The sights were held in London and couldn't be done in the States because the Justice Department considered De Beers to be a monopoly. The rest of the unwashed mass of diamond traders bought and sold the leftovers.

My father took a rough stone from its wrapping and set it on his desk. 'Tell me what you think.'

Most parents worry about their kids learning the ABCs. With my father, I also had to learn the Four Cs: clarity, color, cut and carat-weight, when evaluating a finished gem. The Four Cs also applied as you tried to see the gem-within-the-stone when you dealt in roughs. And dealing in roughs was my father's stock-in-trade. He bought roughs, had them cut into gems, and sold them to dealers who worked the retail trade.

The best way to examine a diamond was under good light and against a white background. If it was a cut diamond, it had to be loose from its setting when examined because the gold or silver setting made it difficult to evaluate.

I started with clarity to determine how 'clean' the stone was, checking it with the naked eye to see how free it was from surface blemishes and inclusions inside. 'Flawless' is a magic word in the business, and that's where the scale started. From there it went a slide downward, from flaws too minute for an untrained person to pick up on, to ones so bad you could see them without the 10x magnification of a jeweler's loupe.

There were blemishes and inclusions visible with my naked eye. More popped up when I examined it under the loupe. No matter how the stone was cut, because there would be so many defects it would be rated down the scale, with defects visible to the naked eye when closely examined.

Next I checked its color, letting the light pass through it and onto the white paper. Some traders pull a white business card out of their pocket, fold it, and put a diamond in the fold to check its color.

With most gems – rubies, sapphires, emeralds – the more color there is, the better. Diamonds were just the opposite. The rarer and more expensive diamonds are colorless, which means they will glitter more because there's nothing blocking the light that enters. The chart starts at colorless and from there goes down the scale to various shades of yellow due to nitrogen content and ultimately to industrial diamonds. As the yellow increases, the value of the gem goes down.

A completely colorless gem was rated 'D', no A, B, or C. Going down the scale, a one-carat 'D' (colorless) could be worth four or five times what a one-carat 'M' (light yellow) was worth – but diamonds were so expensive, that a carat-sized 'M' could still cost you thousands!

The one I was examining was down toward the bottom of the color scale, a dingy yellow and cloudy.

'Tell me more about colors,' my father said.

'There's a funny thing about color – a little yellow takes the value down, but a lot of it sends it up.'

If the gem was really saturated with color, its value shot up. True canary yellows, greens, blues, and pinks were called 'fancy' diamonds, I told him. They were rare and valuable. Big fancy diamonds could sell at Christie's and Sotheby's for millions, just as paintings by the masters did.

'What about a red diamond, are they valuable?' my father asked.

'I've never seen a red diamond.'

'Most people haven't. They say there are no true ruby-reds, only red browns and dark pinks. But I had a ruby-red once, the most fiery red diamond ever found, it was like holding a piece of fire, holding a star in your hand. But that was a long time ago, before you were born, before I met your mother.'

'What happened to it?'

'It was stolen in Lisbon. But I'll never forget it. Like your mother, it was incomparable. Now, what's your evaluation of the diamond you're examining?'

'Junk,' I said. 'Bad color, the faults are so obvious I can see them without a loupe.'

'No, it's not junk. All diamonds have value, this one just isn't as valuable as some others. Even diamonds that aren't gem quality are valuable for industrial purposes. Don't get into a frame of mind that all diamonds have to be D clarity and flawless. We market different grades for different tastes and pocketbooks. A lot of jewelers claim that a man's supposed to spend two months' salary on an engagement ring. Can you imagine how tiny most rings would be if they were all perfect D's?'

'But they'd be good investments. You told me most diamonds sold in this country have too much yellow to increase in value.'

'True, but Americans like big gems, even if they're of lower quality, while the Japanese prefer high-quality gems, even if they're smaller in size. Maybe that's why we have such a high divorce rate. Tell me more about the stone. What size is it?'

I put it on a diamond scale. Diamonds were sold by weight, not physical dimensions. And having its own system of weight was another unique thing about diamonds. The word 'carat' came from 'carob,' the chocolate substitute. In India and the Mediterranean, diamonds were originally weighed by placing carob seeds on one side of a scale and diamonds on the other. I didn't know why carob seeds were chosen; maybe there was more uniformity of weight with them. In modern times, though, it wasn't a very practical method and the diamond industry ultimately standardized a 'carat' as 200 milligrams. Bernie could easily figure my weight in carats because there were 2240 carats to a pound.

In the trade, carats were further divided into 'points,' with one hundred points equaling a carat. A fifty-point diamond was half a carat, seventy-five points three-quarters, and so on.

'One hundred twelve points, a little over a carat,' I said.

'Good, but that's the weight of the unfinished stone. We need to know what it will weigh once it's cut. How would you cut it?'

That was a loaded question. What does an eleven-year-old kid know about cutting diamonds?

I took the stone to a desk off to the side and began to examine it under strong light. I knew the routine, examining the stone with a loupe, looking for the grain, the cleavage lines, discovering exactly the right angle for a cut. If you saw a finished diamond, you would have a hard time imagining that they were sculpted from misshapen stones like the one in my hand.

The most important thing about cutting was being able to envision what the finished product would look like. My father taught me that the people who decide where to cleave, saw, and grind diamonds into their familiar display case have to imagine the gem *within* the stone before they start.

'Imagine you're a beam of light,' my father would say when he handed me a stone to be cut. That's what it was all about, how light traveled. If you could envision exactly how light would react in the diamond, you would know how to cut the diamond to bring out its brilliance.

The first thing you had to know was that all that glitter, the radiance we call diamond fire, those flashes of light, was not from light reflecting *off* the diamond, but from the light entering it and getting processed *inside* the diamond. The cut was just as important as the first two Cs – color and clarity. The three work together to create a dazzling gem.

A diamond was divided into three parts – the wide part in the middle where it's attached to the ring is called the girdle. The area above that is the crown, and the area below the girdle is the pavilion. You had to imagine a beam of light entering the diamond through the table and facets of the crown and getting worked by the facets of the pavilion, the light splitting into different colors as if it was passing through a prism. The light being refracted in the pavilion is the fiery glitter you see.

You couldn't just chop off pieces until you had the familiar shape of a diamond. Even though most stones were cut to create fifty-eight facets, thirty-three in the crown and twenty-five in the pavilion, each stone was unique, and shaping a gem from a rough took careful study. And it didn't always come out the way the polisher planned. That's why some diamonds aren't the bargain they appear on paper to be. Two stones with exactly the same rating as to weight, clarity, and color may have significantly different brilliance because of the way the gem was drawn from the stone. As a rule of thumb, you started with about a three-carat stone to carve down to a one-carat diamond. You might be able to draw a one-carat from a smaller stone, say, a two-carat size, but you may not get the same fire from the smaller stone despite the fact that it has the same stats. Often, the shape and size of the stone was also determined by working with and around defects.

I wasn't going to make my living cutting stones, but if I followed in my

27

father's footsteps and became a diamond trader, each time I examined a rough to see whether I wanted to buy it, I had to keep the biggest 'C' of all in mind – cost. I had to accurately see the gem in the rough to determine how much I should pay for it – and how much the person I sold it to would pay.

So that's how I was trained, to always start by seeing the gem hidden inside the stone, imagining I was a beam of light and following it as it entered and was processed, seeing how facets would refract and disperse the light to gauge how the cut should be.

After determining where to cut, the stone was marked with ink to show where the cleaving, sawing, and grinding are to be done. Using a small mallet and blade, the stone had to be cut precisely on its cleavage to split properly. A hair off and the stone would be damaged or even shattered. That was really the paradox about diamonds – they were hard, but not tough. They were the hardest substance on earth – we all knew only a diamond could cut a diamond. You could put a diamond on an anvil and hit it with a sledgehammer, driving the diamond unbroken into the iron anvil – but it just as likely would shatter because a diamond will shatter when hit along any of its cleave lines.

'Diamond cutting originated in India,' Uncle Bernie told me during an earlier lesson. 'They knew diamonds were hard, hard enough to embed into an anvil when they hit a diamond on one, but they also discovered there were ways to shatter diamonds – if you keep hitting it, by trial and error you'll strike it along the grain and it'll break. They wrapped the stones in sheets of lead and broke them by hitting them hard. They took sharp pieces from the broken stones and imbedded them in the edge of swords when the blades were almost hot enough to melt. It created swords that could cut steel.'

I took the stone in the other room and studied it for an hour, examining it by eye and under the loupe. When I figured out how I thought it should be cut, I marked the lines with ink. Then I reported to my father.

'I would go for a forty-point oval cut. That would be a loss of almost two-thirds of the stone, with some of it recovered as sand.' Sand referred to small diamonds, usually under ten-points. Anything under one hundred-points, a carat, was called a small. 'There's a gletz.' A tiny crack. 'I would cleave it off, taking away about a quarter of the stone. If it's left in, it would probably split the stone during the sawing and grinding needed to create the facets.'

Splitting off the crack would be done with cleaving. It was a procedure that used a mallet and blade to sever off part of a diamond and the process most people identified with cutting a diamond. Cleaving is the way it's done in the movies, but in real life most of the shaping was done by tedious hours of sawing and grinding. Cleaving was risky, though, because the stone could shatter.

I spent the rest of the afternoon and after supper that evening and all free hours between school and sleep the next week examining the diamond and preparing it for a cut. I talked about the diamond to my dad, Bernie, and Emile, a cutter who worked for my father. I put it on a device called a dop and used another diamond to cut a groove in it. Since a diamond could only be cut with a diamond, a pointed diamond was used to cut the groove I needed to set the cleaving knife. I'd cut industrial diamonds, a number of them, practicing on them for the big day when I had to cut something more valuable.

When it came time to do the actual cleaving as my father watched, I began my cut, the diamond mounted and grooved, with a wooden mallet in one hand and the cleaving knife in the other. Before I struck the blow, I looked up at my father.

'What if it shatters?' I asked.

'You'll never know failure unless you try. And you'll never know success until you've experienced failure.'

'So it doesn't matter if I shatter it?'

'Of course it matters. That diamond is worth a year's allowance. If you shatter it, you'll have to come here every day after school for a year to earn your allowance.'

'That's not fair.'

'That's life. You're going to learn something as you grow up. The only justice you get in this world is what you fight for.'

'Why do I have to learn how to cut a diamond?' I knew the answer, but when you're a kid, you keep testing the waters, looking for the answer you want. 'I don't want to cut diamonds when I grow up.'

'You need to know the business. Every inch of it. Otherwise people will take advantage of you, even let you down because they're incompetent.'

Knowing every inch was something he drilled into me. Like the time I won a bike race. Before he let me ride in the race, he made me strip down the bike and put it back together until I could do it blindfolded. 'That's how they train soldiers,' he said. 'They live with their rifles day and night so they have to be able to take their rifle apart and put it back together in the dark.'

I set down the mallet and wiped my hands. They were sweaty.

'Can you imagine how a diamond cutter felt in the old days when he cut a stone worth a king's ransom? They'd often study the diamond for a year or more and have a doctor standing by in case the stone shattered.'

'Would the doctor fix the broken stone?'

'No. The doctor was there to treat the shattered diamond cutter.'

He told me the story of Joseph Asscher, the Amsterdam diamond cutter who cut the Cullinan Diamond, the largest diamond in the world, for Edward VII in 1907. The diamond was 3,106 carats, over a pound and nearly the size of a man's fist, and the royals wanted it cut down to smaller stones, some of which were planned for the crown and scepter. Asscher had a doctor and nurse standing by as he raised his mallet and swung it down to cleave the diamond. Then he promptly fainted as it cleaved smoothly.

The part of the story I liked best was how it was shipped to Britain. When the Cullinan was found in South Africa and it was decided to send it to London to be cut for the king, the mine owners put on an elaborate charade of shipping the diamond in an iron box under heavy guard – but actually sent it by parcel post with a three-shilling stamp. Diamond traders still pulled the same sort of tricks to ship their stones around the world.

I laid the mallet atop the stone again, raised the mallet, and brought it down.

The diamond shattered. I stared at the pieces with a sinking heart. My father's face was expressionless when I looked up to him.

'I want another one,' I said. 'I want another diamond to cut.'

His lips shaped a small smile. 'OK, but you're going to go barefooted if you break it.'

4

Long Island Sound, 1991

Some women love speed. Something gets inside them, triggering more desire than a man's touch. The investment banker's wife was one of them.

She sat across from me in the sailboat's cockpit, creaming her panties as wind and sea hit us. Sailboats actually don't move much faster than a crawl, but when they keel in a good blow and you have to grab your ass – hanging on for dear life from getting swept overboard – it's not much different than the sensation of barreling toward the earth in a stunt plane.

'I'm so excited!' she yelled to me.

Yeah, I could see that. She spread her legs further every inch I keeled the boat deeper on its side. Her pink panties and a line of pubic hair were exposed in the crotch of her short-shorts. Her mouth hung open, inviting. She wanted something, I just wasn't sure where she wanted it first.

An awful moaning came up the companionway from the cabin below. Then the sounds of gasping and gurgling as her husband threw up.

They say there are only two kinds of sailors – those who have been seasick and those who will be. But her husband, Barney, made up a third kind – getting nauseated before we even pushed away from the dock. When he got cross-eyed from vomiting out his guts, I stowed him below, on a bunk with foul-weather straps to hold him in. Last time I looked, he'd fallen off the bunk and was rolling in puke.

'Go faster,' she squealed, 'they're catching up.'

'They' was the *Hedge Fund*, a fifteen-meter cutter we were racing. It should have cleaned the clock of my twelve-meter. Wind and current being equal, a sailboat's speed is determined by the length of its hull. But that's like saying the performance of a golf club is determined by the quality of its manufacturer. Two sailors of unequal ability won't get the same performance out of a boat any more than two golfers using the same club will hit a ball the same distance. The skipper of the *Hedge Fund*, Nolan Richards, didn't have the balls or racing instincts to beat me. A half an hour ago, he followed standard protocol by staying in his line of sail and waiting it out when the wind got spotty and full of holes. That's the conventional wisdom, hang onto that old breeze, because if you cut across the waterway looking for a better wind, you'll lose time and distance. But good sailors also know that every wind has a personality of its own. Like women, some come across and others are just prick-teasers. In my book, you don't win races sailing by the book – you have to adapt to the conditions. My experience on the Sound is that an easterly will shift to a sou-west when the time current tables say that the tide will be at flood. So I shifted over to pick up that wind. The *Hedge Fund* had finally gotten a piece of it, too, but it was too late for them to close the gap.

31

'What'd I get if I win?' I yelled back to her.

She nodded her head and licked her lips. Her face was warm and flush, her lips swollen red and full like the lips of an excited cunt.

I got the idea. And put on more sail. As I turned the winch, Barney's groaning and moaning floated up the companionway. I felt sorry for the poor bastard. Anyone who's never been seasick has no idea of how miserable it is. Not that I cared much for the guy. The boat ride was strictly business. Katarina, my girlfriend, asked me to take Barney and his wife out on my sailboat and show them a good time. She was supposed to be here, too, but a photo shoot for *Vogue* ran overtime and she couldn't make it.

Katarina's a supermodel with a yen to be a Hollywood star. Barney's a paunchy vice president of an investment bank that bankrolls films. A match made in heaven, in Katarina's eyes. I found Barney to be a boring jerk, who reminded me too much of my stepbrother, Leo. When my father and stepmother were killed in an accident fifteen years ago, I inherited a diamond business I had no desire to run. I left it in the hands of Leo and Uncle Bernie. They joked that I thought I owned Citibank, because that was the name on the trust-account checks that came each month and kept me in fast cars, a sailboat, and an apartment in the Dakota on the Upper West Side.

Something dark crawled in me when I lost my father a few years after the death of my mother: a worm called fatalism. You never knew when those Dark Sisters called the Fates were going to grab your ankles and pull you six feet under, so you'd better squeeze every succulent bit you can out of life. What it boiled down to was I didn't give a rat's ass about anything except having a good time. No, having a *great* time – good times were for ankle biters.

Sometimes after I partied hot and heavy, I'd wake up in the wee hours and wonder what my father would have thought of my lifestyle. Neither of my parents lived long enough to wring out all the joys there are in life. But then I'd push the guilt aside – I didn't want to be on my deathbed agonizing over a wish list of things I never did.

The investment banker's wife jerked her thumb at the open companionway and laughed. They had a marriage made in heaven, too. He was rich and a bore – she had expensive tastes and was bored. She was a pulpy blonde, ripe and juicy, with a hot cunt – he'd probably have a heart attack if he ever got a good fuck. 'She's looking after his health,' Katarina had theorized, 'by fucking other men so she doesn't wear him out.'

More sail put the boat's lee side deeper into the water. As the bow exploded waves, the spray came back at us and the blonde giggled like a banshee reeling from a hit of the drug Ecstasy. On the high side of the cockpit, she spread her legs to brace herself as the boat keeled more. She hung onto the lifelines with one hand and her other hand slipped in past the crotch of her panties and worked her clit like the gearshift knob on my Bugatti.

She let go of the lifelines and fell onto me. I was seated behind the big wheel-helm and she landed with her knees on the cockpit floor and her breasts in my lap. She pushed herself back and unzipped my shorts. Her hand dug into my shorts and found my bulge. She freed it from restraint and my long, red, throbbing phallus shot up at her.

'That's why they call it a cockpit,' I told her.

She took it in her mouth with one big gulp. Her mouth was hot and wet. I reared up, driving it down her deep throat.

'Oh, God, I'm dying.'

Her pea-green husband had struggled up the companionway to the foot of the cockpit. He stared at us, dizzy and cross-eyed. His eyes teared and his face gasped as his innards erupted and vomit exploded out his mouth.

5

Katarina was waiting on the dock for us. She carried the couple's day bag as I helped the pulpy bonde get the investment banker into the backseat of their car. Katarina made a point of fussing over the guy until his wife got the car going. As the blonde shot away, she threw me a carnal look.

'What the hell did you do? Fuck his wife and try to kill him?' Katarina asked.

Some women can see right through a man. Maybe it's because Katarina's a redhead. Bruce Springsteen was right about a redheaded woman – she can see every dirty thing you do. Uncle Bernie claims I'm attracted to redheads because I lost my beautiful redheaded mother at a young age. I prefer to think about it like Toulouse-Lautrec did. He believed that redheaded women had a distinctive scent that aroused his prurient desires more than blondes and brunettes. Just because the guy's legs were short didn't mean he was stunted everywhere – his cock was so big, the prostitutes he fucked called him the 'Coffee Pot.'

That little bit of art history was all I managed to get out of Art History 101 before flunking out of college. And I got that from balling the professor, a sorrel filly visiting from the Sorbonne.

'I didn't see your pretty little tush out there when I was entertaining your guests,' I told Katarina.

'The shoot ran late. But, hey, I got terrific news. I'm going out to Hollywood for a screen test. Isn't that exciting?'

'Awesome.' I gave her a hug that lifted her off her feet and a big kiss.

'Your mouth tastes like cock,' she said, 'your cock. A little residue from that blonde bitch?'

I licked my lips. I tasted like the blonde's cherry lip gloss. She was testing me, trying to trap me into an admission of guilt. 'No way, you're putting me on. I had a piece of cherry candy.'

'Yeah, and I know what wrapper you found it in.'

'Come on, you can ride back with me.'

'I brought my car—'

'I'll have it trucked back to the city.'

The few hundred bucks to have the car trucked meant nothing to me. What was important in my mind was that the money bought me a few extra moments of pleasure. I hadn't worked a day in my life and was proud of it. My trust-account checks came in each month from House of Liberte like clockwork. Bernie wasn't any genius at making a buck, though he was good and steady, but he had Leo to back him up. Nose to the grindstone, a two-fisted moneyman, Leo was everything I never wanted to be.

Yak, yak, yak, Katarina went on about her screen test as we walked to my car. Hey, I don't blame her. Her puss has been on the cover of every top magazine in the country, not to mention her pussy on the centerfold of some magazines that are sold in brown paper bags. She came to America from Prague, rising above Eastern European poverty the easiest way a beautiful woman knew. She worked hard, took her career seriously, and did whatever she had to in order to succeed. She had contempt for my work ethic. But what the hell, I wasn't so crazy about it myself.

'I don't know if I have the talent. Other models have tried it, they just don't have the screen magic. A movie camera's alive, it's different than posed shots. It's an animal that eats you up if it doesn't like you.'

'You'll make it, you've got the talent.'

'You should come out to Hollywood, you can be in movies, too,' she said. 'You're not handsome, but you have seductive eyes, just like that actor on the spaghetti jars.'

It took me a minute to realize the spaghetti jar guy was Paul Newman. I should be so lucky to be compared to Newman on any level, though I've been told I could have stood in for an even older time actor, one nobody's heard of today, John Garfield. Except I had a scar down the center of my chin from where I plowed face-first into a tree on my first motorcycle.

We'd be three thousand miles apart if she headed for Hollywood, but Katarina was more of a good-fuck girlfriend to me than a soul mate. Besides, it would give me an excuse to run out to the West Coast more often and check out the action. Maybe I'd buy a place on the beach at Malibu.

My Bugatti had 553 horses. We did zero to sixty in 3.7 seconds. Katarina was pressed back in her seat by the acceleration. When her body caught up with the car, she leaned close to me and rubbed my crotch. 'Let's fuck when we get to your place,' she said. 'My period's coming up and I'm horny.'

What'd I say about speed?

When we reached the Long Island Expressway, I phoned my home recording. 'What the hell?' I said, after listening to my only message.

'What's the matter?''

'That was Big Bertha, Bernie's secretary. She sounded hysterical, told me to call her right away.'

I called Bertha and she gave it to me right away.

'He's dead, killed himself.'

It wouldn't go down my throat or soak into my brain at first. Bernie dead? Suicide?

'Did she say why?' Katarina asked, after I hung up.

'No, she was too damn hysterical.'

I tried to call Leo, my stepbrother, to see if he knew anything, but he wasn't in. I felt bad about Bernie. He was an okay guy, not someone I had a warm family relationship with, but more like the older uncle I only saw on holidays. After my father died, Bernie assumed a lot of airs as head of the diamond company my father built. I didn't mind his airs, not as long as the money came in, but we drifted apart, with the money-trust check and occasional big draws for large ticket items as our only connection.

'Did Bernie have women problems?' Katarina asked.

'No, he was divorced. He had a girlfriend who lives over on Staten Island, but nothing serious. They've been going together for ages.'

'Cancer?'

'Not that I know of, he brags that he's healthy as a horse.'

'Oh shit.'

'Oh shit what?'

'Didn't you tell me Bernie controls your trust?'

'That's no problem, someone else will do it, probably Leo. He doesn't like me, but Bernie got a fat fee for handling the money and Leo wouldn't pass up a buck if it was wrapped around a crocodile's dick.'

'That isn't what I'm worried about. Love, money, and the big C.'

'Come again?'

'Love, money, and cancer. Those are the only reasons why a guy bumps himself off. And if he had money problems and was managing your money . . . Win, you may have money problems.'

Money problems? What the hell did I know about that? The only problem I had with money was finding a letter opener to cut open the monthly envelope that came with a Citibank return address.

'Jeez, Win, you look terrible.'

I fought back tears. 'Fuck it, there's been too many deaths during my life. I'm not going to mourn Bernie. I'm not going to mourn anyone again.'

I left Katarina off and called Bertha. She gave me the name and phone number of a cop who was investigating the death, a Detective Leonard. I gave him a call as I drove home. After we went through the preliminaries of who I was and how well I knew Bernie, I asked how Bernie died.

'Went out the window of his apartment,' he said. 'Five stories up.'

'Out the window. There's no balcony out his windows.'

'Not even a ledge you can stand on. He just crawled out and let himself drop. Went down headfirst.'

Jesus. Headfirst. How much speed does a person get up falling five stories? A hundred miles an hour? Two hundred?

'You're sure it's a suicide? Could it have been an accident?'

'Your cousin-uncle, whatever, wasn't a small guy. And his windows weren't big. They pull up, not slide open. He would have had to kind of crawl through the window and let himself fall. It's not like he could have been reaching for something, slipped, and went "oops" out the window.'

He was right. Bernie had love handles the size of hams. And his apartment windows were old and small. Hell, I doubted he ever opened them. He wasn't a fresh air kind of guy.

The detective asked me the same sort of questions about Bernie's health, finances, and love life that Katarina raised. There was a moment of silence when he finished and I filled it with some thought.

'I don't get it,' I said.

'I know. Suicides are hard for any of us to fathom. But these people have their back to the wall, they can't see the forest from the trees. All they know is the problem they're facing. Suicide is violent and ugly to us. To them it's a release.'

'No, that's not what I don't get. Bernie wasn't the kind of guy who'd crawl out a window.'

'Bud, you never know till you've been there.'

'I'm not talking about his frame of mind, I'm talking about his method. He'd be the type who'd jump into a full bathtub holding an electric heater, even more likely to take pills. The moment he opened that window and looked down to the street, he'd have chickened out, probably puked out his guts.'

I paused, letting the thought sink into my own head before I said:

'You see, Bernie was afraid of heights.'

I had a message on my phone when I got home. It was from my lawyer, asking me to come in tomorrow. His message said he had bad news. I guess he needed to break the news of Bernie's death to me.

6

'You're broke.'

I stared at my lawyer like he'd just stepped out of the pages of a John Farris horror story. With a bloody knife in his hand. We were in his office on the fourteenth floor of the Flatiron Building, a building shaped like a wedge of cheese on Fifth Avenue.

'Broke? I'm a millionaire.'

'*Were* a millionaire.' The lawyer smacked his lips. He reminded me of the funeral director who buried my father. An ankle biter who tries to look sympathetic, but really enjoys other people taking a fall.

'How can this happen?'

'You turned over complete management of your trust to Bernard. He invested unwisely.'

'I turned over shit. My father named him trustee.'

'You outgrew your trust when you were twenty-one. At that point, you had a right to terminate it and take complete control. You chose to leave it in Bernard's hands.'

He was right. I didn't want to manage the money. It would have cut time from the disco scene I was into in those days. Besides, Bernie could be trusted. He was family.

'How do I get it—'

'Back?' He pursed his lips and shook his head. I could tell he was really enjoying it. 'Bernard didn't leave an estate, I'm afraid. Besides everything you had, he sold or encumbered everything he had. You can't get blood from a turnip or money from a deadbeat.'

I'll bet he made that up all by himself.

'How much can I get if I sell the business?'

'What business?'

'House of Liberte. You know, the one that's been paying this firm a big chunk of your salary for years.'

'Win, you're not listening to me. I said you're broke. The House of Liberte was sold last year.'

'What? What'd you mean? How the hell can it be sold?'

'Your brother Leo bought it.'

'First, Leo's my stepbrother. Second, he has no right to it, he inherited a diamond business from his own father.'

'He has every right to it. As a matter of fact, I handled the transaction. Bernard needed cash when the investment went sour and Leo gave it to him, in return for the assets of the business. The firm is now called House of Schwartz.'

'This is fuckin' insane. You're telling me that Bernie went through my entire inheritance and Leo ended up with it? Shit, knowing Leo, he probably helped put the skids under Bernie. Tell me exactly, what do I have left?'

'You mean other than the loose change in your pockets?'

He saw my face go purple and almost crawled under his desk, no doubt remembering the last time he represented me. It was for breaking a bottle of champagne across a bouncer's face at a disco. The judge was so impressed that I used a thousand-dollar bottle of Perrier Jouet – and paid for it – he tossed the case.

He cleared his throat and shuffled papers on his desk. 'As far as I can see, you have the Bugatti and the mine. Your apartment, boat, stunt plane, Corvette, Harley, and all moneys except what you have in your personal account are liened and will go to the creditors.'

'What mine?'

'The one in Angola.'

'Where the hell is Angola?'

'The last time I heard, on the west coast of Africa. It's a former Portuguese colony, rich in diamonds and oil. Communists, also. I believe Castro even has Cuban troops there.'

'I know nothing about a mine.'

'How much do you know about the way Bernie ran the company?'

It was a good question and we both knew the answer, but I was in no mood to have it rubbed in. 'What's the deal on the mine? Is it worth anything?'

'I don't think anyone knows for sure. When the bottom starting falling out from under Bernard's investments, this diamond mine was the first thing he tried to sell or encumber. No one would give him a dime. Angola's a war zone and no one wanted the risk. From what you see in the news, Angola's in constant chaos, with war and revolution. From my written communications with the mine manager, the mine will be shut down in a few months if funds aren't forthcoming to keep it functioning.'

'I thought a diamond mine was supposed to generate cash, not eat it.'

'I understand that the diamonds being brought out aren't of the best quality.'

'How the hell did we end up with this shit-hole of a mine?'

'Bernard purchased it for five million dollars. Using your money.'

'*Five million dollars*! He used my inheritance to buy a diamond mine in a war zone? Was he fuckin' nuts?'

He shook his head and smacked his lips again. I felt like reaching across

39

the desk and spinning his head on his shoulders.

'Win, as someone who has dealt with people in the diamond business for most of my professional life, I can tell you that there is a very thin line indeed between the big successes and the big failures in any business, but especially in the gem one. When a dealer buys a large stone and has it cut, he never knows if he will end up with valuable gems or a handful of dust and splinters. Bernard took a flyer on a mine. He paid perhaps ten cents on the dollar. Had his gamble succeeded, you would have been extremely wealthy.'

'Bernie gambled and lost my money, not his own. I take it he went through his a long time ago. So tell me, can I sell this mine?'

'If you can find a buyer. No one in their right mind would pay substantial money for a mine in Angola, not unless they had the guts to actually run it. And knew how to run a diamond mine. I imagine it's a hands-on business – if you don't get your hands chopped off in a place like Angola.'

'What in God's name motivated Bernie to buy the damn thing?'

'They thought he'd do an end run around the De Beers control of the diamond industry. The House of Liberte has never been a sight holder, that small group of diamond dealers who control most of the world's diamond market under the thumb of De Beers. Your father had a good source of diamonds from an old friend in Lisbon, and Bernie inherited the contact. That source apparently dried up and they got the idea of having his own source for stones by buying a mine. I imagine they thought of themselves as Cecil Rhodes types, the founder of the De Beers empire.'

'A diamond mine in Africa.' I shook my head. Bernie had hardly been out of the tri-state area, as far as I knew. Traveling to the Catskills for weekend fishing and the supper club was the extent of his wanderlust. The mine might as well have been on Mars.

'I might add, the mine came with an extremely positive geological study. I don't know if the mine's never lived up to its potential or if the warring factions have kept it from being developed. But for whatever reasons, they initially invested in the mine, and when things started spinning out of control, Bernard kept hedging his bet with your trust funds.'

Owning a diamond mine sounded like Bernie. It would have been an ego thing, being able to waltz around the Diamond Club and showing off diamonds that came out of his own mine. He had the kind of big ego, lightweight mentality that gets his rocks off from getting one-up on people who hardly knew he existed.

'You keep saying "they." Who was in on this with Bernie?'

'Your bro – uh, stepbrother, Leo, was originally a partner in the mine, but he sold his interest to Bernie a while back.'

'Leo was in on the deal, bailed out before it went sour, and ended up owning my company. Is that what you're telling me?'

He squirmed. 'Leo had an arm's-length transaction with Bernard—'

'And you handled the ink for the deal, I imagine.'

'Win, I think—'

'Leo's a prick who'd rent out his mother's cunt to an army of baboons if he could turn a dime on it. Let's get down to the bottom line. I have a diamond mine in a war zone that's hemorrhaging money instead of shitting diamonds, the Bugatti – probably worth maybe a hundred grand wholesale – and pocket change. Is that it?'

'Man to man, Win, I'm sad to tell you, that's it. And you had better get rid of the Bugatti, because creditors will eventually come after it.'

I got up to leave.

'Bernard had no blood relatives, except for you. What sort of funeral arrangements did you have in mind?'

'Do they still have pauper graves?'

I was at the door when he said, 'Win, you're obviously not aware of it, but Bernard ran up a very substantial legal bill. My senior partner's been on my back about it. I assured him you were a man of honor and would make sure that Bernard's debt was paid.'

I laughed all the way to the elevators. There was some justice in this world.

7

I found Leo in the café at the Diamond Club at the building on West Forty-seventh and Fifth Avenue. He spent his day meandering in and out of the offices of diamond wholesalers, talking to them with one side of his mouth while carrying on a second conversation with his cellular phone on the other side of his mouth. The only time he sat down was to eat, his phone in one hand, fork in the other. When he wasn't eating, pissing, or sleeping, he was making deals.

Leo was built like a stack of rubber tires, with the smaller sizes at the top and bottom – short and wide, with a big, round, basketball-shaped head, fat lips, and the personality of a gnat in a garbage can. Barney the Puke, Katarina's would-be movie backer, had the charm of a lounge lizard in comparison. Leo's dislike for me went way back. When I was fifteen, Leo brought home a girl to meet his mother, my stepmother. I invited the girl, a pulpy redhead, into the garage to see my new hog. I was mounted on the motorcycle and she was mounted on me, when Leo walked in on us.

In retrospect, I'd done the guy a big favor. Pulpy women are great to fuck, but the Leos and Barneys of this world, who don't have the time or desire to take care of a woman's needs, should have women who are more interested in doing their nails than their husbands. That way the women don't get bored and roam.

But despite my good deed, Leo intensified his hatred of me. I've never known the original source for it. I can only believe the basis for his dislike is that I like to have fun. Leo hates fun. He loves work. And money. He can't understand why everyone doesn't love work and money. I don't have a problem with that, different strokes for different folks, to each his own, one person's treasure is another's junk, and all that crapola. But Leo carries it a step farther. He resents anyone being happy, and at the same time is determined not to let a little thing like having a life get in his way of making money that he never spends.

A dealer he'd been dickering with got up to leave as I sat down at the table. Leo's assistant, Karen, was there. Leo barely glanced at me before tapping in a number on his phone. I wasn't important enough to have him give a nod. I took the phone away from his ear.

'What're you doing?'

'I'm going to butt-fuck you.'

'Wha – what?'

I jerked my head at Karen. 'Get out of here. This is family shit.'

She got out. Fast.

Leo's face glowed red. 'You have no right—'

'You fucked me, stepbrother, now I'm going to butt-fuck you. You know what that is, don't you? It's a prison term. Low guy on the totem pole gets butt-fucked. You're not even going to have to take a shower to get fucked.'

'You've gone crazy.'

'Naw, I've gone broke. You know, as in no money. You fucked over Bernie, took the jerk for a ride, got him into a bullshit mine deal, and cleaned him out. I don't think you gave a shit about Bernie, it was me you wanted to break. That fat trust account and me having fun was too much temptation for you, wasn't it, Leo? You just can't stand anyone being happy. You also have to pay for Bernie. I wasn't crazy about Bernie, but he deserved more than a nosedive out a window.'

'Fuck you. You've been too busy sticking your dick into anything that walks to pay any attention to business. What I got from Bernie I got fair and square and there's nothing you can do about it.'

'You made a big mistake, pal. If it had been a stranger that cleaned me out, I'd have shrugged and said I deserved it for not minding the store, but you're family.'

'I'm not your fucking family. Your old man—'

'What about my father?' My temperament went rabid.

'We're not related by blood,' he stammered.

'You're right, you're not real family, but check this out.' I leaned closer and whispered. 'I'm going to be out there, waiting for you. I know how to hurt you and I'm going to do it. Not today, maybe not tomorrow, but I'll be there, you cocksucker, and when you're least expecting it, I'm going to get you.'

After I left, I said kaddish for Leo. Jews say kaddish for the dead. From now on, I'd only think of Leo in the past tense.

8

'Where the hell is Angola?' Katarina asked.

'Tsk, tsk,' I clicked my tongue. 'Such ignorance, Katarina. Angola is a country on the west coast of Africa. Everyone knows that.' I was a little drunk. I picked her up after a photo shoot and took her to Verdi's on Seventy-fifth. I was working on my fifth or sixth vodka martini – or maybe my tenth, I'd lost count.

She squeezed my thigh. 'I'm really happy it wasn't a money problem with Bernie. God, I couldn't sleep thinking you might be broke.'

I didn't have the heart – or guts – to tell her all I had was a Bugatti and a mine that took in more money than it puked out. I made it sound like Bernie was a financial genius and had ended it because he suddenly found out he was terminal with the Big C. She bought the whole act. Besides, her mind was on Hollywood.

'I'm going to miss you.' She gave me a wet kiss, fucking my mouth with her tongue.

'Don't worry, I'm going to be bicoastal.'

'You going to buy that place in Malibu we talked about?' she asked.

'Hell, yes, and a chain of movie theaters that only plays your flicks.'

She giggled and kissed me some more.

'You know what I like about you?' she said. 'You're the only rich guy I know who's fun and real at the same time. I mean, rich guys in this town are a dime a dozen and they all want to be seen with models, but they're all jerks. None of them talk about anything but how much money they made or what they shot in golf. But you're different. You know how to treat a woman.'

She moved her hand to my jade stalk and squeezed, causing it to pump wildly. Somebody told me that a man only had enough blood at any one time for his dick or his brains, and like a little kid, he couldn't chew gum and walk at the same time. That was my problem, I never had enough blood to handle a woman and a simple math equation – like how much money I should spend.

'My Hollywood agent was really jazzed when I told him my boyfriend had an apartment in the Dakota. He wanted to know if it was the one that *Rosemary's Baby* was filmed in. I told him you had Lauren Bacall and Yoko Ono for neighbors.'

'Tell him to drop by, I'll introduce him to John Lennon's ghost.'

Yeah, I'm a hell of a swinger in this town. The Dakota at Seventy-second and Central Park West was the best address in town. Trump's Tower was a ghetto project in comparison. I didn't tell her there was an eviction notice tacked to my door when I got home from my lawyer's office. The building staff shied away from me like I came in ringing a leper's bell. Worse than being ostracized was the looks of loss on their faces – I was the most generous tenant in the place at Christmastime.

'Hollywood's a tough town, tougher than New York,' she said, 'because you've got to put up a front. People here are real, no one cares what kind of car you drive or where you live. Few people have a car, anyway, and we all live like ants crowded into the same hole. But it's all front on the West Coast, all about what you've got – people drive a more expensive car than they can afford, have an apartment with a view they can't afford, designer clothes.'

I tossed the keys to my Bugatti in her lap.

'What're you doing?'

'That will get you an apartment on the beach, bitching clothes, a cherry-red convertible, everything you need to put up a front in L.A. The registration's in the car, I'll sign it over to you. Tomorrow you take the Bugatti to the exotic car dealer where I bought it and they'll write you a check for a hundred grand.'

'God, I was so worried about leaving the right impression out there. What are you going to do, buy another one?'

'Sure, tell the guys in the showroom I'll be in.'

'Jeez, Win, you're so good to me. How can I ever repay you?'

'Fuck my brains out when we get back to my place. A going-away present.'

'Why wait?'

She slipped beneath the table. I spread my legs as she got between my knees. Her head hit the underside of the table and she went 'ouch' and giggled. I quickly scanned the room. Verdi's had that typical dark ambiance, designed so you couldn't see the print on the check or be easily recognized if you were with someone besides your spouse, but it wasn't a blackout. Katarina was wearing a red shimmery dress that literally glowed in the dark, but I figured someone would still have to bend down to see her under the table – so I relaxed to enjoy the ride.

Her hands fumbled with my zipper and I sat up a little to give her a hand. As soon as the zipper went down, her hand went in, searching for the opening to my jockey shorts. She found the exit hole and my phallus shot out.

'Hmmm,' came from under the table, 'I found a diamond in the rough.'

She stroked it like it was a new mink stole. Her tongue flicked at my cock's head, snakelike. Katarina had a cat's tongue, not reasonably smooth like the rest of us, instead of slipping up and down like she was licking ice cream, her tongue clung to my skin and pulled at it. With each lick, a jolt of pleasure hit me.

45

'Hello, Win,' a voice female sang.

I almost shit my pants. Mrs Greenberg, the mother of a guy I went to school with, came up to my table, She didn't speak words, but had an annoying habit of singing them, as if she was a bird. Two other people were with her.

'Hi,' I stammered as that cat's tongue took a big lick.

'I want you to meet friends of mine. This is the Reverend Paul Davis and his wife, the Reverend Mary Davis. They're in the city raising money for their missionary school in Indonesia.'

I gurgled a listening response. The husband-wife missionary team looked like prudish Katherine Hepburn and her missionary brother in *African Queen.*

The cat's tongue took another big lick, one that started at the head of my dick and slowly moved around the ridge separating the glans from the stem. I nearly went airborne off the seat as she stopped licking and her warm mouth swallowed my cock.

'I'm having a fund-raiser for the school,' Mrs Greenberg said, 'and we would certainly love to have you attend.'

I would rather sit in a hot bath and cut my wrists than spend more than three minutes in the same room with the woman.

'Busy,' I got out, smiling weakly. Katarina was chomping down on my dick, pumping it with her mouth. I couldn't talk, I could only sit there with a frozen smile on my face. I was going to explode any second. If I didn't, I would spontaneously combust and there would be pieces of me splattered on the walls.

'You must make time,' Mrs Greenberg said. 'It's such a worthy cause, such needy children—'

A groan slipped by my lips as Katarina sucked and licked.

'Are you all right, Win? You look positively feverish.'

I shook my head, unable to speak. Her mouth was hot and wet and molded around my penis like a glove full of night cream. The top of the table began to vibrate from Katarina's head hitting it. The three people stared at the table like it needed an exorcism. A spoon slipped off the edge and landed at the Reverend Davis's feet.

'Oops,' he said. He bent down to get the spoon and froze as he stared under the table. His eyes went wide and his jaw unhinged.

I'd swear on a stack of bibles that I could see the reflection of Katarina's glowing red dress in his eyes.

9

I woke up at the crack of dawn in my Dakota apartment with Katarina getting out of bed.

'I have an early shoot,' Katarina said.

She sat on the bed and kissed me. I spread open her unbuttoned blouse and kissed her strawberry-like nipples. She pushed me away. 'Stop it, you'll make me late. Did you really mean it about the car?'

'I signed the registration over to you. Take it with you.'

I got out of bed naked and went into the bathroom to take a leak.

Katarina suddenly appeared at the bathroom door. 'You got people in the living room, some woman with flaming red hair claiming to be Scarlett O'Hara.'

'Go to your shoot, I'll take care of it.'

I knew who the woman with a head of fire and a famous name was. Scarlet O'Hara owned an art gallery and was my art procurer. I knew as much about art as Henry Ford did. I left it up to Scarlet to put pieces on the walls.

What the hell she was doing in my apartment and how she got in were a mystery.

She had her back to me when I came into the room after taking my leak. She was directing two workers who were removing a Picasso from the wall.

'What the fuck's going on?'

Scarlet swung around, startled. She gawked at me. I hadn't bothered to put on clothes. The red hair Katarina mentioned was the woman's trademark. It came straight out of a bottle.

'Win – I – I – we're repossessing your art. The check your trustee wrote bounced. I heard you're, uh . . .'

'Broke. How'd you get in?'

'Through me.' The speaker was an uniformed officer. He was on the other side of the room when I walked in and I didn't see him. 'I have a court order for the repossession.' He stared at me. 'You're naked.'

'You're a regular fuckin' rocket scientist. Now get out of my place.'

After the repo crew left, I lay in bed and stared up at the ceiling. I didn't give a damn about the artwork. If I had, I would have chosen it myself rather than leaving it up to Scarlet. I only got it because walls were supposed to have stuff on them. I had more of a connection to the car because I chose it, but giving it to Katarina wasn't a drunken act – it was connected to my folly, a reminder that I had been so stupid, letting Bernie take full responsibility for my money. The truth was, I never gave a damn about money – it was just something that got me what I wanted at the moment. Money was a fickle bitch who never gave a damn about me, either, because it fled the first chance it got.

What are you going to be when you grow up? rolled in my mind.

I remembered that question; it was the only question on a classroom essay that we had to write when I was in the eighth grade. My father had died a few months before and I wrote one short sentence on the paper and threw it on my teacher's desk as I walked out of the classroom: 'It'll never happen.'

Well, I'd certainly managed to achieve my ambition. I didn't have the faintest idea of what I was going to do. I had no education, no profession, no talents. I wouldn't even make a good companion for a rich woman because I wasn't handsome enough or servile enough.

There was something else stunning I discovered about myself. I had no real friends. No college pals, no business contacts. It never occurred to me until now that I was a loner. There had been a lot of women in and out of my life, but nothing that stuck. I had Katarina, but she was on a different planet than I. What I had was a bunch of acquaintances, guys around the yacht club I raced against, the mechanic who took care of my plane, the salesman who kept me supplied in fast cars, bartenders, and headwaiters. But no real friends. No running buddy. No one to back me up if I had trouble coming front and back. And right now trouble was an avalanche. Bernie had even taken cash advances on all of my credit cards, to the tune of a couple hundred grand.

What are you going to be when you grow up?

I wondered what it would be like if I went to a dealership and picked up a car and drove it into a freeway bulkhead at a couple hundred miles an hour. Would I feel any pain as the car accordioned into the size of a shoe box with me inside? Was that the only way out for someone who had managed to completely screw up his life without much effort? What the hell else could I do? Pump gas?

Fuck you and the horse you rode in on. I'd rob banks before I'd give up the ghost just because I was broke. And I'd kill that little fucker Leo first.

There was really only one way out for me. And the more I thought about it, the better I liked it. I never figured I'd live long. My game plan would just speed up the process.

The phone rang. *Katarina's wrecked the car* was my first thought. Hell, I don't remember if she even knew how to drive. Jesus H. Christ, she could take out a city block if she punched the gas pedal to the floor.

'Yeah.'

'Win?'

A man's voice. With a foreign accent. Not Eastern European like Katarina's, but something warmer, French maybe, or Spanish or Portuguese.

'Win Liberte?'

'Who wants to know?' I was getting irritated now. A bill collector already?

'This is João. Do you know who I am?'

I thought for a moment. 'Sure, you got me my first dirt bike, a Honda, top of the line, when I was thirteen.'

It had come after my father died. João Carmona was a diamond dealer in Lisbon. He had been a business associate of my father, a guy my father met during the Second World War when he was in Portugal. I recall Bernie mentioning him, too, so he probably kept up the relationship.

He chuckled. 'I didn't think funeral flowers meant a great deal to a child but the motorcycle might occupy your mind.'

'I rode it only once. Into a tree. But yes, it was a hell of a memory.' I rubbed the scar on my chin. 'Did I ever say thanks?'

'You can now. Drop in and see me on your way to Angola.'

I froze with the phone to my ear. I had made the decision to go to Africa just about thirty seconds ago.

'You must be a psychic,' I said.

'I might be.'

'Or you know more about me than you should.'

He chuckled. It wasn't the sound of amusement, but more of a listening response from someone whose sense of humor ran toward the macabre.

'I was your father's chief source of diamonds during most of his lifetime, and Bernie's source, until Leo started leading him around by the nose. You know, Leo encouraged Bernie to get into the mine deal and when it went sour, he bailed out and left Bernie, ah, as you Americans put it, holding the bag.'

Yeah, I had figured that one out myself. But what I didn't know was João's game. He wasn't an old family friend calling up to help me out. Other than the ill-fated dirt bike, I hadn't heard from the guy since my father died nearly twenty years ago. I remembered that my father used to refer to João as a *ladrào*, a thief, and *crime organizado*, the Portuguese version of the Mafia. But I'm sure much of that was just hyperbole because he continued to do business with him. Calling other diamond dealers thieves was a common practice around the office. It was just part of a business that was competitive, profitable, and ultrasecretive.

My impression was that my father and João were compadres, up to a point – the point where neither one turned his back on the other. My old man had been no angel, that was for sure, no one who wheels and deals in diamonds is. But to refer to João with caution was a sure sign that the man was dangerous besides avaricious.

'So you know I'm broke and it's Angola or bust. Ever been there?'

'Many times. Stop by Lisbon on your way and I will give you some tips on how to survive. With my help, you might even live long enough to make your own fortune. Your best bet for a flight to Angola is through Lisbon, anyway. Few airlines serve Angola directly. Since it's a former Portuguese colony, and the official language is Portuguese, there is still a close connection with Portugal. I have contacts that you will find exceptionally helpful when you reach that African country.'

He told me he'd have someone meet me at the airport if I gave him the flight information. We hung up after he gave me a number to call him back on once I booked a flight. My mind was swirling with questions and scenarios. João knew a lot for a guy several thousand miles and a couple decades away. He also had my unlisted phone number.

João. Leo. Bernie. A diamond mine in Angola. 'Many times,' João had said, about visiting Angola.

I was beginning to get a clue as to how Bernie got into the mining business.

João knew I was broke. So why was he holding out a carrot for me to go to Angola? What did I have that he wanted? Certainly not a mine hemorrhaging money in a war zone.

I wondered what my father would have told me about João if he was still alive.

PART 3

LISBON

10

Victoir Liberte, Lisbon, 1946

Victoir sat alone at a terrace table at a café across from the casino in Estoril. He sipped *garoto*, espresso with milk, and ignored a tray of sweet pastelarias the waiter had set on the table in the hopes they would be consumed and thus charged for. He pretended to read a newspaper, but he was more interested in a man at a table on the other side of the café.

The man sitting across the way had nervous fingers that kept tapping the side of his coffee cup. His wrinkled white linen suit was soiled at the cuffs, his Panama hat had a sweat ring around the crown. His flesh was the anemic gray of the belly of a fish. His unlucky facial features, a small pug nose, weak chin, and watery brown eyes, were marred by a rash on the right side of his neck that his nervous fingers kept leaving the coffee cup to scratch.

To Victoir, the man had the reek of a Nazi. Not one of the goose-stepping horde that terrorized Europe and murdered millions with its blitzkrieg and death camps, but the scared, whipped-rat variety, crawling for cover after the Allies kicked them in the ass. The war had been over less than a year, but the rats had started abandoning the leaking Nazi ship even before that. They still tried to convey a sense of superiority, as if their loon-crazy leader had accomplished anything besides the death of innocents and his own cowardly suicide to avoid a hangman's noose.

Lisbon, a neutral haven for all sides during the war, was now host not only to half the royalty in Europe that had lost their thrones, but for ex-Nazis who came to the port as a jumping-off point for Argentina and other South American countries where the Nazi hallucination hadn't been crushed under Eisenhower's heel.

Victoir sighed and tried to focus on the newspaper he had already read earlier. A moment later João Carmona sat down across from him.

Victoir ordered another espresso for himself and *vinho verde* for João.

It was still morning but João had the peasant's habit of dipping bread in the green wine for breakfast. João was short, thin, and wiry, with dark olive skin, flinty eyes, a flared nose, and cropped, tight black hair. Not pure Portuguese, he was a mulatto from Cape Verde, islands off the west coast of Africa. Small, but dangerous, is how Victoir thought of him. Tough and fast, João always carried two knives – one under his coat, the other in his boot. A natty dresser, he habitually wore high-collared white shirts, a hand-painted silk tie, and a flashy gray suit tailored in a shiny material called sharkskin. He smoked thin, black, foul-smelling Havana cigars.

He thought of João as a fighting cock and himself as a cautious dog. Although Victoir was several inches taller and thirty pounds heavier, he was neither as strong nor as fast as João. Good living in Lisbon had already puffed out his waistline. He was intelligent with a good business sense, cautious but ready to take risks after thinking out the situation, unlike João, who relied on a gambler's instincts – and a quick knife thrust when words failed.

João also had a good business sense, but it was a different type of intelligence – the kind learned on the streets. The survivor instincts of thieves and Gypsies. He was ready to take risks without always thinking them through. And ready to fight his way out of a corner when backed into one.

He needed a man like João in his jewelry business. A couple years younger than Victoir's twenty-six, João was an old soul by street standards. Raised in the Alfama quarter by a mother who was both a *fado* singer and a whore, João grew up mugging people in back alleys and picking pockets at Rossio Square. He got into the jewelry business at the age of twelve the old-fashioned way – robbing drunks of their watches, rings, and *dinheiro*.

Victoir had gotten into the jewelry business through blood. After the First World War, his family migrated to France from a Polish area in the Ukraine, fleeing the Red takeover and pogroms of the region. His mother passed away when he was five and he spent his childhood and adolescence working in his father's jewelry shop. He entered the French army in 1939, lying about his Jewish background, and was in the Vichy sector after the fall of France, with his father in Paris. His father killed himself rather than be taken prisoner in a roundup of Jews. In 1942, after the Allies landed in North Africa and the Germans occupied the Vichy territory and began rounding up Jews for the camps, Victoir escaped on a Portuguese fishing boat that dropped him in Faro on the southern coast of Portugal.

False identification papers secured his way to Lisbon where he survived with his knowledge of jewelry, at first stopping just short of practicing his profession at the end of a knife, as João had done. He didn't bother asking where his jewelry came from. One of his first buys of questionable merchandise occurred when a street tough approached him while he was sitting at his usual sidewalk café along Avenda da Liberdade. The seller was João.

Victoir, with his instinct for gems, and João, with his street sense, were a natural team. Soon, they were working together almost full time. Fencing stolen merchandise didn't sit well with Victoir and he directed their energies toward purchasing and reselling legitimate goods. Or at least gems that had some facsimile of legitimacy. Occasionally there was some question as to the prior ownership of jewels, but diamonds and other precious gems were an international form of money for the hordes of refugees that escaped to Lisbon – including the ones who had reasons to still be running after the war ended.

He taught João how to evaluate gems and the Portuguese took to it. Victoir worked with jewels because it was the only profession he knew. João genuinely loved gems for themselves, especially diamonds, wearing a large diamond ring and diamond tie pin. He was a ladies' man, for sure, but Victoir suspected João's greatest passion was diamonds.

'What do you think of our Swiss friend over there?' João asked.

Victoir shot the Nazi a look out of the corner of his eye. 'The only things Swiss about him are his watch and passport. And they're both probably stolen. What's he selling?'

'A big diamond, that's all I know. Over forty carats, he claims.'

'Forty carats. It would be the size of a walnut. Unless it's heavily flawed, it would be worth a small fortune. Sounds like he has more imagination than I'd give a Nazi credit for.'

'Pedro believes him. He hasn't seen it, but from the description, he thinks it's something really special.'

Pedro was a jeweler they did business with. An old man in a wheelchair, he sent business Victoir's way for a cut. He wasn't a fool and had a good instinct for gems, which gave Victoir pause to think. He gave the Nazi another look.

'How much does he want for the jewel?' The question was almost irrelevant. They didn't know what the gem even was yet, but it was at least a starting point to see if Victoir would even be interested.

'He wants American dollars. One hundred thousand.'

'*Vá para o inferno!* He'd have to have crown jewels to get that.'

João shrugged. 'In this world, maybe he does. We have several ex-kings and twice that many grand dukes exiled here in Lisbon. I bet our waiter was a Russian count before the last war. The question is, now that you've seen him, do you want to do business? Sometimes you get fussy about dealing with Germans.'

'But you don't. You have the morality of a sheep-killing dog, João.'

He grinned. His teeth were glistening white and perfect. 'For the past six years we've lived in a world in which millions of people killed millions of other people for no good reason that anyone can tell me. In which a not-too-bright Austrian corporal was permitted to conquer most of Europe and murder at will before he killed himself. Tell me, *amigo*, what part of what's happened to this world is moral?'

'Invite him to join us,' Victoir said.

'Pedro says he won't talk in public. If you tap the side of your leg with your newspaper when you leave the café, he'll follow us. We'll take a ride somewhere we can talk quietly.'

'Does the guy speak Portuguese? My German's terrible.'

'He speaks some French.'

Victoir padded his leg on the way out and the man followed them to the parking lot where João's prewar 1934 black, ragtop Hispano Sousa was parked. The car, made in Barcelona, Spain, was his pride and joy. He claimed it attracted more women than his twelve-inch cock. Victoir believed the part about the car. With the world's car production shut down since 1939, anything running on four wheels was princely. Victoir had no use for a car. He had never learned how to drive and found taxis more convenient than the obligations of ownership.

They waited for the pale-faced man to catch up to them in the parking lot.

'We'll go somewhere where we can have a private conversation,' Victoir told him in French.

'I have nothing on me, not even money or a passport. It would do you no good to rob me.'

'My name is Victoir, this is João.'

'I am Varte.'

It wasn't a German name and up close, Victoir had second thoughts about the possibility that the man was German. But that didn't mean he wasn't a Nazi.

He motioned for the man to get in the front seat and he would sit in the back, but Varte shook his head and climbed in the back. Victoir grinned to himself as he got in the front seat. Smart man. It was easy to reach over and strangle a man in the front. He couldn't be blamed for being paranoid. The master race was now fair game.

'I don't have the diamond on me.'

'Naturally,' Victoir said. 'But we'll need to see it before we can make a deal.'

'First we talk. You assure me you have the money it takes. And that you're not a thief.'

'*Woher sind Sie?*' Victoir said in German, asking him where he was from.

'*Nein sprechen deutsch,*' Varte said.

Victoir believed him. The man's German was worse than his own. There was a Balkan favor to his accent.

'Romanian?' Victoir asked, taking a shot in the dark.

The man gave him a look of surprise. 'No,' he said in French. 'I'm Finnish.'

Finnish, my ass, Victoir thought. He was Romanian all right. Probably had been in the Iron Guards, the Romanian imitation of the Nazis and SS. King Carol, the exiled Romanian king, lived not far from the casino. For sure, the king had nothing to do with the gem or this low specimen of life claiming to have it. If the king owned it and wanted to sell it, he'd do so in London, Paris, or Antwerp, getting full price, instead of having it pass between thieves.

João drove them down to the shoreline and along the coast to the Boca do Inferno, the mouth of hell, in Cascais. They left the car in the parking lot and walked along the high cliffs overlooking the natural phenomena. The large hole and caves excavated by crashing ocean waves always fascinated Victoir.

Varte, leery of the narrow cliff-side trail, looked at Victoir and João as if he expected them to shove him off.

'My favorite place,' João said, smiling at the nervous man. 'It's beautiful and dramatic, no? Like a woman who will make love to you one moment and scream and tear out your eyes the next.' João's French was worse than Varte's, mixing a little Portuguese into his statement.

'I have a gem,' Varte told them, 'a very special one, very unique, a diamond at least forty carats in weight, perhaps even larger.'

'There are forty-carat diamonds that aren't worth a cup of coffee,' João said.

'This one is worth more than a coffee plantation.'

'What makes it so valuable?'

'It's a red diamond.'

'Rare, for sure,' Victoir said, 'but then again, a heavily flawed red diamond won't buy João his cup of coffee.'

'This is a flawless ruby diamond.'

'Nonsense,' Victoir said, 'you're either lying or you don't know what you're talking about. There's no such diamond in existence. If there was, it would be known – and in some king's crown jewels.'

'Known to who? Europeans? Hundreds of years ago it was in the Peacock Throne of Persia. In the last century, it was in a scepter belonging to the Khedive of Egypt. From there to the treasures of the Sultan of Turkey. When the Sultan lost his throne in 'twenty-two, the scepter was purchased by the Romanian king. The problem with Europeans is that they forget that they are not the whole world.'

'Is the gem still mounted in a scepter?'

'No.'

'Do you have other gems?'

'Not anymore.'

In other words, he used them to buy false documents and passage to Lisbon. Victoir could guess the rest of the story. The Romanian king went into exile, having a fire sale on his way out – or lost the scepter to thieves, probably his own palace guards. One way or another the stone passed from hand to hand until it stuck in the palm of the nervous little man with the white linen suit and Panama hat. Victoir was curious about what happened to the gem since it left the Romanian king, but he didn't want to spook the man by making him account for ownership.

Victoir accepted the man's story that he had a red diamond. Even if flawed, it would be extremely valuable. If not flawed – no, that wasn't possible. A flawless red diamond would be worth a king's ransom because it was so rare.

'How do we arrange to see the gem?' Victoir asked.

Varte's eyes darted to each man. 'When I see the money.'

'How much are you asking?' Victoir asked.

'Two hundred thousand American dollars.'

Victoir kept a blank face, but João whistled. 'Nobody in Lisbon has that kind of money. And if they did, they wouldn't pay it for a stolen diamond. That's what it is, isn't it?'

'Drop me off at the casino. There are others who will give me what I want.'

By the time they got back to the parking lot at the casino, they had agreed upon fifty thousand dollars. It was an enormous amount of money. But Victoir was excited. If the diamond really matched the man's description, it was worth much more. He couldn't handle that much money on his own, but Pedro and others would kick in. João, too, though he usually insisted upon a cut just for bringing in the business.

After they got out of the car, Victoir said, 'We need a couple days to get the money together, but before we do, we need to meet so I can examine the diamond.'

Varte pointed at João. 'You stay here. Come,' he said to Victoir. He led him across the parking lot to a Peugeot with a man sitting in the driver's seat. Victoir recognized the man instantly – Heinrich, a German thug with short hair, a flat square face, and a pug nose. He reminded Victoir of a boar hog. He'd heard the man had been a sergeant in an SS unit during the war. Too broke to get out of Lisbon, he hung around the city, acting as a bodyguard and errand boy for émigrés. He was a dull and stupid man, which made him dangerous. Today he was particularly dangerous – he had a German Luger on the seat beside him.

Victoir got into the backseat with Varte. 'So it's in the car.'

'Only when I am in it.' Varte grinned and took off his hat. 'No one searches hats, not even at border crossings.' He removed a small leather pouch from the inside band, opened the pouch, and shook a stone onto his hand.

Victoir smothered a gasp at the sight of the stone, but he couldn't hide his reaction. His breath was swept from him.

'You thought I was lying, didn't you?'

Even in the dull light of the car, the Old European-cut diamond glittered red hot. It was exquisite. And Varte was right about the weight. Victoir estimated it to be about forty, maybe a carat or two more.

'It's worth many times what I'm asking,' Varte said.

'I don't know, it has to be evaluated. It's too dark in the car for me to examine it.' Even with flaws, the diamond would be immensely valuable. Without flaws – that was unthinkable. The stone was absolutely unique. Varte had not lied, it was a true ruby-red. He doubted Varte really understood what he had. The man knew it was valuable, but either didn't understand it's true value . . . or maybe he was just desperate. At that, the amount of money he demanded would give him a good life in South America.

'Does it have a name?' Victoir asked. Like winds, some diamonds were unique enough to have a name – the indigo blue Hope Diamond, the Koh-i-Nur 'Mountain of Light,' the 530-carat Star of Africa, the blue rose-cut Great Mogul, the great pink Darya-i-Nur, the big canary yellow Tiffany. A name sent the diamond's value soaring.

'It's called the Heart of the World,' Varte said. 'That's the Muslim name for it. You can call it what you like.'

Heart of the World. Yes, it fit.

'Before I saw this one,' Varte said, 'I didn't know red diamonds existed. I thought they were all clear.'

'Diamonds come in many colors – yellow, pink, green, blue.' He didn't add that he had never heard of a true ruby-red, although there were shades lighter and darker. And a ruby itself would not compare to the fiery diamond Varte was selling, because rubies don't have a diamond's glittering fire. He pulled his loupe out of his breast pocket and held out his hand for the stone. 'I can't really judge it in this light.'

Varte indicated a flashlight. 'Use that.' Before handing him the stone, the Romanian nodded at his guard dog, Heinrich. 'Watch his friend across the parking lot, I've heard bad things about that Portuguese.'

'He comes toward us, I kill him.'

'If this one touches the car door while he's holding the diamond, kill him, too.'

'*Jawol.*' He smiled.

Victoir believed the German would do it. A deceptive concept like bluffing would be too complex for Heinrich to handle. 'Hold the light for me,' he asked Varte. Examining the stone under magnification against a white sheet of paper, Victoir could detect no visible flaws. But he equivocated because the conditions were so poor. 'The light is not good enough for a professional examination. I need to—'

'You have had all the examination that you will get. Even if there were small flaws, the gem is worth a fortune. Give it to me.'

He grabbed it from Victoir.

'Get out.'

With Victoir on the pavement, Varte locked the door before rolling down the window. 'You said you need two days to get the American dollars. The exchange will take place inside the casino lounge at exactly eight o'clock on Wednesday. If I see you or your friend before that time, Heinrich will kill you.'

11

João was laying sideways on his car hood, smoking one of his Havana cigars, as Victoir trudged across the parking lot. He laughed as Victoir reached the car.

'*Amigo*, you have the look of a man who just lost his favorite woman.'

'You should have seen it, João, it was extraordinary. Varte wasn't lying, it had to belong to kings.'

'All the more reason to make sure the swine doesn't get away with it.' João made a cutting motion across his throat.

Victoir wasn't usually particular about the source of the gems he bought and sold. Six years of war had turned Europe upside down, killed millions, and emptied the pockets of millions more. But he drew the line at letting someone profit whom he suspected of being a Nazi. After Victoir completed a deal with such people, João followed the seller and relieved the man of the purchase price, splitting the money later with Victoir. Victoir thought of it as a private war. But robbery was one thing – killing was another. Helping refugees by buying their jewelry made him feel good. Making sure a Nazi didn't profit from stolen goods made him feel good. Murder wasn't in his blood. João always claimed he only robbed the goosestepper, but Victoir was never entirely sure. Nor did he press the point.

Victoir shook his head. 'You can't just walk up to him and grab it. He has that big kraut, Heinrich, protecting him. And he's chosen the casino lounge for the transfer. There's no way we'll get the diamond and keep the money. And I don't want to stifle the deal trying. The stone's worth much more than what he's asking.'

'So it's really unique,' João said dreamily, more to himself than to Victoir.

'Like nothing I've seen before.' Victoir's hands were sweaty and he wiped them on his coat. 'Like nothing I've even imagined. A gem that belongs in a royal crown. It's got a name and even a history, like the Great Mogul, only more provocative. Three monarchs who possessed it lost their thrones. Varte seems to want to get rid of it not only for the money but because he's superstitious. He told me death stalks every man who's possessed it – and he said it like a man who knows.'

João grinned and shrugged. 'Maybe our friend has the gift of prophecy – about his own destiny.'

'João, I want this stone. I'd give anything for it. *Everything* for it. There's nothing like it on earth. When I go to America, it would be a calling card into the citadels of the diamond trade. I don't want anything to screw it up.'

That night Victoir lay in bed thinking about the diamond. It put him into a sweat. He never had the inclination to kill anyone, but when he held the Heart of the World in his hand, it created a heat of passion in him, a desire so hot it could explode as violence. What if he'd had a gun with him? Would he have shot the kraut in the back of the head and blown away Varte's face to get the diamond? Was this like the heat of passion that caused angry lovers to kill?

He knew people could get aroused by diamonds as much as sex, but that was true of many things – horse racing and money, to name two. But the Heart of the World kicked his own passion meter sky-high. 'It's not just a stone,' he'd told João before they parted, 'any more than the *Mona Lisa* is just a painting or Michelangelo's *David* is just a figure in marble.' The Heart of the World was unique and beautiful, rightfully the property of kings and queens. And it wouldn't be the first time a fabulous gem remained hidden in a king's vault until thieves got their hands on it.

The Romanian might not be wrong about where the diamond came from, either, he thought. Some of the world's finest gems originally adorned the Peacock Throne. The priceless throne was made for the Mughal emperor Shah Jahan, the Indian ruler who built the Taj Mahal. In 1739 it was seized along with other plunder by a Persian conqueror who captured Delhi and later lost in warfare with the Kurds who broke it up to sell the pieces. The Koh-i-Nur 'Mountain of Light', acquired by Queen Victoria was suspected to have come from the throne, and the same was true of the Darya-i-Nur 'Sea of Light', a flawless pale pink, and its sister, the Nur of-Eyn 'Light of the Eye', two gems in the crown jewels of Iran.

It was also possible the fire diamond was once the eye of an idol. It was believed the Hope Diamond, the forty-five-carat indigo blue, had been stolen from a Hindu idol. It was once a larger stone called the French Blue, stolen from the idol, and left a trail of murder and betrayal as it made its way to France where it ended up on the crown of Louis XVI – who lost his head, his throne, and the diamond at about the same time.

The same fatal history was true of the Orlov Diamond, the egg-shaped, 193-carat stone of the crown jewels of the Romanoffs – before they were murdered by the Reds. Both gems had histories of murder and intrigue, and, as human nature would have it, that just made them all the more desirable and valuable. A name and a history, even bad luck, increased a gem's value. The Moon of Baroda, a twenty-five-carat, pear-shaped canary yellow that once belonged to the Gaekwar rulers of Baroda in India, was said to be unlucky for the owners who wore it crossing water. How much did that reputation for misfortune add to its value? How much did the murderous history of the Great Mogul, the French Blue Hope Diamond, and the Orlov add to their value?

For certain, he had to know more about the diamond, more about its history. After he bought it, he would get it safely to America and into a bank vault. Then he would make a trip to Istanbul, Cairo, and Tehran, places the diamond would have passed through.

In his mind, it wasn't a gem stolen from an idol in India but a piece of a star which had fallen to earth. Meteorites carried diamonds to earth; in fact there was a much greater concentration of diamonds found in most meteorites than in diamond fields. Diamonds were cold to touch, they appeared warm because they drew heat from your hand. But Victoir would swear that the Heart of the World generated its own heat – like a star.

'A piece of a star,' he said aloud. He trembled thinking about it.

12

Heinrich the German was sitting at the bar when Victoir came into the casino's lounge to purchase the diamond. João was there also, but at the opposite end, talking to two women in dresses and makeup that advertised they were in the bar on business. Victoir knew João had his hands in a number of shady businesses. Finding out that João had a string of girls he pimped wouldn't have surprised him.

Victoir stood just inside the entryway, letting his eyes adjust to the mellow light. He didn't see Varte. Heinrich caught his eye and jerked his head toward the back of the room. Sitting at a table in a dark corner, a dim light hanging above the nearby entrance to the *casa de banho* making his fish's-belly complexion glow, was Varte.

'*Olá*,' Victoir said, taking a seat at the table.

'Did you bring the money?' Varte asked.

Victoir raised his eyebrows. 'Did you bring the diamond?'

'The money first. Let me see it.'

Victoir took a pouch out from under his coat and handed it to him. Varte placed the pouch on his lap so others wouldn't see the contents when he opened it. He took out a pack of hundred-dollar bills.

'The Nazis counterfeited these by the millions, using professional engravers and mint employees,' Varte said. 'How do I know they're real?'

'The problem with the Nazis' counterfeit bills is the German obsession with perfection – they made them look better than the originals.'

Victoir was sure many of the bills in the pouch were part of the millions in counterfeits that the Germans printed, but he was also sure that Varte either wouldn't be able to tell the difference – or would be so desperate that he'd take the phony bills, knowing that only an expert could tell the difference anyway.

'These are phony,' Varte said.

Victoir shook his head and reached for the pouch. The man was bluffing. He needed good light and a magnifying glass to tell the difference. 'No, they're all good. Let's not haggle. You keep your diamond and I'll—'

'I must check these under light.'

'Take a few and check them, but the rest stay with me.'

The Romanian removed some of the bills and gave the pouch back. He scurried into the hallway leading to the rest room.

Victoir leaned back and rolled his neck on his shoulders to relieve the tension. Negotiations were tough. It wasn't like talking to a couple about an engagement ring. The exchange of money and merchandise involved levels of fear, distrust, and danger.

He looked back to the bar. Heinrich was still there, hunched over a beer, his elbows on the bar, staring down into his drink. *Maybe he's reading the beer suds,* Victoir thought, *looking for what the future holds for an ex-Nazi with muscles between his ears.* He wondered why Heinrich hadn't insisted upon being at his employer's elbow when the exchange took place. There was one good possibility – that the little Romanian didn't trust the German, either. Not with a stack of money.

Victoir caught João's eyes and shook his head, indicating the exchange hadn't happened yet. He had asked João to stand at the bar and be ready to back him up if necessary. The Romanian seemed to have a healthy suspicion and fear of João, so it was better that he stood off a little.

After several minutes had passed, Victoir began to get worried. What was taking the little man so long? He smoked a cigarette, then looked at his watch again, a nervous reaction since he hadn't checked the time when the Romanian went into the bathroom. It occurred to him that there might be a back way out of the rest room – and that the man might have taken off with the five or six hundred-dollar bills he'd given him.

It wasn't a likely scenario, not when the man had an incredibly rare and valuable diamond, but stranger things had happened since the Nazis turned the world inside out and upside down.

He got up and shrugged his shoulders at João. And glanced at the bar. Heinrich was gone. *What the hell?* He hurried into the short hallway and pushed through the door to the men's *banho*, stopping short as he stepped in.

Varte was on the floor. He lay on his back, his dead eyes staring up at the ceiling, his face in a mask of shock. Blood from his cut throat made a vivid red puddle next to his head and shoulders.

His hat was gone.

The window was open.

13

The sound of a ship's foghorn wailed from the Rio Tejo as Victoir walked along Lisbon's embarcadero. Summer fog had crawled along the bay and went out to sea earlier in the day. The fall of night turned the gloom into a dark shroud that suited Victoir's purpose of being unseen.

Three days had passed since he found the Romanian lying on the floor of the rest room. He had been questioned by the police, but since the dead man wasn't Portuguese and was traveling with a false passport, a reasonable bribe to the investigating officers had stilled any questions they might have had.

Heinrich appeared the next day, his body floating in the large pool created by the sea cliffs of the Boca do Inferno. He would have stayed on the bottom – one of his ankles had been attached to chain connected to a heavy steel truck rim – but a shark had fortuitously bitten off the foot and the chain slipped off.

It wasn't hard to guess the sequence of events. João had bribed Heinrich, arranged the murder of the Romanian and theft of the diamond, and was now erasing the list of witnesses.

Victoir was certain he was on the list – escaping the Nazi beasts in occupied France had instilled in him a finely honed sense of survival.

He thought about the utterly murderous insanity that had gripped Europe for six years. And about everything he had lost. He had lived through the Nazi era in Europe, which they were calling the Holocaust, though the Gypsy expression for the genocide – *the Devouring* – was more accurate. Nothing surprised him. He had no faith in the inherent goodness of mankind. Or friendship.

He was sure the murders and theft were João's work. He felt no anger over what João had done. He suspected that if he confronted João, the Portuguese would only smile and shrug his shoulders and suggest they have a glass of wine and a good woman, rather than answering.

But there were some questions you didn't ask another man. Not when it involved double-cross, murder, and robbery. A man like João could hand you a glass of wine as he slit your throat.

His only regret was the loss of the diamond. He would have given anything for it. Except his life. That poor bastard Varte didn't know how right he was when he said the gem carried a curse. He only hoped that someday the curse would find João. But he didn't think it would – men like João made their own luck. It was the only explanation for people who bet incredible odds to rise from the gutter.

Lisbon no longer was a haven for him.

He found the dock he was looking for and walked along it to a fishing boat waiting for him. He had escaped the Nazis in France in a fishing boat. He would leave Lisbon the same way, taking the boat to England. He had been practicing his English for a year. His papers said he was American. Being American was a good choice, he thought. He wanted to go to

America, where he had relatives who could help him get established in the diamond business.

Besides, it was the one country in the world where a foreign accent did not mean you were a foreigner.

14

Win Liberte, New York, 1991

I went alone to JFK, taking a taxi to the terminal that TAP Air Portugal flew out of. Nobody had volunteered to see me off and I asked no one. The only way to start a new life is to leave the old one behind. 'Alice doesn't live here anymore,' I told Tony, the duty lobbyman, as I passed by. He gave me a puzzled look back. I didn't remember who Alice was, either.

'Gonna miss you, Mr Liberte.'

I gave him an envelope with some cash in it. Tony had been a good guy, helping me up to my apartment more than once when I was too drunk to make it alone.

I felt funny in the taxi and leaned back, trying to figure out what was wrong. Surprisingly, for a guy who never worked a day in his life and only knew how to clip the proverbial coupons, being broke didn't scare me. It was numbing, but I wasn't shaking in my boots. Maybe I was too stupid to be running scared.

Something else was bothering me and I started going down the list. It wasn't the loss of the boat or the cars – those were things that could be replaced. I was never really caught up in possessing things. I bought toys and beat the hell out of them and bought more, to use, not to hoard. I found it easy to give up things. Maybe because I lost my mother and father when I was a kid. Nothing was permanent.

That's how I felt about the apartment in the Dakota. I had a place before that one and I'd have another. The fact it was a world-class address didn't mean much to me. I got it because I had money to burn and the opportunity came up when a rock star fell and needed a quick fix to his finances after too many fixes of another type.

As the cab driver sped down Manhattan streets, playing chicken with jaywalking pedestrians, threatening to leave tire tracks on their backs and teeth marks on his bumper, I realized what was bothering me. I wasn't leaving anything behind that I cared about. Not my glamorous pad, my fast cars, my trophy boat. Not even my trophy girlfriend. I shipped Katarina off to L.A. with a first-class plane ticket and her bank account fat from the sale of the Bugatti. I liked Katarina, but I didn't miss her. I only felt a void about her when I was horny, a good sign that my attraction was more lust than love. Not that she wasn't special to me. The rest of my friends stampeded away when they heard I was broke. Katarina got the word from other people and ran to give me support, but I assured her that it was all a tax-dodge thing with my accountant. It was a good line to feed her. She didn't understand finances any more complex than balancing her checkbook, if that, but she came from an area of the world where governments had corrupt bureaucracies and tax dodging was a way of life.

I tried to think of someone or something I cared about, really cared about, and came up with a blank. I had no family. Bernie was dead and we weren't that close emotionally. My stepmother only invited me for the holidays and I always found an excuse not to accept. My stepbrother was a turd. My 'friends' were all really just acquaintances – I had no blood brothers, no frat brothers.

I hadn't thought of any of this until the merry-go-round suddenly stopped and I was thrown off and landed on my head. Bernie hadn't done me a favor – may the egotistical bastard burn in the everlasting fires of hell. But his screwup had given me more than a wake-up call about my money. Things were still a little blurry because I was still dizzy from the crash landing, but I could see that what I had called living was just a series of isolated events – this week's fuck, this week's fun – rather than a whole performance. Like the title of a book I was supposed to read in college but never got all the way through the Cliffs Notes, my life had been all sound and fury, signifying nothing.

'No friends, no nothing.'

The driver asked me what I'd said. At least, I think that's what he asked. In my father's time, the drivers had hard-to-understand Brooklyn accents. Now they had hard-to-understand accents that came with turbans and green cards. Camel jockeys, sand niggers, towel heads, those were the sort of derisive names my acquaintances – ex-acquaintances – called them. But none of the people deriding the drivers did as much work in a year as these people did in a week. What would it be like to have to drive a taxi and live in a rat hole so you could send money home to your family in the Third World, a family that would starve without it? What goes on in your mind, in your gut, when the rear passenger door of your cab opens at night and you see a guy getting in that looks like he backs out of liquor stores, high on crack, holding a Saturday night special and wearing a ski mask – and tells you to take him to a place where it's dark and lonely and no one hears gunshots and screams? What kind of crap do these people take from johns and whores and druggies and people who puke and piss—

I shivered and shrugged off the idea of ever driving a taxi. When I got that poor, I'd go the *Midnight Cowboy* route and make oral contracts in Central Park rest rooms before I'd take the crap a poor bastard who drove a cab in New York City took.

When I got out of the cab, I tossed the guy a hundred, over twice the fare, and told him to keep the change. My days as a big spender were over, but it was important to me not to feel broke.

15

I was going through airport security when I saw a woman about my age, maybe a couple years older, passing through the metal detector ahead of me. I liked the view from the back and it got even better when I saw the rest of her. She was a redhead, one of my many weaknesses.

A book had slipped out of her open bag as it went through the security scanner. I grabbed it and called after her as she was walking away.

'You dropped this.' I looked at the title. *The Social Economics of Third World Famines*.

'I think I saw the movie,' I said, grinning and handing her the book.

She gave me a look that would chill a rabid dog. 'Did you enjoy the part where children are cannibalized for food?'

Oh, shit. She was *that kind*. Idealistic. Out to save the world.

She joined a group of three men and another woman heading down the concourse. If it hadn't been for the put-down, I probably wouldn't have given her another thought. She was attractive, but definitely subzero. I'm not one of those men who grovel at the feet of women who step on them, but it always makes the chase more interesting when there are hurdles to jump. Besides, there was that red hair.

I got behind the group at the gate check-in. When it was my turn with the young Portuguese woman behind the check-in counter, I indicated the redhead across the room.

'I want her bumped up to first class, with the seat next to mine. I don't care what it costs.' I still had my American Express Card. I couldn't have left home without it.

'Is that your wife?'

'Not yet.'

'What's her name?'

'You'll have to tell me.'

The woman gave me an appraising look. 'Your Portuguese is very good, Mr Liberte.'

'My mother was Portuguese.'

'We have rules about these things.'

'*Americans* have rules about these things. Portuguese have too much soul to let a technicality stand in the way of romance.'

'Why don't you just ask her yourself?'

'I tried to put the make on her with my usual charm and wit and stuck my foot in my mouth. She's a very serious woman with world-shattering matters on her mind.'

'And you?'

'Completely degenerate with a one-track mind.'

The woman sighed. 'Yes, you certainly have Portuguese blood in your veins.' She gave the redhead a look and checked her computer. 'Marni Jones, Dr Marni Jones. She's ticketed with a UN group.'

'How do I get her seated by me?'

'What are your intentions with Dr Jones?'

'To make love with her when we reach Lisbon.'

She nodded. 'Well, that's certainly nothing the airline would object to. As long as you wait until you disembark. The seat next to you is open. *Boa sorte!*'

*

69

I barely acknowledged Dr Jones as she hesitated in the plane aisle, looking at her boarding pass. Still appearing preoccupied, I got up so she could take the window seat. I didn't want to show too much interest at first. It's better to let an ice princess make the first move. We were airborne and served drinks before she spoke to me.

'I've never flown first class before. Thank you.'

I shrugged. 'Can't trust anyone with a secret nowadays. Did she tell you why I wanted to sit next to you?'

'She said you planned to seduce me.'

'And?'

'I took the upgrade. But only for a better meal and a comfortable seat, Mr Liberte.'

'If you knew me better—'

'But I do know you. The check-in clerk gave me this.'

She pulled a *People* magazine out of her attaché bag. The cover proclaimed the Fifty Most Eligible Bachelors. She opened up to the story. ' "Win Liberte loves fast cars and fast women. He is rich, spoiled, drives a car that goes two-hundred miles per hour on public streets, dates super-model Katarina Benes, and has never worked a day in his life." '

'Wow,' I said, 'sounds like a great guy.'

'Mr Liberte – may I call you Win?'

'Mister is fine.'

'Mister, you are irrelevant.'

'Christ, I've been called plenty of things, but what the hell is irrelevant? It sounds like a social disease.'

'In a world in crisis, with wars, revolutions, starvation, injustice, and social upheavals gripping whole continents, do you know where fucking some bimbo while driving two hundred miles per hour on the freeway ranks?'

I had the feeling she was going to tell me, so I cut her off at the pass.

'Do you know what I think about the starving Africans and Asians?' I leaned closer. 'We solve the world's hunger problem by feeding half of them to the other half.'

'I was wrong – you're not irrelevant. You are a completely self-centered, avaricious, and degenerate bastard.'

It didn't take long to find out she was with a UN mission to Angola, stopping off for a conference with Portuguese aid officials before heading down to equatorial Africa.

'Angola suffers from the Third World curse of natural resources, a petro-diamond syndrome. In almost every sub-Saharan country, the discovery of oil or diamonds has brought death and misery rather than peace and prosperity. In Angola, Sierra Leone, the Congos, it's the same story over and over. Rebel warlords grab the oil wells or diamond-mining territories and use the output to buy the arms that keep them in power. They kill not by the hundreds or thousands, but murder, maim, and rape by the tens of thousands, millions have suffered or died.'

'Tell me more about Angola,' I said.

'Why?'

'I don't know, maybe I'll buy the country someday.'

'As I told you, it's a war zone. Until 1975 it was a Portuguese colony. It broke away after years of fighting the Portuguese, but independence only changed who was fighting. From the time of independence up to today, there's been civil war between a group called the MPLA and one called the UNITA. The MPLA controlled the government and was backed by the Russians with thousands of Cuban troops; the UNITA was backed by the CIA.'

'Good guys and bad guys.'

'Bad guys and worse. President Reagan called Savimbi, the leader of the CIA-backed UNITA rebels, a hero. People in Angola call him a homicidal maniac, a psychopath, and worse. He steals children, takes them in when they're starving on the streets, gets them hooked on drugs, gives them army rifles, and turns them into killers. The rebels and the government are supposed to have reached a peace accord, the Cubans have gone home, but no one's serious about peace – war is too profitable. Savimbi has grabbed the diamond area, the government's got the oil fields, they're fighting covertly and overtly, and everyone's happy except the millions of people who are starving.'

'What do you have to do with all this?' I asked.

'I monitor how much UN aid actually reaches the people who're supposed to get it. This is my first trip to Angola, but I understand that if even half of it gets properly distributed, I should cheer.'

She paused and gave me that icy look again. 'I read that your family's in the diamond business. You understand why they call them blood diamonds, Mr Liberte, don't you? Because they're soaked with the blood of innocents.'

I nodded and muttered something noncommittal about my family's diamond business.

'I recall that the House of Liberte is on the list of diamond-mine owners in Angola,' she said. 'Have you even been to Angola to see what horrors the diamond industry has created there?'

That was it, of course, my name was on the shit-list. She knew what a swine I was before she even met me. She looked like she was going to plunge the airline fork she was eating her salad with into my heart. I didn't dare tell her that my present goal in life was to see if there was a way to squeeze enough blood out of my diamond mine to put me back in the style of life I'd had before the Fall.

'Marni, did your mother pack you on her back during the sixties' Berkeley demonstrations when you were a baby?'

'Is that how you view concern for world suffering? As a throwback to the sixties? You are the most completely uninformed individual on the world outside your own selfish pleasures I have ever encountered.'

'I'll change, I promise.'

'Mr Liberte, do you know what I like about you?'

'Nothing, absolutely nothing. But now that we have that out of the way, will you have dinner with me in Lisbon?'

'I'd rather eat with a viper.'

'Is that a yes?'

16

Lisbon

Coming out of customs and into the main concourse, I made one last try with Marni.

'Are you sure you won't have dinner with me?' I asked.

'In all honesty, I should buy you dinner for the verbal assault you put up with for thousands of miles. But I'm going to be terribly busy with UN activities here in Lisbon – meetings every day, dinners every night – so I'm afraid I'm going to have to pass on repaying you.'

'Too bad, it's going to be awful lonely here in Lisbon, not knowing a soul.'

'Oh, I don't think you're going to be lonely.' She nodded over my shoulder. A woman was holding up a handkerchief with WIN written on it in lipstick. She laughed and waved the handkerchief when she saw me staring.

'Good hunting,' Marni said, walking away.

'I'm João's wife,' Simone told me. 'Sorry about the handkerchief but other than your sex and age, I didn't know who to look for.'

She spoke English with an intriguing accent. I needed practice with my Portuguese and lapsed into that after the intro. Simone drove a pearl-white vintage Rolls Royce Silver Cloud convertible. A little too tame and conservative for my tastes in transportation, but she looked good in it.

She radiated naked sensuality. Her black hair, green eyes, and pale skin – which was almost as pearly as the car – accentuated the diamonds she wore. Big ones – on her ears, around her neck, on her wrists and fingers. They all had unique settings but she wore no other gems except diamonds. That was unusual. Most women mixed their jewels, adding some rubies or sapphires for color, although I noticed on a choker several yellow and green and even a rare light pink diamond. While the colors looked good, I knew they were not the best-grade diamonds. The choker would be worth a fortune if the colored diamonds were flawless fancies, not the sort of thing you wore to pick someone up at the airport. But even with serious flaws, the gems would have been worth a hunk.

Rather than appearing ostentatious, the jewels looked good on her, like a diamond collar around the neck of a sleek jungle cat.

I did a quick calculation of the age difference between her and João, who had to be about my father's age, which would make him in his late sixties or early seventies. About twice Simone's age, which I guessed to be around thirty-five.

A hot young woman, a rich old man, probably not a match made in heaven, but I hadn't seen João yet. Maybe he was a Portuguese Jack La Lanne.

Something didn't strike me right about Simone. She had an edge to her. Not so much the hard veneer some women get who've been treated roughly and have had to fight to survive. I saw a little of that in Katarina, a 'don't tread on me' attitude. Simone's demeanor was quieter, more subtle, but infinitely more threatening. While Katarina might be tempted to scratch my eyes out, I suspected Simone was capable of kicking me in the balls and putting a knife at my throat if I pissed her off.

I saw the first sign of it when we stepped out of the terminal. She had illegally parked the Rolls in front of the terminal – the arrogance of the rich. A traffic cop with an attitude written on his face was waiting – being able to chew out an illegal parker was probably the high point of his week. He didn't get three words out of his mouth before she gave him a verbal tongue-lashing. I didn't know a lot of Portuguese street slang, but I got the idea that it wasn't the sort of talk Lisbon traffic cops often hear from women driving Rolls Royces.

'*Bastardo*,' she said as we pulled away from the curve. 'Petty little people with petty little rules.'

'Remind me not to try and enforce any of my rules on you.'

She laughed. 'I'm sorry, but I don't like policemen.' She laughed again. 'I usually don't launch such attacks on them. This one must have reminded me of someone I ran into when I was a girl.'

It made me wonder what kind of past life she led that had brought her into conflict with cops. And if her present life still offered the opportunity.

'You must think I'm horrible.'

'No, actually, I need to improve my Portuguese vocabulary and I just learned some new words. I'm just not sure what sort of people I can use it on.'

She laughed again. She laughed easily, freely, without reserve, just as she went to anger quickly and without restraint. I found myself immediately attracted to her sexually. I've heard it's inbred into men to be attracted to women like United Nations Marni who make a man give chase, no doubt some sort of primeval instinct learned around the cave. Maybe so, but there's also another kind of woman a man is irresistibly attracted to, the same sort of attraction a moth has batting its wings on the edge of a volcano. Women like Kathleen Turner in *Body Heat*, Lana Turner in *The Postman Always Rings Twice*, Barbara Stanwyck in *Double Indemnity*, and as far back as Lorelie and the Sirens, femme fatales have had an animal magnetism that leads a man to his ruin. Some bad men have that fatal magnetism, too, attracting good women to them.

I told myself to keep my zipper pulled up tight. From what I'd heard about João from my father and Bernie, he was tough – not just in a business sense, but in a lethal way.

In my mind, I saw him as the godfather of the Portuguese Mafia. Not to mention that the Portuguese had that Latin machismo that made it all right for a man to screw around, but made it punishable by death for a man to mess with their women. An American husband was more inclined to throw a punch at a trespassing male than a knife or bullet. Getting carved up in Lisbon and suffering a pauper's grave for eternity wasn't on my agenda.

'I'm surprised your father never brought you to Portugal,' she said. 'João and he did business together long before you were born.'

'Probably timing, things just didn't come down right. My mother died when I was eight, my father a few years later. He never made a trip to Portugal after I was born. My mother's health was bad and I understand he and João had worked together for so long it wasn't necessary.'

'I can set you up with her,' Simone said.

'With who?'

'The redhead you were trying to hustle as you got off the plane.'

'Run a dating service?'

'No, I noticed she's wearing a UN food badge. She and her colleagues are here to meet with Portugal's Angola aid society.'

'You know someone with the society?'

'Intimately. I'm the chairwoman.'

Finding out she headed a charitable relief organization was no more surprising than if she had said she was an astronaut. Not that there's a contradiction about a sensual animal being the chairwoman of an African relief society. But Simone didn't seem like the charitable sort. Or a pillar of high society. My instant surmise was a connection between aid to Angola and Angolan diamonds, at least for her husband.

She laughed at the look on my face. 'João has a special interest in Angola.'

'Have you been there?'

She wrinkled her nose. 'Once. I almost died because I wouldn't eat anything or drink anything and left the country as soon as I could. Whatever you've read or heard about it doesn't match experiencing it.'

She indicated the scenery we were passing. 'All concrete buildings and freeway from the airport, but downtown Lisbon is a beautiful old city. Sintra, where we live, is less than thirty minutes from downtown, but it's a different world. The village and its surroundings are considered one of the most scenic places in Europe. The United Nations declared it a World Heritage monument.'

'Any children?'

'You'll meet Juana later, my fifteen-year-old daughter. If and when she decides to come home.' She laughed again.

'Why's that funny?'

'You'll have to be careful.'

'Do I look like someone who would take advantage of a kid?'

'I wasn't worried about *you* taking advantage of her.'

17

Muito mulher. That's what I thought of João's wife, Simone, as she drove from the airport. She was definitely much woman.

The drive from Aeroport de Lisbon to the Sintra exit was a straight freeway shot, about twenty minutes. A few miles off the freeway started the scenic region which Simone said made the area a World Heritage site. It was hilly, with a narrow, winding road, small villages with cobblestone streets, and a castle called the Pena Palace peering down from the top of a hill. We passed through Sintra itself, and onto an even narrower road, hardly fit for two cars. We drove by another castle and further up the road passed an elegant hotel.

'*Palacio de Seteais*, Palace of the Seven Echos,' Simone said. 'Once the home of nobility, now a hotel. We're almost to João's house, which is quite lovely, too. It was the eighteenth-century country place of a Portuguese marquis.'

João's house. Odd way for a wife to express the place she shares with her husband. Their relationship was sounding more like the marriage of convenience that struck me the first time I saw her. A rich old man, a young trophy wife to keep his feet warm at night. The good life.

We turned past a row of ten-foot-tall hedges and turned into the open gateway and down a long driveway lined with regal Italian cypresses. The gray stone house at the end of the driveway was poised at a walled cliff. The Atlantic was beyond. Behind me, on the crown of a mountain, was Pena Palace.

It didn't smell of money – it stank of it.

João was waiting for us by a swimming pool elevated so that a swimmer could have a view of the ocean through a glass partition.

I was right on with my guess about the Portuguese Jack La Lanne. João had the complexion of polished antique bronze, silken white hair, and luxuriously thick white eyebrows. A snappy casual dresser, he was slender built, his skin firm, pulled tight across his facial bones, almost wrinkle-free. His shortsleeved shirt exposed muscles that were hard and thick. Obviously a guy who took care of himself. He was a perfect specimen of a man in his golden years. All except for the wheelchair. I wasn't expecting that.

'Shot in the back a couple years ago, playing cards,' he said, 'just like your Wild Bill Hickcok.'

'Holding aces and eights?' I asked, referring to the hand called bad luck after Hickcok was murdered holding it.

'Just a pair of aces in my hand and another pair up my sleeve.' He laughed. 'Leo fucked you.'

Nothing like getting right down to business.

The portable bar on the patio had a dozen bottles of wine. I sipped a glass of *vinho tinto*, red wine, as I listened. And studied my father's old friend.

Nothing about João was consistent. He was married to a woman half his age. Built like the proverbial brick shithouse even in his old age, he was hostage to a wheelchair. The house he lived in was a genuine antique, a fabulous place that once entertained kings and queens. But the swimming pool beside us was ultramodern, black bottomed with lots of gilt running through it. Greek and Romanesque marble gods hung out around the pool. Large imperial columns separated the pool patio from the ocean view.

The effect was supposed to make the patio look old and rich. It struck me as nouveau riche, tastelessly ostentatious. Maybe João's designer did movies about the Roman Empire and had a spare set left over.

Large sardines, boiled barnacles called *percebes*, and cheese *aperitivos* were set out by an elderly woman I took to be the housekeeper. The sardines were served Portuguese style – I had to gut them myself. I would have expected caviar and champagne from the ambiance of the house. Even the wine was a surprise. It was a good, inexpensive, red table wine, what the Portuguese called *vinho tinto de mesa*.

Simone kissed João when we arrived. Now she sat quietly as he spoke, the good wife.

77

'I'm the one who suggested to Bernie that he consider getting into the diamond-mining business.'

João had a low, liquid voice, like a fine aged wine. It was the kind of voice that massaged you, made you feel comfortable – just before the knife slipped between your ribs. If I hadn't remembered my father's distrust of João, I would have been sucked in. Once I knew there was a relationship between Portugal and Angola, it wasn't hard to put João into the picture. Marni told me on the plane that when the Portuguese colonists left the country in 1975, some of them carried wine bottles full of diamonds out of the country. I could imagine João waiting at the Lisbon airport to meet the planes with cash and a diamond scale.

'I had no idea Bernie would end up sinking your entire inheritance into the mine. I expected him to spread the risk around, but he only brought in Leo, which turned into a disaster. When Bernie had to raise money on a cash call, Leo put the screws to him – and you.'

'Leo knew how to play Bernie. Jerked on his ego,' I said.

'Isn't that how you control a man? Men are controlled either by money or a woman. Most can't pass up either.' He gave Simone a meaningful look.

He was right about Bernie – his trigger point was money. But it wasn't because Bernie was ostentatious. Hell, he probably would have stayed in his rent-controlled apartment if he had won a multistate lottery. No, with him it was a way to get respect and admiration from others. Hell, Bernie wore polyester suits and imitation-leather shoes even in his salad days. Had he spent my money on clothes, cars, and women, I could have understood it better than some screwball mining scheme.

'I have a feeling the mine must have been salted,' I said. 'That would have suckered Bernie in. Leo found out about it and bailed out. Leo's that kind – a nerd, but he knows how to make money. And keep what he makes.'

I never let anything in my voice expose my suspicion that João might have set the whole deal up.

João shook his head. 'You'll have to explain what you mean by "salting" a mine.'

'Tell you the truth, I have little idea myself, at least in terms of a diamond mine. When I was a kid I saw an old movie where the crooks made a mine appear to have gold deposits by shooting gold into the mine with a shotgun. I can't imagine that being done with diamonds. Not that it would have lured Bernie in, anyway. I'm sure he never saw the mine.'

'You wouldn't create a false impression of diamonds by physically plant-ing diamonds in the mine. It would be done through fraudulent geology reports. And you're right, Bernie never saw the mine. He bought the mine based upon my recommendation.'

'Great. Then I can thank you for setting Bernie up to screw me. Is that what you're telling me?'

'You have Bernie and Leo to blame,' João said. 'I didn't know your inheritance was going into the deal.'

'It looks like the mine was a bad investment no matter how you cut it. I still own the mine and I'm told it's losing money. Why'd you recommend Bernie get into something that was bleeding money?'

'The mine was never expected to make money; Bernie knew that going in.'

'Excuse me? Bernie was investing my money in a mine that wasn't expected to turn a profit?'

'It was a way of opening a door to other opportunities.'

'What opportunities?'

'I assume you know how the world's diamond industry works. Most of the diamonds coming out of Africa are controlled by De Beers and their system of sight holders. It's a private club and those of us who aren't members are left scrabbling for stones where we can. I've had good contacts in Africa over the years, especially in Angola because of the Portuguese background of the country, but as people get older and die or retire, and regimes change, most of my Angolan resources have dried up. However, while that was happening, another phenomenon was at work. There is worldwide concern over the conflict diamonds—'

'Blood diamonds. The ones that fuel the wars and civil wars on the continent.' Marni would have been proud of me.

'Blood diamonds, war diamonds, conflict – whatever you call them, it's diamonds for weapons. There are efforts being made to stop the trade.' João shook his head. 'Such naïveté. As if the warring factions wouldn't find other ways to finance their fighting, methods much more cruel than taking part of the diamond output to buy weapons. The efforts to stop the trade have encouraged a boycott of diamonds from the countries where fighting is being financed by diamond production.'

João paused and took a sip of wine. 'As you know, diamonds do not have fingerprints. Whether a diamond was mined in Angola, the Congo, or

Siberia, no one can tell.'

'I've heard that they're trying to develop ways of telling.'

'True, true, but it will never be that precise because there are areas in Africa where the same billion-year-old volcanic eruption created diamonds that are spread over more than one country. Those diamonds will all have the same fingerprint. Regardless, the mounting boycott of conflict diamonds has created a great opportunity for us.'

I caught the 'us' and let it fly over my shoulder. 'Are Angolan diamonds on the boycott list?' It was an important question. I didn't know if my money-losing mine could ever be made profitable, but it was a foregone conclusion if on top of everything else, it wasn't possible to sell diamonds mined from it.

'No. Angola is presently in a transitory period. Savimbi and the government have made a temporary peace. Technically, that makes Angola no longer a war zone.'

'Technically?'

'The peace won't last. I give it a year, maybe two. Savimbi is not sane, he's a complete lunatic, nor is the government truly representative of the people. It won't be long before the honeymoon turns into a violent divorce. They've been fighting for decades, murdering and butchering each other. A piece of paper called a peace agreement can't soak up all the blood that's been spilled.'

'How did Bernie and my diamond mine fit into this bizarre quagmire of civil war and the international furor over blood diamonds?'

'There is a certification process for diamonds. To avoid the boycott, a diamond must come with a certificate that it was mined in a country not on the list of warring nations.'

I put it together. 'Diamonds don't have fingerprints. You mine the diamonds in Sierra Leone or some other place on the prohibited list, get a certificate from a mine in Angola, and you can sell the diamonds in the open market. Because they're tainted, you get blood diamonds much cheaper than other diamonds. Yet they sell the same as other stones.'

'Very good.' João clapped his hands. 'You have your father's intuitive powers. Yes, you get the diamonds much cheaper – but not just because they are conflict diamonds. Even more important than the pedigree of the diamonds is how they're paid for. It is a system of barter, not cash-and-carry.'

'What are they bartered for?'

'The warlords would often rather have weapons than money. Traders who go in and offer them arms and ammunition, rather than just money, are fulfilling a need. Like your American movies, the transactions are probably not unlike the gun runners who used to haul wagonloads of repeating rifles to tribes during the days of the Indian wars in the Old West. Only these war supplies come in jet transport planes and the weaponry often includes battle tanks and ground-to-air missiles.'

'Where do diamond dealers get that kind of weaponry?'

'Just as there is a boycott on buying blood diamonds from the African warlords, there is a prohibition against selling them arms. The weapons are, shall we say, black-market items, many of them purchased surreptitiously in the Soviet Union as that country undergoes massive economic problems.

'Naturally, there is a tremendous markup on the prices, not to mention added expense in getting them from one country to another. The system of payoffs is mind-boggling. A rifle that would sell for three hundred dollars in a sale sanctioned by the government where it was manufactured sells for many times that when it is delivered to a dirt airfield in the middle of a jungle in the middle of a war.'

I sipped my wine and thought about it. It was a clever scheme. About as dirty as it can get. And probably as profitable as the illegal drug trade. 'You pay much less for the diamonds than you would on the open market, and the payment is made by weapons that are grossly overpriced. You then turn around and sell the diamonds for their regular market price. You double-end the deal by gouging both the buyer and seller.'

'*Exactamente!* Now do you see why the mine was not expected to make a profit?'

'Yeah, and I can see why Bernie would have jumped at the opportunity. He would have his own mine. It didn't matter that the mine was hemorrhaging red ink mining diamonds. The diamond production at the mine is irrelevant. The real payoff would be in providing certificates for blood diamonds. Bernie gets to walk around the Diamond District with pockets full of diamonds that he tells people came from his own mine, he gets blood diamonds cheap, and you rack it in as a middleman between the mine owner and warlords.'

João clapped his hands again and Simone let out one of her laughs. 'It was what you Americans would call a win-win scenario, yes?' he asked.

'Yeah, but if it's such a brilliant idea, why don't you tell me what went so wrong that my inheritance got pissed down the drain – and made poor Bernie take a nosedive out a high-rise window.'

João shook his head. His expression was one of genuine regret. 'We could have made buckets of diamonds on the deal and a few pennies' worth of lead defeated us.'

'Come again?'

'The warlord we made our deal with took a nine-millimeter round in his left eye before the matter was completed. I understand it ricocheted inside his thick skull a while before coming to rest.'

'So why would one deal squelch the scheme?'

'These matters are often a three-party transaction – the diamond dealer, arms dealer, and warlord. In order to maximize our profits, we – Bernie, Leo, and myself – decided to supply the weapons used in the transaction. That meant putting out a great deal of money—'

'Especially after Bernie already put out millions for a mine.'

'True, and the arms and transportation cost millions more. Everything went fine until a government army patrol stumbled upon our airfield when the exchange was being made. Shots were exchanged and an unlucky bullet struck our warlord.' João shook his head again. 'The government patrol was run off, but as soon as their leader went down, his underlings started warring among themselves for the diamonds and the weapons. They parked a jeep in front of the plane to keep it from taking off while they argued. The argument turned into a fight and the plane and its contents became casualties. We ended up getting nothing out of the deal.'

'Jesus, this was much too complicated for Bernie,' I said, shaking my head in disbelief. 'He wasn't a bad guy or stupid, he was a pretty good diamond merchant on an even playing field. But this blood-diamond stuff wasn't the business he knew. Everything went to hell and he found himself ass-high in alligators.'

'You have my sincerest regret,' João said. 'I had no idea he had gambled so much. I suffered the greatest loss, but I had other assets to keep me afloat. I didn't realize Bernie basically had only your estate to gamble.'

I wasn't buying João's sympathy act. He wasn't anyone to cry over someone else's spilled blood. But there was still no percentage in taking him on until I knew all the cards he held.

All my logic and reasoning went to hell when I met his eyes. Yeah, he was deadly serious, but there was a hint of amusement in his eyes. He was toying with me. It pissed me off.

'So you got Bernie in over his head and fucked with his mind until he lost everything he had and everything I had,' I said to João. 'Is that the bottom line?'

'Bernie knew exactly what he was getting into,' João said gravely. 'I also suffered a great loss. Bernie paid for the mine, but I covered the lion's share of the purchase of arms. When the deal went through, I lost my collateral, something I cherish more than life itself. I regret that the son of my old friend was inadvertently damaged by the situation.' He spread his hands on the patio table. 'However, the damage can still be undone.'

'I still own the mine, you still have a contact for the diamond–gun exchange. Is that what the invitation to Lisbon is all about?'

João chuckled. Not the humorous laugh that his wife often came out with, but the sound a hunter makes when a funny thought occurs to him as he's about to shoot a deer between the eyes.

'As I said, you have your father's gift of insight. He always knew what I was thinking – even before I did. But yes, as you put it, that's about it. You have a mine that is worthless at the moment, but that can be put to a valuable use. It is a cover for issuing certifications. I have a contact with another warlord who has buckets of diamonds and is in need of weapons. And I have an arms dealer lined up to provide the barter items.'

'I don't have the money to finance a deal,' I said.

'Neither do I, at least not one this size. Besides the disaster that Bernie was a part of, I've had other reverses caused by situations in Angola. This time the arms merchant will be part of the deal.'

'What do you want from me? And what's in it for me?'

'As the mine owner, you can sign certifications for the diamonds we get. The certifications have to be signed in Angola and certified in Angola. Bernie would have flown there once we had the diamonds.'

'That's all I have to do, sign a piece of paper?'

'Basically.'

'I'm not Bernie. Let me have it straight. Unlike Bernie, I won't be taking my own life if I get fucked over in the deal.'

João gave me a humorless raptor's grin. 'Your father was not a physical man. It's one of the things I admired about him. He did everything with his brain. I would hope his son inherited that good sense.'

'Let's leave my father resting in peace and tell me exactly what the deal is and what my part in it is.'

João poured us each more red wine from the carafe as he spoke.

'As you might imagine, in this world there is more than one dealer willing to supply arms for diamonds. Because it is a competitive business,' he gave me another raptor's razor-tooth grin, 'a dirty competitive business, secrecy is essential. Suffice to say that the military person desiring the weapons is in Angola.'

'That doesn't make any sense. Angolan diamonds are certifiable. Why all the secrecy?'

'Let's call the situation one of delicate transnational proportions. The person getting the arms in Angola does not want others to know that he is receiving them. As I told you, there is a temporary peace accord between the rebels and the government. Not everyone is happy with the situation. The diamonds being used for payment are not necessarily ones that can be traced to a mine in Angola – or anywhere else, for that matter.'

That told me a lot – and nothing. It told me that whoever was passing over the diamonds for weapons was either Savimbi or a wild card, someone who didn't want the rebel leader or the government to know.

João went on. 'You will be contacted once you are in Angola by the person buying the arms. Arrangements will be made for the exchange of diamonds for weapons. You will be told the arrangements when they are finalized.'

'How dangerous is it in Angola?'

'No more than waving an Israeli flag in Baghdad or Teheran during Ramadan.'

'I've got a better idea. I'll sell you the mine. You go to Angola, make the arrangements, and send me a check for my share.'

He sighed and looked to his wife. 'Why is it when I am old and tired and confined to this chair that so much *merda* is dumped at my doorstep.' He cleared his throat. 'I am afraid, senhor, that I am persona non grata in that African country. But if you do not want to get involved, that is your prerogative. It will not be difficult for me to find a struggling mine owner in Angola who is willing to participate for the five million dollars you would have earned.'

I sipped my wine and didn't say a word. He had met my price. I don't know how much souls were going for with the devil, but five million would make me rich and irrelevant again.

But I didn't have to say a word. João had spent at least the last half century negotiating deals with other diamond merchants, a breed only exceeded by Persian rug dealers for a reputation of being avaricious.

'Let us drink to our new partnership,' João said.

Simone laughed.

'Do you laugh at funerals, too?' I asked her.

'Only other people's.'

I asked João to explain why he couldn't go back to Angola.

'The last time I was in Angola, I played poker with a rebel leader. I was shot in the back by someone who wanted his job. And even if my physical condition didn't prohibit me from traveling in Angola, my social position would. One tends to make enemies if they stick around the diamond business long enough. The kind of enemies that are bred in equatorial Africa come looking for you with antitank rockets.

'But,' he spread his hands on the table, 'if you are afraid to go, I don't blame you. I can arrange for you to sign the mine over to someone else, perhaps the mine manager. And you would still get a percentage, perhaps as much as ten thousand a month.'

Ten thousand a month was chump change, it wouldn't pay my champagne bill.

'Five million on one deal, that's what you're saying?'

'About two million on this deal. The rest will be earned within six or eight months with more deals. Once we do this one, we will have a steady clientele beating at our door. Shall we say . . . partners?'

'Who's the third member of the team, the arms dealer?'

'A man who is known as the Bey.'

'Sounds Turkish. Algerian?'

'From one of the Soviet Muslim republics, Turkistan, I believe, but he now lives in Istanbul. Formerly a colonel in the Soviet army quartermaster corps. Left the Soviet Union one step ahead of a firing squad, or so I've heard. He apparently got into the black-market arms business while still in uniform. You've heard that expression, "cannon king"?'

'Not really.'

'It's an old-fashioned way to describe a merchant of death, a man who sells weapons to warring parties – and is known to fuel the conflicts to drum up business or even engineer the onset of hostilities. I believe the German munitions manufacturer Krupp was the first warmonger described by the phrase.

'The Bey is a modern cannon king. He doesn't manufacture weapons, of course. He buys stolen ones. No doubt initiating many of the thefts himself. And, like those of his ilk, he is not particular about who he sells to.

85

I understand he supplied weapons to the warring Christian and Muslim sides that turned so much of Beirut into rubble, sells the ingredients for suicide bombs to the Hizbollah and stolen missile-computer technology to the Israelis.'

'Great guy to know – if you want to start a war.'

'Yes, or if you want to trade arms for diamonds. The Bey has the arms, you have the certifications, I have the person who will pay with diamonds. As you Americans say, all the bases are covered.'

I had the feeling that there were more stolen bases in the scheme than João let on. And I wasn't completely buying his contrite confessions about 'poor Bernie' and my lost millions. But right now, João was the only game in town offering me five million dollars.

I saluted João with my wine and gave Simone and him a grin.

'Funny, this will be the first real job I ever had. Look's like it's going to be a real killer . . .'

Simone laughed but João didn't know how to take the remark.

We heard youthful voices and several teenage girls came out onto the patio. They were wearing G-strings and bare skin for bathing suits. It wasn't hard to figure which one was their daughter, Juana. She had Simone's sensuous looks. Younger and skinnier, she had that starved modelesque look of Katarina and so many other fashion-magazine models.

'Jonny, come over here, I want you to meet someone,' Simone said.

The kid sauntered over, full of a sexy fifteen-year-old's conceit and arrogance. No doubt she had a modern fifteen-year-old's foul mouth, too.

'This is Win Liberte,' João said. 'You've heard me speak of him. His father was an old friend.'

She gave me a look up and down. Rude.

'You look better in magazines,' she said, speaking in English. 'But I guess they touch those up.'

I gave it right back to her. 'I'm surprised you read magazines,' I said. 'But, of course, they have big pictures and little words.'

'Fu—'

Simone's laugh cut her off. 'You deserved that, you're a nasty little bitch. Now go back to your friends.'

Jonny muttered a filthy Portuguese expletive about a *caralho*, a man's private part, and gave me a look that told me she wasn't finished with me.

I had to admit though, a surge of desire hit me as my eyes lingered on her baby-smooth buttocks as she walked away.

'I've got a better idea,' I told João, when his daughter was out of earshot. 'Let's send *her* to deal with the war in Angola.'

João grunted. 'She would steal the diamonds and sell them for a new dress.'

'She should be disciplined more, but my husband spoils her and permits her every excess.'

'She is not half as wild and crazy as her mother was at her age,' João rebutted.

Interesting remark. With their age difference, I wondered where he'd found his wife. On a school ground?

18

Simone showed me to a room with a view of the ocean. I couldn't have done better than if I'd stayed at the hotel-palace down the road. The room was luxury-class.

'There's a minibar in case you get thirsty and the buzzer to call the servants is on the end table. We want you to feel at home here. The servants will provide you with anything you want.'

The servants couldn't provide me with an hour of lovemaking to their mistress, but I politely didn't bring up the point.

She paused at the door.

'Would you like me to arrange dinner with her?'

'With your daughter? She's a little young—'

'With the woman from the airport.'

'I'd appreciate getting her phone number.'

'Why don't I arrange it so that she believes she is meeting an important contributor to the cause of world suffering.'

I laughed. 'She already believes that, but I know what you mean. You think she won't go out with me if I call?'

'What do you think?'

'It's easy to say no over the phone.'

'Yes, and I saw her at the airport. She looks like the dedicated type, a person who fights for truth and justice. Not at all the type to waste her time with a man who loves women and fast cars.'

'You're a smart cookie, Simone. Arrange it for me.'

She gave me a parting shot as she left.

'She's not like us, is she?'

I stood by the window and wondered what she meant. Maybe I didn't bleed for world suffering or serve Thanksgiving turkey to winos in the Bowery, but I didn't think I was – then it struck me. Hell, I was just talking about a deal where I'd make a buck – five million of them to be exact – providing arms that killed people. The deal was murder piled upon immoralities and illegalities. All for filthy lucre.

I was no better than João. And probably had less excuses than he did to be involved in bad things with bad people. My father mentioned João had to fight his way off the streets, held back both by poverty and prejudices against his mulatto heritage. My guess is that Simone hadn't come from high society, either. The only thing I had to blame for my willingness to do evil was my own stupidity and laziness in not taking care of my financial affairs.

There was another aspect to Simone's remark that cut me and that I had to think about.

Was I really going to make a deal with the devil? Would I do illegal and immoral things for five million dollars? Acts that could fuel a war?

Look, pal, I told myself, *it's not your fight, not your duty to save the world.*

I didn't create the poverty and misery in Africa and Asia. I know Western imperialism could account for some of it, but mostly, the Third World made its own bed. My job was to make money. If people used the money to hurt each other, it wasn't my fault. If I didn't do it, other people would.

My conscience soothed, I started to unpack. I heard someone at the door and turned. Simone had left without closing it.

Jonny and one of her G-stringed girlfriends were in the doorway.

Jonny leaned over and kissed the girl on the mouth and pulled down the girl's skimpy bathing suit top. She massaged the girl's breasts and smiled at me.

'Want to fuck us?'

I smiled and went over to them.

'Come back when you grow up.'
I slammed the door. I was no fool . . . or maybe I was.
I needed a cold shower.

19

Lisbon . . . Twenty Years Ago

João entered the cool, dark dining room of the private club. It was his favorite room in the building, conveying to him the elegance of the dining room he once saw in a stately old ocean liner – before the ship was chopped up for scrap and sent off to Japan to be made into can openers and cars. Like much of the club, the walls and floors were hardwood, mahogany, and teak. There was a hint of gilt in the ceiling and polished brass strips on the walls. Palms, great ferns, and objets d'art from Portugal's former colonial empires in Africa, India, and China, were scattered about.

He never entered the club called Palacio de la Mar without reminding himself how far he had come in life. Here he was, now a genteel middle-aged bachelor whom bankers and ship owners eyed as a potential mate for their daughters. Not that all respectable Lisbon society felt that way about him. When his membership application was considered, there were many objections to him joining the club. His social background was vague. His financial dealings often questionable. And there were rumors about him, some of which connected him to the *crime organizado* that controlled vice, gambling, and drugs from Porto to Faro.

In the end, it had not been his character – or lack of it – that decided the issue. A large bribe placed with a member who was the country's finance minister gave him a sponsorship boost. And the man who was most vocal about João's suspicious background changed his mind after he received pictures of his college-student daughter having sex with a soccer player – one on the woman's team.

It wasn't that João wanted to socialize with members of the club. He, in fact, did not. A nod and smile upon entry, a salute with his brandy glass or cigar when a member who had been friendly walked by were about the limits of his elbow-rubbing with Lisbon society.

After he became a member, there had been a number of invitations to parties and other social gatherings from members. He knew that the motive behind the invitations was to display him at the event, so that the host could boast about rubbing shoulders with someone they thought was a godfather of Portuguese crime. He refused them all. He also never engaged in business deals with other members, neither in terms of his own diamond business nor investing in their schemes. When a member would propose he enter into an investment, he was always polite – and noncommittal. The same was true of his gem business. When they queried him about diamonds, he referred them to a trader who secretly worked for him.

João's reason for seeking membership had nothing to do with social climbing. He cared nothing for those people. His opinion of them was universally low. Almost all of them had inherited their social and financial positions. Portugal was an old country with established bloodlines – there was little upward mobility. People pretty well stayed at the level they were born into.

João had more than the arrogance of a self-made man toward others who pulled themselves up with family bootstraps – he had the monstrous conceit of a man who had robbed and killed.

But membership had been important to him. His reason was one of personal satisfaction, accomplishing a goal that he had set out as a boy to make. As a twelve-year-old street arab, he had shined shoes near the entrance to the club. He had seen men arrive in chauffeur-driven cars, stepping out onto the sidewalk in their handmade shoes and expensively tailored suits. Even as a child, João had been a clotheshorse – admiring fine clothing on men and women.

Wondering what the interior looked like, the exclusive inner sanctum of a privileged few, led him inside as the doorman was carrying a bag in for a member. Sticking his head in, he smelled the oil polish used on the mahogany walls. He slipped into the entryway and crept down the hall and peeked inside a lounge where men sat around tables smoking fine cigars and drinking aged brandy.

The doorman chased him out, but as he walked down the street, he swore to himself that someday he would walk into the club and have the doorman bowing and scraping. Ultimately, he had bribed and bullied a membership to satisfy that quest. As he grew older, the membership had come to mean less to him.

Frankly, the place bored the hell out of him. He now came rarely, mostly to spend time in the dining room and lounge – the amount required of each member.

Senhora Tavora was at a table waiting for him.

'Senhora,' he said. He kissed her hand before sitting down.

'João, you are so gallant. You would be surprised how few men in this world today know how to treat a lady.'

'I would not. But perhaps you would be surprised how few women in this world know how to be a lady.'

'Like you, I am not surprised, but dismayed.'

They chatted for a moment like two old friends, the gracious older woman, wealthy with pristine bloodlines, the successful businessman. Of course, both impressions were wrong. Senhora Tavora was the biggest procurer in Lisbon – and what she procured were women and men. Whether it was a light-skinned girl for an oil-rich Arab, or a teenage boy with fragile features for a man who preferred entering through the back door, the senhora was accommodating – for a price.

When he told her to meet him at his club, it had occurred to João that someone at the club might have dealt with her in the past and would recognize her. That notion amused him on two levels: they would assume that her scandalous activities were part of his organization – and be fearful that *she* recognized them.

They talked idly over a glass of wine before lunch, really having few interests in common. João knew the senhora first as a customer for his diamond business. And over the years, he had occasionally used her procurement services to find women.

Looking at João, one would wonder why he paid a procurer – a fancy name for a pimp – to provide him with women. In good shape physically, he had grown handsome in middle-age as his youngish face contrasted with his prematurely silver hair. The hair was part of the secret for his look of youthfulness and vitality – it was thick and full, not gray or black-streaked. When he was young, his dark skin and slightly flared nose had been marks of a mulatto and a social stigma. But age and money had been kind to him. As other men grew flabby and thin on top, his genes topped his small-but-powerful, wiry frame with that handsome spray of hair. And his money bought him a manicured, finely tailored look. But the refinements were all on the outside – he still carried two knives.

João's problem was getting women who satisfied his particular need. Each of Senhora Tavora's clients had their own special needs to suit their tastes. The average women bored him. He had no time for the niceties of romance and lovemaking, any more than time and patience for ordinary business affairs. João instinctively went into business deals that offered profits which were rarely available to legitimate enterprises – and he liked the danger and excitement of the shadowy world of business where deals were sometimes made in blood. He was drawn to women from a different world, too, ones with a dangerous edge.

But none of them lasted long around João. Some left because he lost his temper and beat them. Others were caught stealing. Most women simply bored him after the initial sexual conquest.

'I have a very special girl,' the senhora said, after the social amenities had been satisfied.

'If she is anything like you, she would be very special.'

She smiled, obviously pleased, even though at her age she knew it was an empty compliment.

'She came to me from a reformatory up north. I have a person there who knows I am interested in assisting troubled girls.'

João had to take a drink of wine to smother a grin. The person was no doubt a jailer who called the senhora when someone was arrested who fitted the procurer's requirements.

'What makes her special? There are many beautiful women in Lisbon, more than I have time for.'

'She is attractive, though I would not call her beautiful. And her body, though still in the bloom of youth, is more than ample. But you are right, a man with your looks and position certainly has his choice of women. What makes her special, you ask? Have you ever watched a beauty contest? When I see all those beautiful women lined up, I am reminded of the time I went to a horse show and the breeders lined up the thoroughbreds. As your eye moves down the line, sometimes there is something special about a horse that causes you to pause. A look about the horse, the way it holds its head, the way it paws the ground, that tells you it is a champion. That is how I think of this young woman – put her in a beauty contest and she may not win the prize, but your eye would pause once you saw her.'

'What is this special quality?' he asked.

'I can't tell you exactly, I am just a poor woman who tries to bring lonely people together. But if I had to name it, I would say she has spirit. Perhaps even fire. But that is something for you to decide.'

She passed him a hotel key concealed in a napkin.

'I put her into the room at the Alfama hotel we've used before. A small, discreet place I have done business with many times. She is waiting.'

20

João stepped out of a taxi in front of the hotel. He usually drove his own car, but used his Mercedes limo whenever he went to the club. His excuse in his own mind was that parking at the club was difficult. But the real reason was that he enjoyed reliving those days when he imagined that someday he would be the one stepping out of a chauffeured car at the entrance to the club.

He deliberately sent his driver home and went to the Alfama quarter by cab – it wasn't the sort of neighborhood in which one wanted to display wealth. The Alfama, with its old Moorish quarter, was the oldest surviving section of the city, a muddle of narrow streets and alleys and small squares on the hillside below Castelo de Sao Jorge, the castle crowning the hill. He had grown up in the district, his mother working the taverns as a fado singer, living as melancholy a life as the songs she sang. It was in one of these alleys that he committed his first crime when he was eleven, breaking a bottle and stabbing a man after the man pulled his mother off the street and dragged her into the alley to get back money he claimed she stole from him.

He walked past the hotel desk and went directly for the elevator. The lone clerk nodded at him. He got off on the third floor and paused at the door to the room. He was a cautious man. He turned the key in the lock and opened the door, pushing it all the way open, making sure that no one was behind it.

She was on the bed, reading a magazine. She tossed it aside and stood up as he came in. He checked out the bathroom before looking her over.

Senhora Tavora was right – she was a pretty girl, with the potential to be an attractive woman, but too skinny and too young to compete with older, fuller women in terms of sex appeal. It was that other 'something' which the senhora recognized that was special about her. Defiance, was João's first impression. A young woman who had been kicked and beaten by life, according to the senhora, and who had been raped more than once while homeless and on the streets. But like the champion boxer or athlete, she got back on her feet and fought back.

As he looked her up and down, her eyes took on a hardness. She lifted her dress and turned around, pulled down her panties, and shoved her buttocks at him.

'Did you want to examine that?'

'I've seen better asses,' he said.

She spun around, pulling down the stretchy neckline on her blouse, exposing a breast. 'You want a suck? You can take out your teeth, old man, and nibble on it.'

He hit her.

The blow caught her completely by surprise. He swung wide, hitting her across the side of the head, above the hairline so a bruise wouldn't show. She flew sideways into the wall.

She came back at him ready to strike but he grabbed her and slammed her back against the wall, pinning his forearm in her throat. His free hand came up with a knife.

He showed her the blade, twisting it, letting it catch the light and reflect in her eyes.

'My name is João. I am the meanest *bastardo* you have ever met. You are going to be my woman. When I want you, I will snap my fingers and you will come. If I want to fuck you, you will bend over. If I want my dog to fuck you, you will bend over. Do you understand?'

She spat in his face.

He shoved his elbow harder against her throat, feeling the fragile cartilage giving under the pressure. Her face went red and she gasped for breath.

'I like a woman with spirit. But you must understand that there are limits to my patience.' He let up a little on the pressure against her throat and touched the nipple of her exposed breast with the sharp tip of the knife and saw her flinch.

He kissed her mouth. She accepted his lips without responding.

The knife moved carelessly against her breast. João applied pressure and sliced an inch of her breast. Blood streamed down her white skin.

'That's my mark. From now on, you're my woman. Unless I want to give you to someone else.'

He stepped back and put away the knife and sat down on the edge of the bed to take off his shoes. 'Now I'm going to fuck you.'

He saw it coming but she was young and too fast for him. The sharp edge of an ashtray caught him on the side of the neck, leaving a gash.

'That's my mark,' Simone said.

21

Lisbon, 1991

Simone arranged the dinner date with Marni for the following night. The restaurant where I was to meet Marni was near the Rossio, the main square in the middle of Lisbon. I turned down a chauffeur-driven ride and my hosts loaned me a Mercedes. I parked the car in an underground garage around the corner from the west end of the square and walked to the restaurant on the east end. I probably could have found parking closer but I wanted to walk the Rossio – there was a bit of my family heritage on the square. It was where my father had met my mother and fallen in love on first sight.

I smiled as I thought of their meeting, as he looked over and saw her at a sidewalk café, she looking up to meet his eyes. Did what Hollywood call a 'cute meet' occur? As their eyes met, did time stand still, all motion on the street stop, music and voices fade?

As I walked past the big lighted fountain in the middle of the square, I decided that's exactly what had happened to my mother and father. There had been magic that first time their eyes met.

Marni was waiting in the restaurant reception area when I came in. She had her back to me, looking at a painting of a king from some long-forgotten era. I slipped up quietly.

'*Olá, fala Inglés?*' Hello, do you speak English, I asked in Portuguese.

She stared at me, her lips parted in surprise. Then she shut her mouth and pursed her lips as a red color came to her cheeks. She realized she'd been tricked and was struggling between going along with the game or turning on her heel and walking out.

'*Non. Parlez-vous francais?*' she asked.

'*Qui*, I speak French. As a matter of fact, I have French relatives, but let's stick to English, it's much easier.'

'I'm supposed to be meeting a very important Lisbon executive who can help with the aid program. I'm very angry at—'

'No, you're not, I forced Simone to set you up. I told her I'd fallen hopelessly in love with you on the plane and that I'd cut my wrists if I didn't get to see you. She saved my life.'

'If there's a choice, I'd prefer you cut your wrists rather than have dinner with you.'

I grasped both her arms and brought her in close to me. 'Now we can be civilized and adult about this thing, or I can embarrass you in this restaurant with loud and vulgar accusations about how you came off the street and made a lewd proposition to me. What'll it be?'

'You're incorrigible. What do you consider being "civilized and adult"?'

'We have dinner, make love, have breakfast, make love. And so on.'

'You have a one-track mind.'

'That's not true. I sometimes think of other exciting things besides making love to a beautiful woman.'

She laughed. 'Okay, flattery will at least get you dinner. No one's called me beautiful since I was two years old. But I'm buying. That way you won't think you're entitled to dessert because you've bought a girl an expensive meal.'

'Deal.'

After we sat down, she asked, 'You have to explain something to me. Why have you bothered pursuing me? I'm not beautiful, I'm not sexy, I'm a boring teacher-administrator and soon-to-be field worker for a humanitarian cause. You have your choice of attractive women who turn heads when you escort them into a restaurant. So what is it, Win, was my turndown on the plane the first you got in your entire life? Has it traumatized you that a woman could actually not jump into bed with you the moment she saw you? Or are you a masochist?'

I gave serious thought to the question.

'Do you know what I believe in?' I asked.

'Tell me.'

'Nothing. I really don't believe in anything. I've been raised in two religions and the most significant thing I got from them is the vague threat that I have to be good or God will punish me. I can't get up any enthusiasm for social causes.' I shook my head. 'I don't give a damn about politics, religion, humanitarianism, sex education, economic indicators, abortion, earthquakes, plane crashes, or anything else that doesn't affect me *personally*. Maybe that's what intrigues me about you – other than my masochistic desire to have you crush me under your heel. I'm curious about people like you who believe enough in a cause to devote their lives to it.'

'Do you believe in love?'

'I loved my parents and they're both gone. But I've never loved anyone else. If your next question is, am I afraid to love, can it. I don't know, I'll deal with love when I find it.'

'How about all your toys?'

'Easy come, easy go. Now, you've heard my confession, tell me about you. Why did you end up an intellectual instead of a doctor or lawyer or Indian chief?'

'Are you patronizing me? First I'm beautiful, then I'm intelligent.'

'Of course, it's step one in the book I read on seducing eggheads.'

'Is that what I am? An egghead? I don't think the label quite fits me, it sounds more math and chemical than the social sciences.'

'Anyone with more than four years of college is an intellectual to me. Hell, anyone who reads more than the sports page is an intellectual to me. No, I really want to know. How did you get excited about racing off to Africa to save the Dark Continent? How did you end up specializing in Angola?'

'I don't specialize in Angola, my specialties are in Third World economics and African sociology. My interest in Africa was probably from seeing Tarzan movies when I was a little girl.'

'Tarzan movies are for boys.'

'An old-fashioned, sexist attitude. Anyway, when I was at Berkeley, I received a Fullbright to study a year at Coimbra University here in Portugal. My connection to Angola got started because my roommate was from there. She wanted help with her English and taught me her Bantu dialect in exchange. I continued learning the language because I figured it would help get me to Africa someday.'

'You said on the plane that this is your first trip to Angola.'

'Yes. My Third World education has all been theoretical, all in the class-room and working at the UN in New York. My specialty is in the theory of economics, in developing programs that support aid missions. I'm going out into the field to get some practical experience, to see the food-and-medicine chain firsthand. They say that sometimes I'll be knee-deep in crocs, snakes, and swamp water.'

I shuddered. 'Charming thought. Have you had suicidal tendencies for long?'

'The indigenous people put up with those conditions on a daily basis.'

'The indigenous people laugh off insect bites that turn the brains of foreign visitors to mush. Why are you doing this?'

'For the money, of course. I'll get rich handing out bags of rice to starv-ing people. And I can't wait to see firsthand how many atrocities have been committed to keep your diamond mine in business.'

'How is it you know absolutely nothing about me, yet already have tried and convicted me for being a rich, worthless, thoughtless bastard who lives off the spoils from the rape of Third World economies?'

Jesus H. Christ, she had me nailed tight – and correctly. If the woman knew what I was planning with João, she'd go through with that tempta-tion she had on the plane to stick a fork in my heart.

'I must have read it somewhere. But getting back to your original ques-tion about what makes me tick, this may come as a shock to you, but I wanted a career that gave me a sense of accomplishment. Knowing that I will spend my days making life easier for people who have not only been left behind by the modern world, but have been thrown to the dogs of war, gives me as much thrill as you get when you put another million in your bank account.'

'Marni, you have me wrong. I've never gotten a thrill putting money *in* a bank. I am a spendthrift – I waste, squander, and throw away vast amounts of money. I deserve some credit for the fact that I have never *made* a dollar in my entire life. You see me as a capitalist who screws over little people.' I held up my hand in Boy Scout fashion. 'I swear, I've never worked at anything long enough or hard enough to screw anyone.'

She shook her head. 'Why do I get the impression you're telling the truth – and proud of it? Has it occurred to you that you're wasting your life? How can you be proud of having done *nothing*?'

'I expect my reward to come in heaven.'

She choked on her wine.

'Tell me where you come from,' I said. 'Give me your life history.'

'I was born in San Jose on the San Francisco peninsula. My father worked for a computer company. Still does. He's a vice president in charge of research.'

I held up my hand to stop her. 'You don't have to tell me any more about your family. I have a crystal ball. Your father's a computer nerd, your mother a Berkeley feminist radical who packed you on her back to antiwar, antipolluters, antiwhatever demonstrations. The marriage between the computer nerd and the radical didn't work. There was a divorce. You were raised in a commune where people sat around all day smoking pot and making love.'

She shook her head. 'You are amazing. Either you have the blood of Sherlock Holmes in your veins or you had a detective check my background. But you left out the part about how my mother joined the Weathermen and packed me on her back into banks they robbed to finance their revolutionary ideas. And the time she—'

'In other words, I'm completely wrong about everything.'

'Mr Liberte, I couldn't have said it better.'

'I think we're absolutely compatible.' I shrugged. 'Opposites attract. You're an idealistic woman with a string of degrees after your name and a mission to save the world in front of you. I'm an irresponsible never-do-well who needs to be reformed and have nothing to do except squander another fortune.' I leaned closer until my lips almost brushed hers. Her warm sensuality radiated. The moment I saw Katarina, I wanted to fuck her. Marni was a woman I wanted to make love to.

'Win . . .'

'Let's—'

'No. And not because I don't want to.' She pushed me back a little and straightened my collar. 'I want to very much.'

'Do you have someone you have to account to?'

'Yes – myself. I'm not a strong person. I have work to do, mountains to climb, rivers to swim. I can't let myself get involved with a man. I won't be able to function if I did.'

I was talking about making love, not involvement.

She read my mind. 'I'm not like you. I can't explain why, but I just can't get involved with you. Dinner was good, the company was terrific.'

She gave me a peck on the cheek and got up.

I stood up and took her in my arms. 'Don't go. I want to be with you.'

Shaking her head, she pulled away from me. 'It just can't be.'

I watched her disappear out the front door, then threw enough on the table to cover three meals. She forgot to pay. '*Obrigado,*' I told the smiling waiter on my way out.

Marni was a puzzle wrapped in an enigma to me. I could usually classify people, especially women my own age. But every time I put her in a box, she jumped out and hopped into another one. Yeah, she was a socially conscious intellectual, but she was also a lush, warm, sensuous woman who sent my testosterone level racing.

I was just as puzzled about my feelings for her as she apparently was about me.

What the hell – I had rivers and mountains to cross, too. 'And castle walls to storm, dragons to slay,' I told the night. I didn't have the time to ferret out the mystery of Marni Jones.

I was heading for the underground garage around the corner from the square when I saw Jonny. She was with a group near the big fountain in the middle of Rossio. And she wasn't happy.

22

There were eight or ten people hanging out, most of them young – around Jonny's age to college age – and three men who were older, in their mid to late twenties. The kids looked like Jonny – spoiled, rich, purposeless. The three older guys had a harder look to them, especially the one arguing with Jonny.

It wasn't my business and I kept walking, but stopped when I saw one of the hard cases move to the side of Jonny while she argued with his buddy. I had a feeling he was getting into position to grab her. *Shit.* Getting stomped by Lisbon street trash wasn't on my agenda, but I couldn't see the kid get hurt.

I caught the name of the one she was venting at – Santos – and the gist

of the argument as I approached. She was pissed about Ecstasy he sold her
– not high-quality stuff. Wonderful. Now I could get stomped for a good
reason – keeping a fifteen-year-old in drugs.

Santos looked past Jonny as I came up toward them. Most of us think
we live in a civilized society, but at a certain level on the streets, brute
strength counted for more than brainpower. Santos was built like an
artillery shell – not tall, but solid, tapered from the bottom up – big tree-
stump legs, big torso, big neck, small head. I wasn't a pushover but I wasn't
tough, either.

'Hi, Jonny, need a ride home?'

The look on Jonny's face said she wasn't sure if she was going to tell me
to flake off.

'Fuck off, *puta.*'

Santos wasn't calling Jonny a whore – he used the word on me.

'Let's go get—' As I spoke to Jonny, reaching for her arm, I spun on my
heel and threw a right cross for Santos's face, throwing my shoulder and
body weight into it. Just the way I was taught. The punch connected great,
nailing Santos on the jaw. The concussion from the blow ran up my arm.

Santos rocked back on his heels and took a half step backward with one
foot.

It should have knocked him on his ass. The arm still stung – it felt like I
had punched a brick wall.

Santos's eyes glazed over for a second. When they cleared, they focused
on me. Not a human look, but the cold, vicious way a pit bull looks at the
exposed neck of another dog.

I could kiss my ass good-bye.

Jonny was suddenly between us, hitting him with a series of kicks.

'You disgusting bastard, João will rip off your balls and feed them to his
dogs.'

Santos took the kicks and the diatribe without changing his expression.

Jonny grabbed my arm. 'Let's get out of here, away from these stinking
merdas.'

We walked in the direction of the underground garage.

'*Obrigado,*' she said. 'But I didn't need your help. He wouldn't touch me,
he knows João's my father.' She gave me a look of false sincerity. 'Now you
must pay me for the money I lost on his bad pills.'

'Forget it, I'm not into buying drugs.'

She took my arm as we walked.

'What are you into? Sex? We can go to a hotel or fuck when we get back home.'

'Do you think your parents might be a little put out if they find us balling in the living room?'

She shrugged. 'I learned everything I know about sex from watching my mother.'

I looked behind us. Santos and his two buddies were following us.

'Don't worry,' she said. 'They're afraid of João. My father is old but has important friends.'

'They may not hurt you, but that doesn't mean they won't tear my head off.'

The Mercedes was three levels down. We got in and I hit the door locks. As I started the engine, she was all over me. She stuck her tongue in my mouth and took my hand, putting it on the warm patch between her legs.

She bit my ear. 'We can do it here.'

I pushed her off and got the car into drive. 'We're getting out of here. There'd be no witnesses to tell João anything if the two of us were beaten to death down here.'

I navigated the big Mercedes up the ramps. A surprise was waiting for me on the ramp to the street. It was blocked. A small Fiat was parked on the top of the ramp, facing down at us as I came up to the bottom of the ramp.

Santos got out of the passenger side of the Fiat. In his hand was a three-foot piece of steel pipe. He no longer had an expressionless face – he looked ugly, mean, and pissed.

Jonny looked at me. '*Merda.*'

'Yeah, like I said, no witnesses.'

I hit the gas and turned the wheel, whipping the car around, its tires screeching loudly in the underground vault. Instead of racing back down the ramps to get trapped further below, I put the car into reverse and turned in the seat to look back at the ramp the Fiat was blocking.

'What are you doing.'

'I'm going to clear the roadway. Put on your seat belt.'

I hit the gas, burning rubber, as the Mercedes shot backward. Santos gawked as the car came up the ramp. He flattened himself against the wall and dropped the steel bar. The driver in the Fiat gawked at me. I could see his confusion and panic as he fumbled to get the car in reverse.

He had it into reverse when the rear of the Mercedes hit the front of the

Fiat. The collision sent the Fiat flying out the ramp. The Mercedes hit it again as we burst out the exit and into the square, sending the Fiat into a wild spin.

I slammed the Mercedes into drive and took off.

Jonny stared at me, her mouth open.

'Demolition derby,' I said. 'I drove in one when I was a kid. The front end of a car is fragile because that's where the motor is, but the rear can be used as a battering ram.'

'You're crazy.'

'I get that way when people try to kill me.'

She snuggled close to me. 'I like you. I know how to pay for favors.' She reverted to English.

'I'm a guest in your house. Fucking you wouldn't be too polite.'

She laughed. 'You think we're the *Brady Bunch*? João picked Simone off the street – or maybe a whorehouse. He's not even my father – Simone got knocked up by the chauffeur. He ended up in the Boca do Ferno with cement shoes. Or maybe it was the gardener or the man who teaches her tennis. She's fucked them all.'

I didn't say anything. And didn't buy into any of it. Jonny wouldn't be the first kid to hate a parent. Hell, kids sometimes kill their makers. And vice versa. But I knew that João was up to something. My father didn't trust him – and I suspected that Bernie had been too trusting. What I wanted was information from her, not sex.

'You want me to tell you what João's up to, don't you?'

I checked her out from the corner of my eye. 'You into mind reading? Have some Gypsy blood?'

'You're just too honest. I could see the conflict on your face, do you ask the kid to betray her father or—'

'You said he wasn't your father.'

'I don't know who he is and I don't know what he's up to, but whatever it is, people will lose something. Maybe even die. The father of one of my friends has a problem – he is always looking at young girls, younger than me. They say he has a sickness, the kids call it short eyes because of the size of the girls. João has the same kind of sickness.'

'He's a pedophile?'

'No, stupid, he's got eyes for money, even Simone says he's sick.'

'Lots of people like money.'

'Enough to kill for it?'

'Have you ever actually seen him kill someone? Is he going to kill Santos?'

'By the time I tell João about Santos, there won't be any Santos. The piece of shit will get out of Lisbon, maybe go hide in Spain or even Germany for a while. Then he'll have to pay his way back to Lisbon, give João enough money so he'll be in a forgiving mood. If he had hurt me, the price would be his life.'

'How do you know all this stuff?'

'Where do you think I live? In between boarding schools, I hear João on the phone, or when he has his *amigos* over, making deals, talking about people who back out of deals, talking like they're dead people.'

'What's he got planned for me?'

'I don't know, I haven't heard that one. But I think it has something to do with African diamonds and the fire diamond.'

'Fire diamond?'

'João's lover, as Simone calls it. I've never seen it, but I hear them talk about it, a priceless diamond João's had forever. He got into trouble last year, some deal in Africa, and had to give it to the Bey. You have some connection to the fire diamond, I'm not sure what.'

'Who's this Bey guy?'

'Someone he makes deals with. Simone doesn't like him. He lives in Istanbul. Sometimes João sends her there to deal with him. Maybe to fuck him.'

'You have a filthy mouth for a fifteen-year-old. Don't you ever call your parents "Mom" and "Dad"?'

'They're not my parents. I was found floating down a river in a basket. My mother was a princess who got pregnant before she got married.'

'Now I understand you.'

She gave me a questioning look.

'You're a basket case.'

She rested her head against my shoulder and was quiet on the way home. All in all, Jonny was a thoroughly modern kid, hating her parents and all screwed up from all of the hypocrisy around her. Some kids come out the starting gate without a steady stride and never lose the wobble. Jonny was one of them, going around revved up one moment, crashing the next looking for drugs, booze, or sex to make her happy. You could pretty well imagine that she'd be that way the rest of her life. It was hard to pick up the rhythm if you didn't have it out the gate.

23

I parked the Mercedes in the driveway and we got out. The rear end was crunched. 'I'll tell your parents about the damage in the morning. I'll leave you out of it.'

She put her arms around my neck and kissed me on the mouth. It was a good kiss, one of those that stirs a male's primeval reproduction juices. Her body pressed against mine.

'Good evening.'

It was Simone. I tried to break the kiss and pry Jonny's arms off but she hung on. Deliberately.

'Spying?' Jonny asked, finally letting go of me.

'Of course not, sweetie, I was just worried.'

'As you can see, Win got me home safely.'

'I wasn't worried about you, dear. But Win's in a strange country, he's not aware of all the dangers a city like Lisbon offers.'

'If you're that worried, maybe he should stay in a hotel.'

Jonny went into the house.

'I'm afraid your car's damaged.' I told Simone I bumped into Jonny on the street and we went down to the parking lot together and found someone had hit-and-run, damaging the rear end. I wasn't sure if she believed me. I figured that if Jonny wanted to tell her parents about Santos, she would.

'We can talk in the morning.'

Those were good-night words but she wasn't saying good-bye. 'I'm sorry if Jonny has been a bother. It's hard nowadays, for kids. I grew up with nothing, not even love, but that made me appreciate everything I got and to work harder for it. Jonny gets everything free and she appreciates nothing.'

'She's a great kid,' I said. What else could I say? I pulled her out of a street brawl with her drug dealer and she tried to hump me on the way home? Besides, I was beginning to believe she wasn't such a bad kid.

I could feel Simone's heat. The woman had a natural sensuality that radiated sex. I noticed the way her clothes clung to her lush body, the way she walked across a room, her full-shaped lips, and the mounds of her breasts showing above the dress that was cut low at the neck and high at the thigh. There weren't many women in my life that turned me on so fast. I could get aroused by any sensuous woman walking across the room but Simone had something extra, a hint of danger almost.

'She's a little bitch. Did she tell you her father was the chauffeur? Or that she's adopted?'

'Actually, we talked about America. She likes it.'

'You're a liar. We sent her to an expensive girl's school in Connecticut. She hated every minute of it. The only place she likes in America is Los Angeles, and that's only because it's a city of freaks. But that's all right, you are to be commended for refusing to disclose her transgressions. Unfortunately, she will be openly discussing them at breakfast – if she gets up before noon.'

'Well, it's getting late.'

'What did you think of João's proposal?'

'I'm still thinking.'

'It must all be so strange to you.'

'What? African mines, blood diamonds, murderous rebel armies? No, I run into this stuff all the time back home.'

'I've heard you love the danger of fast cars and boats. I suppose if you have to die doing something exciting, it doesn't make much difference if it's in a race car or getting shot in Africa.'

I grinned. 'It makes a difference to me. If I have a choice in the matter, I'd rather die in bed. And choose the woman whose arms I'm in.'

24

The night was warm, with a soft breeze. I pulled open the window, stripped, and took a hot shower. I turned off the light and lay naked on the bed, enjoying the gentle evening air on my body.

An hour had passed when I heard the knock on my door. I knew she would come. She was a woman who loved men. What I didn't know was whether João would send her or she would come on her own. I couldn't deny it, I was horny for her.

She dropped her silk robe at the edge of the bed and crawled on top of me. Her breasts were strong and full, her nipples rock-hard. I leaned up and sucked each succulent nipple. They smelled of rose bathwater. She got my cock between her legs. It strained frantically, already hard, pushing against her pubis, ready to enter her.

'Were you expecting Jonny?' she whispered.

'I was expecting a woman.'

I pulled her to me and kissed her hungrily.

She started down my body, teasing my nipples, sending goose bumps up my spine. She moved her tongue down my hard phallus and around my scrotum and slipped her tongue back up my stalk, moving around it like she was licking an ice cream cone.

I rolled her over and fucked her mouth with my tongue, working my way down to her mound of pubic hair. She was already wet. I took her clit and massaged it with my tongue. I felt her body start to shudder, ready to come. She gasped and let out a moan. I grasped her hips and rammed myself inside her, pumping back and forth until I exploded, her fingers digging into me, clawing my back.

We both lay spent on the bed when I sensed a shadow over us.

'Isn't it just like you, Mother?' Jonny said. 'I bring them home and you fuck them.'

I left the house in the wee hours, before the crack of dawn. I had a taxi meet me at the front gate. I didn't leave like a thief in the night – I crawled out like a worm. I wasn't sure why I suddenly got a dose of conscience. I hadn't thought twice about screwing around with Hot Pants, the investment banker's wife – but then I hadn't been a guest in his house and broken bread with him, either.

As I thought about it on the way into Lisbon, I realized what was really bothering me. It wasn't morality at all. Whatever was between João and Simone wasn't true love. Hell, maybe he had sent her to hump me, softening me up for the blood-diamond deal. He wouldn't be the first guy who used his wife's pelt as a negotiating point. I never made a definite commitment to go through with it – but I hadn't said no, either.

Getting honest with myself, which is no mean trick, I think Simone affected me more than I wanted to admit. I was attracted to Marni, she was everything I wasn't, she had more balls than a four-hundred-pound gorilla to go into a war zone to feed people. But I lusted for Simone. The woman made my blood boil. And like those femme fatales James Cain wrote about, she kicked my good sense out from under me. It wasn't hard to imagine Simone talking me into holding a pillow over her husband's face while she moved a pen in his dying hand across his last will and testimony.

I reserved a seat on a flight to Angola after I called for the taxi. It wasn't leaving until ten o'clock so I had a few hours to kill. I had the taxi drop me off at a fisherman's marina. My father told me he spent his last night in Lisbon after the war walking along the embarcadero. I wanted to retrace his steps.

PART 4

AFRICA

25

Luanda, Angola

Wet-hot heat stinking of petro and ripe fish slapped me when I stepped out of the plane and stood at the top of the portable stairway to the tarmac in Luanda. I started melting on the spot.

'Welcome to equatorial Africa,' a grinning flight attendant said. 'I hope you've had all your vaccinations.'

Yeah, I had shots for cholera, yellow fever, typhoid, hepatitis, TB, polio, and diseases I never heard of before. The only thing I missed was one for boredom. Not that my first impression of Luanda was a quiet boredom. The terminal was crowded with noisy, pushy people. A babble of languages, with some Portuguese thrown in, created a hum like loud radio static in a car crossing a desert. People in stunning peacock robes brushed shoulders with Africans and Europeans wearing Canali and Armani suits and carrying Gucci bags.

The majority of the people I saw were mestizos of a Portuguese–African mix. João had told me that the mestizos controlled the cities and government of the country, while the pure-blood Africans were rooted in the villages and countryside. More important than a matter of race, the geo-demographics were the chemistry for the civil war that the country had engaged in for the better part of the past decade and a half. The rural people felt disenfranchised politically and economically by the powerful mestizo population. Savimbi, the rebel leader, had his main support in the countryside, controlling a large portion of it, including the diamond-mining region.

Besides the civilians in the terminal, there was a conspicuous number of soldiers with lethal-looking automatic weapons. The soldiers stood around in groups of two and three, laughing, talking, smoking, a tough-looking lot, not the retired, rent-a-cop types you would find doing security in the States. The impression in the terminal was of a war zone.

It was a first impression that became a lasting one as I saw the same wartime atmosphere everywhere I went in the country.

A large black man with a big chest, thick arms, and a black cigar that smelled like roasted dog shit was waiting for me as I came into the general reception area.

'Liberte?' he asked.

It wasn't hard to recognize me – I was the only guy who got off the plane wearing a New York Yankees baseball cap.

'I'm Cross, security manager at the mine. Eduardo couldn't make it.'

His English was perfect. He was dressed in tan khakis and the type of leather-canvas jungle boots the army used in Vietnam. Put an Uzi in his hand and he'd look tougher than the soldiers decorating the place.

The missing Eduardo Marques was the mine manager.

'Is he dead?' I asked, inferring that would be the only reason the mine manager shouldn't be at the airport to meet the new owner.

Cross shrugged. 'In this country, being dead is sometimes an improvement over the living conditions.'

His body language neoned bad temper. Like the country, Cross struck me as something of a war zone. Some guys wonder how much money you make when you meet them – others wonder how tough you are. His body language communicated his feelings as I came into the reception area – he'd just as soon stomp me as shake hands.

Things are pretty smelly in Denmark when your employees don't give a shit about you. Three minutes in Angola and I was ready to jump on the next plane out. Only my newfound poverty, innate greed, and the terrifying prospects of having to work for a living kept me from heading for the ticket counter. There was nothing waiting for me back in the States except a job slapping hamburger patties at McDonald's – and I wasn't qualified for that.

Controlling my own sour mood, I ignored the asshole and went for my bags. I didn't know if he was pissed because the mine manager copped out and made him come out to pick me up, or if he just had a foul disposition. I grabbed my bags and followed him. He didn't offer to help. I followed him across the terminal with a bag in each hand and my carry-on strapped over my shoulder. I guess I was lucky he didn't have a bag or I'd be carrying that, too.

A battered old Mercedes that looked like it had lost a few Third World Wars was waiting outside. The dents and bullet holes were rusted. Hell, in this hot, wet climate, people probably rusted.

On the driver's door was a faded sign indicating that it had once been a Lisbon taxi. The driver was smoking and talking to a uniformed guard who was dressed differently than the army personnel inside the terminal and patrolling outside. The guard wore camouflage fatigues without military insignia, had an AK-47 hung over his shoulder, and a cigarette dangling from his mouth. I took him to be a private gun.

The driver opened the trunk for me and stood aside so I could put my bags in. That's okay, I thought, when we got to the hotel, I'd tip myself.

The driver and guard got in the front and I climbed in back with Cross.

'We're going straight to the hotel,' Cross said, as we pulled away from the curb. 'In case you didn't notice the government troops with the machine guns back at the airport or the private one we have riding shotgun, Luanda is not user-friendly.'

The people on the streets didn't seem to have any better dispositions than my companions. The streets were crowded with people, fat cats rubbing shoulders with people who looked defeated. Emaciated people and well-fed specimens carrying umbrellas and briefcases. Squalid mud-walled shacks with tin roofs lined the roadway. Emaciated kids with skinny frames and big eyes squatted in the dirt in front of shanties and stared at us as we drove by.

'A *musseque*,' Cross said. 'Shantytown. There're about ten million people in the country and three or four million of them are displaced by the civil war. They crowd into miserable slums because they have nowhere else to go. A lot of them end up in Luanda. There're a couple million people living in a city that was built to hold forty or fifty thousand. That's a lot of shit and piss in the gutter and water supply. While you're here, drink nothing and eat nothing that isn't completely sanitized. Licking the water off your lips in the shower or washing your toothbrush can give you a dose of something that will give you the shits for a week – if it doesn't kill you. It's supposed to be a modern city but don't let the high-rises fool you. A little glass and chrome doesn't make this place civilized or healthy.

'When you need the velvet rubbed off your cock, you call a number in Amsterdam and they send down a whore for a couple days. It costs a couple grand, but in a country where the four-letter word is AIDS, any other sex except a hand job is suicide.'

He grinned. He seemed to enjoy letting me know what a hell I had stepped into. 'But even healthy people often die from lead poisoning from a twelve-year-old kid with a nervous trigger finger.'

I wondered if he was deliberately painting a bleak picture of the place so I'd tell the taxi to turn around and take me back to the airport. Not that he had to try hard. Luanda was a harrowing experience. If the bugs and filth didn't get you, a bullet might – Marni had told me that a sizable chunk of the rebel army was twelve-year-olds who the commanders deliberately addicted to drugs so they could control them and make them good killers. At the moment, I felt more depressed from the pathos I saw than threatened.

I didn't see much of a Portuguese heritage to the place. Maybe it got blown away and burned up in the colony-era war before independence and the civil war that began in 1975. The only Portuguese flavor I saw was the names of the streets and storefronts. RUA AMILCAR CABRAL, a sign said. The sign had rusty bullet holes.

The streets were paved with ruts, the busses were battered and abused smoking sardine cans with people packed inside, hanging onto the back, and sitting on the roof. Some of the bikes I saw were running on rims.

White paint on a wall proclaimed, SOCIALISM O MUERTE! Socialism or death. A heritage from the heady days of communism, before the fall of the Evil Empire. But someone had crossed out part of it, leaving it to read, SO MUERTE!

Only Death.

There was nothing subtle about the Third World. It stepped right up and smacked you, getting in your face and under your skin. The jokes I made to Marni on the plane didn't seem so funny now. Her lecture on the horrors of war that oil and diamonds brought to Angola came home.

'What do you think of our little capital, bubba?'

'It's crowded,' I said. 'And it stinks.'

Cross gave me a look that didn't conceal his contempt for the rich American he picked up at the airport. 'You're going to find Angola an education, pal. It's a pit stop on the road to hell. Maybe it's even the finishing line.'

'Your English is good. Did you go to school in the States?'

Cross exploded with laughter. 'Yeah, if you consider Michigan City,

Indiana, part of the country. I went to Indiana State and played football. Would have went pro but I fucked up my knee.'

'You're an American.'

'No shit, José.' He tossed his cigar out the window and spat after it.

It was pretty stupid of me. 'Cross' was a long way from being a Portuguese or African name. It must have been the heat that kept me from thinking straight. Or maybe I just hadn't gotten past his attitude.

I leaned closer to him and locked eyes.

'My name is Win Liberte, not José, not Bubba, and I ain't your fuckin' pal. Now, the fact that you're such a prick to me – your employer – means you don't give a shit about your job. Which is okay, because I don't give a shit about you, either. But as long as we're hanging out together, let's have some mutual respect. Or you can go fuck yourself and get out at the next corner.'

Cross slowly lit another cigar, appraising me out of the corner of his eye as he flooded the car with foul smoke. 'Well, you have teeth, I'll say that. You're going to need them. If you want my advice, tell the driver to turn around and take you back to the airport. You may be hell on wheels at the cotillion ball and the country-club dances, but you're into something that would put the fear of the Lord into a Delta Force unit.

'Angola's the kind of war zone those TV talking-heads news people cover sitting in New York or Atlanta while couch-potato Americans switch channels, trying to find news about the latest celebrity divorce because the horrors coming out of this part of Africa are too unreal for them to goggle over. Shit, most news people are too damn scared to come here and cover it. It's not just a war, but a way of life, supervised by all the demons in hell.

'If you're gonna hang around Angola, you better get used to seeing children starving to death in their mother's arms, prostitutes with AIDS doing tricks on street corners, men who can't pick their nose because both their arms were cut off or they're crawling in the dirt because their legs have been blown off by land mines. One of the many records this shithole country holds is more lives and limbs lost to land mines than anywhere else in the world.'

Cross gave me another appraising look. 'I'll give you the benefit of the doubt. Maybe you thought it would be an adventure to come to Africa and see your own diamond mine. Maybe you thought you'd safari dress like Stewart Granger and shoot an elephant or two, and have the natives call you *bwana*. Okay, now that you've had your reality check, get yourself a ticket back to where people don't shit – and die – in the gutters, and kids don't teethe on AK-47s.'

I stared out the window. 'I don't like Angola. And I think you're an asshole with a chip on your shoulder. Not to mention your fucking cigars stink.' I grinned at him. 'But I'm here for the duration, pal. What do you have to say about that?'

He snicked cigar ash on the floor and gave me a calculating look.

'My name ain't Pal.'

I checked into the Hotel Presidente Meridien on Avenida 4 de Fevereiro. I didn't know why the street was named the Fourth of February or why other streets I saw had date names, but it wasn't hard to guess. The dates were victories in war or revolution. And the victors got to name the streets and put up statues.

I took a shower and stood on the balcony, sucking down a cold beer, checking out the busy, noisy, dirty street below. People, cars, bikes, and carts jostled each other like carnival bumper cars. The reflection of the setting sun turned the bay into the black gold of an oil slick.

I never realized until now what a comfortable life I had led. Never worried about money – hell, never even thinking about money because it was always there. So was food, fresh sheets, clean water. I could travel coast to coast in the States and never worry about where I took a drink of water. I'm sure the humidity in Angola probably carried something that wasn't good for you.

When the sun was down, I left the room to meet Cross in the hotel lounge. I was surprised he didn't just drop me off in front of the hotel and continue on to wherever he was headed.

I hadn't made up my mind yet about Cross. I didn't care about his attitude. Probably the only way to survive in this hellhole was to get thick-skinned and mean-tempered. But I needed allies and Cross had one trait that I liked – he was blunt. What you saw is what you got. You'd think nothing short of a mine cave-in would have kept Eduardo, the manager, from meeting the owner at the airport. Which told me I wasn't high on his list, either. Was it that hard to get good help? It was a dumb question. Hell, it was probably impossible.

Which gave rise to the question of what Cross was doing in Angola. And why Eduardo was sticking around, running a loser mine in a war zone. There had to be easier and safer ways to make money. They sure as hell weren't on a humanitarian mission for the mine owner or the warring factions that kept tearing the country apart. That whittled it down to one thing – they were making money. And it had to be plenty of money to make it worthwhile to hang around a war zone and risk murder, kidnapping, and disease.

And that raised another question. If they were making money from my mine, why wasn't I?

In the lounge, I sat down at the table Cross had staked out and ordered a beer, no glass. I had traveled in the Yucatan and Central America and knew better than to order anything that didn't come out of a sealed bottle. If it had to be put into a glass or needed ice, even in a decent hotel, the risk of an attack of Montezuma's revenge went up.

'What's there to do in this town?' I asked.

'Nothing's safe, outside of a few hotels and restaurants. But if you want to tempt fate, for excitement, there are *boites*, discos with American and Brazilian music, and *kizombas*, African-style nightclubs. They have local music and food like goat meat and a sticky ball of smashed yams called stodge. You don't want to go near any of them. Even if you're safe inside, you can be murdered three feet from the front door. And you can figure any cunt you stick your dick into is infected with AIDS. People talk about AIDS like it was the common cold, that's how common it is. If you have a serious death wish that needs satisfying, you can trot through the *musseque*, shantytown, anytime day or night.'

'If this place is such a hellhole, then why are you here?'

'Not for the scenery, that's for damn sure. I came for the same reason other Americans and Europeans are here – money. I got an undergraduate degree in engineering and hired on with an oil company working the Cabinda, an enclave north, up the coast. The area ended up belonging to Angola despite the fact it's surrounded on three sides by the Congo. Working an oil field turned out to be a little too regimented for me. I got diamond fever and left oil to prospect for them.'

'How did you get into mine security?'

'Being broke. Small-time diamond mining is as risky as buying lottery tickets. But it has that same lure, that a little money and sweat will get you the big one. I'm still running some diamond claims on the side, but I needed a job to keep me in beer and beans.'

'You must have hit it big to quit your job as my security manager.' We both knew he hadn't quit. Yet. So far it was still talk.

'I haven't hit shit. I'm quitting so I don't get killed babysitting the absentee owner who decided to drag his pretty ass out of Manhattan to visit one of his feudal domains.'

I looked behind me and around the room. 'Where's this asshole owner you keep bad-mouthing? Let's get him and kill him.'

'I apologize. Your ass isn't pretty. But you don't understand diamond mining in Angola. If you did, you wouldn't be here. Let's start at the top. This country's been at war for over thirty years, first against the Portuguese colonial rule, then rebels supported by the U.S. against the communist regime supported by Moscow and Havana. The C.I.A. and thousands of Cuban troops have gone home and there's a peace treaty, but that's all on the surface. The political pact is nothing but a piece of paper no one cares about and that the leaders on both sides give nothing but lip service to. That's because the fight is not over political freedom, but control of the oil fields and diamond industry.

'When you were a kid, I'm sure you learned in school about the Gold Rushes to California and Alaska, miners packing a six-gun while they stood knee-deep in creeks panning for gold with one hand and fighting off claim jumpers and Indians with the other. Well, bubb— Win, it's the same thing here, only the guys jumping claims in Africa have helicopter gunships, machine guns, tanks, and air-to-ground missiles.'

'The rebels took over the mines?'

'Not the actual operation, but only because they don't know how to run a diamond mine. Let's say they own the mines and lease them back to people like you. And they come by each month to collect a percentage of the take as the rent. If they think you're holding out on them, they kill you.

'Kind of like the Mafia, but those dudes only kill when it's necessary for business. Here, if the rebels or government troops don't like the color of your shirt, they kill you. But only if you're not a big payer. A while back they kidnapped a bunch of Europeans from mines and marched them hundreds of miles into the bush. It wasn't for a picnic. The Euros had been a little slow in their payments.

'But the rebels aren't stupid, they don't kill the golden gooses, except when they feel they need to make an example now and then. Like whacking off the arms of their own people. Do that to the men of one village and a thousand other villages suddenly fall into line.'

'It sounds like organized, legalized murder. And chaos.'

'Murder, massacre, genocide, they cover all the bases. And it is orga-

117

nized. The guy who comes around to collect your rent reports to someone else, right up to Jonas Savimbi himself, the man who heads the rebel organization called UNITA. You heard of him?'

'No,' I lied. He was the guy Marni said was a homicidal maniac, but she threw in a bunch of initials like the UNITA and I couldn't remember who was on first.

Cross threw up his hands in frustration and looked around the lounge as if he was trying to spot an exit. 'You sure as hell did your homework, didn't you, *bubba*? Well, let me tell you about the guy who may be responsible for your death. President Reagan called him a freedom fighter, characterizing him as a regular Abe Lincoln for Angola.'

'That's encouraging.'

'Only if you didn't know Reagan was senile and that his wife's astrologer was running the country. But the American political attitude about Savimbi is a classic example of American politicians being as dumb as they can. If the devil said he was anticommunist, our political leaders would make a pact with him – which they've done at one time or another in most of the Third World.

'People in Angola call Savimbi a psychopathic killer, but not to his face. This is a man who *personally* beat to death the wife and kids of a guy who decided to oppose him. Shit, he even blew up a Red Cross hospital making artificial limbs for people he and others like him had chopped off the arms and legs of – or blew them off with land mines.'

'How can business operate in this atmosphere?'

'Savimbi and the Angolan government opposing him need money to feed their war machines. That money comes from oil and diamonds. As long as you're profitable to the war machines, you're tolerated. If a lower echelon kills the goose laying the diamond eggs, they die, too. And if you're caught screwing them, they kill you, but first you'd get your arms and legs whacked off so you can think about your sins as you bleed to death.'

'Jesus.'

'No, Jesus never came this far south. And all this assumes that your own miners don't kill you because you've caught too many of them stealing. Even if you survive diamond mining, you can get bitten by insects the size of birds or step on a snake that can swallow you whole. The mortality rate for small mine managers and security chiefs is enough to give heartburn to the most cynical insurance underwriter. Not that there's such a thing as insurance in Angola. The best insurance coverage are bodyguards and bulletproof vests.'

'You've managed to survive. What makes you think I'm going to get killed?'

'You're a spoiled rich kid who's never worked a day in his life. You've never done anything more trying than squeezing the steering wheel of a fast car or a pair of knockers on a broad. You haven't got one fuckin' iota of street smarts. You're liable to cash a check with your mouth you can't cover with your ass. You're going to look the wrong way and piss off some twelve-year-old kid high on drugs who has his finger on the trigger of a rusty AK-47. And I don't wanna be standing there when your guts get spewed all over the ground because I'd be next.'

I started laughing.

Cross tried to keep his sour expression, but started laughing, too.

'This whole place is ridiculous,' I said. 'If I promise not to get killed, will you stick around for a while?'

'Yeah, if you give me one good reason why you've come to this hellhole.'

'I'm broke. The mine's all I have.'

That stopped him. And stumped him. The expression on his face cast doubt on my truth and veracity. 'No shit?'

'No shit, José. The guy managing my money sunk everything into the Blue Lady Mine, an investment that doesn't return a dime and no one wants to buy. I don't like being broke, so it isn't going to happen for long.'

He shook his head. 'You think you can drop in and squeeze a few million out of Angola? Man, as black people say in white movies, you be a dreamer. It would be safer for you to go home and rob banks. Or find some broad with more money than brains who'll keep you in the style you're accustomed to in return for keeping her serviced.'

'Don't underestimate me. I've been the best at everything I've ever tried. Money and diamonds are in my blood. I just haven't paid attention to them for a while. When you were playing base ball, my father was making me evaluate diamonds. You said you came here to make a bundle. I want what's mine and what I can earn, but I'm not greedy, not to someone who helps me. Stick by me, show me the ropes, and you won't regret it.'

'Is this one of those "trust me" situations?'

'This is a sure thing.'

'Well, there's just one thing I want you to remember.'

119

'Yeah?'

'My name ain't José, either.'

26

The next morning we took off in a four-seater chartered Cessna puddle jumper for the mining country.

'We're heading for Cuango river country, east of Luana, in the north-east corner of the country. Most planes headed for the diamond country land at Saurimo, but that's too much of a trek for where your mine's located. After we land in a potato patch, we'll drive the rest of the way to the mine, north toward Zaire. The entire diamond-mining area is out of bounds for foreigners unless they're employed in the industry.'

'Is a plane the only way in?'

'It's the safest and fastest. A small plane like this will get us a couple hours from the mine.'

'Tell me about Eduardo.'

Cross shrugged. 'Professional mine manager, a mestizo, born in Angola. His father was a Portuguese coffee planter in colonial days, got into mining after the plantation was burned in the colonial war. His mother was an Ovimbundu, a major ethnic group in the country. Eduardo's been around mines most of his life. He's smart enough not to cheat Savimbi's rep who comes around to collect the rent. If he wasn't, he'd be dead long ago.'

'Who owned the mine before I, uh, bought it?'

'Some corporation with headquarters in Lisbon.'

'Ever hear of João Carmona?'

'I've heard of him.' Cross was curt.

'And?'

He shrugged. 'Carmona's a crook, which is not always a bad thing in Angola, since we're all crooks to one extent or another. I heard he's some sort of Portuguese godfather of the Mafia variety. He's got a bad reputation in the mining country, among mine owners he's cheated. He's persona non grata in the country because he also made a mistake of cheating the government *and* the rebels. I told you about Savimbi. He's not a guy that you cheat. He had Carmona shot in the spine. I was told the idea was to cripple him, not kill him. That way he could spend the rest of his life thinking about what happens to people who fuck over Savimbi.'

'Did Carmona ever have ownership rights in the Blue Lady?'

'I don't know. I've been with the mine less than a year and you owned it during that time. He could have been an owner, through that Portuguese corporation that had it before. If he was, he'd have been anxious to get rid of it before Savimbi found out and took over the mine to get it out of Carmona's hands. Eduardo would know, he's been around a lot longer and knows the corporate crap. If he'll tell you.'

I raised my eyebrows. 'Why wouldn't he tell me?'

Another shrug. 'Eduardo lives in Angola. That means his first order of business is to survive. You're a ship passing in the night. You may be gone tomorrow. Or dead. He's got to keep all his options open. However you look at it, you're a short-timer. He's not going to burn any bridges for you, bro.'

'Why didn't he meet me in Luanda?'

'I don't know, maybe he's like me, he doesn't give a shit and plans to quit anyway. Your mine is not the most profitable one around. I was happy to take his place picking you up because I needed to conduct some business in Luanda.'

'He gets a decent salary. You don't do bad, either.'

'Bullshit. Those are stateside salaries, neither one of us would work in Angola for that kind of money. We're both working claims on the side, buying, selling, trading them, staking other prospectors for a piece of the action.'

João said the people who worked for me would also steal a part of their salary. But I didn't know Cross well enough to bring up the subject. One thing I did catch in his tone — there was no love lost between him and Eduardo. Nor was Eduardo technically his boss. João told me many mine owners keep an administrative distance between the head of mining operations and the head of security, as a balance of power. If the two get together to steal, they could rape a mine. Of course, with an absentee owner like the Blue Lady's had, there had been no one around to keep them apart.

From the coast, the ground beneath us rose in green foothills and highlands as we flew toward diamond country.

Two hours into the flight, we landed at a dirt field outside a small town. The air was hot and almost as humid as Luanda's. I followed Cross's example and stuffed a handkerchief down the back of my collar to catch sweat. I had traded in my fashionable sports clothes for a nondescript khaki shirt and pants I picked up in Luanda. Long sleeves and mosquito repellent were the order of the day. I bought boots that laced almost to my knees.

'Hoping you only run into short snakes?' Cross asked when he saw my boots.

An African driver with a Land Rover that looked like it lost against Rommel in North Africa back during the Big One drove up to the plane after it stopped taxiing. A wooden sign on the side proclaimed MINA AZULA SENHORA, BLUE LADY MINE, in faded black letters. It wasn't hard to imagine how the mine got its name. The place to find diamonds is 'blue' earth deposits.

'This is Gomez,' Cross said, indicating the grinning, sweating driver. 'He drives us, drives for supplies, drives for anything we need. Just think of him as the stagecoach driver hauling loads through Apache country.'

The butt of a pistol protruded from under Gomez's shirt. A rifle was mounted above the front windshield inside the Rover.

Leaving the landing field, on the outskirts of a dusty little town, we stopped where a fifty-gallon oil drum had been set up in the middle of the road. Three men in army fatigues hung out in the shade, smoking and throwing dice. One of them lazily sauntered over to the car to accept the money Gomez gave him.

'Toll,' Cross said.

We passed a house with cement walls and iron bars on the windows and front porch. A fat man sitting on a rocking chair on the steel-caged porch waved and shouted a greeting to Cross as we drove by.

'That's Ortego, the biggest diamond broker in the area. He buys stuff from the river people and thieves. More diamonds pass through his fat paws every month than we produce in a year. He looks like an easy pushover, but he killed two men in the last year who thought that.'

Leaving the one-street town, we stopped at another fifty-gallon drum.

'I wish I had the toll concession,' I said.

An hour out of town as we drove along a dirt road in a winding river canyon we began to see men and women working the river.

'There're two types of diamond gathering in the region,' Cross said. 'At the mine, we burrow tunnels into the ground, trying to find and follow a kimberlite, a diamond pipe, what they'd call a "vein" in gold or silver mining. But what you see here on the river is the most basic way of finding diamonds. Alluvial mining. Diamonds were created deep in the earth, under tremendous pressure. They were brought up toward the surface by volcanic action. Erosion, earthquakes, wind, rain, especially river action, uncovered diamond pipes and pushed the diamonds many miles downstream.

'These people are individual diggers, *garimpeiros*. They wade into the river and haul up mud and gravel in the hopes of finding roughs. Their methods are about the same as used in old-time Gold Rushes a hundred and fifty years ago – a pick, a pan, and a man, or in this case, men, women, and children. Some of the diggers get angels like me who'll throw in a few dollars a month for beans in return for a percentage. But the percentage is usually zero. Some of the better-financed diggers have sluice boxes or vacuums to suck up more of the river bottom. Most of them just work with their two hands and a bucket.'

I knew more about the history of diamond mining than the actual process. Knowledge conveyed again by my father. Up until the mid-1800s diamonds had been the sole possession of royalty and the super-rich because the supply of them, mostly from Brazil and India, had been small. In 1867 a fifteen-year-old Boer farm boy walking along a riverbank picked up a glittering stone that turned out to be a 21-carat diamond. But it was considered a fluke and caused little excitement. Two years later another boy found a diamond, this time an 85.5-carat stone, the Star of South Africa – and the rush was on. Seamen deserted their ships in African ports, gold miners abandoned their claims, farmers pushed aside their plows, tens of thousands of them, mining thirty-foot-by-thirty-foot claims, 'ten coffin-size,' as the saying went.

Ultimately the mining industry also went underground, in search of those kimberlite pipes Cross mentioned. All diamonds, except for the ones that rode to earth on meteorites, came from deep in the mantle of the earth, created when carbon was put under tremendous pressure and temperature billions of years ago. Violent, cataclysmic eruptions drove the diamonds up in carrot-shaped 'pipes' of volcanic material bluish-gray in color. The material that brought the diamonds up was called kimberlite, named after the 'big hole' in Kimberley, South Africa, one of the first diamond mines.

Kimberlite pipes that reached to or near the surface became eroded from weather and earthquakes over billions of years and diamonds in them were carried hundreds or even thousands of miles along rivers and into the sea.

An African family, a man, woman, and two small children came up from the river as the Land Rover approached. The older man's right arm was missing.

'A *mutilado*,' I said, using a word I'd heard describing amputees. 'Car accident?'

'Machete,' Cross said. 'Some of the river miners were late with their payment to a rebel strongman a couple years ago. It didn't matter which ones hadn't paid, Savimbi's men just pulled a dozen out of the water and chopped off arms. Just one arm per man, though, so they could still work. If they didn't die from the wound.'

Cross got out of the car and approached them as an old friend, shaking hands, chattering. He pulled a handful of candy out of his pocket and gave it to the kids. To my ear, newly tuned in Luanda, it sounded like they were speaking a mixed pot of Portuguese and some African language. Portuguese was the official language of the country, but it wasn't heavily spoken outside cities and towns.

After the social preliminaries were over, the man handed Cross several stones. Cross held them up to the light and used a loupe to examine them. After more dialogue, Cross gave them money and got back into the vehicle.

'One of my partners. I grubstake some of the river people, usually just for food and supplies, for a percentage. Other times I buy up claims and get people to work them, again for a percentage.' He handed me the diamonds. 'Any idea what they're worth?'

It was a test. I took out my father's loupe and gave them a once-over. 'They're flawed but workable. In New York, maybe a thousand, fifteen hundred. I have no idea how much here.'

'Less than ten cents on the dollar to what they'll be worth wholesale in New York or Antwerp, probably a hundred dollars from Ortego, the diamond man. And that's a couple month's haul for that family, and a good one, and they only get half after expenses. But a few dollars is a lot of money to people who have nothing. I'll sell these to Ortego and pay a tax on them to the rebels.'

Cross sneered at me. 'I pick up an extra thousand each week with my outside activities, not even tip money to a rich guy like you, but it keeps my feet in the business.'

'Waiting for the big one.'

'Waiting for the big one. And the gods like to play games with the big one. There're just enough decent stones found to whet your appetite, keep you sweating and cussing, but not enough to get rich on. And every once in a while lightning strikes. Couple months ago a woman working a claim found an eighty-carat stone, flawed, but still worth a couple hundred thousand, even to the fat man. But I don't know how much the woman and her husband got – if anything. Some people say they're in Luanda living like kings. Others say their bodies are buried in back of the fat man's house. Or in some mass grave the rebels dig periodically.'

'What do you say?'

'I say I'm going to make it big, kick a rock and find out it's a thousand-carat flawless blue. I'm going to sell it to one of those Silicon Valley billionaire computer nerds and buy me an island somewhere in the South Pacific with palm trees, beautiful native women, and my own microbrewery. Just like in the movies.'

27

The mine was on top of a hill. It looked like a prison from the bottom of the hill and the impression wasn't far from the truth. It had a ten-foot chain-link outer fence with barbed wire, plus an inner fence made of solid wall, eight feet tall with another four feet of barbed wire at the top. Between the two fences I spotted a guard walking a Doberman. The first thing we came to was a guardhouse.

'Jesus. I feel like I'm about to serve a term at Alcatraz.'

'There are three things you have to know about diamond mining,' Cross said. 'Security, security, security. If there is any way anyone anytime can get their hands on diamonds, they'll figure out a way to steal them. They swallow them, stick them up their ass, fly them out with pigeons, throw them in garbage that their wives will pick through at the dump, wedge them into the tires of a supply truck, or drop them in the gas tank for their accomplices to pick up later. And those are just some of the ways.

'The workers sign on for three-month stints and never leave the compound during that time. Because diamonds are small and can be swallowed by the dozens, not to mention stuffed in other orifices of the body, when they quit or leave the mine for R and R, the workers get X-rayed. So does anyone else and anything that comes into contact with the miners, except Eduardo and me. Work here long enough and you start to glow in the dark. And hell, that isn't anywhere near foolproof. They make deals with the X-ray technician to phony up the results of the X-rays or even mess with the machines.'

Eduardo wasn't in the office when we arrived. His bookkeeper, Carlotta Santos, a top-heavy woman in a dress that barely constrained her well-nourished body, was surprised to see us. Cross mentioned that Carlotta was also of Portuguese – Angolan mix.

From the appearance of the woman, I immediately latched onto the idea that she was something more than clerical help to Eduardo. Cross told me Eduardo's wife and kids were living in Luanda. One look at the bookkeeper and I was sure he kept his bed warm here at the mine with her. I admit to being a little more sensitive about who is or isn't doing it than most people.

For a lowly bookkeeper, she was wearing some fine stones. One on a necklace was a good two carats. To the naked eye, it looked like more than a couple years' salary for her, even at the rate of inflated salaries in the diamond region.

It wasn't hard for me to imagine that Eduardo was keeping his honey in *my* diamonds.

'Eduardo is below. A piece of equipment broke and he must inspect it. I will send a message that you are here.'

'Never mind, I'll go find him,' Cross said.

She gave Cross a look of derision. 'We were not expecting you until tomorrow. You did not call and let us know you were bringing Senhor Liberte so soon.'

'Sorry about that.'

He kept his face blank when he spoke – which gave me the impression that Cross had deliberately brought me back early as a surprise to Eduardo and the woman. I didn't know if he was trying to catch the mine manager or someone else skimming or just did it to keep everyone on their toes.

There was a third possibility – that Eduardo and he were in on something and Cross just wanted to throw around his weight.

Cross left to find the man and I made myself at home in the manager's office while I waited. Laid out on top of his desk was a packet of ten stones and I examined them while I waited. The stones had the slightly 'soapy' feel of diamonds pulled from the earth. Each diamond was of high quality and could be polished into a gem of at least a full carat or more.

Ten- or fifteen-carat diamonds were a drop in the bucket considering what had to be taken out of a mine to make it profitable. Tons of earth had to be moved for every carat. But diamonds weren't supposed to end up on the mine manager's desk. Their ultimate destination, before being transported from the mine with high security, would be a safe in the sorting room.

I was also struck by the uniformity of the stones. Diamonds that can be polished into a carat are a cross section of what you pull out of a mine. To the contrary, they represent only a tiny fraction of diamonds missed. The Blue Lady was pulling more industrial-grade stones out than ones of gem quality. This packet was obviously hand-picked. From my cookie jar.

Cross came back with Eduardo a few minutes later.

The mine manager rushed in, looking flustered. He was reed-thin, about fifty, with copper skin and rows of bumpy yellow teeth. While Cross came across as a blunt and brutally honest mule, the mine manager struck me immediately as a slippery weasel.

After introductions in Portuguese, I continued in the same language and indicated the diamonds I found on his desk. 'Good stones.'

'They're not from the mine,' Eduardo said, quickly. 'They're alluvial diamonds, I have river claims, like Cross.'

'Yeah, but your claims pay a hell of a lot better than mine,' Cross said. 'I've been lucky.'

'I wish the mine had been that lucky,' I said. 'It brings up some decent-quality roughs, but they're mostly small, less than a carat, and a lot of sand-size, along with a huge number of industrial-grade stones. If we could consistently bring up stones like these, the mine would turn a profit.'

'We bring up what the earth provides,' Eduardo said.

I grinned. 'If Mother Earth doesn't get more generous, I'll be better off getting a bucket and going down to the river than pouring money into the mine.'

'I suspect, senhor, that after seeing Luanda and now the mining country, you will very soon conclude you would be better off back in New York.'

'Why don't we take a look at the mine,' I said.

'Now? Perhaps tomorrow after you have rested and become oriented—'

'I came thousands of miles to see this pig-in-a-poke. I'd just as soon get it over with right now.'

Cross bowed out, saying he had security matters to attend to. I followed Eduardo through the security gate that separated the office building from the diggings themselves.

'How long do you intend to be with us?' Eduardo asked.

'As long as it takes,' I said. 'If I'm going to own a diamond mine, I want to know how it operates.'

He gave me a look that left little doubt that he thought I was mentally deranged.

'I'm the curious type,' I said. 'When I get behind the wheel of something, I want to know everything that makes it tick. I know zero about diamond mining – other than it's costing me a lot of money.'

'Diamond mining hasn't changed a great deal over the last century,' he said. 'There are diamonds and there is dirt. You still have to dig up and process the dirt to find the diamonds. That means you must go through tons of earth for each little carat of diamond. A hundred years or so ago, Rhodes and others started scraping the surface of the earth and the riverbeds for the stones. Soon they were digging shafts into the earth, hauling out millions of tons of dirt, and examining dirt for what is often no more than a tiny speck of diamond.

'Today, it's still done much the same way it was during the last century. The big mines owned by De Beers and others may have more modern equipment, especially in the processing stage, but most mines are like the Blue Lady. The methods are tried, true, and basic. Diamond mining is not as dangerous nor as dirty as coal mining, but it still must be done with caution.' With that, he gave me a hard hat to wear.

I listened to Eduardo as if I knew nothing, but I already knew the way diamonds were mined from my father's lectures. Besides, I only really knew book learning. Seeing the real thing was an eye-opener.

'If we invested in better equipment, would it increase our take?' I asked.

'It would increase the amount of dirt processed, and thus increase the "take," as you put it. But it would be good money after bad. A diamond mine can be a hole in the ground that money is thrown into.'

We stepped into an elevator cage. Eduardo continued talking as we descended.

'The objective of diamond mining is to find the kimberlite pipes, the veins of blue earth where diamonds are found. Diamonds form in the tremendous pressure about a hundred miles under the earth's surface and are coughed up when volcanoes erupt. When the volcanoes brought up the blue earth millions of years ago, some of it reached the surface, but most of it stayed buried or got buried over time.'

He waved at the ground we were passing along the descent. 'The ground surrounding a pipe is called a reef. The reef here is about a hundred feet thick, so originally the mine had to go down at least a hundred before hitting any diamonds.

'After the reef, before you get to blue earth, is an area we call yellow dirt. This yellow dirt is a mixture of gray-blue earth and common, non-diamond-bearing soil, created when other soils mixed with and diluted the blue ground over an eon ago. Diamonds are found in yellow ground, but the richest hauls are in the blue earth itself, the pay dirt.

'And that, senhor, is the problem with your diamond mine. We have only hit *yellow* dirt. Blue earth isn't here − or it has evaded us. We have tried tunnels in all directions in the reef, but have never had enough funding to dig the number we need.'

'What if I came up with more money?' It was a bluff. I didn't have the money and it wasn't the type of place you got bank financing. I was just testing the waters.

'As I said about new equipment, good money after bad,' he said. 'The Blue Lady is a *puta* with a dry hole. She wants money but gives little of her charms. We scrape out just enough to keep paying the rent and overhead. You can find better and safer investments for your money in America. And a safer place to spend your life.'

The elevator groaned to a stop. We stepped into a shaft that was white-washed and lit with dim electric lights.

'We paint the walls and ceiling to reduce the need for lights.'

He took me through passageways to a tunnel where we ran out of white walls. Eduardo indicated the miners and a pile of rock debris at the end of the tunnel. 'This area was blasted this morning. First we drill holes in the wall to be blasted, then pack the holes with explosives. After the blast, the debris of rock and dirt is loaded into wheelbarrows. We will follow them.'

The wheelbarrows were rolled back down the tunnel. Along the way, they went through special doors that were closed in case of flooding. The rock and dirt was dumped into small carts on a rail track. It was hot, sweaty work.

'Now we will follow the rail cars to the crusher.'

As we walked, Eduardo told me an old joke about diamond mining.

'One day, a miner came out of the mine pushing an empty wheelbarrow. The act made the guards highly suspicious and they thoroughly searched the man. And found nothing. The next day, when work was over, the miner came out, again with an empty wheelbarrow. Again, a thorough search and nothing was found. This went on day after day, and even the mine manager and security director got involved in the searches, but they never found a single diamond on the man. Do you know why, senhor?'

I did, having heard the story as a kid from Uncle Bernie, but I pretended ignorance.

'Because he wasn't stealing diamonds,' Eduardo howled, and slapped his leg, 'he was stealing wheelbarrows!'

The rail carts were dumped onto conveyor belts that carried the ore to a crusher. Once the ore was crushed to reduce it down to dirt and gravel, conveyor buckets carried it to the surface.

'You will ask, can diamonds be crushed in this contraption?'

I wouldn't ask, but I was still playing stupid and I nodded like the visiting yokel Eduardo had taken me for.

'Yes, even diamonds, the hardest substance on earth, can be shattered if hit right. There is always a possibility of damage to huge stones, but such stones are extremely rare. Also, all along the process, the miners themselves are on the lookout for anything that reflects light. They get bonuses for finding stones before they enter the crusher.'

We took the elevator back to the surface. There, we followed the ore to water tanks.

'These are the churning tanks where the ore from the crushers are dumped. The heavy gravel and diamonds sink while the rest is washed away. Large rocks are separated off and from here the residual ore, gravel, and diamonds go back onto a conveyor belt to be carried to the grease tables.'

The 'grease tables' were a series of vibrating aluminum terraces coated with about half an inch of grease. The ore was washed over the tables.

'The special characteristic of a diamond is that it will attach itself to the grease while other stones and gravel will wash off.'

130

Eduardo had the water flow shut off for a moment and scraped off some of the grease with a trowel. He used his pen to poke in the grease and brought out several small stones. 'Here you see diamonds truly in the rough.'

He spoke to me as if I was a schoolchild being given an educational tour of the mine. He wiped the trowel on a metal basket that resembled a kitchen sieve, but with much finer holes. 'The grease is scraped in the baskets that have extremely fine holes in them, and the baskets are stuck in boiling water to remove the grease. Then the stones are sorted and graded.'

In the grading room, workers with good lighting and magnifying glasses examined the stones and graded them. While Eduardo explained the grading process, I made polite listening responses.

After we left the sorting room, Eduardo said, 'You Americans always like to get down to the bottom line, so this is it. Diamond mining is mostly a simple, mathematical proposition. Once you have found pay dirt, it becomes a question of how many thousands of pounds of dirt must be removed for each carat of diamond recovered. The less earth moved and the more numerous and higher quality the diamonds are, the more profit is made.

'Our profits are affected both by the fact that we operate in a war zone, where we must pay bribes and everything costs more, plus the elementary fact that we have not hit a blue pipe. There doesn't appear to be a blue pipe anywhere near this mine. Much more yellow ground per carat must be removed to recover diamonds than mines operating in rich blue soil. Obviously, the more dirt to be dug, moved, and processed, the more it costs per carat. We must process almost twice as much dirt per carat as most other mines. Which is why this mine can barely turn a profit despite my full-time efforts.'

I listened and said nothing. I was still processing everything I'd heard and seen since arriving only hours ago.

He brought up another subject as we walked toward the administration building. 'I've been approached by a syndicate who is interested in buying the mine. I expect to get the final details very soon, probably sometime tomorrow. I'm told that the offer will have a short fuse; you would have to decide immediately. I've stalled them already as I awaited your arrival.'

'Why are they interested in buying a losing mine?'

'They believe they can run it more cheaply. And perhaps they can, using literally slave labor, or even prison labor provided by the UNITA.'

I added the new twist to the information I was digesting. Eduardo was as sincere and truthful as a Luanda whore. And less honest. That he was stealing from me, skimming diamonds, was obvious. He was a thief. My real question was whether Cross was in on it with him. And whether I would get out of Angola alive once I confronted them.

The other issue I was processing was the offer to buy the mine. Someone obviously thought that the mine could be operated at a profit. So why wasn't it? I was eager to see the details of the offer, but I wasn't getting any hopes up. Eduardo wasn't the type to pass on something good to me.

Before we parted, I asked Eduardo a question that had been buzzing around my head.

'Have you ever heard of a big red diamond, an actual ruby-red?'

He shook his head. 'If such diamonds exist, I have never seen one. There is one I've heard of, a flawless stone that once belonged to a king, but I don't know if it actually exists or is just a legend.'

'How about João Carmona?'

That caught him by surprise. 'Carmona? A real crook, believe me. I suspect he was behind the Portuguese corporation that once owned the mine. He is held in disfavor in Angola. He made the mistake of cheating Savimbi.' Eduardo grinned. 'A very bad mistake. Savimbi is not just crazy, but loves to kill. A very bad combination if he is your enemy.'

28

I settled into the room assigned to me in the building that housed the mine's management employees and added up the score.

For a certainty, Eduardo was skimming from the mine. That was a no-brainer – he lied to me about the source of the roughs I found on his desk. The stones had a soapy feel. Diamonds that come out of the ground have an oily film on them. I suppose that's why they stick to the grease table. But the oily coating on alluvial diamonds is washed and rubbed off by exposure to water and other elements – another diamond fact my father taught me during those after-school sessions.

The stones handed to Cross by the river miner which Cross had me examine in the Land Rover didn't have a soapy feel. Eduardo's stones did. They had come from my mine and bypassed the sorting room. Usually by the time they reach the graders, the soapy film is boiled off, which meant the stones went into Eduardo's pocket inside the mine. And the best candidate for the source of the thefts was the grease table.

Was Cross in on it with Eduardo? They had two different personalities – one blunt, the other innately deceptive – but they both worked for an absentee owner who was thousands of miles away. It also would be harder for Eduardo to steal without letting the security manager in on it. And Cross was blunt about the fact that he was in Angola for one reason only – to go home with a poke. Of course, that was my only reason for being in the country.

I had to assume that they had a skimming operation going and that the undercurrent of animosity between the two was an act for my benefit. One thing I was sure of – if Eduardo was skimming, the bookkeeper was in on it, too. Stealing at work was something you shared with your lover, not your wife.

The next morning I watched at the window until I saw Eduardo go through the gate in the mine. Then I left my quarters and arrived bright and early at the bookkeeper's office.

'I want to see the books, Carlotta.'

She stared up at me like I'd just been beamed down by Scotty.

'The books? Why?'

'Because I own the place.'

I could see from the way she pouted that she wasn't used to people at the mine snapping at her, which nailed it for me in terms of her relationship with Eduardo. People are more likely to tiptoe around the boss's girlfriend than his clerk. She was a hot item, pure animal in terms of her body and sex appeal, too hot for a man to work around without having his testosterone heat up. And Eduardo didn't strike me as a man who was above a little sin. But the real tip-off was how formal they were to each other, 'Senhor Marques this . . .' and 'Menina Santos that . . .'

Calling each other 'mister' and 'miss' wasn't how two people who worked together in an office all day, every day acted, not unless they had something to hide and were putting up a front.

Sitting down in front of the accounting books, I realized I knew zero about how to read them. I hadn't flunked out of accounting at school – I just hadn't taken any business courses in the first place.

I stared at the books and wondered what the hell to do. I could proba-bly get the gist of them, even though some of the terminology might throw me. But I realized all they would tell me was the present state of the mine. To really understand the figures, I had to have something to compare them to. Past histories of the mine. Other mines with a similar production.

I dug in as best I could. There were monthly and annual summaries, and from these it wasn't hard to get an overall picture of the business. On paper, at least, the place was just creeping along, turning a bare profit one month, losing money the next.

The books confirmed Eduardo's explanation that the mine wasn't making money because of bad luck in finding diamonds. We were simply moving too many tons of dirt per carat. That was it in a nutshell.

It would have been okay if I hadn't suspected he was cheating me.

By the same token, I didn't know if Eduardo was stealing enough to make the mine significantly less profitable. It was almost a given that Eduardo and Cross would skim a bit as a perk for working in a war zone. And that I should overlook it. And it was a given that Eduardo could skim a little without Cross knowing about it, but if he was taking out diamonds in a large enough quantity to affect the profitability of the mine, Cross would have to be in on it with him.

Skimming wasn't the only thing I was looking for. I was still bugged by the way Eduardo had dropped the news that there was an offer to buy. The iden-tity of the buyers was vague. And the part about having to make an immediate decision was hardly the way the sale of a mine was done, even in a war zone. Not to mention that no one would make an offer on the mine if they hadn't come here and examined it thoroughly. And had it re-examined during the escrow.

The thought occurred to me that Eduardo could be in on the sale, a silent partner, maybe even deliberately keeping production down in order to drive the selling price of the mine down.

As I was going through the books, I started looking for inconsistencies, something that would tell me that more diamonds were being taken out than were being accounted for. I checked the tonnage of ground dug up and processed compared to the number of carats month after month, but it remained reasonably consistent. I went over the quantity and quality of stones reported from the sorting room and compared them to what was sold to wholesalers, but again there was little inconsistency.

I decided to check the books for prior years to see if there was a pattern.

'Give me the accounting summaries for the past ten years,' I told the bookkeeper.

'There aren't any.'

'Why not?'

'Senhor, the mine has only been open for two years!'

Now why hadn't I thought of that? *Be just as dumb as you can, Win*, I told myself, sticking my head back in the accounts.

I spent all morning re-examining the books, looking for some inconsistency that would reach out and poke me in the eye, but nothing took a shot at me. I had to be missing something.

Finally, I concluded he wasn't cooking the books. The real tipoff for that conclusion was not my inadequate accounting knowledge, but the way the bookkeeper reacted to my request to see the books. She was surprised, even irritated, but not fearful. And Eduardo came by once to say hello during my examination and wasn't sweating it, either.

He had to be stealing the diamonds before they were accounted for. And Cross had a part in it.

When I was finished, Eduardo asked me into his office.

'Are you satisfied with your examination of the records?'

'Yes, everything appears to be in order.'

'Good, good. Now that you've confirmed again the mine's poor financial condition, I must encourage you to accept the offer to sell. I received it by telephone this morning. Regretfully, I must also inform you of my own plans to leave your employ. My wife and children are anxious for me to return to our house in Luanda.'

'I'm sorry to hear you're leaving. That, of course, would have some effect on my consideration of the offer. What exactly am I being offered?'

'Basically, it is a cash payment to you of five hundred thousand American dollars. Naturally, half of any sale proceeds would go to UNITA.'

'Who's making the offer?'

'A South African corporation. I understand it is only recently formed, a partnership of several wealthy businessmen with experience in diamond mining. Since the offer is for cash, they do not see fit to provide further information about themselves.'

'Frankly, Eduardo, the quarter million I'd net out after giving half to the rebels wouldn't pay my liquor bills. And that doesn't mean the government in Luanda won't grab the rest as I try to board a plane. What do you get out of the deal?'

'Nothing, of course; you own the mine, and I will be leaving anyway. The amount on the paper is just their public offer. Arrangements could be made for a direct deposit into a Swiss bank account of half a million dollars, in your name alone. Conversely, on paper, the UNITA would see that you are only getting half that amount, thus you would owe them only one hundred twenty-five thousand. I shouldn't say this, but I suspect the new owners could be induced to pay the fee to Savimbi's people, letting you net out the full half million.'

I pretended to think about it while I tried to sort out how many layers of deceit I was facing. For a guy who wasn't getting anything out of the deal, Eduardo not only knew a hell of a lot, but had all the angles covered – right down to upping the ante.

My bullshit detector was wailing like an air-raid siren. The guy was too eager to see me walk away with money in my pockets, even if it was chump change compared to what I used to have. *And he didn't even ask for a bonus for working up the deal.* He was doing it out of the sweetness in his heart.

I didn't like it.

Eduardo had a connection to the offer, something that was going on under the table. The threat to quit was to pressure me into selling. I didn't need any pressure, but I needed a hell of a lot more money than clearing out a few hundred thousand. For a mine I had over five million invested in.

'Let me think about it.'

'The buyers need—'

'Christ, I need some time, Eduardo, I just got here. I'm not kicking the offer out of bed, I just want to let it mull around my mind a bit, maybe talk to my lawyer and accountant. Just tell the buyers I'm giving it some thought. The mine's not going anywhere.'

29

I decided to check out the mine on my own – without Eduardo hand-feeding me what he wanted me to see. I wanted to learn every detail of the operation. I might soon be running the mine by myself. It wasn't something I could do in a few hours, but a diamond mine didn't take a rocket scientist to supervise, either, especially when I would only do it until I could find another manager or get a legitimate offer to buy.

The most complicated thing about a diamond mine was to not do something stupid and flood it, cause a cave-in – or, most commonly, get caught without spare parts and a mechanic for a piece of critical machinery that closed down the whole mine when it went out, like the elevator, conveyor belts, and crusher.

Unlike a coal mine, there was little risk of explosion at the Blue Lady, nor were there the miles of tunnels that are often found in other types of mines. Geological studies and test bores gave clues to where diamonds and dangerous sources of underground water might be found and determined the direction tunneling took. If I could keep the machinery running, the workers on the job, and cash coming in from sale of the production, I could keep the mine afloat until lightning struck. Or so I hoped.

I needed to learn enough basics about the operation, and names, faces, and functions of key personnel, so that if Eduardo walked out, I could keep the mine going until I found a replacement. Most of the time, the guy who oiled the gears of the conveyor belts and elevator, or knew how to keep them going with a wrench and a kick, was more important to the daily operation than the mine manager, who spent 99 percent of his time in his office on the phone or shuffling paper. Or humping the bookkeeper.

I took the elevator cage down to the operations level and grabbed the duty foreman.

'Let's take a walk, I want to learn the operation.'

His Portuguese was limited, but he got the idea. With a little Portuguese, a few local expressions I'd picked up, and a lot of hand signals, we were able to communicate as I asked him about everything I saw.

Before the crusher, I spotted a small rough and rubbed it between my fingers, feeling the soapy film that would cause it to stick to grease down the production line.

Four hours later, after getting the general idea on how the explosives are handled, learning how to set the crusher, close flood doors, lay a rail track, replace an elevator cable, and a hundred other nitty-gritty procedures, I got to the grease table. Along the way, I showed a mechanic how to diagnose a problem with the gas engine of a small tractor that pulled train cars. A gas or diesel engine was something I understood better than anyone at the mine. The only thing I knew better than an engine was a woman's working parts.

As I watched the grease-table worker put the grease-and-diamonds concoction into the sieved baskets, he carefully removed a stone about two carats in size and offered it to me. I smiled and thanked him. Then I practiced removing the grease-and-diamonds muck and greasing the table, to make sure I knew exactly how it was done.

He knew less Portuguese than the foreman, but between the two, I got across the question of how often the grease-table worker put aside stones for Eduardo as he had just done for me.

'He says a few stones a week, perhaps, that's all,' the foreman said. The foreman wasn't stupid. But he was honest. He kept a blank face when he confirmed my suspicion that the grease table was where Eduardo was skimming the diamonds. I told the foreman I would add a bonus onto this week's pay for each of them – if our discussion stayed under a hat.

I did some quick calculations on the stones I had seen in Eduardo's office, from what I was just told by the grease-table worker, and how much the fat man who buys diamonds pays for them. I figured Eduardo was pocketing maybe a couple thousand a week in diamonds. Not an insignificant amount, nor was it petty cash in Angola. But considering that half the mine's reported output ended up in the pocket of the government or the warlords, had the money gone back into the mine's production it wouldn't have amounted to a hell of a lot.

There was no way that Eduardo's grease-table skimming was changing the financial picture of the mine.

I wondered if the South African offer was nothing more than a blood-diamond laundering scheme like João had in mind – blood diamonds for weapons. That was a good possibility. It was a losing mine and could be bought at a cheap price.

But as I went to the sorting room to check out the operation of weighing and grading the stones, a thought nagged at me.

The mine is worth every dollar Bernie paid for it.

Bernie had his faults, but he wasn't a fool, even though he acted like one sometimes. *Hey, Bernie, put everything you have into a blood-diamond mine in a war zone halfway around the world! Throw in the kid's inheritance, too!*

In New York, when I was stunned by the fact I was broke, I bought into that scenario. But after talking to João in Lisbon, seeing the mine, and thinking about Bernie, it didn't ring true.

I said it aloud to hear what it sounded like: 'Bernie was no fool.'

Bernie knew my father didn't trust João. He wouldn't have jumped into bed with him. Not on a whim. Yeah, big profits in blood diamonds and owning a diamond mine was the right kind of *pizzazz* for Bernie. *But Bernie was no fool.* Hell, Bernie ran the business for over ten years after my father died. He was no ball of fire, but he kept it running – without driving it into the ground until this Angolan deal raised its ugly head.

I had to accept the premise that Bernie was too conservative to risk everything in a diamond-laundering scheme with João. The only way that Bernie would have risked so much was if he thought it was a sure thing. I could see how it probably came down. He would have been attracted to a blood-diamond deal with João. It was quick profits, a big return on investment, and an element of criminal conspiracy that Bernie would have enjoyed.

Bernie wasn't my dad, he wasn't as smart in making deals or as personable in selling himself. Bernie had an Achilles heel – his ego. But he also had a sharp eye for the diamond business. What he lacked in innate intelligence he made up for in osmosis – the diamond business was in his blood since he'd spent a lifetime in it. Until the mine deal, he hadn't just maintained my trust fund, he increased it each year despite my high rate of spending. I'd been so angry at him after finding out I was broke, I hadn't given him the credit he deserved.

The blood-diamond deal from João would have been too risky for Bernie to have gambled everything on. Mulling it over, I couldn't see Bernie risking the whole nine yards without a backup plan. He must have thought he had a fallback position. But it failed.

What the hell did Bernie, Eduardo, and the South African syndicate know about the mine that I didn't know – and I was sure João didn't know, either?

And what happened to turn the deal so sour that Bernie did the big Dutch? Or did he have help out that window?

Another intuitive flash hit me.

Bernie must have known something about the mine that made him risk big money on it. That had to be it. Bernie was too smart to have bought into a business hemorrhaging red ink without a backup plan.

There was one more thought that nagged me. I wondered where Simone was during the negotiations with Bernie. Bernie wasn't stupid when it came to money, but how was he when it came to women?

If there was anyone in the world who could talk a dog like Bernie off a meat wagon, it was Simone.

Simone. Bernie. Blood diamonds. The Blue Lady.

It gave me a headache.

I went to my room and drowned myself in a bottle of *vinho verde*.

30

The following morning, as I was deciding what to do about the mine bleeding red ink, I received a visit from the devil.

I hadn't finished my learning process so I went into the mine with the incoming day shift. Few of the miners spoke much Portuguese, but I latched onto the same foreman from yesterday who could communicate well. I had deliberately avoided Cross and Eduardo the prior evening, taking dinner alone in my room – and drinking most of it.

'Have you worked other mines?' I asked the foreman.

He shrugged. 'A few'

'Anything different about this one?'

'Maybe some have better equipment, some have worse, some hit blue earth, some yellow, some just plain brown and no diamonds. This mine is about the same as most, not rich, not poor.'

'We have to hit a kimberlite pipe for it to be rich, correct?'

'Very much so. We hit blue dirt, everyone happy.'

He meant both the owner and the miners because the miners got a bonus when the haul exceeded certain limits.

'Has the mine ever hit blue dirt?' It was a shot in the dark.

He shook his head. 'No blue, just the yellow. But there are diamonds in the yellow. Only not rich like the blue. But we will hit the blue dirt someday, eh senhor? That's why we call her the Blue Lady. A lady isn't a *puta*.'

'I hope she lives up to her name.'

I made him show me everything again, twice over. I knew from car and boat engines that if the gods willed it, it wouldn't be the big motor part that was going to cost the race when it blew – it would be the one-inch rubber hose or the paper-thin gasket that would go south.

'I want to see all spare parts, too,' I told the man who handled the inventory of parts and equipment. The backup inventory was slim, not only because of the mine's finances but the difficulties involved in importing equipment. About half the time shipments disappeared between the plane's belly and the customs warehouse.

'We often buy back from thieves the parts that get shipped to us,' the parts man told me. 'And then there are the taxes. The government collects one tax, the rebels collect another. If the equipment has to be hauled overland by truck, there are many tolls to be paid, also.'

Bartering with other mines for parts was also part of the game. It wasn't an organized process. I soon learned that despite my arrogance, I had a lot to learn. Yeah, I knew more about repairing the engines used to run mine equipment than Eduardo did. But I was completely ignorant regarding how to get a replacement belt for a generator, when you couldn't call the local parts store and have it sent over.

There were mostly empty shelves in the wire cage where the parts were kept. The parts keeper said that Eduardo had slowly been reducing the inventory of spares, telling him that the mine couldn't afford to carry backup parts. It made my blood boil because I realized it was part of Eduardo's plan to keep the mine in the red. Equipment cost many times more here than in Europe or the States, but most of it was still a small-expense item compared to the overall cost of running the mine. A broken fifty-dollar pulley on the elevator could put the entire mine out of business until it was replaced. The mine would be down, but most of the overhead would keep piling up because the workers remained on-site.

The parts keeper had a cousin who did much of the gofering and negotiating for him when parts were needed. He worked the entire mining region.

'Give me a list of everything we need,' I told the parts keeper. 'And everything that typically goes out on us. You know from past history what we need most of the time. Put your cousin to work filling the list now, before we need the stuff.'

A thought struck me. 'Will your cousin take roughs instead of cash for parts?'

The parts keeper gave me a noncommittal shrug but I saw that I had hit a home run. The mine paid UNITA out of its proceeds from the *sale* of roughs. By buying the equipment with stones that didn't go into the UNITA pot, I'd be getting the equipment at a big discount. And the cousin would be happy because he'd be getting a greater value in diamonds than he could have gotten in cash. I wondered how many other mine expenses I could pay with diamonds. Maybe I'd talk to Cross about paying him off in roughs. After I figured out what I was going to do about Eduardo – and found out whether Cross was in on whatever Eduardo was pulling.

I was watching the blasting process when one of the miners came along and handed me a message. Cross wanted to see me.

He was waiting in the elevator. 'Hop aboard, the devil's waiting topside.'

'This goddamn country is too hot for the devil.'

'True, but this guy is called El Diablo – except to his face – because he'd scare the balls off Satan himself. Colonel Jomba is the regional enforcer for Savimbi and his UNITA.'

'What does he want?'

'What do these people ever want? It's rent time. Eduardo will let him check the books and give him the percentage of what the mine produced, but Colonel Jomba made a specific request to talk to you. Privately.'

'Why?'

'Beats the hell outta me.'

'Some fuckin' security chief you are.'

Cross grabbed my arm before I stepped off the elevator and pulled me aside so he wouldn't be heard by a group of miners waiting to descend.

'Watch your mouth with this guy Jomba, you've never met anyone like him. He's a wild beast and hardly human, a chip off the old block of Savimbi. The closest thing to these guys would be a three-hundred-pound Chicago Bears lineman with the appetite of Jeffrey Dahmer. If you looked cross-eyed at him he'd have your arms cut off. If you cheated him out of fifty cents, he'd have the amputations done very slowly. That way you can think about how you fucked up as you bleed to death. Millions of people have died in this crazy war and guys like Jomba have personally killed hundreds, maybe thousands.'

I had an idea why the colonel wanted to speak to me. But it wasn't something I could reveal to Cross. João intimated I would be contacted about the diamonds-for-guns deal. I suspected this was it. It made my knees weak. What the hell had I gotten myself into? Running guns and blood diamonds had a totally different connotation in Lisbon than in Angola. If I wasn't careful, some of the blood staining the diamonds would be my own.

A line of jeeps with mounted machine guns and antitank rockets were parked at the gate to the mine. About thirty or forty rough-looking soldiers hung around the vehicles. There was an unkempt grimness to the lot of them that made them seem more like the marauders they were rather than government troops.

Cross grabbed my arm again. 'You're on your own, bubba, I didn't get an invitation. Don't piss off this devil, I can't help you if you do. Keep your mouth shut, your wallet open, and try to look scared. If you shit your pants, that'll impress him more than tough talk.'

'Looking scared will be easy.'

'One last thing. If he invites you to a barbecue, you're probably on the menu. He once burned a *garimpeiro* at the stake for holding out on him. The guy probably cheated him out of fifty cents.'

Jesus H. Christ. As I got closer to the man, I realized Cross was not exaggerating – the colonel could kill the appetite of Hannibal the Cannibal. He was a bull, big girth, big arms, short legs the size of tree trunks. Big bald head completely free of hair. Bull neck. Put it all together and it added up to a guy who could rip off my arms and legs and beat me with them.

As I got within spitting distance, the picture worsened. *He had devil's horns tattooed on each side of his head. And a tattooed necklace of barbed wire was around his neck.* I didn't miss the knife slashes on each cheek.

The deliberate mutilations were probably not designed to scare anyone. This guy was already scary. No doubt he added the horns and barbed wire necklace because he liked the artwork.

Now that was *really* scary.

He carried a British army officer's swagger stick under his arm. His boots shined like mirrors. Medals bristled on his chest. A 9mm semiautomatic sat in a black holster on his right hip. Another gun was holstered under his left arm. On him, the guns looked like children's toys – he probably teethed on them when he was a baby and only a hundred pounds or so.

He had 'dangerous son-of-a-bitch' written all over him.

I couldn't imagine any mine owner being late with their rent. It was like missing a payment with the Grim Reaper.

What do you say to a guy who has devil's horns and barbed wire tattooed on him?

'Hi. I'm Win Liberte,' I said in Portuguese.

'I am Colonel Jomba,' the man said.

143

'Glad to meet you.' I started to offer a handshake, but let the hand flap by my side. I wasn't sure I would get it back.

He had sharp teeth, what you'd expect to see in a shark. I wondered if he had them sharpened deliberately. Maybe it was a fashion statement, like the barbed wire and devil's horns. And maybe the teeth got ground down chewing on the bones of his victims.

The jeep he was standing next to had a human skull for a hood ornament.

Another fashion statement.

He snapped the swagger stick against the side of his leg as we walked and talked. His Portuguese was excellent, cultivated and educated, better than my kitchen dialect.

'Senhor Carmona told you in Lisbon of the plan?'

I was right. This was the contact about the blood-diamond deal.

'Not really. He said he wanted to work out an arrangement involving certificates for diamonds that come from areas where there has been, uh, conflicts.' I didn't mention that I was undecided about going through with the deal. The colonel was not a man you disappointed with a refusal or even a little ambivalence.

'Pressure is great. If we wait too long, there will be open civil war. Once that happens, Angolan diamonds will be defined as conflict diamonds and subject to boycotts. When that happens, your certification will be useless.'

'I see,' I said, seeing nothing. What was this colonel up to? He was subordinate to Savimbi. And João was persona non grata in deals with Savimbi and the UNITA. The word 'coup' came to mind. I got the suspicion that the colonel planned to trade diamonds for weapons and use them to carve out his own piece of the rock. The fact that it might be a rogue operation was not encouraging. That would bring down both the government in Luanda and Savimbi's UNITA rebels on me if it failed.

Colonel Jomba went on. 'The Bey also cannot come to Angola, at least not publicly. He was Carmona's partner in the attempt to cheat Savimbi. Thus, you will need to take a more active role in the arrangements, filling in the duties that Carmona and the Bey cannot perform.'

'I don't want—'

He stopped and faced me, tapping his swagger stick against the side of his leg. 'We understand each other, do we not?'

'Of course,' I smiled. I understood perfectly. My head was going to get mounted on his jeep's hood if I pissed him off. João had left out a few things when he explained the deal to me in Sintra – mainly that my ass was going to be on the line. Cross had said Savimbi personally murdered the wife and children of an opponent. I couldn't even imagine what he would do to an American caught plotting against him. This guy Jomba was supposed to have burned someone at the stake. Alive. Not to mention chopping off arms.

The expressions, 'getting skinned alive' and 'the torture of a thousand cuts' came to mind as I pondered my own potential fate.

'I will be back again to discuss the specific arrangements with you.'

He looked back to where Cross was standing by the guard shed, watching us. 'Have you told your security man that we will be dealing with each other?' He asked the question smoothly, inviting a slip of the tongue from me if I lied.

'Not a word. He thinks you are talking to me about the contribution we make each month.'

He eyed me. 'Very good. If I doubted your word, I would kill him now.'

'I'd like to have some idea of how the deal will come down. I know it's diamonds for guns, but I have no clue what my part—'

'No clue is exactly what is best for you. Do you understand what I mean?' He gave me an appraising look out of the corner of his eye. 'You Americans have contempt for the mental capacity of people of the Third World. Dr Savimbi has a doctorate from a Swiss university. I hold a degree in economics from a Portuguese university. I also studied economics in London. I know how to count beyond my fingers and toes. But I also deal with betrayal in a harsh, old-fashioned way. Do you understand what I mean?'

I stopped and faced him. 'I understand that you're passing out a lot of threats to someone who you want to deal with. I understand that I intend to maintain my part, but that there are other people involved, not all of whom might hold up their end. I also understand I don't want to be left holding the bag when everything goes to hell because someone in Lisbon or this Bey character doesn't produce.'

Jomba grinned and nodded his head to the cadence of the swagger stick beating against the side of his leg. 'Then we understand each other. You do your part, and no matter what happens, you will be in the clear. And well rewarded for your efforts.' He nodded at the Blue Lady mine. 'Much more than you will ever get digging in that barren hole.'

We parted company, with me clear on one thing: the odds of my surviving long enough to make a killing in Angola had just gone up. It was no longer a question of whether a twelve-year-old kid high on drugs pulled the trigger of his rusty AK-47, as I stood in the way of the bullet. Now I had enemies in high places. Men who handed out barbaric punishments that would have scared the balls off of Torquemada, the beast of the Spanish Inquisition.

If a river miner got burned alive for cheating on a few dollars' worth of diamonds, what would they do to an American mine owner who screwed up a blood-diamond deal? Or who stood around when everything went to hell?

I hadn't seen Savimbi, but if Jomba was just a chip off the block of the UNITA leader, I was getting caught between two savage demons.

I didn't think an actuary would give good odds of me surviving to a ripe old age – or even to my next birthday.

I knew one sure thing: João had never walked a straight road in his life. He was the type who would cheat me out of whatever I had coming if it increased his share. If the Bey was João's pal, he would walk the same crooked road. No matter what Jomba said about me coming out all right if I did my part, I didn't want to be around when anyone else screwed him.

As I walked back toward the guardhouse where Cross waited, I was careful to keep my features blank. The colonel had left me with many unanswered questions, but one thing was perfectly clear – it was a lose-lose scenario for me. Once I signed the phony diamond certification, and did whatever else Colonel Jomba wanted me to do in order to get guns into his hands, I would go from a needed ally to a material witness to his shady deals. Not to mention walking away with a big chunk of money that would fit better in his pocket.

As Cross might say, there were three possible scenarios for me from this mess: *dead, dead, dead.*

Cross hadn't bought into any of this and I wasn't about to endanger him by getting him involved. Not that he would be stupid enough to dig a hole for himself in Angola.

When I came back, he gave me a puzzled look. 'Well, bubba, there's a lot more to you than meets the eye. And don't give me any horseshit about you and the colonel discussing the rent – you two were as thick as thieves out there. If that prick wanted to talk money, he would have done it in front of Eduardo; he isn't that subtle.'

'Do you really want to know what was said?'

146

'Fuck no. If that crazy bastard comes back to kill everyone at the mine because whatever was supposed to come down didn't, I want to go to hell knowing I was an innocent bystander.'

31

That night after dinner I knocked on Cross's door. He didn't look happy to see me. He was packing his bags.

'Going someplace?' I asked.

'I'm bailing out, like I told you I would. You walking around with the devil's cock in your hand today was the last straw. If you've come here to ask me to stay on the job, you're wasting your time. I'm quitting, pronto. In the morning, I'm getting on my horse and riding into the sunset.'

'What's your real reason for leaving me high and dry? Is it just the usual prissy-ass crap about your impoverished childhood and the silver spoon up my ass?'

'I told you I don't like your choice of friends. Having to do business with the Jombas of this world is bad, but at least it's just business. If we weren't paying Savimbi's boy, we'd be paying the thugs on the other side of this political quagmire. But from what I could see from the body language of you and that fuckin' gorilla in a uniform, you have something else cooking.'

I sauntered over to an end table where Cross had several bottles of booze and poured myself a Scotch. His holstered 9mm semiautomatic pistol hung from a belt hooked around the bedpost. Convenient. He could reach down and grab it in the middle of the night without hardly taking his head off the pillow.

'What do I have cooking?' I asked. I sat on the bed, sloshing the whisky around in the glass.

'I don't know and I don't want to know. But being human, and knowing the vices of man, I can take a guess. Colonel Jomba has something up his sleeve. He has the worldview of a pit bull, so it's probably just some simple plan involving murder and thievery. What scares the crap out of me is the secrecy. These guys aren't subtle about collecting the rent. Which makes me wonder whether he might be thinking of skimming from Savimbi. And that you're involved in it.

'If you think the colonel is a mean bastard, I can only tell you that compared to Savimbi, he's a pussycat. Savimbi catches you and one of his boys skimming, he'll shove a hot poker up your ass and make you drink Drano to cool off. In Angola, guilt by association is proved just because you're close enough to get dragged in when a couple hundred UNITA gunmen start rounding up everyone in the neighborhood.'

'Cross—'

'No – no – no, don't tell me what you got coming down, I don't want to know. But I knew some shit was up when you dropped Carmona's name on me. He tried to cheat Savimbi once and the way I see it, he's sent you back down here to finish the deal.'

I had a feeling he was right. The colonel didn't want the war to end, it was much too profitable. Peace meant getting a real job. And there were probably a bunch more in the rebel camp like him, chafing under the peace plan Savimbi had agreed to. That made it open season for João and his pal the Bey to trade weapons for diamonds. Cross was no dummy. If I gave him half a chance, he'd come up with the answer that it was a blood diamond deal. But I wanted to steer him away from the truth until I figured out what my moves were going to be. And besides, I had come to his room for a different reason than to ask him to stay at the mine.

I reached down and pulled his 9mm from the holster.

'Hey, don't play with that.'

He started for me and I pointed it at his gut and said, 'I told you, whatever I do, I'm the best at. That includes shooting.'

'What the fuck you doing, man? You point that fuckin' gun another way or I'll shove it up your ass.'

'Get your roughs.'

'What?'

'Your roughs. I want to see them.'

'What do you care about – oh, I see, you think I've been ripping you off, is that it?'

'I know Eduardo's been doing it. I still have a small question in my mind about you.'

'Prick.' He took a book called *The Secret Garden* off the shelf and flipped it open. The book was hollow inside. He threw a pouch from the book onto the bed.

'Everyone of those came from the river. Not that you'll be able to tell. Diamonds don't come with fingerprints, bubba. You can't tell if those came from the mine, the river, or the moon.'

I felt the stones, rubbing them in my hand. All different sizes. A few were a carat or more, but most 'smalls' were less than a carat. Some were even industrial-grade. Even with the naked eye, I could tell few of them would be flawless. And all of them lacked a soapy feel.

'That's right, they're not oily, they're smooth,' he said, 'just like river stones. But that don't mean they couldn't have come from the mine. Once they go through the boiling point to wash off the mess from the grease tables, you can't tell a river stone from a mined stone. Unless that old man of yours taught you something that you can't find in geology books.'

'He did. None of these came from the mine.'

I slipped his gun back in its holster and got up. 'You're not stealing from me. I didn't think you were, but I had to be sure. Eduardo's roughs had the distinctive feel of mined diamonds. He lied when he said he got them from his river claims.'

I handed him back the stones. I should have seen it coming when he reached for them with his left hand. He buried his right fist about three inches into my gut, knocking the wind out of me. I flew back onto the bed and curled into a fetal position.

'Now don't you go puking on my bed,' he said, 'or I'll make you change the bedding.'

He filled a water glass almost to the brim with Scotch. 'Want another shot?'

I sat up, holding my stomach which hurt like hell. 'I want a gastroenterologist.'

'Hey, now don't you go complaining. I deliberately hit you in the stomach so I didn't knock out any of your pretty teeth. You know how hard it is to find a dentist in Angola? One without AIDS?'

'Thanks, pal.'

'I figured you had a right to be suspicious.'

'I don't want you to quit.'

'Fuck you. Why?'

'Because I need you. But I'm going to fire Eduardo.'

'Who's going to run the mine with him gone? You know how hard it is to find a competent mine manager?'

'I'm going to run it.'

'Shit, the heat here has gotten to you, or maybe you got bit by a bug that carries the crazies. Eduardo may be an ass and a thief, neither of which are grounds for being fired in Angola, but he also has a degree from a mining school and twenty years of experience.'

'I didn't say I was going to run the mine forever, just until I can get a replacement. And I know it's not a piece of cake, but it's not impossible, either. Diamond mining isn't that complex. Half the job revolves around keeping the machinery going. And machines are something I understand even better than Eduardo.'

'It won't work.'

'It has to, I can't have Eduardo around.'

'Tell him to stop stealing. And give him a raise.'

'It's not the skimming. Look, I have a feeling about this mine and about Eduardo. You know that old line about something smelling rotten in Denmark? Something stinks with this whole setup. Something about the mine, about Bernie getting in over his head, something more than your suspicions about João Carmona and Colonel Jomba. And I won't know until I get rid of Eduardo and get down and dirty in the mine and really find out what's going on.'

Cross lit a cigar and sucked on the end. 'Man, I don't disagree with you. I knew Eduardo was skimming, but, hell, that's just a perk for working in this hellhole of a country. I never figured he was stealing enough to really affect things.'

'I don't think he is. He's skimming a grand or two a week, not enough to make a difference in the long run.'

'Then what do you think he's up to?'

I shrugged and shook my head. 'I don't know. But I can feel the con in my bones.'

'Tell me what your bones are saying.'

I told him about Eduardo trying to get me to sell the mine. And not wanting a bonus for setting up the deal.

'He didn't ask for money? Holy shit, bubba – uh, Win, you're right. That motherfucker wouldn't pass up a nickel if it was wedged between a croc's teeth. I can think of one thing he might be doing.'

'Holding back production to reduce the price of the mine?'

'You guessed it.'

'It's a possibility. At first I thought the mine was salted to take Bernie to the cleaners. After I got rid of the notion that the mine had been salted, my next bet was that it was being skimmed blind. That's not happening either, probably because Eduardo would have to have you and every other supervisor in the place in on it.

'Then I figured maybe he deliberately keeps production low to reduce the mine's output, but I've talked to foremen who have worked other mines about how much they pulled out. Eduardo seems to be about on par in terms of how much dirt they haul out per man-hour. And we haven't hit blue dirt, that's a certainty. You can tell we're still in the yellow stuff just by looking at what's coming down the conveyor belt.'

'But you still think he's got something up his sleeve?'

'He could have asked for ten percent of the sales price as a finder's fee, fifty thousand in his pocket even if he was getting a fee from the buyers. If I didn't think something was up, I'd have agreed.'

Cross blew smoke rings. 'Yeah, he's got something going all right. Hell, for that kind of money, you could *almost* buy my loyalty.'

'I told you, if I make it, you make it.'

'Yeah, trust you? A guy who's never worked a job or made a dime in his life? You're gonna start running a mine tomorrow and get us rich?'

'Cross, one thing you need to learn in life, people are consistent. Losers never make it big. And achievers succeed at anything they try. Running a diamond mine isn't any more complicated than winning a race in a sailboat.'

'You are full of shit.'

'True, but go back to the consistency thing. I'm a winner, in everything.'

'I guess you're telling me that I'll always be a loser.'

'No—'

'Forget it, I was just falling back into my usual prissy-ass crap about my impoverished childhood and that silver spoon up your ass.'

'Well, are you going to give me a hand with the dirty work?'

'Where do you want to start?'

'You gave me an idea when you talked about how Savimbi dealt with insubordinate employees. We could stick a hot poker up Eduardo's ass and make him drink Drano.'

'I'll drink to that.' Cross chugged down the last half of his glass of whisky. Afterward, he wiped his mouth on his sleeve and eyed me quizzically again.

151

'Okay, wise guy, tell me, how do you know that my diamonds didn't come from the mine? They feel the same as river diamonds once the oil's been boiled off. What's this secret your old man taught you?'

'Eduardo had choice roughs, all over a carat, all flawless. Your stones were a mixed bag, some good, some bad, nothing really sensational, just the sort of stuff the *garimpeiros* pull out with their shovel-and-bucket method.'

I got off the bed.

'What my old man taught me was that people are consistent. A thief is a thief his whole life, even if he only indulges once. And an honest man doesn't steal. If you had had one flawless diamond larger than a carat I would have known you got it from the mine. And I would have shot off your left nut.'

32

Cross used his security keys to open the door to Eduardo's quarters. The living room was dark. Light came from a crack around the door to the bedroom. We crept across the room and I listened at the door. I recognized the sounds – the groans and moans of two-legged animals humping.

Having less finesse than me, Cross kicked open the door. Eduardo was sprawled spread-eagle on the bed and Carlotta was on top of him in a female superior position. Both were naked. Carlotta screamed and Eduardo bucked her off, moving his hand under his pillow.

Cross pointed his gun at Eduardo's face. 'Take your hand out, slowly.'

I retrieved the gun from under the pillow while Eduardo and his woman squawked.

'Did you know that humans are the only animals that fuck face-to-face?' Cross said. 'I read that in a book somewhere.'

'This is—'

'Grab your clothes,' I told Carlotta, 'and get out of here.'

Eduardo struggled into his pants. 'This is outrageous, you will pay for this intrusion, I have powerful friends, you will be dead by morning.'

Funny – in America or Europe, people would threaten to call the police. In Angola, the threat is that you'll be murdered.

'Let me give it to you in simple terms, Eduardo,' I said. 'You have been stealing from me, stealing the mine blind. You've been skimming the cream of the crop off the grease table.'

'Fuck you.'

'No, pal, it's butt-fuck *you* time. Watch him while I take a look around.'

He had a three-foot-high black safe in the corner of the bedroom. 'We'll need to persuade him to give us the combination,' I said.

'Forget the safe,' Cross said. 'They're loss leaders in Angola, nobody's stupid enough to put anything in them except junk. With this guy, I'd look for a secret compartment, floor, wall, ceiling.'

He was right. I found the hiding place under the sink in the tiny kitchen. I removed boards from the bottom of the sink cabinet and found a cigar box full of wrapped diamonds and a waterproof pouch containing paperwork.

The look on Eduardo's face told me I'd hit pay dirt. Cross whistled as I unwrapped diamonds.

'This *bastardo* wasn't a piker, was he?'

'Fuck you,' Eduardo said.

Cross hit him in the mouth. 'You've been stealing on my watch, *compadre*. And you didn't even offer to cut me in on it.'

'These are superior roughs,' I said, 'all will cut down to at least a carat, all flawless or near flawless, fifty grand worth at least, even the ten cents on the dollar you get here.'

Eduardo started mouthing another threat and I sat down beside him, shook my head, and gently told him, 'It won't work, pal. Colonel Jomba isn't going to be happy at all.'

Eduardo's face went gray-green and his eyes bulged. 'Jomba doesn't have anything to do with this, you know that.'

'I can't keep it from him.' As I spoke, I began examining the paperwork in the pouch. 'When he came by, he took me aside to talk about you. He got word that you were skimming from the mine and not kicking back to him. One of the foremen tipped him off that you've been treating the grease table like your own private cookie jar. Jomba wasn't happy at the news, Savimbi himself told him to straighten out the mess.'

'Jomba is insane. Keep the diamonds, I don't care, I'll go to Luanda and be with my family.'

'That's really nice of you to let me keep what you stole from me. Hey, what's this?'

I pulled out the deposit history to a Swiss bank account. 'Over three hundred thousand dollars.'

Cross shook his head. 'Holy shit, this guy is something else.'

'How long's he been manager?' I asked.

'Two years,' Eduardo said, 'but half of the money came from the last mine I ran.'

'Okay, so with fifty grand in the box and half of three hundred thousand in the bank, you've ripped me off for a couple hundred grand. Which means you ripped Jomba and Savimbi off for a hundred grand. Not to mention what you owe them on thefts from the last mine you ran.'

Eduardo was sweating bullets. 'Jomba will kill all of us if he finds out.'

'Actually, he offered me a reward, half of whatever I recover.' I looked up at Cross. 'What do you think Jomba will do to him?'

Cross laughed. 'You don't have to threaten him. He knows. Don't you, Eduardo? What do you think? Maybe slice pieces off your arms and legs, an inch at a time, and toss them to his dogs? Slice your tongue down the middle for lying to him? When you're nothing but a bloody stump, he'll hang you up in the middle of town for the flies to—'

Eduardo slumped forward and I caught him before he hit the floor in a faint. We got him back into the chair and I shook him awake.

'I'll tell you what we're going to do, Eduardo. When the banks open in Switzerland tomorrow, you're going to do a telephonic transfer and transfer everything in your account to my account. And then you're going to get a head start before we tell Colonel Jomba.'

We tied up Eduardo so he couldn't go anywhere and left the room. Cross would sack out in the room to make sure Carlotta didn't help Eduardo escape.

When we were out of Eduardo's hearing, Cross asked, 'You really plan to tell Jomba? He'll take a big cut if you do.'

'And if I don't, I'll be the one taking a cut. What do you think the chances are that Jomba has someone at the mine on his payroll or just scared shitless enough to keep him advised?'

'It's a sure thing someone at the mine's reporting to him.'

'And Cross.' We stopped and faced each other. 'You get ten percent of whatever is left after Jomba grabs his piece. The rest will go to run the mine.'

'Thanks. And hey, I think you're right about Eduardo. The diamonds he bled from the mine weren't enough to make a big difference to the bottom line. That means he's up to something else.'

I held up the pouch of papers. 'I'm going through these tonight. Maybe he left tracks in them.'

33

Eduardo and his honey took off after I supervised a money transfer from his Swiss account to my New York bank. It felt like something foul had been swept from the mine. With the threat of Jomba after them, I figured it would be a long time before they raised their ugly heads.

My first official act was to promote the foreman who had been giving me lessons in diamond mining. I put him in charge of the daily operation of the mine, reporting directly to me.

I had coffee with Cross out on the verandah of the living quarters.

'I found a geologist's bill in Eduardo's paperwork, someone from Cape Town,' I said. 'There's no report, just the bill.'

'It wouldn't be unusual for an Angolan mine to use a South African geologist. Was it for the mine or someplace else?'

'For the mine.'

Cross shrugged. 'Probably nothing to it. The mine gets geological studies now and then to direct the tunneling.'

'I know, I saw them in the mine files. But there are two things unusual about the bill. It's not from the firm that has done studies in the past. More importantly, the bill says it was for the Blue Lady but Eduardo paid for it out of his personal funds.'

Cross snorted. 'Eduardo was so cheap, he wouldn't pay for his mother's funeral out of his own pocket.'

'Another thing, he had the bill hidden with his cache of stones. It must have been awfully important to him. And something he wants to keep secret.'

'Why don't you call the geologist and have him send you a copy of the report?'

I shook my head. 'No, I don't think so. Eduardo claimed that the people who want to buy the mine are a group of South African businessmen. He might have been lying, but he might just be thick as thieves with this geologist and this South African group. I want to check the geologist out first, hire an investigator, see if he's legit, what his reputation is, maybe even pay a cold-call visit on him in Cape Town. It's harder to say no or lie face-to-face in person.'

'I have a friend who's security chief at a South African mine. Mining's a small world. He might know something about the guy.'

'See what you can find out. In the meantime, get ahold of Jomba. Eduardo and Carlotta should be in Luanda by now if they hired a charter. We have to show him Eduardo's paperwork and settle up with him. I don't want him to get the idea that we're slow at paying.'

'Uh, bubba, don't look now but I think you have a problem.'

The shift foreman was running toward us. Cross and I got up and met him at the bottom of the stairs. He was so excited that he burst into an African language.

'Portuguese,' I told him, 'speak Portuguese.'

'He's telling you there's a problem in the mine,' Cross said.

'Slow down, what's the problem?'

'Water is coming into the tunnels.'

'From where?' It was a stupid question, water from underground rivers and streams was a constant problem with the mine.

He jabbered again so fast in Portuguese and an Angolan dialect I couldn't understand him.

'That bastard,' Cross said.

'Who?'

'Eduardo went down into the mine before he left and had the graveyard shift remove the latches from all the watertight doors. He's flooding the mine.'

'What? What do we do?'

'We? You got someone in your pocket? You're the new mine manager. *Start managing.*'

PART 5

MARNI

34

Clipboard in hand, Marni watched Angolan workers unload a truck into a UN aid warehouse in the small town of 9th de Outubro. The town name of October 9th had once been named 28th de Julho, July 28th, for the day it was liberated from the Portuguese during the war of independence, but had changed several years before when the UNITA renamed it for the date they 'liberated' it.

A worker let a sack of rice fly off his shoulder. The sack ripped open as it hit the truck's bumper and rice spilled out onto the ground. A crowd of women and children watching the unloading made a mad dash to grab handfuls of the rice.

'Damn it!' Marni threw her clipboard on the ground. 'That's the third bag you people have broken. I saw you, I know it was deliberate. Sonofabitch!'

She stormed away, heading for a cold-water dispenser set under the shade of a tree. She patted sweat from her face with her handkerchief, then poured cool water on it to cool her neck.

Michele LaFonte, another aid worker, picked up the clipboard and joined Marni in the shade. She laughed as she handed Marni the board.

'I see you're following the training manual on how to deal with indigenous workers.' Michele's English was overlaid with a heavy French accent. She was Marni's supervisor and teacher.

'Aren't throwing tantrums in the manual? Sometimes it's the only language they understand.' She nodded toward the truck being unloaded. 'They've been dropping bags deliberately, aiming them at a jagged edge on the bumper so they'll burst. That food is sent from halfway around the world to feed them and their people and they sabotage it. The people scooping it up are in league with the ones dropping it.'

'Let me guess, they demanded more money for unloading, were late starting, are dragging their feet—'

'All of the above. And they especially don't like to take orders from a woman.'

'It's a loss of status for them.'

'That's how it started, they demanded more money just because I'm a woman and then they turned to sabotage when I refused. I just wish there was a dose of reality in those manuals I read about Third World relief before I got here. The books left out the part about the fleas that leave ugly sores on your ankles, the food that turns your stomach into a volcano until you're puking lava, the mosquitoes thirstier than the Vampire Lestat. They don't even mention the time difference. There is no concept of time here, at least not one I understand. These people come and go when they please, work when they damn well want to, and only show up for sure if it's time to get paid.'

'Tell them what I've been telling my crew – the cost of every damaged bag will be deducted from their pay.'

'Good idea!'

In a jumble of Portuguese, Umbundu, and the international language of hand signals, Marni got across the fact that she was going to deduct broken bags from their pay. A howl went up from the workers but they went back to work, handling bags more carefully, after she threatened to fire the whole bunch of them.

'Good work!' Michele said when she came back into the shade.

'I'm still learning. I wish I had your command of the language in dealing with these people. And your balls.'

'You will, it's just a matter of practice. And survival.' Michele's features turned grave. 'Word has come from the south that two of our people and ten Angolan workers were killed in an ambush of a food convoy.'

'Oh, no.'

'The names haven't been released yet. I'm praying none of my friends was killed.'

'Jesus, what an awful way to die. Being murdered when you came here to help. Do they know who did it?'

'There's no word yet, but they usually never really know anyway. Oh, the government will send out patrols, or Savimbi's UNITA will send them out, there'll be some fighting and an announcement that renegade government troops or renegade rebels or someone else did it and has been punished, but we never know who's telling the truth. Things will be quiet for a while and then in a month or two there'll be another attack, food and trucks will be hijacked, and some of us will be killed.'

'You have a wonderful sense of fatalism, Michele. The kind that makes me want to pack up and head home.'

'It is a paradox, isn't it? UN, Red Cross, missionaries, we all come here to help these people who have been so brutalized by war and the food and medicine is hijacked to be sold on the black market by some of the people we've come to help.'

'You can throw in nasty pests, terrible diseases, insufferable living conditions – hell, I am going to pack!'

The two women laughed.

'It's discouraging,' Marni said. 'I need a bath, a cool glass of lemonade, dinner with a man who doesn't smell as badly as I do, maybe a few tender moments with him between pure white sheets—'

'You can have my vibrator!'

'I'd prefer your husband next time he's in town.'

'He's never around, that's why I have a vibrator.'

Michele's husband was a helicopter pilot who ferried aid workers and supplies into isolated areas.

Marni wiped the sweat on the back of her neck with a handkerchief. 'It was so different where I went to school in California. Reading about the misery in books, watching documentaries, talking to people who'd been in the field, it just doesn't prepare you for the reality.'

Michele nodded. 'You never know how terrible things really are until you see a child with AIDS being eaten alive by flies, or having to teach someone whose arms have been cut off how to wipe themselves after they've gone to the toilet. But you're being too hard on yourself. You've only been in Angola a couple months and you already have a reputation for getting the job done and refusing to budge, whether you're up against lazy workers or corrupt officials.'

'What amazes me is that we all continue to function in the face of threats and chaos. You just told me that some of our coworkers were murdered a few hundred miles from here. But other than shedding some tears if we knew any of them personally, we will continue to function and get the job done.'

'*Qui*, we will.'

'And you and your husband have been doing this for years.'

'We will die in the saddle, as your cowboys say. Hopefully, not for many years from now. My only wish is that when the time comes, my husband and I will go at the same time. Very quickly.'

'God, don't talk like that.' Marni shivered.

'It's a fact of life. Anything can happen when you're working in a war zone.'

'Sometimes it seems so hopeless. Distributing food, getting people vaccinated, you see instant results. I wonder if we're having any effect at all, if it's possible to have an effect in this sea of misery.'

'*Ce n'est pas la mer á boire.*'

'It's not the sea to drink,' Marni said, translating Michele's favorite expression. 'Okay, it's not impossible, but maybe we'll drown in human misery.'

Michele squeezed her arm. 'You're so sensitive, so idealistic, maybe too much. You came here to save the people of Angola but you found out a lot of people aren't worth saving because they're part of the problem. And the rest of them are so downtrodden, so broken and beaten, they can't help themselves and often become part of the problem because they bite the hand that feeds them.

'My skin is thicker,' Michele went on, 'my ideals are buried deeper. I've been at this for over twenty years, in the Congo, Sierra Leone, Rwanda, Bosnia and the Palestinian camps. I know I can't save the world and I don't try, I just help as many people as I can today and hope that it makes a difference in the long run. Besides, the job pays well.'

That got Marni laughing so hard she started coughing. 'The pay stinks,' she gasped, 'and the working conditions suck, but I think you're one part Mother Theresa, one part Joan of Arc, and a little Simon Legree.'

'Simon Legree?'

'A plantation overseer, literally a slave driver. He's a character in a book. Now teach me some more of that Umbundu profanity that gets the workers to shut up and do their jobs.'

Just then an aid worker, a woman Marni's age, waved and yelled as she came by before walking out to the road.

'I see Rita is wearing her uniform of the day,' Marni said.

Michele glanced at the woman's miniskirt with distaste. 'I've met a Rita at every aid mission I've been on. There's always one who'll wear short-shorts and a tank top without a bra underneath to the marketplace, confirming to Third World men, all of whom are pigs when it comes to women, that Western women are all whores.'

'She gave me graphic details about the male parts of the Angolan military commander she's sleeping with. She calls it a black mamba. I've seen the commander driving around with a couple local whores in his jeep. I'd say Rita's risking it.'

'I always wonder if it's really a sex thing when I see a European woman like Rita jump into bed with the local men in countries I've worked, from the Balkans to the Far East. I suspect the men back home never gave Rita the respect she needs – probably because she was too easy. The Ritas of this world look for fulfillment in a man's bed. It's not there, regardless of who the man is. And here, she's putting her whole life on the line.'

Marni shook her head. 'It's pretty sad, but she'll learn there are two things you can't get vaccinated for – stupidity and AIDS.'

After the truck was unloaded, Marni went into the long tent where the food and medical supplies were stored before distribution. With Venacio, her Angolan assistant, she began a count. Auditing aid was half her job, the easy part. Trying to get as much of it as possible into the hands of the people it was intended for was the tough part. Food and medicine would mysteriously disappear from the warehouse overnight, trucks would arrive with less aid than they had started with. Even worse than common thievery was the blatant theft by corrupt government officials, rebel warlords, black marketeers, and gangs of hijackers.

Countries are like people, Marni thought. They develop personalities and emotional distress, just as individuals do. They can go schizo like Germany did under the Nazis, paranoid like Russia under Stalin. Angola she saw as a beaten child, whipped and starved, raped and tortured, until it no longer knew what a normal existence was. Traumatized, the whole country acted psychotic, often hurting itself and those who were extending a helping hand.

They should audit the misery, she thought, and gather it up and shove it down the throats of the companies and people feeding the war frenzy with oil and diamond dollars. Starvation, disease, deaths and injuries from bombing, shelling, and land mines, looting, hijackings, ambushes, rape, kidnapping, murder – it would be an audit of hell, she thought.

'*Menina*,' Venacio said, addressing her with the Portuguese word for Miss, 'I just counted eighty-six bags of wheat and you wrote down rice.'

'I'm sorry, my mind is somewhere else.'

'Your mind is so full of your many duties, you don't have room for your own thoughts.' He took the clipboard from her. 'Go for a walk, go for a dinner and movie.'

They both laughed at the joke.

'Okay, I do need some air. Finish up the counts. When you tell me how much was stolen between the airport in Luanda and here, lie to me so that I can feel better about the world.'

She left the tent and the small UN encampment, walking along the dirt road that ran beside the river. Women offered food – oranges, ears of corn, sticky balls of yam – and polluted drinks to the drivers of the trucks and busses using the road. She knew that some of the women offered more carnal pleasures, too, and that AIDS was not just a deadly disease to these people, but a fact of life. So was poverty, crime, and murderous warfare.

Yet so many of these women had easy smiles and took delight at the littlest things. And often she saw acts of generosity and kindness. The only noticeable malice was in the arrogance of the men who carried automatic weapons and acted more like bandits than soldiers.

Under the shade of a eucalyptus tree, she paused and watched *garimpeiros* working the river for diamonds. An altercation broke out between river miners as one man used a piece of wood to drive back others from what he considered to be his claim. There was more shouting and splashing than bloodletting.

She turned away from the dispute and watched a boy helping his father search for diamonds in a deeper part of the river. The older man dove down with a bucket in hand and a plastic tube in his mouth. The boy pumped on a bellows connected to the tube, sending air into the line. Or at least, that was the theory – the driver came up frequently, gasping for air, so she wondered how well the improvised air line worked.

But for the grace of God go any of us, she thought. She had picked up the expression from her grandfather, Jack Norton, on her mother's side, a man she had only met as an adult. He used it whenever he saw someone less fortunate than himself.

'An accident of birth,' she said aloud to herself. That's what kept her from being one of the women in the river hunting for diamonds in the murky water with a baby strapped to her back, or lying on her back in a shanty along the road, earning food money for her children by satisfying the sexual needs of a truck driver – while she slowly and painfully died from disease. She thanked God she wasn't one of them.

She turned from the river and leaned against the tree, looking down the row of shanties lining the dirt road. Down the road, a man vented his anger at a woman selling oranges. Probably his wife, she thought, as the man yelled at the woman. She knew enough of the language to realize it had something to do with money, probably the money the woman had collected from the sale of the fruit. Her knowledge of an Angolan tongue had not been as beneficial as she'd thought it would be. Language differed, almost from village to village.

As Marni watched the angry man's lips moving, she got an image of her own father. And her mother.

She was born in San Jose, the capital of California's Silicon Valley, an hour's drive south of San Francisco. Her father had been an aerospace engineer who retrained himself into a computer engineer when the defense industry imploded and the computer industry exploded.

Her father's name was Brian. Her mother's was Rebecca. There was a time when her mother was called Becky, but after they were married, her father insisted that her mother only be called by her proper name.

Their marriage took place in Salt Lake City. The capital of the Mormon world.

35

Salt Lake City, 1961

Jack Norton, the father of the bride, waited outside the Mormon Temple in downtown Salt Lake City. The temple was the biggest and most prestigious in the Mormon world. Jack was a lifelong Mormon, born to parents who themselves were the children of Mormon Utah pioneers. Despite his birth pedigree, he was not permitted into the temple to participate in or observe the wedding. His daughter Becky, the bride, was standing a little apart from him, with her mother, nervously awaiting the call to enter. Marital problems with his wife kept the distance between them.

His daughter broke away from her mother and came over to Jack. She kissed him on the cheek. 'I'm sorry, Daddy, I wish you could come in the temple for the ceremony.'

'I wish I could too, only because I want to be with you and watch my baby on the most important day of her life.'

'If you had only—'

'That's over with, Becky, I am what I am. I try to be a good person. If that isn't good enough for my family and my church . . .' He hunched his shoulders. 'What can I do?'

She put her fingers to his lips. 'You promised not to call me Becky.'

'Oh, I forgot, it's Rebecca now'

'Brian says nicknames are for children, that I'm a woman now.'

Jack only smiled but he had a few opinions of his own, mostly about the dictates of his very soon-to-be son-in-law. He was more than twice Brian's age, and hated the feeling that he had to get up and salute when the young man entered the room. Brian had that kind of personality, treating people around him like he was a Boy Scout leader and they were Cubs. Jack took it with tight jaw, for the sake of his daughter.

There was an expression about people with steel-trap minds; the implication being that, like the jagged jaws of an animal trap that clamps onto an animal's leg and can't be shaken off, some people latch onto ideas that they won't budge on, no matter what others say or how wrong they are. Brian Jones was that type – about almost everything. He was locked into his view of the world. And what he saw was a sloppy world that needed its ducks to be lined up – in the order he prescribed. He was neat and orderly to an extreme. Fresh out of engineering school, he seemed to lead his life and planned to lead Jack's daughter's life as if he was guided by the markings on a slide rule.

As Becky left her father to greet friends arriving for the ceremony, her mother came over to speak with Jack. She was angry and didn't hide her feelings.

'Do you realize what an embarrassment you are today? I don't mind you embarrassing me, but you have humiliated your daughter because you can't be with her in the temple on the most important day of her life.'

'Funny thing,' Jack said, 'that I can't be with my own daughter in my own church. I don't drink to excess, don't smoke, haven't killed anyone or stolen anything, I can't think of anything of the list of sins that would make me a bad person.'

'You know what you did, I'm not going to stand here and argue with you. And you do drink alcohol.'

'I drink a little wine, yes. I figure that if it was good enough for Jesus, it's good enough for me.'

'Oh, yes, I know, when the offering of bread and water is made in church, you told Rebecca that Jesus turned water into wine and the only miracle of Mormonism is that they managed to turn wine back to water.'

'While you're thinking about all my imagined sins, have you thought about the guy you've pushed your daughter into marriage with?'

'Brian is a respected young man, he's already a successful engineer.'

'They're a match made in hell. What Becky lacks in confidence, Brian overcompensates for with arrogance. He's going to make her life hell and she'll suck it all in without fighting back.'

'I'm not going to listen to you run down a fine young man. You should be worrying about your own actions, not Brian's.'

She left him and joined her daughter and the friends. It was time for the ceremony.

Jack waited outside, walking along the street to pass the time. Yes, he knew what he had done, but he wasn't thinking about that. He was wondering what was going to become of his daughter. Brian Jones was a guy with no screws loose – he had everything bolted so hard, there was no room in his head for anything but his own tightly ratcheted-down view of the world.

As he walked around the great temple, he thought about the Church he, his wife, and his children had been raised in.

The Mormon religious movement began in western New York state about a hundred and fifty years earlier. During a time of intense religious revivalism in America, a twenty-two-year-old farmer's son claimed an angel called Moroni gave him 'golden plates' which contained religious revelations. The plates had remained buried for fourteen hundred years. The young man, Joseph Smith, claimed that through revelations, he translated the writing on the plates into what came to be called *The Book of Mormon*. According to Smith, the plates were returned to the angel.

The Book of Mormon, which is accepted by Mormons as holy scripture in addition to the Bible, relates that a 'lost' tribe of Hebrews, led by the prophet Lehi, migrated from Jerusalem to America about six hundred years before the birth of Christ, over two thousand years before Columbus stumbled onto the continent on his way to India. Since the Mormons consider the American continent to be the true land of the early Bible, in Mormon tradition, the Garden of Eden is located somewhere near the present city of Independence, Missouri.

On the ancient American continent, the Hebrews multiplied and ultimately split into two groups: the virtuous, hardworking, industrious Nephites, and the sinful, heathen Lamanites. The Nephites prospered for some time, building great cities, and were even taught by Jesus, but eventually they were wiped out in wars with the Lamanites. Over two hundred thousand Nehphites were killed in the last great battle between the two forces.

In the Mormon tradition, it's believed that the Lamanites, who forgot their beliefs and turned into heathens, were the ancestors of the American Indian.

Combining elements of Jewish and Christian mysticism, the Mormon movement grew with Smith periodically pronouncing more revelations.

One of the key points of early Mormonism was the practice of polygamy. Smith himself was reputed to have married fifty wives. He was arrested after he had the newspaper press destroyed in a town he had founded after the paper criticized him. Hostility grew against the movement and Smith and his brother were taken from the jail by a mob and murdered.

It occurred to Jack more than once that the biggest lure of Mormonism in those days was the desire of some men to have more than one wife and the willingness of some women to be domestic slaves.

Another of his followers, Brigham Young, led a migration to the Great Salt Lake in Utah. The Mormons prospered in the desert and Utah ultimately became the only state dominated by a particular religious sect.

A dented, smoking VW camper-van coming down the street backfired, interrupting Jack's thoughts. The van's rear end was plastered with bumper stickers. One caught his eye: *A CLEAN DESK IS A SIGN OF A CLUTTERED MIND*.

In terms of his new son-in-law, he considered the words prophetic.

36

Inside the temple, Rebecca nervously accompanied her mother and friends to a room where the marriage would be solemnized. Like her parents and the man she was marrying, she had been born and raised in the purview of the Church. While she didn't have the intense dedication to religious matters that Brian and her mother had, she tended to be obedient with a huge desire to please. Leading her life in a way that gained approval from her mother and husband-to-be was important to her. She tended to be nervous about things, to equivocate and lack confidence. That was one of the reasons she was attracted to Brian. He was completely in charge of everything around him. From the moment they met, he was telling her what to do and how to act. Besides insisting that she be called by her proper name, he had her change her hairstyle and dress more conservatively to make her appear reserved and mature.

Much of her religious fervor was also directed toward gaining approval. Deep down, she had little interest in religion. But the Church was important to the people around her and that made its teachings and approval important to her.

Women in the Church were raised to be good wives and mothers. Careers outside the home were not emphasized, but hard work in terms of providing a wholesome environment for the family was. To produce many children, enriching the Church's blood pool, was a duty instilled into Mormon girls. That and duty to the Church.

She knew the history of the Church, could probably recite it by rote, but the impression on her was little more than what she knew about the American Revolution or other important pieces of history. It was her father and Brian who really knew Church history, and their ideas and concepts conflicted with each other.

She had been in the temple the day before, going through another ritual which young people raised as Mormons and new converts receive. It was a sort of initiation called 'endowment' where the person is ritually washed, anointed with holy oil, and dressed in temple clothes, after which they watch a dramatic performance of the story of creation, learn secret passwords and handshakes, and receive a secret name.

Joseph Smith had been a Mason, and many of the endowment rituals were similar to that practiced by the Masons. The dress code was simple: white shirts and pants for the men, long white dresses for the women, and white slippers for both.

Rebecca had received her endowment into Church membership during a two-hour ceremony the day before the wedding ceremony. Brian had received his before setting off to Germany for a two-year-long 'mission' to bring the word of Mormonism to people in that country. Brian, as a man, had been told the secret name that Rebecca received during the endowment ceremony. Rebecca would never know his.

Rebecca and Brian entered the 'sealing' room of the temple. These special rooms were used to solemnize a marriage for eternity under the rites of the church and to seal children everlastingly to their parents.

The endowment, wedding, and other Church ceremonies were performed by male members who had been elevated to positions in the Church. Since the Church did not have a professional clergy, it relied on its male members to perform the traditional functions of a clergy. At the age of twelve, all worthy males became deacons in the Aaronic priesthood. They became teachers when they reached fourteen and priests when they reached sixteen. From there, many of them moved into the hierarchy as bishops and other positions. Women could not become clergy and African-Americans were denied admittance into Church membership.

The thought of her father having to wait outside flashed in Rebecca's mind. She wished he was there with her. The problem had to do with who was allowed entry into the temple.

Non-Mormons and members not in good standing were not admitted into the temple. In order to gain entry into the temple and be married there, Rebecca, Brian, and the others with them had to present temple recommendation cards from their bishops. Cards were issued after an annual interview in which the member was signified as being an active member and paying the tithe demanded by the Church.

Rebecca's father was refused admittance in the temple for the wedding because he had stopped regularly attending functions at their local church. When his wife and children questioned him about the destination of his soul, he told them, 'I have faith in God, but I don't think I need my passport to heaven stamped by mortals.'

In kinder moments, Rebecca's mother said her husband was going

through a midlife crisis. When less generous, she said he was possessed by
the devil.

37

San Jose, California, 1968

'This hallway is completely out of kilter. It's so far off the mark, it makes
me dizzy to stare down it.'

Seven-year-old Marni sat in a corner of the living room and watched
her father, Brian Jones, speak to the building contractor who had built their
house. She ate chocolate pudding from a plastic cup as she listened.

Her father's tone with the older man was the same one he used when
speaking to her and her mother. He did not raise his voice, but there was a
certain arrogance that let the listener know that he was irritated – and
superior.

The contractor, an older man with a ruddy, sun-wrinkled face, shook his
head. Trying to keep the irritation out of his voice, he said, 'Mr Jones, there
is a one-inch variance in seven feet of hallway wall. That's well within
customary construction tolerances—'

'It isn't in my house. This is not a *tract* house, it's a *custom* house.' He
spoke the words as if instructing a child. 'If I used that sort of sloppy variance in my own work, I'd be driven out of my profession.'

An employee of the contractor, a young man with a beard and long hair,
tapped the head of a hammer in the palm of his hand as her father spoke.
The young man eyed her father with undisguised anger.

Her father either didn't realize it or didn't care that he was antagoniz-
ing the contractor and his worker. He turned his back on them and went
across the living room to where Marni's mother, Rebecca, was sitting.

Marni heard the bearded young worker say to the contractor, 'That
dude needs to get his nuts cracked.' The worker grinned at her and winked
and then started helping his boss tear out the drywall and framing that was

guilty of being an inch off over a seven-foot run.

Her four-year-old brother, Brian, Jr., was asleep on the couch beside her mother, who was heavily pregnant with her third child. Her mother was not a physically strong person and the strain of the marriage, family, and current pregnancy showed on her face. Each pregnancy had been difficult and the problems had increased with each. Brian had not been sympathetic to his wife's pregnancy woes. 'I have to go to work every day whether I feel like it or not. You have your duties like any other wife. Your problem is that you think like a loser, so you are a loser.'

Marni finished the cup of chocolate pudding and put it aside as she picked up her doll and hugged it. The spoon in the now-empty cup fell out and chocolate smeared onto the beige carpeting.

Her father had been speaking to her mother about plans for the backyard when he saw the offending spoon on the carpet.

'*Rebecca*! Your daughter has stained the new carpet.'

Her mother hurried off of the couch and across the room, her husband's words hammering at her.

'You have to learn to run an organized household and train your children to act properly and not like spoiled little animals!'

Marni wanted to scream at him, 'Leave her alone,' but was too afraid. Coming toward her, her mother looked so overwhelmed, Marni began to cry.

Two years later, Marni's grandmother came from Utah to stay with the family and help out when Rebecca was pregnant with her fourth child. Marni was now nine years old, her brother, Brian, Jr., was six, sister, Sarah, almost two. The most recent pregnancy had been a surprise. When it came, Rebecca had not recovered from the difficulties she had experienced from her past pregnancies. She needed a break but her duties dictated otherwise.

'It's all in your mind,' Rebecca's mother told her.

Rebecca, breast-feeding Sarah, nodded numbly. It was a phrase she had heard often from Brian. Her facial features exposed the strain and toll life had piled on her.

Marni and her brother sat on the floor nearby and played with a puzzle their grandmother had brought them as the two women talked.

'I know, Mother, I know.' It wouldn't do any good to tell her mother that it didn't matter if the sickness was in her head or her big toe – she was depressed and felt emotionally and physically battered from the daily routine that many women found they could take in stride. A neighbor woman had suggested she see a psychiatrist. When Rebecca posed the idea to Brian, he had gone ballistic. He asked his mother-in-law to pay a visit and help get Rebecca's mind thinking straight.

'You don't need to see a psychiatrist,' her mother said. 'You just have to tell yourself that you must do your duty to your husband and your children and then simply do it. You come from strong stock. There's no excuse for your house to be a mess, and look at you, you haven't washed your hair in days. How do you expect your husband to respect you and treat your properly if you can't respect yourself?'

Sometimes Rebecca thought it would have been better if her mother had been the one who married Brian instead of her. Her mother was the perfect Mormon wife Brian wanted – hardworking, uncomplaining, orderly, with a respect for the authority of her husband and the Church. The Mormon way of life was a wholesome one, with a vital family life filled with children who were raised to be strong and healthy.

The only thing wrong with their family was her inability to do what was expected of her. And that was no more than what was expected from other Mormon women. She knew she was a failure and hated herself for it. But as she tried harder and harder to live up to her husband's expectations, she found herself failing more and more, falling behind in her housework, barely able to attend Church functions. She had no desire to do anything.

She hadn't wanted another child. And she knew that the growth of the family would not end with the termination of her current pregnancy. Brian wanted six children – a number he said would satisfy him that they had fulfilled their obligation to their Church.

'I don't understand you, Rebecca. Your sisters are all happy and their families are all doing well. Your husband is more successful than either of theirs, yet you let yourself go and sit around the house feeling sorry for yourself. You remind me more and more of your father.'

Her father was no longer a part of their life. Brian considered her father's lax attitudes about the Church and life in general a bad influence on Rebecca and forbade her from communicating with him.

'No wonder your husband has complaints about you. Look at the way your older sisters handle their families, their children are constantly taking part in Church activities that your sisters organize.'

'I go to church, Mother.'

'You show up at church, but Brian says you go there like a zombie. You don't participate, organize any events, and when you've been appointed to monitor a function, you do it with such little enthusiasm that the other people lose patience with you.'

'You're right, you're right,' Rebecca said.

Marni looked up from the puzzle as her grandmother denigrated her mother. Rebecca's face and eyes had become blank. All of the tension in her appeared to have flowed into her hands which were twisting a baby diaper.

Marni had stayed with her grandparents on her father's side in Utah the previous summer. While there, she had seen her grandfather wring the neck of a chicken for the supper pot. As she watched her mother, it reminded her of her grandfather and the chicken.

38

San Jose, 1971

'You can't do anything right!'

Marni sat on the couch in the living room and watched her parents in the kitchen as her father yelled at her mother. Marni's knees shook. She wanted to cry at these times when her father shouted at her mother, but her father told her a ten-year-old doesn't cry. But the baby laying on the table beside her mother didn't know the rules and cried as her father's voice raised. Brian, Jr. and Sarah were on the living-room floor watching cartoons on television.

'You spend every minute of your day in this house and you still can't get anything right. You can't shop, cook, care for your children, or do the things to make my life easier.'

There was no expression on her mother's face. Her features were dull, her eyes dark and hollow and lifeless. She kneaded dough as her husband scolded her. She squeezed the dough over and over, her knuckles white. The baby had not stopped crying.

'Look at these children, they're all a mess, you can't even take care of them, they're filthy, you feed them junk, and put them in front of the TV for it to raise them. If I had known what a loser you were, I would never have married you. I'm going up in my career and instead of you helping, I have to keep dragging you along. Even your mother and sisters can't understand you. My mother says I should take a belt to you, that if you're going to act like a child, you should be disciplined as a child. If you don't get yourself together and start acting as a mature, responsible adult, I'm going to send you back to your mother to be trained as a wife and mother!'

Her father left the house, slamming the front door behind him.

'Milk,' three-year-old Sarah said.

Marni got up and went into the kitchen to get her little sister milk. At ten years old, Marni was taking care of her younger brother and Sarah. Her mother had become less and less attentive toward them. She knew her mother was also inattentive toward her new baby. When the baby cried, Marni would tell her mother it was time to breast-feed. Her mother was listless and would spend hours staring blankly at the TV. More and more often she heard her mother talking to herself, mumbling about what a bad mother and wife she was. As her mother's mumbling became more frequent, Marni understood less and less of it. Sometimes it sounded like her mother was talking to someone beside herself, someone who was telling her to do things that her mother didn't want to do.

Marni took the carton of milk from the refrigerator and poured a glass for Sarah. She put the carton back in the refrigerator and turned to go back into the living room.

Her mother was still sitting at the table. She had stopped kneading the dough and was doing something with the baby now. Marni caught the movement out of the corner of her eye and turned to look.

Her mother's hands were around the throat of the baby. She was wringing its neck. Her mother let go of the baby and it dropped to the floor. It lay still, lifeless. Marni saw her mother staring at her with eyes no longer dull but feverish. Her mother stood up and reached for her. Marni screamed. She dropped the glass in her hand and ran.

PART 6

AFRICA

39

Gomez, the mine's delivery driver, took me into Lurema to ransom a generator that had been diverted from a Luanda shipment to the mine. Buying the generator from the police, who were probably the original thieves, was much cheaper than ordering a new one and waiting weeks for it to come. It probably wouldn't have managed to get through the second time, anyway.

Sometimes I shook my head and asked Cross how the country functioned with everything so messed up. The answer was always the same – it didn't.

The Blue Lady was up and running with me at the helm, although it seemed like each day God kicked the hurdles up a notch to make me jump a little higher. I was learning some of the rhythm of dealing with the people. Back in the States, everything operated off the clock. One o'clock meant one o'clock or a few minutes either way. Time took on an entirely different meaning in equatorial Africa. The people, commerce, and transportation were not all cogs geared into the same giant time machine that ran the Western world. There were many different ideas about what an appointment set for one o'clock might mean. An appointment at one o'clock didn't even mean that it was to happen on the day previously arranged.

Overall, I was feeling good about myself. My acquaintances in New York – ex-acquaintances – would have laid odds that I would have walked away from running the mine or failed at it because it just wasn't fun. It wasn't fun, but it was a challenge, and as Cross said, it put bread on the table. I enjoyed the challenge, there was nothing like a mine flood or cave-in to get your adrenaline pumping, but my nights were boring – and lonely. And horny. There was no way in hell I'd touch a woman in a country where AIDS was epidemic. Hell, there was so much AIDS around, Cross claimed a guy had to be careful even practicing the sin of Onan.

The jeep was dodging potholes near a UN aid compound when I spotted a woman leaning up against a tree near the river and did a double take.

'Pull over,' I told Gomez.

She turned when she heard my footsteps approaching.

'Oh my God, I can't believe it, the Playboy of the Western World, in Angola.' Marni clapped her hands. 'And in work clothes. Or are those soiled khakis a new type of leisure suit?'

I held up the palms of my hands. 'Calluses, too.'

'From golf clubs?'

'In Angola? Where the sand traps are quicksand? And you get eaten by a lion if you go into the rough to look for your ball?'

I gave her a hug. 'It's good to see you. I can't tell you how – how—'

'How what?' she asked.

'How horny I am.'

That got her laughing.

'What are you doing here?' I asked.

'Distributing food and medical supplies. At least, the portion of it that doesn't get stolen and ends up on the black market. Sometimes I forget who I'm working for – the relief agency or the local thieves. What are *you* doing here?'

'Buying back equipment from the police who stole it.'

That got us both laughing.

A line of jeeps came by and a horn honked. Colonel Jomba grinned and waved with his swagger stick as he went by in his chauffeur-driven jeep with its skull hood ornament.

Marni shuddered. 'The man's a monster. We pay him under the table to see that our food trucks don't get robbed. And then we pay him for return of the stuff when they do get robbed. Do you know him?'

'Vaguely.' The colonel looked like a very happy man. He ought to be – he took half of Eduardo's nest egg. You can bet Jomba considered it an extra bonus that didn't need to be reported to his UNITA bosses.

'One of our aid workers is actually dating him.'

I shrugged and kept my face blank. Considering the barbedwire necklace and head horns, what he might have tattooed where the sun doesn't shine wasn't even imaginable.

Marni studied my face, taking my jaw and moving my face side to side.

'Hmmm. You've changed.'

'How so? It's only been a few months.'

'You look older, wiser, more serious and introspective. You've lost some of your irrelevance.'

'Sounds serious,' I said. 'It must be the water. Or the stuff that swims in it. If the microbes don't get you, the crocs will. You've changed, too. You always were serious, but it was sort of a scholastic gravity, the look of the nearsighted teacher or professor who rarely peeks out of their rabbit hole. Now you've got sweat stains instead of academic cobwebs. You look like a veteran of the real world.'

'Of a war, you mean, one that I lost.' She indicated her baggy army fatigue pants and dusty boots. Her white blouse was smeared with something dark. 'Chocolate from a candy bar I gave a child. It's probably the first time in the child's life he tasted a piece of candy. And he'll be dead in a few months from AIDS.' She brushed back her hair. 'I look like hell. I need a bath and—' She started laughing, and ended up crying.

I pulled her into my arms. She tried to push away but I squeezed her tight.

'Christ, you must go through hell every hour of every day. I don't know how you keep your sanity dealing with all this human misery.'

'Do I look like I've kept my sanity?' she sobbed.

'You look like a woman who's been carrying the world on her shoulders. Has it occurred to you that mere mortals couldn't do what you do? I probably would've dropped the kid and ran like hell if I knew he had AIDS.'

We sat on a log and I held her hand.

'Sometimes it just builds up inside me. We heard today that some aid workers were killed down south. They may even be friends.'

'I'm sorry. You must be in danger yourself, every day.'

'Being murdered I could handle, at least if it came quickly. But dealing with poor people, starvation, disease, mutilation, add that to the dangers and – and – I'm not a strong person.'

'Like hell you're not. I couldn't do what you're doing for five minutes. I put on mental blinders whenever I leave the mine, just to keep my sanity. And I don't leave the mine without an armed guard. I've been hiding in my safe hole while you've been out on the front lines in hand-to-hand combat.'

'No, I'm a weak person. I thought I could handle anything, but the misery is getting to me. Everything we do gets undone. We try to help people, and if their leaders aren't screwing them, they're screwing themselves because they don't know any better. But there are aid workers who've been doing this for years. They don't sit around and cry.'

'Then they've hardened to it. I imagine they had some good cries before they got thick calluses on their feelings. This country has to change anyone who comes into contact with it. Hey, look at me, I'm a changed man, I don't even make jokes anymore about war and famine.'

She stood up and offered me her hand to shake. 'Enough self-pity. I've got to get back to work, my foodstuffs are probably going out the back door faster than they're coming in the front. It's my job to make sure that they get into the right mouths.'

I took her hand and pulled her to me.

'I'm not shaking hands and driving off'

'Win—'

'No, this isn't Lisbon, you can't step out of the restaurant and into a taxi. We're the only two Americans around, I like you, you like me, we both need some TLC. Besides, have you ever seen a diamond mine?'

'Didn't I tell you that diamond mining—'

'Yeah, yeah, I know, diamond mines are evil. I'll give you an opportunity to tell that to the miners who work their butts off to support their families and everyone else in the neighborhood. You can also tell those poor bastards who spend their days in rivers trying to muck up enough diamonds to stay alive. In case you haven't learned this about Angola, diamonds aren't evil, people are.'

She looked deeply into my eyes. 'I don't know. What are your intentions, Mr Liberte?'

'To make up for lost time.'

40

Cross used some profanity I hadn't heard since I was in high school.

'I hate your guts. You're gonna get the velvet rubbed off your dick and

I'm still getting calluses from beating my meat.'

'It's because I live right – good wholesome food, lots of sleep, avoiding the ruin of alcohol.'

'You're full of shit.'

'Yeah, but I smell sweet.'

I splashed an extra dose of cologne on my neck and cheeks. I was in Cross's room, getting cleaned up. I'd turned my room over to Marni so she could freshen up after the trip to the mine. Three days had passed since I bumped into her on the river because she insisted on finishing up an inventory before she would come. I finally picked her up and brought her back to the mine.

The three days gave me time to send a plane to Luanda for champagne and food that didn't taste like mine food and to have my room cleaned and painted. Yeah, I was putting on the dog, but what the hell, this was the first available woman in a thousand miles. And as it turned out, it was a woman I genuinely liked.

'On top of that, you're sending me to Luanda because you're afraid she'll take one look at me and kick your skinny ass out of bed.'

'I'm also afraid the mine's going to drown if we don't get that water pump in Luanda. Make damn sure you're standing at the cargo door to the airplane when it's unloaded and you never let it out of your sight until it's installed in the mine.'

Cross threw his hands up and appealed to heaven. 'Did you hear that, God? This candy-ass bastard who didn't know shit from shinola until I taught him is now telling me how to run a security operation.'

I knocked on the door to my room. When Marni opened it, I handed her a hard hat.

'What's this for?'

'Mine regulations. You're going down below.'

'Into the mine?'

'Don't you want to see how a mine operates? The real action takes place in the hole.'

'Yes, but . . . are you going to X-ray me when we come out?'

'We'll see. Sometimes we do a search instead.'

I took her through the security gate and across to the mine elevator. She stared at everything with wonderment. And smiled at everyone.

'Is it dangerous below?' she asked.

'Compared to what you've been dealing with it's a piece of cake. You do have to watch out for the giant diamond worms. They make holes in the tunnel floor and eat you when you fall through.'

She asked intelligent questions in the mine, curious to know how everything worked. I was a little condescending at first, smug that I was teaching her something. She watched an explosion to create ore. We followed the debris all the way back to the surface to where it was processed and the diamonds weeded out.

'These men work so hard,' she said. 'It's too bad their hard work is so used and abused by the government and rebels.' When we were topside again, I pointed to a diamond on the belt coming out of the crusher.

'Aren't you a little amazed that a diamond in the rough looks so plain?'

'I am amazed. I thought they came out of the ground shaped like a diamond, you know, like you see in Tiffany's window.'

'You're kidding,' I said.

'Yes.'

I thought about her statement as we followed the workings topside to the grease table. 'I was being smug and superior down below.'

'I know, but it's all right. I think it's great that you're finally doing something useful with your life – until I remind myself that you're raping a Third World country of its precious resources.'

'Precious resources? Ever try eating a diamond? Don't blame the Western world or Western entrepreneurs for all the evils of the underdeveloped nations. The evils and oppression were here for thousands of years before we came along.'

She started lecturing me on Third World economics, a subject I was singularly uninformed about, and I cut her short.

'You should save that speech for Colonel Jomba,' I said. 'I understand he's got a degree in economics from London – and an advanced one, the Third World kind where you do a body count instead of ledger entries. Isn't that the kind of economics you find in most of the Third World?'

'Just when I think it's safe to like you . . .'

I stopped and kissed her on the mouth. She didn't resist. 'You're right, I'm still a swine, but at least now I'm a hardworking one.' I showed her my calluses again.

When we reached the grease table, I told her to grab a handful of grease.

'Are you sure I won't come up with a diamond worm?'

'Do you have to question everything I ask?'

'Are you trustworthy?'

I let that one pass.

I scooped the grease out of her hand and into my own and poked through it with my finger.

'What's this?' I brought out a rough, larger than a pea. 'Let's take it into the sorting room and see what we have.'

We stood by while a grader cleaned the stone and carefully examined it.

'It's a D,' the grader said.

I carefully examined it with my own loupe and then let Marni look through the loupe.

'Amazing, I didn't realize that a diamond had that much fire in it.'

'You have good taste,' I said. 'It's flawless and of the highest clarity. It'll be graded a D.'

'Only a D? Not an A?'

I laughed. 'D is the highest rating for a diamond. This is a perfect diamond, colorless, with a hint of blue. When it's cut down to more than a carat, it'll sell for top price. On Fifth Avenue it would cost as much as an economy car. It's an exceptionally good stone.' I handed it to her. 'It's yours, a gift from the diamond worm.'

'Oh my God, I can't take it.'

'Of course you can. It's the luck of the draw. You might have walked away with just a handful of mud.'

That wasn't exactly true. I had set the whole thing up. I selected the best stone we'd pulled out of the mine for over a week. I switched it for the industrial-grade stone Marni pulled out of the gook.

'Did that give you a different view of diamond mining?' I asked, when we were walking back toward the security gate.

'Yes, it's hard work, and I'm sure the miners earn every dime they get, twice over. But the mine owners are still partners with petro bandits in being the ruin of Angola.'

'There you go again, tripping over that excessive education of yours. You've dropped the blame for the state of the underdeveloped world and the wars on every continent, on oil and diamonds. Don't you realize that people kill each other not just for greed, but principles? The IRA isn't killing over diamonds, India and Pakistan aren't beating each other over the head because of diamonds, the Israelis and—'

'What's your point?'

'I keep telling you. People are evil. Not diamonds, not oil. It's not America's fault that people in the Third World are ruled by dictators. Is there a single democracy in the Third World? Can you name one? Is that our fault? We didn't make this world.'

She started laughing.

'What's so funny?'

'Do you realize we're arguing economics and politics at a diamond mine in equatorial Africa? When you were a kid, did you have any clue that this was what you would be doing later?'

'I never thought I'd live this long.'

'What? Why do you say that?'

I shrugged. 'My mother died young, my father a few years after she did. I just assumed that I wouldn't make it to a ripe old age.'

'How strange, my mother died young, too.'

Something in her voice told me that now was not the time to ask her for the details.

We paused at the X-ray machine.

'You're going to X-ray me?'

'Yes.'

'I thought you were joking earlier.'

'You have your choice – X-ray or a body-cavity strip search.'

'Who does the search?'

'It's a prerogative of the mine owner,' I grinned.

'I'll take the X-ray.'

'Sorry, I just remembered the machine's broken.'

41

We lay in bed the next morning, Marni's body pressed snugly against mine. I felt warm and comfortable.

I didn't have a rating system for all the women I've fucked but making love to Marni had been different than the others. It wasn't that my blood boiled hotter, or even the number of times I got it up and we got it off. It was something else. As I lay in that warm, cozy twilight between sleep and being awake, I tried to understand what it was exactly.

Then it came to me. *Peace.* I felt at peace, as if being with Marni satisfied some deeper urge than I've ever felt with any other woman.

She stirred beside me and squeezed my penis. 'How's my diamond worm?'

I was getting a hard-on. 'Getting ready to attack you again.'

We had breakfast on the patio.

'That was the first good night's sleep I've had since I arrived in Angola,' she said.

'You're letting the place get to you.'

'I know, my friend, Michele, says that if you open your heart to the horrors, pretty soon they eat your soul. I think what bothers me most is seeing babies dying of disease and hunger while that creepy Colonel Jomba goes around collecting protection money and living like a fat cat.'

Jomba wasn't a subject I wanted Marni to explore too deeply. If she found out I was involved in a blood-diamond deal with him, she'd whack off my diamond worm, rather than suck it.

I was relieved from going deeper into the subject of the colonel when the phone rang. It was Cross calling from Luanda.

'I hope I'm interrupting something,' he said.

'Not really, we've been discussing the socio-demographics of Third World demand-centered economic foundations and—'

I removed the phone from my ear as Cross made an obscene sound. I handed the phone to Marni.

'Say hello to Cross.'

I didn't know what he said to her, but when she handed the phone back to me she was blushing and giggling.

'Listen, bwana,' Cross said, 'I got some interesting information for you about that geology bill you found in Eduardo's papers. The land not only adjoins the Blue Lady,' he said, 'but you own it. It's one of the parcels belonging to the mine, but it's in the direction opposite from where most of the tunneling has been.'

'You said something about knowing a guy in South Africa? Can you check out the geologist, see what kind of reputation he has?'

'I'm in like Flynn with the security manager at a De Beers diamond mine. We do Cape Town when I get down there for some R and R. I called him but he's on vacation. I'll keep trying.'

After we hung up, Marni asked, 'Trouble?'

'I'm not sure. The mine manager didn't handle everything around here kosher. He not only had his hand in the till, he jumped in up to his neck.' I nudged her foot under the table. 'What did Cross say to you?'

'Sorry, he swore me to secrecy. But, he let me know there are bigger fish to fry.'

'When you're hanging around the fish market, remember it's not the size of the fish that counts, it's the taste.'

We were back in bed on a fishing trip when Cross called back. 'My friend knows who the geologist is. He's a mining engineer with a quirky reputation. He's developed a system he claims can find blue earth better than anything else out there. Some people say he's a quack, others think he's a genius. One thing they all say – he's eccentric. He's got a feud going with some of the big mining outfits and won't let them use his equipment.'

'Do one more thing,' I said. 'Get me the flight schedule to Cape Town.'

I hung up the phone.

'Something's up,' I told Marni. 'When I used to race, I always got this feeling when I knew I was about to break out and take the lead. I'm getting that feeling now.'

'You're going to Cape Town?'

'*We're* going there.'

'I can't go right—'

'Yes, you can, you told me you had leave coming.'

She started out of the bed and I pulled her back.

'You don't understand, I have a job, a duty—'

'Didn't you tell me you're snapping at everyone around you? When you're not walking around in a daze. You need to get away for a few days. Shop, dance, eat in a French restaurant, make love on a warm beach.'

'Okay, you've convinced me.'

'No, I think you need more convincing. Come under the covers. I have something for you.'

42

Cape Town, South Africa

'Cape Town is one of the most beautiful cities in the world,' Marni told me as the plane made the descent for the capital city near the tip of Africa. She had a guidebook in her lap. 'The ocean water is icy cold because it comes from the Antarctic, but the beaches are warm and scenic.'

I leaned over and took a look down at flat-topped mountains with almost vertical cliffs and beaches and made a polite listening response. My mind had been on other things during the couple-thousand-mile trip from the mine. I had paid Cross's South African security manager to compile a quick dossier on the engineer I had come to see. I was going through the information for the third time.

Marni noticed the name of the subject of the report. 'Christiaan Kruger, is that the geologist you're going to see? Sounds like an Afrikaan name.'

'What's that?'

'People who originally had a Dutch background. They fought a war with the British, the Boer War, about a hundred years ago, and the British ended up with all of South Africa. But the Boers, called Afrikaans now, are still the most powerful white political group in the country. They're known to be tough, carry guns, be very religious, and dislike blacks and other whites. They have their own language, called Afrikaans, and culture. The whole population of whites in South Africa, Afrikaners, British and other-wise, amounts to less than fifteen percent of the country.'

I kissed her. 'How come you're so smart?'

'I read the guidebook. The place you chose to stay, the Nellie – officially the Mount Nelson Hotel, is world-class. You have good taste.'

I shrugged modestly. Actually, it was Cross who told me where to stay.

'I want to take a ride on a Tuk Tuk and go to the beach,' she said.

'What the hell is a Tuk Tuk?'

'A three-wheeled taxi, built around a motorbike. It got its name from the sound the engine makes. Tuk, tuk, tuk—'

I went back to my papers.

Kruger sounded like a textbook, hardheaded, rebellious Afrikaner. He became a geologist-mining engineer for De Beers early in his career. He left the big company and worked as an independent in the Kimberly area. He filed for a number of patents for inventions in regard to gold and diamond mining, and frequently ended up in lawsuits over unauthorized use of his work. For the past decade, he'd been locked in litigation with an outfit that he claimed was infringing on his patented method of finding blue earth.

The report stated that Kruger had been arrested for punching the attorney representing his opponents and on another occasion, for taking possession of the company equipment in the field – at the point of a gun.

As part of his probation on the gun charge, he left the mining area and moved to Cape Town.

There was a handwritten note at the end of the report: *Idealistic bastard – principles more important than money.*

I closed my eyes and gave it some thought as the plane made its descent. How to approach Kruger had been on my mind since Cross got back to me with his name. I hadn't called to let him know I was coming – it was too easy for someone to say no over the phone or get out of town in a hurry. I was going to cold-call him, show up at his door without warning. The fact he had a love affair with guns didn't boost my confidence level.

But the handwritten notation at the bottom of the report gave me an idea.

43

We checked into a suite at the Nellie. Marni marveled at the elegance and quaintness of the luxury hotel. 'It's from the days when the *Orient Express* went from Europe to Asia and men like Cecil Rhodes and Barney Barnato battled for an empire in diamonds.'

'Great,' I said, pulling her to me. 'Let's have dinner in bed.'

'No, no, this is my chance to eat in a real restaurant, where I don't have to worry about the water, fleas biting my ankle, or a stray bullet.'

We ate at the best French restaurant in Cape Town. We ended up having dessert in bed.

The next morning, we took a taxi downtown to a gem dealer Cross told me about. I parked Marni outside for a few minutes while I went in to sell some roughs. When I came back out, I shoved a thick wad of rand into her purse.

'What's that for?'

'Exotic see-through lingerie, captivating perfume – hell, get a tiger-skin coat or something.'

She gave the money back to me. 'They have lions in Africa, not tigers, and they're an endangered species.'

'So are you. I'm not taking the money back. Put it in a poor box if it bothers you so much. I'll meet you back at the hotel in a couple hours.'

'It's too much money.'

'Don't worry, it's not my money, I stole it.'

Kruger lived in what South Africans called a Coloured neighborhood, 'Coloured,' according to my taxi driver, being the official designation of people of mixed European and African blood. 'That's half of us in Cape Town,' he said.

As we pulled up to a small, unimposing house with a chainlink fence and overgrown yard, I asked the driver, 'What would you call this neighborhood? Poor, middle-class?'

He thought for a moment and spit out the window before he decided. 'Not poor, not middle-class. Maybe better than poor people, not as good as middle people.'

That's about how I had tagged it. Which brought up an interesting point – why was a successful engineer-geologist, with a bunch of inventions to his name, living in a run-down house in a run-down neighborhood? I thought I knew the answer. If I didn't, he'd probably run me off the property.

'Stay put,' I told the taxi driver. 'If you hear shots, call the police.'

'If I hear shots, I'll call them from home.'

There was no lock on the gate, but I looked over the yard before I entered. Chain-link fences usually meant there was a big dog in the picture. I got across to the house without being attacked by Cujo and knocked on the door. After a couple more knocks, the door was answered

by a black woman in her forties or early fifties. Too attractive to be a
housekeeper, I took her for Kruger's wife.

'*Ya?*'

'Good afternoon. I'm here to see Mr Kruger.'

She frowned as she looked me over. 'Mr Kruger doesn't see anyone
without an appointment.' She had an Afrikaner accent.

'It's rude of me to call like this, but I don't have your phone number. I
have information for him about his blue-earth exploration system.'

My answer stymied her. Which was my intent. I probably could have
told Ed McMahon sent me from a sweepstakes company with a million
dollars and she'd have slammed the door in my face. But I said the magic
words.

'Wait.'

She closed the door. A minute later it was opened by a middle-aged
man. Kruger was small-built, ruddy-complexioned, and sported a permanent frown.

'Who are you? What do you want? I'm busy.' *What* came out 'waat' with
his accent.

'I can help you with your fight over your blue-earth technique.'

'How?'

I held up a five-carat rough. It wasn't as primo as the one I gave Marni
at the mine, but it was worth thousands of South African rand.

'I want five minutes of your time because I think we can help each other.
I'll leave if it turns out I'm wrong or you can throw me out. Either way, you
keep the stone.'

'How can you help me?'

'Five minutes,' I said.

He hesitated. As he did, a big Rottweiler or some other lethal-looking
breed that would have scared the dog poop out of Cujo stuck its head out
between Kruger's leg and the door frame.

'Five minutes,' Kruger said. 'Then I put Hannah on you.'

I hoped Hannah was his wife.

I followed him into a room cluttered with equipment, books, and dust.
The dog followed me.

He sat on a stool next to a desk piled high with papers and books. I
remained standing. So did the dog.

'I own a mine in Angola, the Blue Lady. You did a report on property
adjoining the mine, property that belongs to me. The person who ordered

it was my manager, Eduardo Marques. I want to see that report.'

'If the report belongs to you, you must have it.'

'I don't have it. I think Marques was pulling a fast one, having a report made behind my back, then trying to buy my property cheap.'

'If the report was paid for by Mr Marques, then it belongs to him, get it from him.' He stood up. 'This has nothing to do with the litigation I am involved in over my invention.'

'It does on two levels. First, like you, I'm being screwed by someone I trusted. I worked hard for what I have,' I almost choked on the lie, 'and Marques is trying to steal it. And I need money to keep the fight going. If it turns out you can help me, if there's money to be made, I'll be willing to cut you in. You've been fighting thieves for years. I don't know your personal circumstance, but you may need money for that fight.'

I did know his circumstance – he designed a system that should have put him on easy street and instead, he was living someplace between poor and 'middle.' I waited while he pondered my words. It was obvious that his first inclination was to throw me out, or sic Hannah on me, but I hoped I had pressed the right button. He was idealistic and fanatical about the technique he invented. From what I gathered, he was offered plenty to settle his lawsuits, but refused – unlike yours truly, he was not willing to sell his soul to the devil. He wanted truth and justice. Rather than offering him money, what I was offering was a way to keep fighting.

'I don't understand your request. You say you want to see the report. What the report says, the report says. Offering me money won't change the results.'

'You're right. The report might say it's a dry hole. But the present mine operation is a dry hole – and there's an attempt to drive me out of business and take it over. My gut tells me there's something else out there.'

'I consider my work for clients as confidential. You are not the one who paid me, you are not my client.'

I pulled papers from my inside pocket. 'This is a copy of government records showing that the property belongs to the Blue Lady and that I am the owner. I am fighting a thief who has no right to my property – the same as you are.'

He put on glasses and examined the papers.

'You know what?' I said. 'This whole thing can be settled by a quick look at the report. I'm assuming it shows positive findings for diamonds. If it doesn't, I'm wasting both our time.'

'I can't show you the report.'

'Fine, fuck it, if you want to help crooks, go ahead.' I turned to leave.

'I can't show it because I don't have it. He took it.'

'He?'

'Your mine manager. He was here yesterday.'

44

Marni lugged packages to the elevator. A nice man with a smile held the door for her and inquired as to her floor.

'Top level,' she said.

'Mine, too,' he said.

He seemed to be the nervous type, smiling, but a little hyper. It occurred to her that in Angola, he would be called a mestizo – half-African, half-European ancestry. In South Africa, by a law intended to discriminate, he was a Coloured.

'Looks like you bought out the stores,' the man said.

She laughed. 'Not quite, but I did put a dent in a few of them. I've been in the backcountry for a while, and I'm afraid I went wild when I saw shelves and racks full of clothes.'

'You're an American.'

'Yes. You have a slight accent that almost sounds like what I hear in Angola.'

'I am Angolan.'

'Really? What a coincidence. I flew in from there yesterday.'

'On business?'

'My friend is here on business, he's a mine owner, but I'm taking a few days off from world food-mission duties.'

He held the door open for her after the elevator doors swung open on the penthouse floor.

'Such a worthy organization, you food people, I have seen your staff distributing food many times.'

He grabbed one of the bags she was losing her grip on.

'Here – let me take that.'

'Oh, thank you.'

He followed her down the hall, carrying the bag.

She stopped at the door to her suite, put her bags down, and got the card key out of her purse.

'Thank you, I can handle it now,' she said, intending it as a good-bye, as she pushed the door open and put some of the bags inside. But he still stood there and handed her the remaining bags. After she put them down and turned around, he stepped in and swung the room door shut behind him.

He pulled a gun from his coat pocket.

45

I stared at Kruger like he'd just told me I had the Big C.

'*Eduardo Marques* was here?'

'Right where you are standing, Mr Liberte.'

'You gave him my report?'

'I gave him his report. He paid for it.'

'Sonofabitch.'

Hannah growled. Maybe she didn't like bad language.

'Okay, that's fine, give me a copy, too.'

'He paid me a bonus to give him the original and not keep a copy. He told me that there was going to be litigation over the land and that it would be to my benefit if I didn't have a copy. I lost most of what I accumulated over the past thirty years in litigation. The idea of not sitting on court evidence appealed to me.'

'There's no litigation. Marques was nothing but a mine manager, he has no right to anything. He's got someone with money behind him trying to keep the report a secret to drive down the price of the mine. You never kept a copy?'

'No. I've done hundreds of reports over the years, thousands actually. If

I kept copies of them, I would need a room to store them.'

'And I suppose you can't store the results in your head, either. You don't know your exact findings?'

'Of course not, it was a long, complex study.'

'Okay, sorry I—'

'But I can give you my overall opinion.'

That stopped me. 'Which is?'

'Inconclusive. But I saw some indicators that blue earth might be present.'

'What did you find?'

He shook his head. 'I can't tell you much. The report was inconclusive. I didn't have all the materials I needed to make a full analysis. I assume that as a mine owner, you know how the hunt for blue earth is made.'

'I sort of inherited the mine.'

'I have my own technique and equipment for analyzing the materials, but geologists all use the same raw materials in making the search. I examined earth samples, taken from the surface and from drilling cores down to a hundred feet. I was looking for "indicators," clues that there is blue earth in the area.

'To understand an indicator, you have to realize how diamonds are formed in the earth. All the diamonds that will ever exist on earth were formed billions of years ago deep in the earth. But,' he held up his hand, 'at the same time diamonds were being formed, and shoved up in kimberlite pipes, other minerals were being formed and moved up with the diamonds. Kimberlite pipes are not enormous in size and are usually buried, making them hard to find.'

Kruger grabbed a glass jar containing a number of stones.

'Hunting for these small deposits in the vast earth would be like searching for the proverbial needle in a haystack – unless we had clues. The clues are that other mineral objects are created and scattered in the same process by which diamonds are created and shoved upward.

'We call these materials "indicators" because they can indicate that diamonds are in the same general area. Since some of these indicators are much more widely spread than diamonds, they are easier to find.'

He pulled some stones out of the jar.

'Some indicators are these green chrome diopsides . . . and here, there are garnets of many colors, pink, purple, green, yellow, orange. These gems are related to diamonds, having been created in the same cata-

193

strophic convulsions of the earth as diamonds. But, they are not as rare as diamonds, or hard, nor do they have the brilliance of a diamond. In my opinion, the indicator that provides us with the best clues that there is a kimberlite pipe of blue earth in the area is a stone designated G-ten, a class of garnet called "pyrope." ' He rummaged through the jar and came up with a dark red stone. 'This is a pyrope. The name is derived from an ancient Greek word for "fiery-eyed." '

'Did you find pyropes when you examined my property?' I asked.

'I never examined your property. The peace treaty had not been reached in Angola between the rebels and the government and I wouldn't risk my life by going there. Your Mr Marques had samples taken and he shipped them to me to be examined. I can't tell you exactly what my findings were without seeing my report, but I remember very well that it was both promising and inconclusive.'

'What was promising?'

'There were indicators present. The report was inconclusive because I told Marques that I needed more raw materials, more drilling for core samples. That was over a year ago. He said a new partner was coming in and he would get back to me. I never heard back from him until yesterday. Like you, he showed up without an appointment.'

The 'new partner' was probably Bernie. João hustled Bernie into buying the diamond mine, but Bernie must have somehow gotten wind of the exploration Eduardo was conducting. It wasn't the sort of thing that Eduardo could keep as an absolute secret – drilling required large equipment.

I had an idea of how Bernie might have found out that Eduardo was drilling for core samples. You can't do anything in Angola without getting a permit – and paying both a license fee and a bribe. Bernie would have a record search done in Luanda before buying the mine. That search could have brought up licensing for the drill equipment. With that knowledge in hand, he might have confronted Eduardo, even if it was by telephone, and learned that there were indicators. For all I knew, Bernie had come to Angola and met with Eduardo.

'You understand,' Kruger said, 'more work must be done, more tests, before the matter can be pinned down. If a kimberlite pipe is found, it may turn out that you can tunnel to it from your present mine, or that you must start from scratch and open an entirely new mine. You'll need expert engineering and geological advice during the whole process.'

'Can you come to Angola and conduct the search?'

'I wouldn't go to that hellhole for all the tea in China.'

'I'm not in the tea business, Mr Kruger, but I suspect that diamonds are eminently more valuable, pound for pound. You didn't want to come into a war zone. There's peace now, if nothing else, a hiatus in the fighting. It's a window of opportunity.'

'For which of us?'

'Both of us. Eduardo Marques is not a fool. He spent his life running diamond mines. It's in his blood, he can smell them. You've confirmed that they're probably out there, it's a matter of pinning down the spot. You're both a mining engineer and a geologist. You can find the pipe and find the best way to reach it.'

I took the jar of minerals from Kruger and set them on his desk. I wanted his full attention. Hannah growled as I leaned toward her master.

'Shut up,' I told Hannah. 'Look, Christiaan, your balls are to the wall and you're almost broke from fighting those bastards who stole your process. They got the gold mine and you got the shaft. You come to Angola, like a couple of Texas wildcatters, we'll bring in a diamond pipe that will blow the lid off the mountain. You come back here and kick ass on those thieves – and we'll both live happily ever after. What do you say?'

Hannah snarled as my voice rose.

'Shut up,' Kruger told her.

46

I was in a good mood when I got back to the hotel. Kruger was lined up. He'd come to Angola in a month. In the meantime, he gave me a list of the equipment I had to acquire. I stopped at the front desk and had the list faxed to Cross at the mine.

Going up the elevator and down the hall, I was almost skipping. Everything was coming up roses. I opened the suite door and stepped in, grinning like a banshee.

I lost my grin as I saw Eduardo and the gun in his hand.

'Close the door,' he said. 'I don't want to disturb the other guests if I have to shoot you.'

I closed the door.

Marni was in a chair by a window.

'You okay?' I asked.

She nodded. 'We've been chatting about things. Mostly how much he doesn't like you.'

'You have ruined my life,' Eduardo said. 'But now you will reconstruct it for me.' He gestured with the gun at papers on the desk. 'First you will sign the papers selling me the mine. You will find that the price of the mine has dropped. It is now one rand.'

Eduardo didn't look like he had fared well since the last time I saw him. His suit and shirt needed freshening, his eyes were bloodshot from too little sleep or too much liquor. Worse, his hands were trembling – not a good sign when he's holding a gun pointed at me.

'That's about two bits where I come from. I would be crazy to sell it to you for that price.'

'No, no, not crazy, you are erasing the errors of your past ways. I would be dead now if I had not gotten out of the country before your friend Colonel Jomba caught me. Don't think I don't know what the two of you are up to. Or that you wanted me out of the way so that the two of you will have no interference with your schemes. And that *puta* you make schemes with, I know what you and her and her husband are up to.'

'What if I won't sell you the mine for pennies?'

'That would please me very much, very much. I would first shoot you in the foot, the top of your foot, where all the bones are. Then I would shoot your kneecap—'

'I get the idea. Where do I sign?'

'It is not that easy, senhor. You may sign the paper and then as soon as I leave, call the police and claim you were forced to sign.'

That thought had occurred to me.

'Do you recall that you put a gun to my head and made me call my bank and transfer to you all the money I had in the world? Do you recall that, senhor? Do you recollect making me give you all of the money I spent a lifetime earning?'

'I recall taking back the money you stole from me.'

'*Exactamente*! That is exactly it. And now, I will take back what you stole from *me*!'

He came closer and nudged my arm with the gun. He was wide-eyed. His movements had a nervous intensity to them, as if he was wired from something besides life.

The crash of breaking glass suddenly sounded – a riveting, stunning noise.

Eduardo and I both froze. Marni had smashed a large window, swinging a chair into it. The chair disappeared from sight, on its way down a dozen stories.

I recovered first. I grabbed his gun hand at the wrist. The gun went off and a bullet went into the floor. Marni screamed out the window – '*Fire!*' – as we struggled. The guy was wiry and stronger than I would have guessed. I tried getting the gun from him and it went off again. I butted his face with my forehead, smashing his nose, and twisted him around until he went down and put my knee in his stomach. Flat on his back, nose gushing blood, wind knocked out of him, the bastard stuck his thumbnail in my eye. I flinched back, feeling his gun hand twisting out of my grip—

Marni hit him on the head with the base of a lamp. It caught him off guard and he went limp for a second and she hit him again. He went real limp. I took the gun from his hand. Breathing hard, I told her, 'Get me something, a necktie, I'm going to tie him up. And call the police.'

'I don't think that's going to be necessary.'

She was right – that smashed window had probably been heard by ships at sea.

We had dinner in our room that evening – after we changed rooms.

The police had taken Eduardo away. We killed the rest of the day until early afternoon giving statements and signing papers, including a promise to return to Cape Town if needed by the justice system.

When Eduardo came out of the daze Marni put him in, he cursed me – and put curses on me – using various Portuguese-Angolan words and phrases you see on bathroom walls. When he called Marni a *puta*, I kicked him in the stomach.

'He's tied up,' Marni said.

'Yeah. Makes it easier to kick him.'

I wasn't sure if she was going to laugh – or cry. Actually, she did a little of both.

'What's funny?' I asked her.

'I was so happy to be in Cape Town where we wouldn't get murdered.'

During dinner that night, she was quiet and melancholy.

'Still thinking about Eduardo?' I asked.

'No, I was thinking about death. You told me that you lost your mother early. So did I. My mother killed herself, after she strangled my baby brother and tried to kill me.'

I was stunned. 'Jesus.' I didn't know what else to say.

Marni shrugged. 'She was crazy, mentally ill, maybe driven that way by my father. He was very demanding and critical, she was submissive and lacked confidence. As strange as it seems, she didn't kill out of malice. I think she couldn't take it anymore and wanted to kill her children because she didn't want them to suffer like she had.'

'Marni, I'm sorry—'

'There's nothing to be sorry about. It's something I have to deal with, mostly avoiding contact with my father.'

'Maybe it makes you frightened to get involved with a man.'

'Is that what we are, involved?' she asked.

'I don't know what we are, sometimes I don't know who I am. The death of my parents left me fatalistic about life, I thought I had to fill it with good times, wring out as much fun and joy as possible before the grim reaper came knocking. Now, I don't know. Doing an honest day's work and seeing the result makes me wonder if I don't want to accomplish something more permanent than seizing the moment.'

I lay in bed that night with her head on my shoulder, her soft, warm breathing against my neck. Neither of us was in any mood for wild, passionate sex. We just cuddled close.

I tried to imagine the horror of watching your mother murder your sibling and then try to murder you. The Medea Syndrome, Marni called it, named after the goddess in the play by Euripides and Greek mythology who killed her children to punish her husband, Jason, leader of the Argonauts and seeker of the Golden Fleece, after he deserted her for another woman. The spurned Medea killed their children in revenge.

I tried to analyze my feelings for Marni. Was it lust? Sympathy? Now that I had gotten what I wanted, the velvet rubbed off my dick as Cross would say, was I ready to move on?

No great revelation came, but one thing puzzled me. I wanted to be with her, not just for the moment. I wanted to make her proud of me and to protect her. But I had never felt this way before.

47

We took a flight back to Luanda two days later.

Almost being murdered had put a little damper on Marni's R and R. At first I thought she was more traumatized by the incident than she would admit, and that her emotions were raw after she revealed her family secret; we were on the plane before I found out what was really bothering her.

'Win, what did Eduardo mean when he said you were involved in something with Colonel Jomba?'

'I cut Jomba in on the money I retrieved from Eduardo. It's a form of paying taxes. If I hadn't done it, he would have hung me from a meat hook and used me as the hood ornament on his jeep.' That was the truth. At least part of it. The other part was that Eduardo had gotten wind of the deal with Jomba, but Marni would have thrown me out at 38,000 feet if she knew I was involved in a diamonds-for-weapons exchange.

'It sounded to me like he was referring to something else, something he wasn't involved in.'

'I pay the UNITA the usual protection money all the mine owners do. Jomba is the bagman for the collection.' That was true, too. So far I had managed to neatly evade her questions by making statements that were unimpeachable.

'Eduardo also said something about a woman you were involved with, he used the Portuguese "whore" word to describe her – and me.'

I kissed her hand. 'I don't ask questions about your past.'

'I'm not questioning your past. He made it sound like there was something up. I know that you stayed with João Carmona in Lisbon. His wife, Simone, is influential in a Portuguese-Angolan relief organization because her husband has donated money, but everyone knows that Carmona has been involved in the blood-diamond trade.' She held onto my arm and looked at me with earnest eyes. 'You wouldn't get involved in anything like that, would you? You know the suffering, the horrors that blood diamonds have brought to Africa.'

I kissed her cheek and brushed her lips with mine. 'Sweetheart, Eduardo was on drugs and hallucinatory.' Another brilliant end run around the truth. I should have been a lawyer.

She shook her head. 'We're approaching Luanda. Now tell me the truth, the moment you get off this airplane, you're going to forget you even know me. I'm going tromping back to the jungle to hand out food packages, and you're going to head back to New York where women don't smell of mosquito repellent.'

'Never.' I kissed her nose. 'I've never felt about anyone like I do about you.' That was the truth.

We left the plane and walked together into the terminal. A surprise was waiting for me. A woman was holding up a handkerchief with the name WIN LIBERTE chalked on in lipstick.

It was Simone.

Oh shit. I thought I muttered it under my breath but it came out. 'I can explain,' I told Marni.

The look on her face told me there was no way I could explain.

'Hello, forgive me for my little joke.' Simone shook hands with me and Marni. She said to me, 'I'm sorry, I showed up unexpectedly. I tried to reach you, but your man at the mine said you were out of town. Some things have come up in regard to our deal with Colonel Jomba that require immediate attention.'

'I'll be with you in a moment.'

I escorted Marni to a taxi. I gestured at one of the guards-for-hire and gave him money to ride shotgun into town with Marni.

'You've slept with her, haven't you.'

It wasn't a question.

'And you've got a dirty deal going.'

There was nothing I could say.

She left angry and hurt. As I watched the taxi leave, Simone appeared beside me.

'Did I say something wrong?'

'You are a bitch.'

She kissed me on the mouth. 'Of course, I am. But at least I'm good at

200

it. It's the only way a woman can deal with men who think they are in charge of the world.'

'What are you here for? Drop in on your broom to ruin my life?'

She laughed. 'Oh, no, please, don't tell me that the dashing and glamorous Win Liberte has fallen in love – and with an idealistic little bookworm. At least you could leave me for a movie star.'

'I can't leave someone I never had.'

We got into a taxi together.

'Is it going to complicate matters if I stay at the same hotel that you and Marni are in?' she asked.

'Marni's meeting friends from work and flying back to diamond country this afternoon.'

'Good. I was worried I was going to spoil your evening.'

'You're not. I'm taking you to your hotel and dropping you off. I have an afternoon charter upcountry, too.'

She put her hand on my upper thigh. 'You're angry at me. I really am sorry.'

'Let's get down to business. Why are you here?'

'All right.' She spoke low, so the driver and guard couldn't hear us. 'The timetable for the trade has moved up. The political conditions in the country are deteriorating. Savimbi and the government are constantly at each other's throats, the peace accord could go up in smoke anytime.'

'What do you care? These people will still need bullets to kill each other with.'

'If open war breaks out, Angolan diamonds will get designated conflict diamonds and the certification will be useless.'

'What exactly is Jomba up to?'

She shrugged. 'War, a coup, a revolution, who knows? These people have any number of ways of killing each other. Our deal is with Jomba, alone. We can't deal with Savimbi without alienating Jomba, who is looking to take over the UNITA. Many UNITA leaders are of the same mind as Jomba – tired of Savimbi's leadership. If the peace process is completely implemented, the rebels will have to disarm. And they will lose their diamond money.'

'So we arm Jomba so he can kill Savimbi and turn the country into a bloodbath. Is that about the lay of the land?'

She padded my arm. 'What's the matter, Win? Did your United Nations girlfriend tell you how terrible it is to trade diamonds for arms? Haven't you been down here long enough to understand how this place works? If we didn't provide tanks and guns for these people to kill each other with, they'd be doing it with spears.'

'Did you ever meet Bernie?'

'What?'

'Bernie – the guy I called my uncle, the one who invested my inheritance in the mine – did you ever meet him?'

'No, I don't think so, I don't remember.'

She was a good actress, but I could tell she was lying. My question rattled her.

'What's so important about this deal that you and João are willing to risk more money in a blood-diamond deal that might go south? From the way you live, you don't look like you have to worry where your next meal is coming from.'

'It's the fire diamond.'

'The fire diamond?' I knew what she was talking about, my father told me a ruby diamond had been stolen from him, but I pretended ignorance. It wasn't hard for me, in this game where there are puzzles wrapped in enigmas and surrounded by mystery.

'The Heart of the World, a diamond that's ruby-red, very rare, perhaps the most valuable diamond on earth that isn't in a museum. João told you he got into money troubles in that deal that broke your uncle, but he didn't tell you that the Bey was holding his fire diamond for the debt. There's going to be an exchange in this deal with Jomba. The Bey is giving Jomba weapons for diamonds, and the Bey will give us the fire diamond. But the Bey can't be trusted.

'The Heart of the World is worth more than the whole diamond deal put together. João is afraid that the Bey will try to keep it, or Jomba will find out about the diamond. If he does, he will grab it.'

'What would prevent Jomba and the Bey from getting together and doing a deal behind João's back?'

'They don't know each other. Jomba doesn't know who's supplying the weapons and the Bey doesn't know who he's delivering them to. João won't even reveal the time and place until the last moment.'

'No honor among thieves?' It was looking more and more like I was going to be left holding the bag. An empty one.

'Maybe you can explain something to me.' I counted on my fingers. 'Jomba's getting guns, the Bey's getting blood diamonds, João's getting the world's most valuable gem, and I . . .'

She squeezed the top of my leg. I disliked and distrusted this woman, but her touch sent my testosterone level up. What fools men are.

She said, 'I have some information that might surprise you. That man who used to manage your mine – what was his name?'

'Marques, Eduardo Marques.'

'Yes, him. He approached João recently about the mine, asking for his help to buy it.'

I kept my face blank, but it was tough. My instant reaction was that they were in on it with Eduardo. João would play all ends against the middle.

'Win, you're sitting on a gold mine, as you Americans would say. Marques had a geological report done that revealed a kimberlite pipe on the property.' She hesitated. God, she was a good actress. But I wasn't a good actor. 'From the look on your face, I think you know what I'm talking about.'

'I know Marques has something up his sleeve. He tried to buy the mine before I fired him for stealing. He claims he has a South African group behind him. He made another offer to buy the mine recently, wanting to trade lead for diamonds.'

'Lead for diamonds?'

'He had a gun. Why didn't you and João tell me Marques was a crook when I was in Lisbon?'

'We didn't know, he called João few days ago. João turned him down, of course. João was a friend of your father's and is now your partner in diamond trading. He wouldn't dishonor his relationship with you.'

It was getting harder to keep a straight face. Not only did my father consider João a world-class thief, but João stole the fire diamond from him. It wouldn't surprise me if he was in on the deal to steal the mine from me. I expected to hear from the South African lawyer that Eduardo's partners included João.

We pulled up to the hotel.

'Are you through with me?' I asked.

'Not quite. I told you the time schedule has moved up. You will have to be in Istanbul in three days to finalize the arrangements.'

'Excuse me, there must be a problem with my hearing. You didn't say I was to be in Istanbul in three days?'

'The Bey wants to meet you. He doesn't like dealing with someone he's never seen. He wants to look you over. And he and João have to make the final arrangements for the weapons delivery and marketing the diamonds.'

Istanbul. I tried to envision where it was at. Portugal was by the straits on one end of the Mediterranean, Istanbul, Turkey, I think was on the other end, the east side. Yeah, I hadn't hung around my geography class much, either.

Her hand went back to my thigh and squeezed. 'I'm sorry, Win, but it's necessary. If any of us cause this deal to fold, I'm afraid the Bey and Colonel Jomba both would seek revenge.'

She didn't add João into the equation, but he'd probably be at the head of the pack, snarling at my heels as I ran from the hounds of hell.

She leaned against me and kissed me. Her lips were warm and lush.

'What can I do to make all this up to you?' she asked.

I started laughing. I kept laughing as she got out of the taxi and slammed the door. She started to walk away and turned back, speaking to me through the open window.

'João will wire your instructions on Istanbul to the mine.' She hesitated. 'Don't hate me.'

Bitch.

48

Simone's phone was ringing as she entered her room.

'*Está.*'

'It's me,' João said. 'Did you tell our friend where he has to go?'

João was speaking in code because he was certain a room phone in an Angolan hotel was not secure.

'Thanks for asking how I am.'

João chuckled. 'How are you, my love? Did I tell you that I miss you? That I count the hours?'

'You're a terrible old fraud. How is Jonny doing?'

'Probably "doing" every boy in Lisbon. She has the morals of an alley cat. Like her mother.'

'Don't bother taking any blame for how your daughter turned out. And yes, our friend was told.'

'How did he take it?'

'How would you take it?'

'I wouldn't.'

She thought for a moment. 'I'm not sure he will, either.'

'Will he show up for the meeting?'

'I'm sure he will. At this point, he has no options. The question is, what control will you have once he has an option?'

'That's simple, my love. We make sure he never has any.' João's voice took on a chilling edge. 'I think there will be a time in the near future when all this hassle about modern life gets our friend Win to the point where living's not worth it.'

Neither spoke for a moment, then João asked, 'Have you spoken to our friend, the colonel?'

'We met – briefly.'

'And?'

'He insists we meet the new timetable.'

'And we will, we will, if that's what we have to do to get my baby back.'

There was no pretense that João cared more for the fire diamond than Jonny or Simone.

He went on. 'I heard an interesting thing about tattoos and the colonel. Besides the bizarre ones that are visible, a member of the Angolan embassy staff told me the colonel is reputed to have had his penis tattooed so it appears to be a lion with a mane when the foreskin is pulled back.' He paused. 'Have you tasted any lion meat while you were in Luanda?'

'Is that what you want me to do?'

'My love, you know I never tell you what to do. By the way, be careful. Our man is asking for a bigger cut.'

There was a knock on her room door.

'Someone's at the door. I'll call you in the morning before I go to the airport.'

She opened the door. A maid handed her an envelope. It contained a room key.

She undressed and took a bath, then showered afterward and applied bath oil to her damp body. Sitting naked in front of the mirror, she finished putting on her makeup. She lubricated her vagina with a sperm killer, then put on lacy white panties and bra. The color contrasted well with her copper-tone complexion. Before she put on her dress, she posed in front of

205

a full-length mirror. And let out a sigh. Men would describe her as sexy and sensuous, but like most women, Simone was her own worst critic.

She chose a red, strapless cotton dress, nice enough for evening, but not as provocative as she would have worn for a cocktail party.

When her preparations were done, she left the room and took the elevator up two floors. Rather than use the room key she had been provided, she knocked on the door.

Cross opened the door. Without smiling, he stepped aside and let her enter.

'Is Win going to wonder where you're at?' she asked.

He shook his head. 'I left a message that I went upriver to look at a claim. I do it all the time.'

She took a seat on the couch.

'What's your pleasure?' He gestured at a tray full of liquor bottles.

'*Nada*. Tell me what Win said about Eduardo.'

'The same thing I told João on the phone. Win called me from Cape Town, said Eduardo came to him with a gun and a paper to sign.'

'Signing over the mine.'

'That's the size of it. Eduardo's in jail. Considering he's a foreigner, he'll probably stay in jail for a while since he'd be a flight risk if bailed out.'

'Is that all he told you?'

Cross sat on the arm of the couch and grinned down at her as he swished the ice and whiskey in his glass. 'What's the matter? Afraid Eduardo will tell Win that you and your hubby were in on the deal to steal his mine?'

Simone smiled up at him. Her lips were friendly, but her eyes were cold and calculating. 'Don't let your imagination run away with you, Cross. João and I can't get involved in ownership of a mine in Angola, not while Savimbi's still alive.'

'You could if you used a dummy South African corporation as a cover.'

'As I said, don't let your imagination run away with you.'

'It already has.' He leaned down and kissed her on the mouth. He ran his lips down her neck and breathed in the floral essence between her breasts.

'Hmmm. You smell like a woman should.'

She returned his kiss, this time with eagerness. He slipped off the arm of the couch and onto the cushions. He pulled her dress up, then bent down and kissed her white panties.

'You want some Portuguese pussy?'

His face came back up. 'What do you think? I already have a hard-on. Before I eat your pussy, there's something we need to discuss . . . while I still have control over my senses.'

He sat back on the arm of the couch.

'João said you wanted a bigger cut.'

'No, that's not the right way to put it. "Wanted" sounds like I'm asking. I'm not asking, babe. This deal is getting hairier. When I got into it, I didn't know Jomba would be bucking Savimbi. That's kind of like a slow way to kill yourself − like using a machete to hack off your own toes and working your way up.'

'Savimbi's human, he doesn't live up to his reputation.'

Cross howled. 'Honey, you obviously haven't spent enough time in Angola. Savimbi is insane and he's got an army, half of whom are crazy from drugs and the other half are just plain crazy. What do you think the chances are of Jomba beating him?'

'That's none of our business. We deliver weapons, get the diamonds, and leave the dogs to scrap over their bones.'

'*You* leave, you mean. No one's going to notice that you don't belong here. But if Savimbi smells a rat, he'll immediately start looking for the ones running. And I'll be the one taken off the street and dropped at his doorstep if I try to run.'

'What's this all leading up to? How much?'

'Our deal was a quarter million for helping you pull off the deal with Jomba,' he said.

'And making sure our friend Senhor Liberte doesn't back out of the deal or try a double-cross.'

'And spying on Win for you. I want a half million.'

'All right. I'll let João know that it's now a half million.'

She stood up and took the glass from his hand and put it aside. He spread his legs as he sat on the couch arm and she moved between them.

'Are we through with business?' she asked.

'What if I'd asked for a million?'

'What are you talking about?'

'I'm just wondering why you agreed so quickly, no argument, *nada*.'

'There's plenty to go around. What is it you Americans say? Don't look a gift horse in the mouth?'

'Yeah, well, it kind of makes me wonder when someone is too easy.

207

There're promises and there're promises, and they don't always get taken care of. Makes me wonder whether you and that husband of yours really intend to pay me off. I could just get stuck here in Angola after everything goes to hell. But you will be in Lisbon.'

She unbuttoned his shirt, taking his nipple in her mouth. 'I want you to fuck me.'

She heard the bedroom door open and turned her head. It was a young person, white skinned with short blond hair, dressed in baggy clothes.

Simone asked, 'Who is this?'

'Someone I imported from Amsterdam. You can't trust the pussy in Luanda.'

Simone frowned at the person. 'Is it a boy – or girl?'

Cross laughed. 'That's the fun of it. We'll find out together.'

49

Istanbul

I hired a high-speed boat that took me out onto the Bosporus, into the Sea of Marmara, and down the Dardanelles to the town of Canakkale on the Asian side of Turkey. I picked up the car I had reserved, first stopping at my hotel before starting for the hour-long trip. I was headed for the ruins. When I arrived I got out of the car and walked to the edge of an ancient wall along a cliff and stared down across the Dardanelles to Europe.

It was here, on the wall in the city of Troy, that Odysseus, Hector, Achilles, and Paris had fought over the fickle and beautiful Helen.

Istanbul was one of the great cities of East and West, a fascinating, mysterious, throbbing city at the crossroads of history. It was a city of political intrigue and conspiracy, of clashing cultures and ambitious empires. But it was to these ruins on the other side of the straits, an unimposing place of gray stones battered by war and time, that I was drawn.

It was a place where men had died in fierce battle, where a woman was determined to follow her own heart even if it meant death, destruction, and the fall of kingdoms. There were few places on earth where men had died so valiantly and so much had been wrought in the name of love.

I thought about Odysseus leaving Troy after the war, doomed by an angry god to embark upon a dangerous journey, in perilous waters. That's how I felt about my New York-to-Lisbon, Africa-to-Istanbul venture. Damned by the gods. And the one-eyed Cyclops was João. I had inherited his machinations from my father like a genetic defect. And I was pretty sure that Bernie had died from the same disease.

I called Marni before I left for Istanbul. I asked her to come with me. The request was insane. How would I have ever explained that I was meeting the conspirators in a blood diamond deal? She said, 'No,' and hung up.

I think I made the call because I knew she would say no. It was my weak-kneed way of pretending that I could back out of the deal. Yeah, back out. But I couldn't claim for the sake of my everlasting soul that it was because of my concern for what Jomba would do with the weapons. I had Simone's attitude about Angola – if they weren't killing each other for one reason or in one way, they'd find another. And five million dollars soothed a lot of guilt for me. Hell, I'd even make a donation to an Angolan relief fund.

No, it wasn't a sudden case of morality – it was the possibility that the Blue Lady was a gold mine – metaphorically speaking. If Kruger found more indicators in the test drilling we planned, the five million dollars I was getting – that I would probably never live to enjoy – could be chump change. If the money came out of my own legitimate mine, I would be as safe as the proverbial golden goose.

Life was so damn complicated. Besides having to fend off João the Cyclops and an Angolan colonel with a barbed-wire necklace and a human hood ornament, I was resolved to the fact that Marni would never be a part of my life.

Bottom line, I was a shit. And she knew it.

As I looked across the narrow strait dividing Asia and Europe and thought about Marni, I couldn't remember what happened to Helen at the conclusion of the Trojan War. But I did recall that Paris was killed.

'You have a good view of the Sultanahmet from here,' the Bey said.

The Bey and I were on a balcony of his house. Spread out before us were the narrow straits of water called the Golden Horn and the Bosporus, along with the old, walled part of Istanbul.

The Bey was a small-built man, no more than five-six or five-seven and slender, probably a hundred and thirty or forty pounds. Bald, without even a hint of shaved hair around the sides, no eyebrows, and without wrinkles on his face, I had no idea of how old he was. When I had visited João and Simone in Lisbon before I went to Angola, Simone told me that the Bey was ex-KGB but João had scoffed. 'They all use that as a subtle threat,' he said.

I wasn't so sure. There wasn't much subtlety about the Bey's threats. I was picked up at the hotel by a limo. The driver and the guy riding shot-gun looked like they had teethed on guns and barbells. I saw several more scattered around the grounds, two with big mastiffs on short chains. My impression of the Bey was that he was a careful man who had enemies.

Simone and João were in another part of the house having a drink with friends of the Bey.

The Bey struck me as more Russian than Turkish, only because his skin was lighter, and I heard him claim earlier he was born in Georgia. The dinner conversation had been about the fall of the Soviet Union and the independent status of some of its former republics. Simone saw the question on my face and explained that Georgia was a small country on the Black Sea between Turkey and Russia. No one offered any explanation as to how he got to be called 'the Bey,' and I didn't ask. I didn't know what a bey was, anyway. Besides I think João told me the Bey was from somewhere else. I came to the conclusion that the Bey's background changed with the tide.

'What I love about the view from this balcony,' the Bey said, 'is you see so much history of the world. You have the great dome building of St. Sofia, the second church of Christendom before the Sons of Islam took the city and massacred the last defenders in the church. Topkapi Palace, the seat of the Ottoman sultans, is there, to the left of it. Royal princes were kept away from the palace because so many of the sultan's wives tried to gain the throne for their own sons by murder. To the right is the Blue Mosque, one of the great religious edifices of Islam.'

I made listening responses and sipped a vodka martini. I didn't know why the Bey had invited me out onto the balcony to give me a personal tour, or even still, why I had been commanded to come to Istanbul.

'I can see that I'm boring you,' the Bey said. 'Before you came, I asked

João to explain to you that I insist upon meeting face-to-face with people who I am investing a great deal of money in. That's why I asked you here.'

'I wasn't aware you were investing anything in me. My only role in this action is to certify the diamonds that get turned over to us.' I had been warned not to mention Jomba's name to the Bey. João was keeping him in the dark to insure that the Bey didn't cut him out and make his own deal.

'I was under the impression your role would be larger than that.'

I smelled a rat. 'What do you mean?'

'That you will take possession of the diamonds from the buyer of the arms and hand them over to my representative. You understand how this sort of arrangement comes down, don't you?'

'No, I don't.'

'The exchange will take place in stages. Three days before the delivery, you will check the buyer's goods and insure they are as represented in terms of the total carats, quality, and quantities. You will then notify me and I will set the exact time for the exchange. An hour before my planes are set to land, you will confirm that the same diamonds are at the landing field. A few minutes before the exchange, my reconnaissance plane will check the area for traps. When the actual exchange takes place, the diamonds will be turned over to you and you will turn my share over to my representative. What you do with João's share is between you and your friends.'

'João isn't my friend, this is strictly business.'

'My apologies. I was led to believe that your relationship with him and Simone was almost of a family nature.'

'I trust João as much as you do.' I let that sink in for a moment. 'And I don't know him as well as you.'

The Bey chuckled, the throaty rasp of a death rattle. 'You are blunt, Win, I like that.'

'Then let me give you the other barrel. My agreement is to certify the diamonds. To me, that means I sit in a nice, safe, warm place and sign my name. There was no mention of me standing in the line of fire in a jungle clearing while your people and the buyer decide if you're going to go through with the deal or shoot it out.'

'I'm afraid that you have inadvertently brought the matter upon yourself. You eliminated the person who was going to monitor the exchange.'

I caught it immediately. 'You were going to have Eduardo do the exchange.'

'Yes, he was perfect for the task. Like you, he's an expert on diamonds, near the exchange site . . . and obtainable. At least he was, until you had him locked up in Cape Town.'

Other things were falling into place. 'I hired a lawyer in South Africa to trace back Eduardo's partners who were planning to steal my mine. He came up with a Swiss corporation and ran into a brick wall.'

'The Swiss are very practical about business matters. As long as you do the stealing and killing outside their borders, they don't ask questions about money you bring them. But your suspicion is correct. I was the money behind Eduardo's attempt to buy the mine.'

'And to kill me.'

He chuckled again, another death rattle. 'Not at all, although had it succeeded, I would not have lost any sleep over it. I'm very practical, too, especially with people I don't know. Or with ones like João, who I know too well. I didn't know Eduardo was going to try to get you to sign over the mine at the point of a gun. It was a stupid move. When you fired Eduardo, as far as I was concerned the affair was closed. I let him know that, which is perhaps why he became so desperate. I had loaned him money, an advance, you see . . .'

'I see.' In other words, Eduardo couldn't pay it back now that I had raided his bank accounts. And he would have the Bey's men on his tail.

'I owe João an apology,' I said. 'I thought he was behind Eduardo.'

'You owe João nothing. Eduardo went with the highest bidder. He approached both of us, but João could not guarantee the money needed to buy the mine and explore for more diamonds. João came to me as a middleman and I cut him out.'

'God, the tangled webs we weave. This scheme has more facets than a diamond.'

'It goes without saying that I now have no interest in obtaining your mine. You are aware of the potential, I wish you luck in developing it. You may get rich, or find out the exploration was a hole in the ground you threw money into.'

'I appreciate the fact that you're going to let me have my own property, but I still have no intention of being the stakeholder.'

'Oh, but you must. You seem to be forgetting something.'

'What?'

'Your share of the transaction is coming from the diamonds that Colonel Jomba will be handing over. Do you plan to permit your share to come into my hands – or João's?'

Jesus. What a pisser.

I had a question as we started to go back inside. I locked eyes with him. 'Who murdered my uncle?'

Nothing showed in his eyes. I might as well have asked him the time.

'I don't know,' he said.

Of course, he did. One thing I had learned – the Bey knew everything. Including the fact that Jomba was the arms buyer. My gut told me that the suspicion I had was right. João had killed Bernie. I didn't know how, I wasn't even quite sure of why, other than it had to do with diamonds, but I could feel João's hand in it.

After dinner we gathered in the center of the Bey's high-domed library. The room had the ambiance of a museum. Simone came up beside me as I stared at a fully wrapped mummy.

'The Bey is known to collect – and deal in – antiquities. I'm sure there are custom inspectors from Giza to Angkor Vat who would like to get a peek in this room and the Bey's vault.'

The Bey gathered us around a small table covered by a white cloth in the middle of the room. As he spoke, bright strobe lights came on over-head.

'As you know, my friends, I am an avid collector of rare treasures. Let me show you what I presently consider the crème de la crème of my collection.'

He whipped off the cloth. Simone gasped at the display.

A crystal bowl, party size, was filled with diamonds. On top of the diamonds, in the center, was a single gem, about the size of a walnut.

The Heart of the World.

With lighting from above and beneath the table, the display sprayed the room with glittering light, making the Heart of the World convulse with volcanic fire.

I didn't gasp aloud like Simone, but I was also stunned. Like my father, I had diamonds in my blood. And, like my father, I had never seen a gem like this one. Diamonds were masked in myth and mystery. Hard enough to cut steel, yet dazzling and sensuous on a woman, a diamond never struck me as being of this world. Looking at this one, I thought it was misnamed – it wasn't the heart of the world, but the blazing heart of a star. To a diamantaire, it would be better than owning the *Mona Lisa*.

Across from me, the glittery spray played on João's features. It was like looking into the face of the devil and seeing the most deadly sins neoned – greed, murder, lust. It was inhuman, even terrifying. João stared at the fire diamond, a man possessed. I now knew why his wife called the gem his lover. When it came to the diamond, he wasn't just a lover, he was a possessive demon-lover, the kind who followed his wife to her lover's bed and then hacked them both to death, letting them see the wicked edge of the ax before it struck.

A drama soon played out in the room. João tore his eyes away from the Heart of the World and looked up at the Bey. The two men locked eyes, two predators coming face-to-face in a jungle, each digging its claws into the territory they claimed. Now another emotion appeared on João's face – *hatred*. Violent, murderous, vicious malevolence.

Some devil gripped me, too. I thought about the fact that João had stolen the gem from my father. That he had murdered Bernie. And now he was trying to steal my mine – if he didn't get me killed by Jomba.

'I understand you want me to act as the middleman in the exchange.' I directed my words at João. 'I'll do it, but my price has gone up.' I turned to the Bey. 'I want the Heart of the World. It was stolen from my father and I want it back.'

João stared at me like I'd just cut off his balls. The Bey stared at me like I had just gouged out his eyes. Simone just gawked – for once, she didn't emit that laugh of hers.

'That's the deal. You don't like it, go fuck yourselves.'

I walked out. I wasn't sure I was going to make it to the limo that I had waiting for me outside. There was a chance that the Bey would hang me from a meat hook and let his thugs take target practice. And João was inflamed enough to walk from his wheelchair and grab my throat. But I didn't give a damn. I was tired of being played for a fool and being threatened.

After having pissed off two of the most dangerous men in the world, all I had to do now was return to Angola and deal with murderous warlords while I tried to strike it rich.

I thought about the time I was in a New York bar and met a guy. He talked about a strange type of financial deal. It was called a 'viatical investment.' The guy found people who had a short time to live and offered to buy their life insurance policy at a discount. If the dying person had a $100,000 policy, he'd buy it for $50,000. It was a win-win deal – the buyer made a killing when the person died and the dying person got an infusion of cash for their last days. The deals only went sour when the dying person made a miracle recovery.

If I called the viatical investor up and described my current problems, he'd be foaming at the mouth for a chance to invest in my imminent demise.

50

Angola

Marni stared at the people in the distribution line. The nausea she had felt earlier was welling up again. She had thrown up soon after rising. The only thing left in her stomach was the tea she drank to settle it, but she still felt ready to heave. *I've got a dose of something*, she thought. The question was whether it was something that would put her on her back for a few days − or kill her. The third possibility was something like malaria that remained chronic.

Her job this morning was to watch the workers hired to watch the people picking up food packages. The idea was one package, one person, but the way she felt, they could throw open the storage sheds and turn the food over to a mob.

'There are a hundred ways to cheat,' she told her assistant, Venacio, 'and these people know all of them.' It was an unfair assessment and she knew it. Most people in line were honest, like most people everywhere. But desperate conditions made even the most honorable try to grab whatever they could.

Finally, she gave up the ghost and handed her clipboard to Venacio. 'You're in charge, try to keep them from stealing the store. I'm going to see if Dr Machado will give me something that will put me out of my misery.'

She reported to the small infirmary where Machado, a mulatto from Luanda, and his staff, tried to provide medical support to the thinly spread medical facilities in the region. Machado also provided medical assistance for aid workers.

She gave samples of blood and urine and laid back on a cot while she waited for the results. The luck of the draw, she thought, that's what the aid workers called getting a dose of something wicked. Everyone got sick, usually more than once, but her real fear was that it would be something permanent.

The woman who took her temperature noted the uncut diamond stone Marni wore on a necklace. 'Very nice,' she said. 'Is it flawless?'

'Yes,' Marni said.

She knew what the woman was thinking – it was foolish to wear something so valuable. She wore it because it made her feel close to Win. She rubbed the stone and thought about Win, feeling sad and lonely. That she was in love with him was not at issue. He was not a hard person for a woman to fall in love with. But she felt a betrayal of her and the people she was in Angola to help. Blood diamonds were not an abstract economic-political issue to her. She had seen too much of the 'blood' that flowed from the evil trade, too many orphan children roaming the streets, too many amputees.

She could forgive Win his ignorance when he was in New York or Lisbon, but he had spent enough time in Angola to see the terrible consequences of supplying arms for diamonds. It was murder, mass murder on a large scale.

Dr Machado came in. He was frowning.

She groaned. 'Give me the bad news, tell me the truth, I've caught something permanent, a bug that's going to eat me alive.'

'It's only permanent if you want it to be. They invented the condom for this sort of thing.'

'*Oh my God, I have AIDS?*'

'I believe the old-fashioned expression is that you are with child.'

She gaped at him. 'I'm pregnant?'

He shook his head and clicked his tongue. 'Please, don't tell me this is another immaculate conception. Or that you caught it off a toilet seat.'

She leaned back, her head on the pillow. 'My God, I'm pregnant.'

'A time to rejoice . . . or for an abortion.'

'An abortion? I don't know, I haven't thought about it.'

'When you do, realize that you must leave Angola as soon as possible if you decide to have the baby. This is not a healthy environment for the local women who become pregnant, and at least they have a resistance built up to some of the maladies lurking in every drink, bite of food, or exposed skin.'

216

There wasn't any significant thought process involved in her decision. She would keep the baby. She loved Win Liberte, with all her heart and soul, even though she didn't want to admit it. The child in her was a part of him.

She made another decision. Not to tell him about the baby. It was not selfishness on her part. A man who was untrustworthy and a liar could not truly love a child. She was sure that her own father didn't love her. She was not going to let her child be emotionally abused as she was.

51

I tried to contact Marni as soon as I got back from Istanbul and was told she had returned to the States. That stunned me. Down deep, I suppose I thought that we'd still get together. I guess I had overestimated her depth of feeling for me – and underestimated mine for her.

I had been back from Istanbul for a week when I went to Luanda to meet Kruger's plane when he flew in from Cape Town. We never went into town. I had the hotel deliver a gourmet lunch to the airport and my chartered plane took us to diamond country. I didn't want him to take one look at Luanda and take the next flight back to South Africa.

It was dangerous for Kruger to putz around the diamond area alone. I told Cross to stick to him. The way the mining country operated, if anyone found out Kruger had a system for finding blue earth, they'd kidnap him and keep him on a short chain while they took him out prospecting.

When a shipment of equipment came in for Kruger, I rode out with Gomez to deliver it. While Kruger was getting the equipment set up, I took Cross aside.

'How's it look?'

'Who can tell? All the guy does is walk around and talk to himself and tell the men where he wants equipment set up. I wouldn't be surprised if he pulled out a divining rod used by water witches. From the looks of that drilling rig he's set up, we may hit oil.'

'That would be okay with me. Listen, we need to talk.'

I laid it out for him, the whole shebang with João, the Bey, and Jomba, starting with the death of Bernie, right down to me demanding the fire diamond and walking out. Cross listened, blank-faced. I didn't know how he was going to react. I needed Cross, he knew more about dealing, double-dealing, and dirty-dealing in Angola than I had time to learn.

'Well, what do you think?' I asked.

'Interesting. If I was a priest, I'd tell you to say a hundred Hail Marys and start thinking about what I'd say at your wake. If I was a doctor—'

'I get the idea. The bottom line is that you're going to have to come to a decision. You're either with me in trying to survive the Jomba situation – or pack your bags. If you're in for the duration, you'll get a piece of the action.'

'A "piece of the action" has a different connotation in equatorial Africa than other places in the world. Around here, they take Shylock's pound of flesh, literally. I wouldn't stick around for a million bucks.'

'How about two million?'

That stopped him in his tracks. 'Holy shit.'

'That's my offer. You stick around, help me get through this mess in one piece, when we hit blue earth you'll be a rich man.'

A chuckle came from deep in his throat. 'I knew there was a catch – and there're several of them. You not only have to live, you have to be in one piece. And then there's that little contingency about hitting pay dirt.'

I looked over to where Kruger was yelling at the workers helping him. 'Kruger has something good enough for people to want to steal. This mine is good enough for people to line up to steal. That sounds like a winning combination to me.'

'Enough to bet your life?'

'That's what I'm doing. But you've stuck your head out far enough, already. If you want to bail out, I won't blame you.'

'It's kind of a rough fall when you bail out without a parachute. If I go back to the States, I'd head for L.A. where my sister has moved. I didn't exactly leave the oil business on good terms, so it'll be tough to get a decent job. Without money, I'd just be another guy hanging around street corners, wondering where my next fix would be.

'Bubba, you told me that the devil met the price of your soul when João offered you five mill in a blood-diamond deal. My soul's got a lot more dents and scrapes on it than yours.' He slapped me on the back. 'You got a deal.'

He grabbed my arm and held me back as we started to walk back toward Kruger. 'It's occurred to me that you might be smarter than you look. There're an awful lot of players in this game, from Cape Town to Istanbul. You haven't pulled one of those cons where you've sold more than a hundred percent of the mine, have you?'

'You have to trust me.'

'Fuck trust. You think João and Jomba are mean bastards. You get between me and my money and I'll rip out your heart and feed it to my dog.'

'What I like most about you, Cross, is I always know where you stand – on the winning side.'

'Did you have a plan?' he asked. 'Or were you going to just throw yourself on the mercy of the gods?'

'What do you think Jomba's chances are of knocking over Savimbi with a coup?'

'I've seen Jomba, I haven't seen Savimbi. From what I've heard, Savimbi would have Jomba for breakfast. Savimbi is a national hero, at least among the rebel faction, which is most of the backcountry. Jomba's a pit bull with a brain, and he's balking at the choke chain Savimbi jerks whenever he wants to keep the colonels in line.'

'Coups by colonels have been notoriously successful around the world.'

'Yeah, but they're usually marching in and taking over a civilian government. Savimbi may not advertise his meanness with tattoos and hood ornaments, he's too smart to appear as a murderous maniac, but from what I've heard, he's murderous in terms of the big picture and keeps up a statesmanlike front. That's why President Reagan and the CIA pumped so much money into him. They thought he was an idealistic patriotic. People in this country knew better.'

'Then Savimbi's our man.'

'Our man for what?'

'To handle Jomba.'

'Shit, has diamond fever melted that little brain of yours? When it comes between choosing between you and Jomba, Savimbi will take his colonel's side on several counts, not the least of which is your being a foreigner without an army.'

'When Savimbi finds out Jomba's plotting against him, Jomba will be history.'

'Maybe, and maybe you're making the mistake of thinking like a Westerner. Try this for a scenario. Savimbi finds out Jomba is plotting against him. But Jomba has his own army. So the two of them sit around the campfire and reach an accord on how to deal with their mutual enemy, the government in Luanda, while they roast you over the hot flames.'

'Then we'll have to sweeten the pot for Savimbi, give him a good reason not to deal with Jomba.'

'What's the good reason?'

I shrugged. 'He gets the weapons that were intended for Jomba.'

'How do you manage that?'

'We punt.'

'Bubba, you only punt when you have a kicker that can reach the goalpost. If the ball drops short around here, they whack your kicking leg off.'

'Okay, I haven't got a plan yet. I need to know more about Savimbi.'

'That I can arrange. I got a pal in Luanda, he used to be a CIA contact with Savimbi, back when the Luanda government was commie and Washington thought Savimbi was an African George Washington.'

'He still with the CIA?'

'Nope, he went on the disabled list and settled down in Luanda with his Angolan girlfriend.'

'Got shot?'

'Got AIDS.'

Kruger approached us. 'You dug in the wrong direction.'

'I don't understand,' I said.

'The tunneling in your mine, we have to change the direction.'

'You found a pipe?'

'I've found the same indicators I examined before, but now I know the direction they are spread in.' He pointed off my property. 'The pipe may be on your property, or on the property next door. We'll find out after we tunnel.'

'Pray,' I told Cross. 'Promise Him anything, but ask Him to let us win the lottery.'

52

Kruger had to fly back to South Africa to get equipment he needed. I didn't want to leave him without Cross or me at his side. His sudden need to leave the area worked out well. Cross called his CIA friend in Luanda and set up a meeting for us after we dropped Kruger off at the airport.

We flew together to the capitol. I made sure Kruger was safely on a plane to Cape Town before I would leave the terminal.

'You afraid someone's gonna kidnap him from the airport?' Cross asked.

'This is Angola.'

Cross nodded. 'Good point.'

We talked about Kirk, the ex-CIA agent, on the way to the meeting. The meeting was to be held at Kirk's apartment. 'Less chance of being seen than if we met him at a bar or restaurant.'

'How'd you meet Kirk?' I asked.

'Hoosier T-shirt. I was wearing one in the lounge at the Presidente Meridien in Luanda. This guy comes up and says he went to Indiana State, same as me. We start comparing notes and find out we lived in the same dorm, one semester apart.'

'Kirk's black?'

'What do you think, bubba? Would the CIA send a white-ass with black-face to pass themselves off as Angolan?'

'You have a bad mouth. Someday I'm going to stick my foot in it. You said Kirk's tight with Savimbi from the days when the CIA was running a covert operation in the country. You think he's still tight with him?'

'He used to feed Savimbi the guns and money that kept him fighting the government. It's not the sort of thing that Savimbi would forget. Especially when he tells Savimbi that he has a dude who wants to talk about guns and money.'

'Why'd he stay in Angola?'

'Why not? As far as his wife and kids back home are concerned, he's dead. As long as he can keep the disease under control, he can live a relatively normal life here. His Angolan woman's infected and so are a million others. He doesn't have to put up with the prejudices he would at home.'

Cross and I had settled on a story that we wanted to talk to Savimbi about 'diamonds and guns.' We figured that was vague enough. I was inclined to tell Kirk the whole story, get his opinion of what we should do about Jomba, but Cross had howled with laughter.

'You are a naïve bastard. Kirk has to survive in this country. You tell him you're double-crossing Jomba, and Kirk would tell Jomba to protect himself and his old lady.'

'You have any faith at all in anyone?' I asked.

'Yeah, I have faith in Washington, Lincoln, Jackson, and whoever's face is on the hundred-dollar bill – the bigger the denomination, the more faith I got.'

Kirk's apartment building, located in an area with harbor views, was being renovated. The first thing I noticed was the security. The doorman who buzzed us in was behind a counter topped with bulletproof glass. I didn't doubt that he had an AK-47 or two under the counter.

We took the elevator to the fifth floor and walked down the hall to his apartment door. Kirk opened the door. I was in for a surprise. I had expected a duplicate of Cross, a big-chested man with broad shoulders, from the steel mills of Indiana. Kirk was short and skinny. I didn't know if he had shrunk from his disease, or if he was just a much smaller man. He had thick glasses and salt-and-pepper hair. He looked a little scholarly, not at all the James Bond type.

The surprise was that he was a double amputee. Both his arms were gone halfway between the elbow and wrist. He had a prosthetic on the right side.

His wife, Maria, was an attractive woman in her mid-thirties. A cute little girl of about ten poked her head in for a second before Maria disappeared after her as we sat down to talk business.

'Cross says you want to meet with Savimbi and talk business. And that you're a relative newcomer in Angola. What do you know about Savimbi?'

'I've heard he's tough and mean.'

'He's that and much more. A charismatic political leader beloved by a couple million people in this country. Honored at the White House as a head of state when all he had was a ragtag army. He's got university degrees from Portugal, Switzerland, and China and speaks a half-dozen languages. And he's burned people at the stake.'

'Wonderful qualifications for leadership,' I said. 'He must be nuts.'

'He is. To understand Savimbi, you have to understand why this country has been going through nearly two decades of civil war, following a war of independence against the Portuguese. Guerrilla warfare to gain independence started around '61, and continued for fourteen years until Portugal's colonial hegemony was thrown off in '75. Portuguese colonial rulers were sent packing, but the same thing happened here in Angola that happened in Mexico and South America after the Spanish were tossed out. The mestizos, the mixed bloods, most of whom are city dwellers, inherited the government and the economy. The villagers were exploited economically and kept from exercising political power. That created resentment and a political vacuum.

'Savimbi filled that vacuum. He became the champion of the villagers, millions of them. With the backing of Cuba, the government attacked Savimbi. He retreated into the bush in his own "Long March" reminiscent of Mao's. He regrouped there and kept up guerrilla warfare against the regime in Luanda. He was the son of a railroad stationmaster and he knew the operation of Angola's rail system intimately. He used that knowledge to attack the rails and disrupt the flow of troops and military supplies. And, with the Commie block supporting the regime in Luanda, Savimbi became the darling of Washington.

'Pretty soon the Luanda government had Soviet MIGs with Cuban fighter pilots on hunt-and-destroy missions against Savimbi's troops, and Savimbi had Stinger missiles to shoot down the MIGs. Besides foreign aid, the government financed the war with its oil fields and Savimbi grabbed the diamond mining area.

'He claims to be a devout Christian, but if he has any serious religious views, they're the kind that Satan holds. I suspect that he's something of a Marxist at heart, but leaned toward capitalism when Washington opened its checkbook. He likes to tell a little joke about how religion affected Angola. He says that when missionaries came to Angola centuries ago, they had Bibles and Angolans had the land. Now Angolans have Bibles and the missionaries have the land.'

'From what I've heard,' I said, 'the peace agreement between Savimbi and the government won't last.'

'It's already in shreds. It's just a matter of the actual shooting starting up again. The government will never give Savimbi substantial power. Remember, this is a guy who has burned opponents at the stake, who has personally murdered the wives and children of men who opposed him. What do you think he'd do if he got a position of power in Luanda?'

'Take over the government by murdering everyone else,' Cross said.

'Exactly, and he'd do some of the killings himself. Think about that, the political leader of millions of people, with blood on his hands. Nuts like Hitler killed millions, but never with his own hands. About the only killer rulers I can think of offhand are Genghis Khan, Stalin, and Saddam.'

I said, 'If everything is going to hell between Savimbi and the government, this might be an opportune time to approach him with a, uh, merchandising deal. How well do you know him?'

'I was the CIA point man with Savimbi during the mid-eighties. I traveled with him, hiding my head when the bullets flew and the bombs dropped.' He laughed. 'I saw the look on your face when I opened the door and you saw my arms.'

I nodded. 'Cross didn't tell me.'

Cross shrugged. 'Hell, I never noticed you didn't have arms.'

Kirk sprayed out a mouthful of tea he was in the process of swallowing and broke into a gale of laughter. When he was done laughing, he wiped his mouth. 'Sorry. Okay, let's get down to business. I don't know what your business is with Savimbi, and even if you wanted to tell me, I don't want to know. I can introduce you to Savimbi, set up a meet. Whether he kills you or does business with you, that I can't say. I want fifty thousand dollars, U.S., in advance. I want another fifty if you come out of the meeting alive.'

We made a deal for diamonds instead of dollars and left the apartment. When we were in a taxi, I asked Cross, 'What happened to Kirk's arms?'

Cross laughed, almost a giggle. 'Haven't you guessed?'

It hit me. 'Savimbi?'

'Savimbi. He caught Kirk and one of his own men with their hands in the till. They were diverting CIA-supplied weapons and reselling them. Savimbi personally chopped off Kirk's hands.'

'Jesus. But he was CIA.'

'Yeah, but remember what Kirk tried to get across, the guy's psychotic. You don't burn people at the stake unless you've got a serious personality disorder, one that you don't find in the average textbook on abnormal psychology.'

'What happened to the other guy?'

'He wasn't CIA. Kirk told me Savimbi had the guy impaled on a sharp stake – alive. And raped his wife in front of him as he was dying.'

Cross leaned over and nudged me with his elbow.

'Just think of it this way, bubba. You've got so many enemies, Savimbi would probably be doing everyone a favor killing you.'

53

The meet with Savimbi was set up for the following week in a rural area in the Moxico region in the southeast of the country. Savimbi's headquarters were in a place called Jomba – no relationship to Colonel Jomba – but Kirk told us he was not always there.

'We fly into a landing strip in the jungle,' Cross told me, relaying Kirk's instructions. 'The pilot won't even know the precise location until we're in the region. Once there, we'll be transported to another location for the meet.'

We were getting ready to have Gomez drive us to the airfield where we would meet the puddle jumper arranged by Kirk, when Cross gave me the bad news.

'Jomba is here to see you.'

'Oh shit.'

'No shit, José. If Jomba got word of the deal with Savimbi, we can all kiss our asses good-bye.'

Jomba was waiting out by his jeep. I sneaked a look at the hood ornament. I wasn't sure it was the same skull.

He slapped the side of his leg with his swagger stick as we walked.

'I received a call from João Carmona. He tells me you have created a problem in regard to the exchange.'

'He's a liar, there's no problem.'

'Why would he say that if it were not true?'

'Like I said, he's a liar. There's no problem with the deal, there's a disagreement between us over a diamond. He stole a valuable diamond and I'm getting it back in the exchange. That's all there is to it.'

He stopped and faced me, giving me that horrible grin. His tattooed horns glowed. 'Your troubles with Carmona must not interfere with the arrangements that have been made. I will be most unhappy if they do. Do you understand that?'

'I understand that we have a business arrangement. If João fucks it up, go after João.'

He tapped my chest with his swagger stick. 'If João fucks it up . . .'

I pushed the stick away. 'I don't perform well when I'm being threatened. Look, we're in a deal together, we all need each other. Coming over here and stepping on my tail won't help either of us.'

I swear those goddamn horns turned purple. I was sure that the big bastard was going to kill me on the spot. But I was gambling that getting the arms deal through would be more important to him than stomping a bug like me.

He looked at the mine and back to me. 'Understand this, senhor. I don't care what you do with Carmona, you can kill him if you like. But if you do anything to harm my arrangement for the weapons, I will not just destroy your mine, I will take you down below, into a dark tunnel, and give you such pain that even your soul will cry. Do you understand me, senhor?'

'Understood.'

Cross was waiting for me at the mine entrance when I finished with Jomba. He snicked ash from his cigar and examined the burning end before looking up and shaking his head.

'What is it you don't understand about pissing off that devil? I could see from his body language that Jomba was teetering on the edge of getting himself a new hood ornament.'

'Only the fact that I'm instrumental in getting him weapons kept him from squeezing my head till my eyes popped out. Why kill one man for a little personal satisfaction when he can get an infusion of guns and kill thousands?'

'Jomba doesn't have to kill me,' Cross said. 'Everytime he shows up, I lose a few years off my life. Pretty soon I'll die of old age.'

We flew over five hundred miles of equatorial Africa, mostly above the great plateau that occupies much of the east and south of the country once you get away from the coast. Kirk wasn't with us. 'He says he can't afford to lose his legs, too,' Cross said.

We landed on a stretch of dirt road where a Hummer and a jeep were waiting. It was an area more like a savanna, not as thick and lush as the rain forests closer to the equator, but still humid and thickly wooded.

'Put these on,' the pilot told us. He handed us cloth masks that were similar to Halloween items.

'Why are we wearing masks?' I asked.

'Orders. Don't take them off until you are told. Don't talk to the soldiers or anyone else until you see Savimbi. They speak to you, just make short replies.'

As we walked toward the vehicles, I took a guess about the masks.

'Kirk wants to make sure that we aren't identified,' I said. 'Jomba may have spies at headquarters. Two American visitors would raise talk.'

The soldiers waiting for us must have had orders to keep their mouths shut, too, because other than a '*Boa-tarde*,' no other conversation ensued between us. The driver and guy riding shotgun in the Hummer chatted away to each other in a Bantu tongue while Cross and I sat in back and looked at the scenery. I expected that it would be a short drive to Savimbi's headquarters, but I didn't get my expects. We traveled for an hour on the narrow dirt road and then left it for a grassland hardly scratched by wheeled vehicles.

'From what Kirk told me,' Cross said, 'Savimbi doesn't hang around one place too long. He figures the government could settle their political differences with a little carpet bombing if they know where he's staying.'

It was turning dark when the Hummer entered a small village. In the thick foliage surrounding the village, I saw military vehicles and scattered encampments of soldiers.

The Hummer pulled up to the headman's house and we got out. A full-sized poster of Savimbi wearing a beret with general's stars and wearing military fatigues was on the wall of the hut. The picture showed people cheering him while he shook his clenched fist at the world.

We were greeted by an officer wearing a UNITA uniform. 'Follow me,' he said in Portuguese.

We stepped into the house and the door was shut behind us.

'You can take off your masks now.'

The room was lit with temporary lighting hanging from the ceiling. The hum of a generator could be heard coming from behind the house. A table was set for two.

'Please,' the officer, a major, gestured at the two chairs. 'Our leader will be here shortly. He asks that you enjoy a meal in the meantime. Wine or beer?'

We both took beer. Wine would be iffy in the backcountry. The beer turned out to be cold. 'That generator must keep a refrigerator going, too,' I told Cross.

Once we had eaten, the same officer reappeared and offered cigars and brandy. Moments later, Jonas Savimbi entered, accompanied by the major. He was a powerfully built man, in his late fifties, with tight, short-cropped hair. Unlike the poster, he did not have a full beard – his cheeks were beardless. He still maintained facial hair in a circle around his mouth and down to his chin.

I expected to see him in a military uniform, but he had on a leisure suit and a shirt unbuttoned at the neck.

My first impression of him was a man full of energy. His eyes, body language, handshake, all conveyed a sense of powerful dynamism. Far from nervous energy, there was sense of deliberation about him. He was charismatic. Unlike the politicians back home who buy their way into high office with promises and deals, this man had stirred the hearts of millions of people with his rhetoric – and went into the bush with gun in hand to fight for . . . his beliefs? Naked power?

I looked into his dark cold eyes as I smiled and shook hands, reminding myself that this was also a man who burned people at the stake.

He got quickly down to business. His Portuguese was better than mine.

'Why did you set up this meeting?'

I cleared my throat. 'I've got myself into a bind. I own a diamond mine in Colonel Jomba's area.'

'I'm the colonel's superior officer.'

'Yes, that's why we're here.' I took a breath and let it all hang out. 'Something's up, I'm not sure of all the ramifications. Jomba has worked out a deal with a diamond trader in Lisbon named João Carmona. And an arms dealer in Istanbul who calls himself "the Bey." Diamonds from somewhere else, I suspect Sierra Leone, are being brought in. My job is to certify the diamonds as Angolan, so they don't have a blood-diamond taint.'

I paused and glanced at Cross. He swished brandy in his glass and shrugged.

'Go ahead, put the other foot in your mouth,' he said.

'I think that Jomba's planning a coup.'

Savimbi exchanged looks with the major. Neither revealed any emotion.

'Why do you believe Jomba is plotting against me?'

'That's the way we've sized it up. I was told by João's wife that Jomba plans to take over UNITA once he gets his hands on the weapons.'

Savimbi nodded. 'And what did Jomba tell you?'

'Nothing. He just looks at me like he's sizing me for a coffin.'

Savimbi chuckled. 'I doubt it. He usually doesn't leave a large enough piece to bury.' He leaned back in his chair and folded his hands on his chest. 'And, senhor, please tell me why you have come to me with this information, rather than simply going along with the arrangements.'

'I don't get along with João Carmona. There is bad blood between us, going back to the time when my father lived in Lisbon and did business with him. He stole a gem from my father, a family heirloom,' I lied, 'and I want it back. It's part of the deal between João and the Bey.

'Look, let me get down to the bottom line. In a nutshell, I get along fine with the Bey. He'll deliver the weapons, I'll take care of the diamond end of the exchange. We have no problems. But I'm afraid Carmona will have me murdered, for my share of the deal.'

Savimbi smiled. His face revealed nothing, but I thought I caught a hint of amusement in his eyes.

'Your assessment of Senhor Carmona is no doubt an accurate one. I once had the opportunity of applying ultimate justice to him. I let him live, bound to a wheelchair, because it suited my purpose.'

'I suspect the world would be a better place without him,' I said.

'What is the status of your mine?' he asked. 'I understand it is a losing entity.'

I hesitated. I didn't want to open any cans of worms by telling him we were prospecting for a kimberlite pipe. But my instincts told me not to lie to the man. 'The mine is bleeding money. But I'm pursuing a positive geological report that says there are diamond indicators on the property. If we tap into a pipe, it will increase the payments to UNITA.'

'What do you want out of the transaction you say is coming down between Jomba and the others? Carmona's share?'

'Nothing, I don't even want the share promised me. I want nothing to do with Carmona. I'll never see the share anyway; Carmona will have something up his sleeve to cheat me out of it. I think he was involved in the death of my uncle in New York and creating a serious financial hardship for me. I don't want anything to do with him. I want the gem he stole from my father and to be left alone so I can get my mine to start turning a profit.' I didn't volunteer the fact that the Heart of the World was immensely valuable. It would be like waving a hunk of raw meat to a lion.

Savimbi stood up. 'My advice to you is to go back to your mine and act as if nothing has changed.'

'What about Jomba and the blood-diamond deal?'

'You have managed to get yourself entangled with very dangerous people, several of them, Carmona, the Bey, Jomba. I suggest you don't let any of them know that you've spoken to me. And that you play the part you have agreed to.'

'But what—'

Savimbi turned and walked out.

The major indicated two bunks. 'You will stay here tonight and be driven back to the airplane in the morning.'

After he left, Cross and I stared at each other.

'What the hell,' I said. 'I don't know what just happened, but there's one positive side to it.'

'Yeah, what?'

'We're still breathing.'

54

When we got off the plane at the landing field in diamond country, Gomez, my driver, was waiting for us. So was someone else.

'Jesus H. Christ, she's here,' Cross said.

'She' was Simone. Wearing a safari jacket, boots, and a white shirt, she looked like she had just stepped out of a safari movie. The X-rated kind.

'This is an unpleasant surprise,' I said truthfully.

'I was in the neighborhood and dropped in.' She gave me a kiss on the cheek. She smelled good.

She shook hands with Cross.

'Do I still have a mine?' I asked Gomez. 'Or did this woman sell it while I was away?'

He grinned and shook his head. 'Senhora arrived yesterday. She stayed in your quarters.'

Wonderful. They assumed Simone was my girlfriend. If I had any secrets, she was privy to them now. A goddamn ant couldn't get near the mine without being strip-searched, but they give a beautiful woman the keys to the place.

I rode in the backseat of the Rover with Simone.

'The arrangements have been made for the exchange,' she said. She spoke English so Gomez wouldn't understand her.

'When?' I asked.

'Tomorrow.'

Cross glanced back at me. Tomorrow would be too soon for Savimbi to field troops or however he planned to handle Jomba. I'd have to call Kirk the moment I got back to the mine and hope he could contact Savimbi. From my point of view, it looked like things got worse every time I turned around. Now my life was going to hell in a handbasket.

'How's it supposed to come down?'

'Jomba has prepared a field for the planes to land on. Before they set down, Jomba is to give me the roughs. We'll inventory them on the spot and notify the Bey by satellite phone it's all clear. You're to certify the stones. The Bey will be along with the shipment. We give him his cut of the stones and your certifications.'

'What happens to you and the rest of the stones? You leave with the Bey?' I asked.

'We don't trust him. I have a chartered plane back at the field.' She padded my arm. 'Don't worry, you can take your cut before I leave.'

'What happens if things don't go well between the Bey and Jomba? Suppose Jomba decides to keep the diamonds and the guns?'

'The Bey is not stupid. He will have a number of men with him. And he'll have the transports rigged to explode if Jomba tries anything.'

I leaned back and closed my eyes, relaxing against the back of the seat. Life was full of surprises. Simone had flown in on her broom. The time schedule for the exchange had gone to hell. And I had found out I could- n't trust my backup.

Cross didn't make any lewd remarks or bother to ask who the woman was waiting at the airfield.

He knew Simone.

Now wasn't that a pisser.

55

The gate guard at the mine ran to the Rover as we pulled up.

'The mine has flooded!'

'*Merda*! Where's Kruger?'

'In the mine, with the foreman, trying to get the pumps to work.'

'Show the senhora to my quarters.' I started for the shaft and his words followed me.

'Colonel Jomba was here earlier. He became very angry when he found out you were not at the mine.'

'You're right,' I told Cross, 'you can't punt when you're not even on the playing field.'

As the elevator went down the shaft, the operator told me that the lift could only go down halfway.

'What do we do? Jump the rest of the way?'

'No, senhor, you climb down the ladder.'

'Don't worry,' Cross said, 'if you break a few bones, it will only reduce the time Jomba needs to pulverize you. Uh, look, bubba, there's nothing I can do to help you. I'm going to check on my people.'

I knew he was lying. He was probably going to knock off a piece with his babe Simone and figure out a way to feed me to Jomba.

I wasn't in a good mood as the lift dropped. I was having a hard time keeping track of the players in the game João had started. The only thing I knew for sure was that they were all on the *other* team.

The reception area at the bottom of the shaft was wet but not knee-deep in water.

'The water is farther in,' a foreman told me, 'but watertight doors are holding back most of it.'

I found Kruger knee-deep in water, banging a wrench at a water pump and cursing it. He looked angry and frustrated enough to use the wrench on me.

'Where the hell did you get this pump? It looks like something Cecil Rhodes would have thrown out in the 1890s.'

'It came with the territory. What happened?'

'Your dynamite crew blew into an underground stream. They're lucky it wasn't a watery grave for them. You're lucky they didn't destroy the whole damn mine. When you said you didn't know anything about mining, you weren't kidding. Did it occur to you that you can't just turn workers loose underground?'

He had more to say, but he was working on the pump and talking to it. I left him and went back topside.

Cross was waiting for me.

'Jomba was here, Simone talked to him.'

'Good. When do I give blood?'

'Tomorrow. People like your pal Bey and Jomba like to catch everyone flat-footed. I don't think it has anything to do with us seeing Savimbi. If it did, Jomba would have been waiting for us and we'd be crying in hell by now. They just want to pull a surprise on everyone. But hey, you know, you have a great attitude. No shit, most guys would be pissing their pants. There's some hairy stuff coming down.'

'I'm crying inside,' I said. 'I want you to take Kruger to Luanda until this thing blows over. We'll come up with an excuse, something we need to check at the mine ministry.'

'You're sending me to the dugout just as the game's starting? No way, José.'

'That's the way it's going to be. I'm more worried about Kruger than I am about this deal.'

'And I'm worried about our deal. Two mil, remember?'

'From the look on your face, you don't think I do. I don't screw people. I told you two million. Whether you're in Luanda, or at the exchange, your deal with me is the same.'

I walked away. Getting him out of range when the exchange came down was just an excuse. I didn't want to have to watch my back for one more knife. When I told him the two million was still on the table for him, I wasn't lying. Unless I found out he had been lying to me.

I knocked on the door to my quarters and let Simone answer it. She had changed into pants and a blouse that didn't expose anything – and hid nothing.

'You're a cunt,' I told her.

Her eyebrows went up. 'Such language to a married woman. If we were in Lisbon, João would have your throat slit for calling me that. I want your apology.'

'You're right, it's no way to talk to any woman. So, okay, you're a fuckin' bitch. And your husband has put more rental mileage on your cunt than a rent-a-car. Did you blow Jomba when you saw him?'

I went to the minibar and poured myself a stiff shot of Eduardo's aged brandy. She followed me, but kept her distance.

'You're in a foul mood.'

'Who the fuck do you people think you're screwing with? Do I strike you as someone who just fell off a lettuce wagon?' I went to her bag and took out her satellite phone. Then I ripped the mine phone out of the wall.

'What do you think you're doing?'

'From now on, think of me as your shadow.' I got in close, too mad to let her sensuous femininity play games with my mind. 'You're going to sit down and tell me exactly what is coming down with Jomba, the Bey, and your dirtbag husband.' I held up the phone. 'Just think of me as your secretary. You get any calls, I'll be sure and monitor them for you.'

She had green eyes, not black, but Shakespeare's description of the Dark Lady, the femme fatale who ran amuck with his emotions, came to mind. The Bard of Avon seemed to be more inexorably attracted to the Dark Lady – and almost fearful of her.

'What are you going to do if I don't cooperate? If I tell Colonel Jomba you're not cooperating?'

Good question. But I had an answer. 'I'm going to tell him that we don't need you and João, that when he's got his guns, he can keep your portion of the diamonds.'

She started laughing hysterically.

'What's the matter with you?'

It took a moment to get her breath back. And she started laughing again. 'I already told him,' she gasped, 'that he can have *your* share.'

56

In the morning, I sent a scowling Cross in a pickup truck to take Kruger to the airfield.

'I feel like I'm being left out,' Cross said. 'I could at least stick around so I can identify your body parts after the colonel gets through with you.'

I took Gomez, my driver, aside.

'Senhora Carmona and I have to go to a meeting,' I told him. 'We'll take the Rover.'

'*Sim*, Senhore.'

'I'll give you a choice,' I said. 'You can drive us or you can stay at the mine.'

'What choice? I am your driver, senhore.'

'There may be trouble. There's going to be a delivery of merchandise to Colonel Jomba. If things don't go right . . .'

I didn't have to draw him a picture. He knew Colonel Jomba and the Angolan war system far better than me.

'No problem, senhore.'

'OK. If I live through this, you get a year's pay.'

That brought a smile to his face.

Simone came out of my quarters dressed in a different safari outfit than the one she wore yesterday, even down to the boots.

'You look like you're on your way to a fashion shoot,' I said.

'Let's hope there won't be shooting of any kind.'

I had slept in the room that Eduardo's girlfriend, Carlotta, had before I canned her. I had to confess I was tempted to sneak back into my own room and climb into bed with Simone. Hell, for all I know, it might have turned out to be my last meal.

She held her hands up, away from her body. 'Aren't you going to search me?'

'No, I trust you.' I laughed about that all the way to the Rover.

When we were settled in the back, she asked, 'Did you plan on telling me about your conversation with the Bey?'

'He just gave me time and place,' I lied. Besides the arrangements for the exchange, I told him I had to have the fire diamond in my hand before I signed a single certification.

We were halfway to the field where the exchange was to take place when the satellite phone rang. It was the Bey.

'Jomba has changed the landing spot,' he said. He gave me the new location. It was a strip of road, ten miles in the opposite direction.

I gave Gomez the new rendezvous.

'Better for landing planes,' Gomez said.

I shook my head and said to Simone, 'These people don't take chances, do they?'

'Not when they're betting their lives. If Savimbi or the government get wind of the exchange, there will be bloodshed. Some of it would be ours.'

We were stopped three times at checkpoints that Jomba's men had set up. We had no paperwork but each time the soldier in charge stared at me carefully and compared my description with that written on a piece of paper.

By the time we neared the stretch of road chosen as the rendezvous point, the area was bristling with rebel troops and weapons. Not just machine guns mounted on jeeps – I saw tanks and rocket launchers in the bushes. It looked like Jomba was ready for an all-out battle. It occurred to me for the first time that the weapons being delivered could affect a war in which an entire country was at stake.

A black helicopter, a military gunship with rockets in its belly, circled overhead.

'The Bey,' I said. He had told me he would personally check out the terrain before letting his planes land. I knew he wasn't just talking about the lay of the land.

As we came into the landing area, I saw Jomba at a command post speaking on a telephone. We headed in that direction, but were stopped by an officer.

'Senhore, follow me, preparations have been made.'

He led Simone and me to a tent which had all four of its sides rolled up so only the top shaded the interior. In the middle of the tent was a table covered with a white cloth, a chair, diamond scale, and battery-operated lamp, as well as gallon buckets with lids.

The officer put a bucket on a table and removed the lid. I kept my face blank, acting as though I saw a bucket full of diamonds every day. They were roughs, of course, uncut, unpolished, but each bucket had more value than most people earned in a lifetime.

The officer pointed at a pile of diamond certification documents. 'Please begin.'

'How much time do I have?'

'One hour.'

I sat down and got started. No matter how you hacked it, twenty million dollars' worth of diamonds was a boatload. It would take days for me to make even a cursory examination of them. And I had an hour.

I shook out a portion of the stones from the bucket onto the table. Determining the size was easy – by eyeballing them I could see that they were all two carats or more. The stones I examined with my loupe were all nearly flawless and the color of most of the stones leaned toward white. There were a number of coloreds, mostly yellow, and even they were good. I was only able to do a random sampling, but I made sure that I examined stones at every level of the bucket. As soon as I had evaluated and weighed one bucket, I went onto the next one.

When the hour was up, the satellite phone rang.

'I'm overhead,' the Bey said.

I stepped out of the tent and waved up at the hovering gunship.

'I could only do a random sampling, but the goods appear to be as represented,' I shouted into the phone.

'Good. Do not let the goods out of your sight. I don't want to get home and find I have cans of rocks. My transports will land momentarily. After Jomba inspects the weapons, I will be given half the diamonds and certifications for them. You and João get the other half.'

'You get your certifications when I get the fire diamond.'

'Of course. Don't worry, Mr Liberte, it is not to my advantage to cheat you – or kill you.'

After I hung up, I saw Simone staring at me.

'You are a fool. João would never let you get away with the red diamond.'

'João's a long ways away.'

The transports came in, three of them, fat prop jets that landed one at a time on the long, narrow strip of dirt road. As each plane landed, army trucks came out of the bushes and lined up by the cargo doors. I had considered Colonel Jomba little more than a cunning gangster in a uniform, but as I watched the operation, it struck me that at the very least he was an efficient military leader. Everything seemed to come off with precise clockwork.

While the planes were still being unloaded, the Bey's chopper touched down a few hundred yards from the tent. The officer who was supervising me received the call to proceed. 'The colonel has authorized the release of the payment.'

Half of the buckets were loaded onto a truck. I signaled Gomez. He brought the Land Rover over and we loaded the rest of the buckets into it.

We drove out to the Bey's chopper. Four of his men were standing by the chopper. They looked as lethal as Jomba's. I was the only one without an army.

The Bey stepped down from the big gunship as we pulled up. He smiled and gave Simone a little bow. 'Senhora.'

She gave him a tight smile back.

Another table with a battery-powered lamp was set up. We watched as another man came out of the chopper, sat down at the table and began to examine stones from the cans.

'I trust you,' the Bey said, 'but we have to make sure the buckets were not switched behind your back.'

He trusted me about as much as I trusted him.

After the diamond examiner finished, he gave the Bey a nod. The Bey held out a small pouch. I took it and felt its contents. It was the fire diamond. I didn't open the pouch. Jomba's men were standing by and I didn't want them to see what I had gotten. I gave the Bey the certifications.

'*Adeus*,' he said, waving as he climbed into the chopper. '*Boa sorte!*'

Good-bye and good luck. My sentiments exactly.

'Let's get the hell out of here,' I told Gomez. Simone and I climbed into the backseat and Gomez got the Rover moving. Jomba was busy getting his weapons. I wanted to be out of sight, out of mind before he thought about other things. And if Savimbi's men arrived, there would be outright warfare.

The change in landing spots could be the death of me, I thought. After I was told by the Bey that the location had changed, I never had a chance to call Kirk and tell him. Simone and Gomez were glued to me. Either one could have tipped off Jomba that I was playing a double hand.

My days were numbered in Angola. They would be numbered period, if I stuck around and Savimbi got his hands on me. Once he found out there was a new location for the exchange, he'd think that I double-crossed him, deliberately misled him.

We hadn't gone more than a couple miles when I saw a familiar-looking pickup truck parked along the road. It was the mine truck which Cross used to take Kruger to the airfield. Cross was standing by it. He must have dropped off Kruger and had come back. Someone tipped him off that the landing point had been changed. It hit me in a flash – the Bey told him. That's why it was so easy to turn over the diamond to me rather than João. No one expected me to keep it.

Gomez started to pull over. 'Keep going,' I yelled.

'Pull over,' Simone said.

'Yes, senhora.'

Yes, senhora?

Something jabbed me in the side. It was a small, black pistol, the kind of automatic my father used to call a 'woman's purse gun.'

'I told you to search me.'

'Gomez, whatever she offered you, I'll double.'

He shook his head as he brought the car up next to where Cross was standing. 'I'm sorry, senhore, but what she offers only a woman can give.'

Cross opened my door.

'Get out,' he said.

I got out. Gomez got out of the driver's side and Simone scooted out behind me. As she climbed out, Cross grabbed her gun hand and twisted it behind her. He took the gun away from her and shoved her away. He put her gun away and pulled out a bigger gun.

'What are you doing?' she asked.

'Get on the ground,' he told her and Gomez, 'facedown.'

When they were both on the ground, he asked me, 'Where are the diamonds?'

I nodded at the back of the Rover.

He opened the back and twisted the lid off a bucket. 'Jesus Joseph Mary.'

It was an awesome sight, buckets of diamonds.

He grinned at me. 'How much are in these cans?'

I shrugged. 'Maybe eight, ten million.'

'Partners?' he asked.

'I told you two million. That's about half of my share. If you take João's, you won't live long enough to enjoy it.'

'I might take that risk.'

'There will be no place on earth where you can hide,' Simone said from the ground.

He ignored her. 'You make the call, bubba. Do we take the whole nine yards? Or theirs, too?'

The 'we' gave me a dose of relief. He was on my side.

'Let's just be rich, not greedy.'

'You got it. You can get up, bitch.'

She got up, howling at Cross with street language that would have even surprised her daughter Jonny.

We suddenly had company. Jeeps pulled up. The first person I saw was Jomba in his jeep with the skull hood ornament.

Then I saw who was sitting beside him and nearly shit my pants.

It was the major, the one who had taken care of us at Savimbi's. Cross picked up on it, too. He looked at me. 'I think we are fucked.'

Jomba and the major got out and walked up to us. Both were grinning. 'You left in a hurry, Senhore Liberte. But you took my diamonds with you. We were on our way to the mine to get them back, but you saved us the trouble. Get the buckets,' he told one of his men.

Simone stepped forward. 'Those diamonds belong to my husband. If you touch them, there will be a telephone call made to Savimbi, telling him that you are plotting against him.'

They both howled with laughter at her. Jomba was slapping the ground with his swagger stick, bent over with laughter.

Cross and I looked at each other again. We both got it. Simone still didn't get it. I grabbed her arm and pulled her back from Jomba. Her mouth would get us both killed.

'Shut up,' I told her.

She wasn't stupid – she shut up.

When the buckets had been transferred, Jomba called over Gomez. I could see the beads of perspiration on the driver's forehead as he walked over to him. Jomba put his arm around Gomez's shoulders and walked him to the side of the road.

He shot him in the head. Gomez's body flew backward, off the road.

Jomba put away his gun and shook his head. 'He was my eyes at the mine, now I will have to replace him. He would not have betrayed me for money, but like all men, he was weak when it came to a woman.'

He tapped his swagger stick against my chest. This time I didn't try to push it away. I expected to die.

'You want the woman dead?' he asked.

'No.' My voice had shook. 'No, I don't.'

'OK. I give you the woman.' He laughed and grabbed his crotch and did a humping motion. 'And Savimbi says you keep your mine. But I get the diamonds.'

Jomba and the major roared with laughter as they returned to their jeep.

My knees were weak. I jumped in behind the wheel of the Rover. Cross started to get in the front passenger seat but changed his mind. 'You ride up front,' he told Simone. 'For all I know, you have a gun up your snatch.'

'That fool Jomba,' she said. 'João will let Savimbi know he's plotting against him. He'll never enjoy what he stole from us.'

'You still don't get it,' I told her. 'The weapons were for Savimbi. Jomba's not working against him, he's working *for* him.'

'What are you talking about?'

'The peace accord between Savimbi and the government is going out the window. Savimbi needs weapons, he has diamonds to buy them with, but he can't buy them openly. He sets up a deal, using Jomba as a front. And he uses Angolan diamonds, ones he's been collecting from the mines for years. There was no need to certify the diamonds, they were all Angolan. It was all a charade in case the government found out. If that happened, Savimbi would claim Jomba was plotting against him.'

We drove directly to the airfield where Simone's charter was waiting. No one spoke during the entire ride. When we got there, she got out without saying a word. Cross and I were halfway back to the mine when he let out a big sigh.

'Fuck, I was rich for a minute. A shitload of diamonds, they were all mine. I had my own island, the Riviera, beautiful women, the whole nine yards, right in my hand. Now all I got to keep me company is pulling my pud.'

'You still have a piece of the mine.'

It was his turn to howl with laughter. 'Yeah, and all the fuckin' muddy water I can drink.'

57

Kruger came back the next day, cursing me for having wasted his time with a trip to Luanda. 'I'm sick of this goddamn bloody country and your goddamn bloody mine. When I get this thing dry, I'm out of here.'

I barely saw Cross for the first couple of days after we got back. Neither one of us wanted to talk about how we lost the Big One. I got enough out of him to understand that I had been the high bidder, otherwise he would have thrown his lot in with Simone. 'I made a deal to help out with the blood-diamond deal before you arrived in Angola,' he alibied. And he was right. He had agreed to screw me *before* he met me. I'm sure screwing a stranger is on a higher moral plane than screwing a friend.

Cross didn't know that I had the Heart of the World. I kept that entirely to myself. When I was alone in my quarters, I pulled out the gem and examined it like a little boy surreptitiously looking at girlie magazines. Jomba didn't know about the diamond either or I would have joined Gomez along the road.

I could feel the power of the gem as I rolled it in my fingers and it sprayed me with fire. Looking at it with a loupe was like staring into the heart of a volcano. None of my possessions – cars, boats, money, women – affected me like the fire diamond.

Giving it some thought, I believed I would kill anyone who tried to take it away.

I finally got together for dinner with Cross three days after we got back. I invited Kruger, too, but he sent a message from down in the mine that I could shove dinner up the same hole he planned to shove my entire mine up.

Dinner was as cheerful as a Baptist's wake. Cross was moody and had too much to drink. And I didn't try to be the life of the party.

'I'm going home,' Cross told me. 'When Kruger goes, I go.'

'You've had it with Angola, too.'

'I thought things were tough in Michigan City, but let me tell you, bubba, my old pals who get recycled in and out of prison are choir boys compared to the bastards running – and ruining – this country.'

The door suddenly burst open and Kruger rushed in. I groaned. He looked like he had just crawled out of a muddy hole, which he had. I had never seen the man smile.

He came up to the table with a muddy chunk of mineral in his hand. I thought for a moment he was going to hit me with it.

'This came out of the goddamn tunnel that flooded.'

'Did it cause the flooding?'

'You are the worst goddamn mine manager I ever saw. You don't know your ass from that hole in the ground out there.'

I sighed. I had brought the poor bastard into a war zone and stuck him a hundred feet below ground for weeks. All on a wildgoose chase. I would-n't blame him if he did hit me with the chunk.

'You know what?' I said. 'Eduardo was right, putting more money into this place is good money after bad. And I'm out of good and bad money. I think we should all bail out and go home.'

'Bail out, my ass. Not after I hit a pipe.'

Cross and I froze. I looked at the chunk of gray-blue earth Kruger was holding.

'You two are so goddamn stupid you don't even know blue earth when you see it. You're one very rich man, Mr Liberte.' His face broke out into a wide grin. 'Damn if we all aren't.'

PART 7

ANTWERP
AND
PARIS

58

The Blue Lady made me rich, but did nothing toward extending my life expectancy as the fragile peace – what Cross called a *bleeding peace* – between Savimbi's guerrillas and the government slowly dissolved.

It took a year to reach the kimberlite pipe of blue earth. When we did, the horn of plenty started flowing.

'We gotta get out of this acreage in hell that passes for a country before we're too dead to enjoy being rich,' Cross told me, after a firefight occurred on our doorstep between conflicting warlords who wanted the same 'rent.'

The only comfort I got in Angola was the fact that it would be harder for João to kill me there. I had done everything but piss on his grave, and I'd do that if I outlived him. One thing I knew from the blood I inherited from my mother: the Portuguese don't forgive and don't forget. And they love a good blood feud, which is how I'd come to think of the fight over the fire diamond.

I knew I'd hear from João again. I just hoped to hell I'd see the knife coming when he shoved it in my back.

'We're leaving,' I told Cross. 'Get us a plane.'

'Where are we going?'

'Antwerp.'

'Where the hell is that?'

'France, Holland, Belgium, hell I don't know, one of those countries, I was never good at geography. All I know is that most of the best diamonds in the world go through there. Bernie and my father had dealt with a diamond merchant at the bourse in Antwerp. I gave him a call the other day and asked him to find me a buyer for the mine. He has an offer.'

'Who the hell would want to buy a diamond mine in a war zone?'

'Bernie did.'

Cross chartered a big executive jet from a French company. When I came aboard, I found out he had rented one with frills. There was champagne, caviar, a master chef, bedroom suites, and four women of easy virtue.

'Four?' I asked Cross.

'Two for me, two for you.' He grinned and blew smoke in my face. 'You wouldn't begrudge a starving man two steaks, would you? Bubba, it's been so long since I've been sucked or fucked, my cock's liable to strike one woman dead, so I need a backup.'

Who the hell was I to begrudge a starving man?

59

I showed the fire diamond to Cross on the plane.

'You smart sonofabitch,' he said. 'Why didn't you tell me?'

'I'm telling you now.'

There was a reception committee waiting for us at the airport in Antwerp. Asher van Franck, my diamond contact at the bourse, came aboard with a customs inspector. He spoke English with a heavy accent. He had arranged for us to clear customs privately because of the value of the fire diamond.

'I have the armed car, additional guards, and even the TV camera crew from CNN you requested. The people with cameras were harder to get than the men with guns.'

Franck was a tall, skinny man, six-six at least. Now over sixty, I imagined that in his youth he could have played basketball in the days when white men still played the game – if anyone played the game in Belgium, which by the way I found out from the plane's cabin crew was where Antwerp was located. The other geography lesson I learned was that the city was the second largest port in Europe despite the fact it was on a river, fifty miles from the North Sea.

Franck's beard, temple locks, and yarmulke advertised the fact that he was an Orthodox Jew, not a surprising cultural statement since historically, most of Antwerp's diamond trade has been under their control.

I introduced Cross to him and noticed that Franck looked askance at the feminine foursome standing by to disembark.

'Don't worry, I'll make sure they wait until the news cameras are gone before they leave the plane,' I reassured him.

'What's all the excitement about?' Cross asked. 'Wouldn't it have been better if we had just snuck into town?'

'Publicity never hurt a diamond. I've got one that belongs in a king's crown. I'm going to play it to the hilt. Hell, let's let the reporters know that a king has made an offer.'

'Which king?' Franck asked.

'It's confidential. So confidential I haven't figured out yet which one it is.'

Cross gave me a look that told me he wasn't happy about the fact I hadn't discussed my plans with him. But he'd made it plain that he'd had it with diamonds and only wanted to see them on a woman's fingers – wrapped around his dick. He jerked his thumb at me. 'When I met this guy, he didn't know his ass from a hole in the ground. Now look at him, Mr Wheeler Dealer.'

Poor Franck. He looked a bit distressed. I don't think several decades of working with Bernie and my father had prepared him for the entourage I'd arrived with.

I still hadn't decided what I was going to do when I grew up. If the sale of the mine went through, I'd walk away from the Blue Lady with over forty million dollars in my pocket. And one of the most valuable diamonds in the world – one that wasn't for sale. The fire diamond was a link to my father.

I wasn't the same person anymore. Angola had changed me. I didn't know what had happened to me in that ravaged land. Maybe working for a living changed a person. I was more thrilled about keeping the mine alive and functioning than I was about the payday. And now that I had my blood warmed up, I wasn't sure I was ready to walk away and go back to being the irrelevant, irresponsible ass Marni believed me to be. Not that she was wrong or that I wanted to change for that reason. Mostly I liked the sense of accomplishment. It brought meaning to my life. My father and mother would have been proud of the way I had run the mine and made it a winner. That meant more to me than the money or anyone else's opinion.

'The diamond's in this briefcase,' I told the lead security man when he boarded, speaking to him in French. Franck translated my statement into something that sounded a little like French, but the security man understood me. 'I want your automatic weapons at the ready when you take it down the steps and put the diamond in the armored car.'

'We do not have a security problem, your diamond is safe here in Antwerp,' he said.

'I don't care about security problems. I want the transportation of it dramatic enough so it makes the evening news and tomorrow's papers. You don't have to point your guns at the news people, just make sure they know you're ready to start spraying lead.'

When we were secure in the limo and on our way to the hotel, Franck told me about the arrangements he'd made at the Antwerp bourse. A bourse was the French term for a diamond exchange.

'Your fire diamond is the talk of the bourse. I deliberately limited the invitations to the reception where the diamond will be on display. People are scrambling for invitations like it was a royal wedding. It will shoot up your asking price.'

'I'm not ready to sell the diamond.'

Franck raised his eyebrows. 'Really? Then why all the promotion and showmanship? I heard you had an offer from that American computer tycoon, the one that people claim is the richest man in the world.'

'Yeah, if it's not for sale, why all the hoopla?' Cross asked.

'I'm thinking about going into the diamond business. The Heart of the World would be the centerpiece of the business.' I hadn't told Cross about what I wanted to do.

'But you've been in the diamond business all your life,' Franck said. 'You were born into it.'

'It's been in my blood, but not my mind. I'm considering reviving House of Liberte, perhaps even extending it into retail.' Franck looked at me as if I'd just told him I wanted to start a snake farm.

'Retail? That is a whole different world than anything your father or myself were ever involved in. Cartier, Tiffany, Winston, Bvlgari, they are years – centuries – ahead of the competition. I can understand it if you want to become a sight holder—'

'I'm not going to become a sight holder, I don't like the restrictions.' I didn't tell him, but it was too much like being in business. Diamonds can be exciting, but negotiating, wheeling and dealing, really wasn't for me. What I wanted to do was build something, as I had done with the mine. Being like Leo, spending my day with a phone glued to my ear buying and selling had less appeal to me than running that snake farm.

'You may not like the restrictions of being a De Beers sight holder, but it would be a route for you to get into the diamond trade in a big way. As the owner of a diamond mine and someone who possesses one of the great diamonds in the world, you would have no problem getting an invitation to join.'

I knew the sight-holder routine. Sight holders were the only people permitted to attend the ten sights – sales – of diamonds held by De Beers. A large percentage of the world's diamonds passed through those ten sales De Beers held in London yearly. From there, most of them came to Antwerp to be cut, although Israel and New York did some cutting. India cut more diamonds than anyone, up to 80 or 90 percent, but most of their output was smalls and sand.

There were only a limited number of sight holders, around a hundred and forty or fifty. With thousands of diamond merchants in the world, to be one of the few who were privileged to buy from De Beers was prestigious. And profitable. Leo would have given his left nut to be a sight holder. But it wasn't for me. It was too much the same-old, same-old every day. And there were rules you had to follow. Like joining the army, it was regimented – and I wasn't good at saluting. Besides, I had my father's maverick attitude about De Beers and its stranglehold on the world diamond trade. I wanted to carve out my own empire and not be under the thumb of Big Brother.

'I'm not going to be a sight holder and I'm not going to buy exclusively from De Beers' people. I want to take on De Beers.'

'Jesus,' Cross whistled, 'you're fuckin' nuts.'

Franck turned coronary purple. 'You are talking about a company that owns or controls most of the diamonds in the world. Taking them on, as you put it, would be equivalent to a bicycle rider racing a Ferrari.'

'You see them as king of the road, I see them as fat and vulnerable. They can't even do business in America because they're a monopoly.'

'They still control most of America's diamond trade. They may not sell any diamonds inside the country, but the diamonds that are brought in and sold are mostly from De Beers controlled stock.'

'How you plan to do this?' Cross asked.

'I'm not sure yet, but I know that if you're going to grab a big piece of the diamond business, you don't go after little guys – and you don't fall into line and take orders from De Beers. De Beers has the business – billions of it. I want a chunk of it.'

'How is De Beers able to control the world diamond industry?' Cross asked Franck. 'There are other outfits mining out there.'

'Bottom line, they control the world price by controlling production and distribution.'

'They don't control Win's mine. We sell those diamonds without getting De Beers' permission.'

'True,' Franck said, 'you can buy and sell diamonds everywhere in the world without De Beers' permission, but you are literally doing so *on their terms.*'

'Come again?' Cross said.

'Diamonds are a commodity, particularly on the wholesale level. Like corn or wheat or petrol, wholesalers pay essentially the same price for the same quantity and quality of diamonds. They are mined and graded and valued the same everywhere in the world. Every hundred years someone may come up with a unique diamond, a huge stone or the rare ruby diamond that Win possesses, but otherwise rough diamonds of the same quality are indistinguishable from each other, like ears of corn or stalks of wheat. They may be a fashion item once they are cut and placed in unique settings, but unlike the clothes a woman wears, the reasonable price of a diamond is not based upon who is selling it or how fancy the setting is but on the diamond's size and quality.

'At the wholesale level, since they are indistinguishable, a diamond of the same size and clarity sells for the same price as millions of other diamonds of the same quality. Diamonds from Africa sell for exactly the same price as those mined in Russia, Canada, or on the moon. Because diamonds are a commodity, like pork bellies and cotton, the prices for them are very much subject to the vagaries of supply and demand. When there is a bumper crop, literally all diamonds of the same size and quality go down in value. When supply is low, they all rise in value. You cannot avoid the whims of the marketplace because your diamonds are better than someone else's.'

'And that's how De Beers controls the market,' I said. 'They can manipulate the supply and demand.' My comment was directed to Cross.

'Exactly,' Franck said. 'Let's assume that House of Liberte wanted to compete with them. De Beers has vast resources, it is a multibillion-dollar company. It can reduce the supply of diamonds on the market, increasing the price per carat that House of Liberte has to pay for its diamonds.'

'And,' I said, 'once I pay top price, they can flood the market with stones, bringing the price per carat crashing down, leaving me holding the bag – literally.'

Cross shook his head. 'They have that much control?'

Franck said, 'They have that much control. Not that they use it in that manner. We are talking about a hypothetical situation. Let's say House of Liberte challenges them for control of part of the world's wholesale diamond market. Manipulating supply and demand would be a powerful weapon in their arsenal during the battle.'

Cross nudged me. 'Maybe you'd be better off cornering the market in pork bellies, bubba. You can at least eat 'em if you're stuck with 'em.'

I shrugged. 'Who knows? Maybe I'll go to Russia. They have diamond mines there that aren't controlled by De Beers.'

Franck shook his head. 'My friend, if you thought it was dangerous in Angola, you would find it even more so in Russia. Angola is a young country, populated by unsophisticated people who do not know how to handle the natural resources and governmental responsibilities thrust upon them suddenly. Russia is an old country that, over the centuries, has perfected greed and murder into a fine art.'

60

The next day I walked with Franck down Hoveniersstraat in central Antwerp. Like the exchange in New York, the Antwerp bourse was nondescript. Falling between three or four narrow streets, there was no glamour, no glitter, nothing really to distinguish the area from other downtown areas.

'It's difficult to conceive that most of the diamonds in the world, perhaps as many as nine out of ten, have passed through Antwerp,' I said.

'Yes, but we have been cutting diamonds for over five hundred years, before America was discovered – and plundered. New York, Hong Kong, Taiwan, Thailand, the Ramat Gen outside Tel Aviv, the vast output of Mumbai and Surat in India have all nibbled at the pie, but Antwerp is still queen of the diamond ladies.'

We were on our way to a meeting with the broker who had a buyer for the Blue Lady. I had assumed the broker would be an Orthodox Jew like Franck, since they controlled the Antwerp industry. But that wasn't the case.

'You are going to meet the Prince of the Sinjorens,' Franck said. 'Sinjoren is an expression dating back to the time when Antwerp was part of the far-flung Spanish empire. The aristocracy in the city came to be called Sinjorens, a word derived from the Spanish word *señores*. The men of the old families of the city with money are still called Sinjorens today. Maurice Verhaeven has the oldest blood and thickest wallet. Surprisingly, he has made much of his money himself, having inherited little beyond his lineage and patrician nose.'

'You said you couldn't use a Jew to broker the mine. I assume that means the buyer is Arab.'

'Yes, yes, you assume correctly.' He glanced sideways at me. 'An astute observation. I spread the word in the exchange that you were interested in selling, but there were no takers because of the situation in Angola. I also let Verhaeven know because he has contacts in Eastern Europe, Russia, and the Middle East. I do not know who the buyer is, but I suspect that he is either a Russian or an Arab. Those are the only two nationalities with the kind of money it takes to buy a diamond mine. Verhaeven has brokered many diamond deals between Arab and Jew, so it would not surprise me if he turns out to be an Arab.'

The meeting took place in an office in the Beus voor Diamanthandel, the diamond club called 'the casino.'

Franck paused as we entered the building. 'I have to give you a word of advice about Verhaeven. Be cautious. I recall an expression in your country about dealing with a sharp negotiator, some thing about counting your fingers after shaking hands with the person. The same is true about

Verhaeven. But in Antwerp you would count your hands.'

He chuckled and explained as we walked. 'Antwerp has a legendary giant named Antigon. Antigon guarded our Scheldt River in the days of old and demanded a toll from all boats that went up or down it. If the captain failed to pay the fee, Antigon chopped one of the captain's hands off. That is how the city came to be called "Antwerp". It means something like a taking or throwing of a hand.'

It occurred to me Antigon the giant would have done even better if he'd packed his bags and moved to Angola or Sierra Leone. Savimbi and his ilk could have taught him a few things about collecting tolls.

Verhaeven did have a patrician nose. And he looked down its slope to the rest of the world. He carried off the role as Prince of Sinjorens with real flair. He wore a gray silk suit, light blue shirt with a white collar, yellow tie, and dark brown wing-tip brogues. He looked like he'd stepped off the set of a 1940s movie. His handshake was warm, his eyes piercing, his French perfect.

I liked him immediately. But I could see why Franck warned me. There were two ways of selling in this world: the soft sell and the hard sell. Verhaeven was definitely from the soft-sale school. I got his measure immediately because my own father was from that same school.

'I have a buyer,' he said. 'At a price which Franck indicated you would accept.'

'I told Franck to consider it a fire sale. I need money for something else. What are the terms?' I asked.

'Cash.'

I grinned. 'That's a term I never argue with. Who's the buyer?'

He coughed gently into his handkerchief.

'Naturally, the terms will include your commission and Franck's,' I said.

'Thank you. The buyer is Arab, Saudi. Have you heard of the bin Laden family?'

I shook my head. 'No.'

'A very prominent family in Saudi Arabia, which means they have ties to the royal family, as most prominent families are related to the royal family. I believe the moneymaker was an illiterate camel merchant who built a difficult road for a prior king and went on to become the major building contractor of the oilrich kingdom. One of his many sons, Osama, is the purchaser. He knows what he is getting into, everyone knows the situation in Angola and he would be especially sensitive to the chaos. I understand he spent some time in Afghanistan fighting the Russians.'

I didn't know why a rich Arab would want a diamond mine in a war zone and didn't really care.

'How fast can we wrap up the deal?'

'Very fast. Arrangements are already in progress for transfer of the purchase money. So is the legal documentation. There might be one problem. If the Angolan government has to approve the sale—'

I shook my head. 'Not a problem, everything in Angola has a price and can be obtained quickly if the payment is kicked up a couple notches. I thought of that before I left Luanda. I have the permit for selling the mine back at the hotel. I'll send it over. We just need to fill in the buyer's name.'

'I'm certain there'll be a corporate entity taking ownership,' Verhaeven said. 'I'll find out and give you the information.'

We went over other details, the most important one being the transfer of money. Things were going amazingly well considering that I was selling a problem in a war zone.

Verhaeven sipped wine and wiped his mouth delicately with his napkin. 'In regard to your ruby diamond—'

'It's not for sale.'

'I could get you a very substantial price.'

'I've decided to keep it. I'll see you at the reception.'

On the way back to the hotel, I said to Franck, 'I understand there's some painter that Antwerp's particularly famous for, a guy named Rubens.'

He smiled. 'Yes, there was a Flemish "guy" named Rubens who painted.'

'Buy me one of his paintings.'

He stopped and stared at me. 'Just like that, buy you a painting? Did you have a particular one in mind? A particular stage of his art—'

'Just get me a painting with Rubens's name on it.'

'I see. Something with Rubens's name on it,' he muttered. 'Do you know what it would cost to have something with Rubens's name on it?'

'I don't care what it costs. It's business. I'm going back to America with a world-class diamond. A world-class painting would look good beside it. Americans are snobs, especially for old European stuff.'

We parted at the hotel, with Franck still muttering to himself.

61

The driveway outside the hotel where the reception for the fire diamond took place looked like the lineup for Cannes or the Academy Awards. Limos pulled up and deposited well-dressed bodies, some of them women with almost more jewelry than clothing. A crowd had gathered, cameras were rolling.

Inside, Franck looked high enough to have been sampling some of the Ecstasy neighboring Amsterdam was famous for producing.

'It's the social event of the year,' he said, rubbing his hands. 'The social event of the century.'

He introduced me to a young Flemish artist, a friend of his daughter's who had planned the reception and had salted it with European film personalities. 'Hugo's worked on Dutch and German films as an art director,' Franck said. 'He's also an interior designer. Does sensational work. You said you wanted a Hollywood flair, Hugo is the closest we get to Tinsel Town in Antwerp.'

Franck almost giggled as he made the introduction. 'Mr Liberte told me today to buy him a Rubens. As if he were asking to purchase the newest brand of car.'

I stood with Hugo in front of the centerpiece he had designed to house the fire diamond when it arrived. It was a crystal bowl full of what appeared to be 'diamond ice,' pieces of clear crystal that glittered.

'I had not seen the diamond except for a picture you sent Asher, so I designed a centerpiece which I thought would best display its features.'

'I like your design.'

'When the red diamond is placed in the bowl,' he said, 'it will stand out very strikingly. Underneath,' he pointed at the bottom of the bowl, 'hidden in the podium, is a powerful beam of light that I'll turn on after the diamond is set in the bowl. That will send the light from the crystals and the red diamond up to the revolving ball, which in turn will spray it around the room.'

The Heart of the World was a small object, about the size of a walnut. It was hard to appreciate something that small, even if it was a diamond. I liked Hugo's design of spreading the diamond's red glitter all around the room, giving the stone a powerful impact on the assembly.

'Watch yourself,' Hugo whispered, 'the two women heading this way are both aspiring actresses. They read in the tabloids you're the former boyfriend of Katarina Benes.'

Cross came over and grinned salaciously at the women surrounding me. 'Owning a diamond mine is guaranteed to turn up the lust in the coldest women on earth.'

I heard my name and turned around to a surprise.

Leo – prick, dick, shithead, evil stepbrother Leo – grinned at me. He gave me a big hug.

'Win, I can't tell you how thrilled the family is about your success.'

He patted me on the shoulder.

'My brother's success is my success, that's what I tell people around the bourse in New York. Remember how Dad called it the bourse, but then, he was really French, wasn't he?'

My brother? This dickhead was calling me his brother in public?

Dad? This prick was calling my father 'Dad'?

The family is proud of me? I felt like asking him if that was the same family who couldn't remember my name when they found out I was broke.

This was the first I'd heard or seen of the bastard since I left New York for Lisbon and Angola.

'What are you doing in town, Leo?'

'Came over to visit my money in Switzerland.' He gave me a big wink. I recognized the wink. It was the same one he and Bernie used when mentioning secret Swiss bank accounts. Leo made a couple trips a year to Switzerland, taking over cash and stashing it out of sight of the tax man. Diamond and narcotic dealers shared a common affinity for cash transactions.

'Actually, I moved the account to Luxembourg – better interest. And you know, the IRS is always snooping around the Swiss, especially with all the Nazi gold scandals. I didn't know you were in Antwerp until I spoke with Franck's secretary this afternoon.'

After introducing him to Cross, I asked, 'Making a buy in Antwerp?'

'You know it. The usual delivery plan.' He grinned.

Ah, yes, the old hollow shoe-heel delivery plan. I remembered that was how Leo got his buys past customs, through a cavity in the heels of his shoes. The guy had cheating customs and the IRS down to a science.

'We brought a truckload of flawless roughs in from the mine,' I told Leo. 'Internally flawless D's, all three carats or more.'

'Well, maybe we should talk—'

'No talk, no bargaining.' I put my arm around his shoulders and squeezed. 'You're family, guy. I want you to have as many as you can fit in your shoes. I'll tell Franck to give them to you at half market price.'

Leo almost swooned in my arms. It took me another five minutes to unglue him from me.

After he was gone, Cross gave me a funny look.

'What's with you? Isn't that the stepbrother you've always hated?'

'It's butt-fuck time.'

'Man, you can butt-fuck me like that anytime. That guy's gonna make a bundle off of those diamonds you gave him for cheap.'

'He's going to need it,' I said, grimly.

The arrival of the armored car stopped the chatter in the room. A representative of the armored car company brought in the briefcase. I had to smother a grin at the sight of the guards carrying their weapons as if they were under attack.

The representative followed me into an adjoining room where I took the briefcase and excused him. Alone in the room, I opened the briefcase and took out the pouch.

It was empty.

I took another pouch from a secret pocket in my coat and shook out the Heart of the World. I hadn't even told Cross about my deception.

I figured with all the attention focused on guards and the armored car, no one would think they were carrying around an empty briefcase and that I actually had the diamond on me. It wasn't really something I dreamt up – valuable shipments of diamonds were made around the world in packages marked as other items.

Hugo was a genius. When the Heart of the World was placed in the glittering bowl and hit with the beam of light, the diamond looked like the heart of a volcano.

I was listening to the 'ah's' and 'ooh's' when a waiter stuck a portable telephone in my hand. 'Sorry, sir, but the caller said it was urgent.'

'How are you, Win? I've missed you.'

There was a snake in every paradise.

'The only thing you missed was putting a slug in my heart, Simone. I hope you called to tell me that João has died and gone to hell.'

'We're your family, Win. João and your father were like brothers, you shouldn't talk like that about family,' Simone said.

'You're a murderous, double-crossing, thieving, fucking bitch. What do you want?'

'You know what we want. You're displaying João's fire diamond and we didn't even get an invitation. We have to watch the reception on CNN.'

'Let's not play games, Simone. João stole the diamond from my father. Even if I decided to let bygones be bygones and pay João a few bucks to smooth the pain of loss, after you fucked me over in Angola I'm not willing to give you shit.'

'You don't understand, Win. It's not about money. João loves that diamond more than anything, more than me. Now it's about blood. Your blood.'

62

JFK, New York City

Leo flew first-class. He had no idea what it cost Win to get him upgraded from the super-saver fare that he always used, but he'd tell Win not to do it again. It was a waste. He'd rather Win just gave him the money instead. He heard about a guy, one of the biggest dealers at the New York diamond exchange, who always flew coach and donated the difference between a first-class ticket and his cheap ticket to charity.

That kind of mentality Leo couldn't understand.

But as long as he was in first-class, he scarfed up the champagne and hors d'oeuvres. The food was served on china rather than the plastic-wrap crap they gave you in coach and the utensils were silver.

Real class, he thought.

He put a knife, fork, and spoon in his briefcase, along with a bottle of wine and champagne. Also in his briefcase were statements from his Swiss account and new Luxembourg account. He'd saved over a million dollars in taxes the last five years by going offshore with many of his business transactions. He'd conduct the sale in New York and have the other party wire his offshore account from their offshore account. He cheated, they cheated, and everyone was happy. And what the IRS didn't know wouldn't hurt him.

The heels of his shoes were packed with the diamonds Win sold him at half of market price, literally giving them to him. He always considered Win to be an arrogant prick, but Leo put a price on everything and as far as he was concerned, Win was now family.

He stuck another bottle of champagne in his briefcase.

Life was good.

He handed over his customs declaration at passport control.

'Nothing to declare today, sir?'

'No, had to attend a wedding in Paris.'

That's how he always travelled, flying in and out of Paris rather than Antwerp or Switzerland. When the customs people saw the diamond capital or the name of the world's money capital on the declarations, they literally strip-searched and body-cavity searched you. But nobody went to Paris on business.

He was passing through the customs area exiting to the concourse when he was stopped by two men.

'Agent Wilson, Customs,' the man said, flashing a badge. 'This is Agent Bernstein, IRS.'

'Wha-what do you want?'

'We'll start with your briefcase. And your shoes.' Wilson grinned. 'After that, things will get interesting if we have to bring out the extractors.'

Leo gaped at them.

'How – how did—'

'A little birdie told us.'

63

Paris

I pulled the same stunt at Orly airport in Paris that I had in Antwerp, having an armored car pick up an empty briefcase with cameras rolling, while I carried the diamond in my pocket.

The Heart of the World's reputation followed it from Antwerp, attracting much more news coverage. A public-relations person hired by Franck met the plane and handled the news briefing, handing out a videotape that showed the diamond in the spectacular setting at the reception.

I parted with Cross in the airport. He took a taxi to Charles de Gaulle to catch a flight back to the States. 'I'm not going back to Indiana, there's nothing there for me. My sister's living in L.A. and she says it never freezes and hardly even rains. I'm going to camp out on the beach with a beer and a babe. Make that *babes*.'

I wished him luck and told him to keep in touch.

A limo driver was waiting for me after I cleared customs.

'*Bonjour, monsieur,*' the driver said.

'My cousin's supposed to be here,' I said.

'I'm sorry, *monsieur*, there was some confusion and my dispatcher failed to tell me to pick her up. We will be picking her up on the way.'

There was something odd about the limo driver's coat – it didn't fit his muscular arms and shoulders, nor his paunch. He had a southern European look, dark eyed and dark complexioned, and a heavy accent to his rough French. I wasn't sure where it came from, something European, but I was lucky I understood his French – most of the time I hit Paris the taxi drivers were of Southeast Asian ancestry and something always got lost in the translation when I tried to communicate.

I climbed in the passenger compartment. A bucket with champagne was waiting for me. I grabbed one of the newspapers that the limo came stocked with, scanning it quickly to see if there were any stories about the diamond. My French was pretty good, much better than what I heard from the limo driver. During my teens, I sometimes stayed with my Parisian relatives, people designated as 'cousins' although their familial relationship was only vaguely defined.

The family was in the jewelry business and I'd arranged for them to introduce me around and prepare the invitation list for the gala reception that I was planning. I hadn't seen Yvonne, the cousin who had planned to meet me at the airport, in years. I remembered her as a serious young woman who worked hard at the family business in the St. Cloud district. She had recently taken over management of the firm when her father retired.

I grabbed the champagne bottle and started unwrapping its head when the limo suddenly pulled over to the curb where a man was waiting. My curbside door opened and a man got in.

'What the—'

He had a gun and a bad temperament.

'Shut your fuckin' mouth.'

He spoke Portuguese. I now realized the source of the accent that underlined the driver's French.

'João sends greetings.'

'I don't have the diamond.'

I was scared shitless. The guy's gun hand was shaking bad. He wasn't scared. His dull eyes and tight facial muscles had the look of someone who smoked too much crack.

He hit me in the face with the gun.

'Listen carefully, *amigo*, and you might live. We're going someplace where there's a telephone. You're going to arrange to have the diamond delivered to us. If you make a mistake with the phone call, I'm going to cut off your nose. If whoever you call makes a mistake, I'm going to cut off a piece of you for every hour that we're delayed, starting with your balls. *Entendez?*'

Yeah, I understood. My brilliant fucking plan to divert attention away from me with the armored car routine left me exposed. I should have been in the fucking armored car with the diamond I had in my pocket. As soon as these street trash found the diamond on me, or I turned it over when they started to cut off my nose, they'd kill me.

'Stop thinking.'

I wasn't thinking, I was sky-high with adrenaline from *panicking*. The fucker raised the gun and slammed it down on my knee. I yelped and bent over with pain. When I uncoiled, I pushed aside his gun hand and came around, swinging the champagne bottle. It hit him in the face, across the nose, splattering me and the interior with blood.

His head snapped back and the dull light in his eyes went completely dark.

The driver hit the brakes and twisted around with a gun in his hand as I turned to him. I ducked down. My hand reached the door and I pulled the handle, hitting the door with my head and shoulder, flying out face-first, landing on the pavement in a belly and elbow flop. I bounced on the asphalt and rolled, arms and legs flying.

When I stopped rolling, I lay dazed, my head spinning, ears ringing. I got onto my knees. I felt no pain – my body was numb from shock. The sound of tires screeching spiked my adrenaline – *I'm going to be run over.*

There were plenty of cars on the freeway but I was on an overpass, in the shoulder of the road – no cars were coming at me. A car engine revved and burned rubber behind me. I jerked around. The limo – the sono-fabitch was coming back at me. I got to my feet and dove for the railing, bellying over it, facing a thirty or forty foot drop down to the freeway below. With no place to go, I hung on with both hands as the limo backed up, scraping against the side of the railing. As it pulled up to where I was, a bloody face with his nose flattened appeared in the side window.

The guy was trying to get the door open but the car was too close against the railing. Screaming at me, he brought up the gun and started firing. I ducked down, still hanging on as the window exploded. My head was still spinning and my ears were filled with a fuzzy siren.

I looked up as the gunman knocked glass away and stuck the gun out, pointing it at me. The limo suddenly lurched away from the wall and the gunman disappeared from sight as the limo moved into traffic and then swerved violently to avoid a collision. It was about fifty feet from me when it hit the railing again with its front passenger-side fender then bounced off and headed down the freeway.

A couple seconds passed before I realized that what I heard was an actual siren. The limo driver must have heard it, too.

But it wasn't a police car. An ambulance sped by, the paramedic in the front passenger seat staring at me as I clutched onto the railing.

64

'Very, very smart,' my French cousin, Yvonne, told me. 'That's exactly what you should do when you're kidnapped, fight back immediately.' She spoke faster than a speeding bullet and my French was tested in keeping up with her.

'I took a kidnapping class,' she said. 'I had to when I made a trip to Japan with diamonds sewed into the hem of my coat. That's the only way the insurance company would sell me kidnapping insurance for the trip, if I took security training. They told us at the class that the best and probably only time you can make an escape is in the first few moments of the kidnapping. That's the time when the kidnappers have just grabbed you, they're still in an unfamiliar and uncontrolled environment, and are distracted looking around to see if there are police or witnesses. Once they take you to their hideout, you're finished. That's their territory, a secure, controlled environment without witnesses.'

'I'm afraid I can't take credit for outsmarting them. I just happened to have a bottle of champagne in my hand when I panicked and reacted to being slammed in the knee with a gun. If it wasn't for the champagne, a Taitinger Blanc de Blanc Nineteen—'

She broke out laughing. Yvonne was the cousin who was supposed to have been with the limo that picked me up. Fortunately for both of us, the thugs had left her out of it. The limo was found abandoned near a freeway off-ramp. The real limo driver was found tied up and gagged, but otherwise unharmed, in the trunk of the limo.

It was late afternoon by the time I got through with the police. I told them truthfully everything I observed or heard during the kidnapping attempt – except for the mention of João's name. Nothing was going to happen to João if I gave the name, he obviously didn't leave his wheelchair to direct the actual crime and he'd have an iron-clad alibi. What I wanted to avoid were a million questions about my own connections to João, from blood diamonds to a fire diamond.

The story I gave out about how I came into possession of the Heart of the World – that I'd bought it off a mysterious vagabond who flagged me down one night when I was returning to the Blue Lady mine – had no truth to it, but no one could make it out to be a lie. Not that anyone would go to Angola to find out.

Yvonne had picked me up at the police station and took me for food and drinks afterward. I needed the drinks.

'One positive thing came out of this,' I said. 'The publicity generated by the robbery attempt won't hurt the stone.'

'Did you stage it for that purpose?'

I rubbed my sore knee. 'If I had, I would have passed on having my kneecap knocked off. Tell me about Rona. I read that she's straight, a lesbo, a nympho, that she's a hermaphrodite, bi, and that she's had a sex-change operation, that her name was originally Ron.'

We were on our way to a fashion show. Rona, no last name, was one of the world's top fashion designers.

'The stories about her sex and sexual preferences are probably true – all of them. She claims her sexual preferences and desires change with the phases of the moon. Or is it her astrological sign that changes monthly? Whatever it is, Rona started out with having the nose and ended with the eye.'

'The nose and the eye?'

'Perfume takes a nose, that's how she started. She worked for Nicholas Romanov, the perfumer who claims to be a descendant of the czars. When Romanov died, his wife took over the line and Rona left when the woman started pushing her out. Bad mistake, because it was Rona who had the nose for choosing the scents. Rona came out with her own line and it was a hit. After her perfume line made her name well-known, she moved into fashion and turned out to have an eye for that. She's only been at it a couple years, but her clothes are the talk of the fashion industry. You probably saw some of her designs barely clinging to some of the almost-nude actresses at last year's Academy Awards show.'

'I'm afraid I was knee-deep in mine muck during the Academy Awards.' I glanced at the gem case in the backseat. She was taking jewels to the fashion show; 'rent-a-gem' Yvonne called her deal with Rona. She loaned the jewelry to the designer for the models to wear down the runway and in turn got free publicity for her jewelry business.

'Any jewelry in there worth anything?' I asked.

'Nothing,' she said. 'I wouldn't risk valuable pieces on these models. They're liable to slip out the side door after the show and take the next plane back to Barbados or wherever they hang out between shows. No, it's all pretty and flashy, but most are pastes of our better designs.'

'Fifty cents' worth of scent can sell for fifty dollars.'

'What?'

'I was thinking about a conversation I had with business associates, about going into the diamond business. I want to come up with a new approach to this old business. Pennies of scent can sell for pennies or many dollars, depending on how it's packaged and advertised, but the problem with diamonds is that they're a commodity like pork bellies.'

Yvonne screeched. '*Pork bellies?*'

'Pork bellies are all the same.'

'Not to the pigs, they're not.'

'To the bacon eater, they are. Anyway, the example I was giving about diamonds is that they're not a fashion item, at least not at the wholesale level, because they're all the same. But perfume and clothes are different. Fifty cents' worth of scent can sell for—'

'Five hundred.'

'And a dollar's worth of cotton can make a dress worth fifty dollars for a trip to the supermarket or five thousand for a trip to the Academy Awards.'

'I see what you're saying. Diamonds are subject to the laws of supply and demand, fashion isn't,' Yvonne said. 'Fashion creates its own demand, but a diamond is a diamond is a diamond. Except of course when it's a flaming ruby-red no one has ever seen before.

'You're spoiled. With the Heart of the World, you got a taste of the sort of markup you find in the fashion world. The stone is worth a hundred times or a thousand times its ordinary carat value because it's unique. But a diamond like that, one that grossly exceeds its carat value because it's unique, comes around once in an eon. You're trying to find a way to make other diamonds worth more than their book value and it's not going to happen. People have been trying to do that for a long time.'

I nudged her with my elbow. 'There's an old expression about never saying never.'

'Well, Win, when you come up with a new way to market diamonds, let me know. I want to cash in, too.'

65

Rona was of indiscernible age and sexual preference, to my eye. Maybe if I saw her with her clothes off, I'd have a better idea of who and what she was. We went backstage and Yvonne introduced me.

'So you're the man with the fire diamond who fights off thieves,' Rona said. 'I saw it on television. You must bring it to my party after the show. You were foolish to fight with the thieves. Let them take it and collect the insurance. Bring it tonight and I will steal it from you.'

She spoke twice as fast as Yvonne and her French was only half as good. She was off and running without waiting for a reply. She was one part tornado, one part tyrant. She moved from model to model backstage at the fashion show, adjusting this and that, yelling commands, arguing with the girls, shouting at her assistants. She operated off of high-octane adrenaline, the kind that could fuel a Concorde.

Word spread that I was the man who owned a diamond mine and the most valuable diamond, and women who wouldn't have given me a smile on the street eyed me like I was a movie director looking to cast a starring role – on the casting-room couch at that.

Yvonne thought it was funny. 'We women are so attracted to a man's wealth and power, that's what's sexy for us. At first it was the caveman who carried the biggest club, now it's the man who has the biggest bank account. But at least there's a practical reason behind the attraction. Men are much more basic and frivolous – give them tits and ass and they don't care what's in the bank or in the brains.'

Watching the fashion models in various states of chaotic undress reminded me of the times I went back to see Katarina when she was modeling. Modesty was not a part of the modeling gig. What was surprising about the profession is that many of the women looked better with their clothes on than off. Their tall, slender figures with modest bustlines suited designers presenting clothes, but were too skinny for my taste. Once in a while there was a Katarina who had a lush, full body that was perfect with or without clothes. The top model for the show, an Italian woman Katarina had worked with and said was temperamental, was living up to her reputation. Like Katarina, she wouldn't wear just anything but had the right to refuse if she didn't think the clothes complimented her.

'This is not the outfit I agreed to wear,' she told Rona. 'You've made a change at the last minute.'

'You'll wear it or you'll never model again.'

That brought out an explosion of Italian, French, and English expletives. The women stood face-to-face, flushed and angry. It was the show's grand finale. Rona tried to adjust the dress and the woman pushed her hands away.

'It makes me look like a cow! I won't wear it!'

'You are a cow! You contracted for three runs. You wear the outfit or you can go down the runway naked and mooing!'

'Fine, good, fuck you, you bitch, I'm going naked.'

She began ripping off the clothes, taking everything off until she stood naked.

'There! I am ready to go onstage!'

Rona faced her, red in the face and her fists balled up.

I stepped in, pulling the pouch containing the fire diamond out of my pocket.

'I have the perfect complement to end your show with,' I told Rona. 'She can wear this.'

I held up the diamond. I had placed it in a simple setting with a thin gold chain making it easier to handle – and harder to lose.

They both gawked at the gem.

'Oh my God,' the model said, 'it's the fire diamond.'

Rona shook her head. 'It says nothing about my designs.'

'Yes, it does. It's launching your new line of fashion diamonds.'

I put the diamond around the model's neck.

'It's the most valuable diamond in the world,' I said. 'You're wearing a hundred million dollars. If you run for the door, my guards will shoot you in the back.' I made up the price, but it was a nice rough figure.

'Oh my God.' She held up the diamond to look at it and then looked at me. 'I love diamonds,' she purred.

Her vocabulary was limited, but her nipples stood at attention and saluted me. I got an instant hard-on. Like Yvonne said, it wasn't what was between the ears that interested a man.

66

'Pork bellies?'

Rona's face twisted in a sour expression.

We were alone in her Ile St Louis apartment overlooking the Seine and Rive Gauche. The Heart of the World had brought down the house at the fashion show. That and the fact that it was all the model wore. Rona took the stage right behind the model, and announced her new line of fashion diamonds. That's all she said, which was smart, since we hadn't figured out yet what exactly a line of 'fashion diamonds' was.

'Pork bellies,' she repeated.

I laughed. I'd given her the 'diamonds are a commodity' lecture I'd heard every time I mentioned starting a fashion line.

'But they don't have to be pork bellies,' I said. 'I realized that when I watched you take pieces of cloth and with a snip here and a tuck there, change the entire appearance of a dress.'

'We have unique cuts,' she said. 'Every one different. Is that possible?'

'Within limits. Most diamonds are given fifty-eight facets, which is called a 'brilliant' cut. That number was chosen because it maximizes light that gives a diamond's fiery glitter. But there are other cuts that can be used. The Tiffany Diamond has ninety facets. Bottom line, there are dozens of ways to cut a stone. The fifty-eight rule is used most often because it produces a good result. Sometimes the diamond itself determines how it should be cut.'

I could see her mind working away, she hadn't interrupted me. I kept going.

'I don't want to leave you with the impression that all diamonds of the same size and clarity sell for the same price after they're cut and hit the retail market. A prestigious jewelry store will sell comparable merchandise at a higher price than a discount store. But at the wholesale level – between dealers – prices are pretty much standardized based upon size and quality. A stone with the same color and clarity and cut can sell for more than another one because it has more fire – it may be that the stone started out larger and the cutter whittled away more diamond to get a better result. It depends upon how much leeway there is for a cut and how much rough you want to cut away, thus reducing the carat size. Most people are more interested in the size of the finished product than the glitter because the brilliance is often too subtle for someone to notice unless they make a close examination.'

'But you can come up with a Rona cut, a unique cut that no one else uses?'

'Yes.'

'Then we need a unique cut,' she said. 'That's what fashion is all about. Women don't buy my dresses at Bon Marche or Macy's, they buy them in shops where only one-of-a-kind dresses are sold.'

'I'll get the best cutter in the world and we'll come up with a design that will be unique and meet a high standard of brilliance. It may be we'll need to increase the number of facets substantially, over ninety perhaps, in order to get the right glitter. It'll cost more and will only be practical on larger stones.'

She waved away the extra cost. 'The cost of merchandise means nothing in fashion. You said people would pay more to buy the same diamond at a high-end store like Bvlgari's and Tiffany's than from a chain store.'

'That's true, on the retail end people are willing to pay more for the privilege of shopping where snob appeal is part of the purchase. But the prices won't be radically different for exactly the same stone with exactly the same brilliance. High-end stores sell better merchandise. Like I said, two stones with the same clarity and cut aren't necessarily equal in brilliance.'

'Buyers are all fools when it comes to fashion,' Rona said. 'Each woman thinks she's buying one-of-a-kind when she buys my dresses. For my more expensive designs, I may only send one of each design to a shop, but there are thousands of shops from Paris to San Francisco to Tokyo. When an actress is seen wearing the dress in a national magazine or awards show, I load up the stores with that design. Women believe it's okay to imitate a woman that is considered well dressed and sexy.'

'Maybe we'll let the buyer chose the design,' I said.

'Pardon?'

'That would really make it exclusive.'

'How would you do that with diamonds?'

'People are used to walking into a store and choosing a diamond that's already been cut and mounted. But what if we offered something really unique? Let them come into the store, choose a rough based on the size and clarity they can afford and then choose the shape and cut they want.'

'Can that be done?'

'With expensive stones it can. And using a computerized program to design the cut would not only impress people but show instant results. We'll only deal in roughs of a certain shape and whose brilliance can be brought out with a limited number of different cuts. We can have computer models that show the end result of different cuts to the buyers. They can either choose a Rona cut, the standard fifty-eight brilliant, or a totally unique cut that is one-of-a-kind.'

'I'll leave the cutting to you. We need to talk about three more important things. First, why should I get involved in this?'

'Exclusivity. People have had clothing and perfume named after them. No one has ever done diamonds. As the best advertising slogan in history says, diamonds are forever. They're the hardest substance on earth, harder than steel. When your line of perfume has evaporated and the clothes you've designed are shreds, the diamonds bearing your name will live on. A thousand years from now a Rona diamond will sparkle as brilliantly as it did today.'

Her eyes lit up at the idea of name-recognition immortality. What I didn't say was that I intended to get a lot more mileage out of her name in the long run than she ever imagined. Of course we'd have stores in New York, London, Paris, and Beverly Hills to cater to the rich. But someday I'd make even more money selling a Rona line to people who buy their engagement rings at the jewelry counter of places like Wal-Mart. Now wasn't the time to bring up that idea. Rona had terrific snob appeal because she was the biggest snob in the world. Getting her to go for mass production would have to wait until she needed the money.

'All right, the second question is, how much will I receive for the use of my name?'

I grinned. 'I thought you'd want to let us use your name for the sake of art, sort of a gift to the world.' I put up my hands to stop a flow of profanity. 'Just kidding, but this is a win-win scenario for you. You're basically licensing your name and leaving all the work to me. We'll take a look at other licensing agreements and come up with terms that will be more than fair.'

'The agreement won't be just for money, but my name is my stock-in-trade. I will insist upon controlling how my name is used – and that it is not abused or involved in anything that will tarnish it.'

271

'That's fair. What's the third thing?'

'Let me see that red diamond.'

We had been sitting at a safe distance from each other, but now she moved closer, sitting almost on top of me.

'It's back in the vault—'

'It's in your pocket. You are too much in love with it to let it out of your sight.'

Smart lady. I handed her the Heart of the World.

She rotated the diamond in her hand, picking up the light.

'Incredible. It really looks like a fire is glowing in it.'

She put her hand on my lap. She squeezed my penis with one hand and the diamond with the other.

'We'll seal the deal with a fuck,' she said. 'Mars is in Capricorn, Mercury is in ascension. I'm heterosexual and horny this time of month.'

PART 8

HOLLYWOOD

67

House of Liberté, Beverly Hills, 1998

I stood on the corner of Rodeo and Little Santa Monica and looked down Rodeo in the direction of Wilshire. It was a singularly unimpressive street. One- and two-story buildings, for the most part. It had none of the powerful facade and elegance of the upper-end shopping districts of New York, London, and Paris. But there was more snob appeal in a few hundred yards of Rodeo than on the entire eastern seaboard of the United States, with maybe some of London and Paris thrown in.

That was because snob appeal was easier to obtain on the West Coast than anywhere else. The only thing that counted out West was money. And it didn't have to be 'old money.' Leaving out the carpetbaggers who brought their money with them, there was no 'old money' in California, at least not the way they counted 'old' in Europe. California's version of old money came from mining, oil, and real estate, none of which were ancient history. New money came from entertainment, the defense industry, and Silicon Valley, and engendered real contempt from the European and eastern seaboard old money because the person who possessed it actually *worked* for it.

The snob appeal of Rodeo Drive was even more focused in terms of its basis – it was almost exclusively centered around 'the industry.' The fifteen or sixteen million people in the Los Angles basin worked in many different industries, but universally, when 'the industry' was mentioned, it meant the entertainment industry. A guy with ten thousand shoe stores spread across

America could move here and buy a twenty-million-dollar house in Beverly Hills, but in terms of snob appeal, he ranked far behind the actress who appeared periodically on a cable TV show and lived in a West Hollywood walk-up.

Not that the shoe guy's twenty-million-dollar mansion was that impressive either, especially if you drove by and saw it going up piece by piece. You can bet about 95 percent of the cost went into purchase of the lot alone. The remaining 5 percent was used to raise a plywood mansion. That's what all these big Beverly Hills houses were, good old pine framing with plywood walls. On top of the plywood went a façade that hid the house's cheap construction.

You could get away with that kind of cheap construction in the warm, dry Southern California climate. On top of that, anything grew here, because the climate's basically warm desert turned into an oasis by stealing water from communities hundreds of miles in every direction. I watched the landscaping go up one day on a new Beverly Hills plywood mansion. After the house was done and the concrete driveway was dry, trucks loaded with trees, bushes, and flowers pulled up. Full-grown trees and bushes went into the ground, blooming flowers were planted, and grass rolled out. Literally in hours, bare dirt around the house was turned into a small rain forest. I especially like watching the grass being rolled out. It reminded me of the old movie Dick and Jane from the 1970s starring Jane Fonda and George Segal. Segal, who played Dick, was an aerospace executive who got laid off about the time he and Jane bought an expensive new house. As their financial woes rose, they didn't just lose their expensive furniture and cars, but the landscaper came back and repossessed their plants and rolled-up lawn.

Yeah, the town was phony, tacky, plastic, a cheap imitation of quality, a place with a Styrofoam soul.

And I couldn't wait to jump into the middle of it.

I don't know what it was about L.A. that attracted me. It wasn't even a real town with a main street – mostly it was just one giant strip mall. If you had to choose a main street, I guess it would be Wilshire Boulevard which ran twenty miles and went through three different towns.

But I had the same emotional response to *the industry* that everyone else had. I came here to mingle with the stars, maybe even make love to one or two – hopefully not an action hero pumped up with steroids.

It was amazing how well I fit the L.A. mode. I ran my diamond busi-

275

ness like a movie studio when it came to promotion – no one pulled more stunts or got more free publicity. What it had taken the old names in the diamond industry over a hundred years to build up in terms of name recognition, I had done in the five years since I left Angola. Now I was doing the same play as I walked down to meet my staff on Rodeo Drive where House of Liberté was getting its finishing touches. Yeah, I kept the accent over the 'e.' It had snob appeal. Isn't that what diamonds were all about?

I had opened stores in New York, London, Paris, and Rome. I saved Beverly Hills until last because I knew it was the hardest nut to crack. People here were more used to hype than anywhere else. That meant the hype had to be mind-blowing to get their attention.

The Rona Diamond was still our mainstay, but Rona had quickly lost interest in diamonds as soon as she found out it was dull work, discovering that you couldn't lift a hem or put a tuck here or there and create a different look. It took a guy with a magnifying glass and diamond cutting tools and machines several hours to make any difference.

Basically, I rented her name, which was fine with me. I was slowly weeding the Rona name away from my high-end customers, saving it for people who couldn't spend a hundred grand on an engagement ring. My game plan was someday to take the Rona name national, selling engagement rings in the under-five-thousand market through retailers, but keeping the wealthy clientele for my exclusive stores.

I even picked up a trick from Beverly Hills banks that I was using in my stores. They called it 'personal banking.' Small banks in downtown Beverly Hills – all six or eight blocks of it – had cubbyholes for its tellers. Rather than a customer walking up to a wide counter, they were assigned to a particular teller who they got to know by name. I did the same thing in my stores, turning my sales people into 'gemologists' who were assigned rich customers and 'advised' them as to all aspects of their jewelry. It added another layer of the mystique and vanity that surrounded the diamond trade.

The woman who was to manage the new store and my PR person were across the street from the store giving it the eye when I approached.

'It's almost finished, Win,' Cameron Reed, the manager, said. 'I'm so excited.'

She was a petite blonde, about five feet tall, not counting three-inch spiked heels. I didn't know women still wore those things, you didn't see them often, but I had to admit that high heels did something for a woman's body that turned me on. But I didn't hire her for sex. I stole her away from Bvlgari's in London, where her British accent was wasted. A British accent went a long way in pretentious Beverly Hills, especially if there was a blonde with good T & A behind it.

'We're talking about the window display,' Pat Weinstein said. Pat, who was six inches taller and fifty pounds heavier than Cameron, was my PR person. She worked for a firm that handled stars and I stole her away because she brought with her a computer printout of the private telephone numbers and addresses for the top movie stars in Hollywood. If I was selling shoes, I'd put my money into advertising – marketing diamonds to the rich and famous called for a PR person who could shovel bullshit.

'Window display is an art,' Cameron said. 'At Bvlgari—'

'Then let's get an artist,' I said.

'We have display people.'

'I don't want an ordinary jewelry-window display. I want something that will cause a sensation, something Pat can use to get us news coverage and a buzz on about the store.'

'I'm not sure I know what you mean when you say an "artist." Display people are artists in their craft,' Cameron said.

'I mean a *real* artist, someone famous, an Andy Warhol. If we got Warhol to do the display, wouldn't it be a sensation?'

'More like a miracle,' Pat said. 'He's dead.'

'Then find someone else – or dig him up. Listen, I remember my father telling me way back when that a New York jewelry store hired some top painter of the day to decorate the store window. It caused a sensation. Find out who are the best-known painters in the country. Hell, there are a dozen galleries within a hundred yards that can provide the information in five minutes.'

Cameron frowned. 'To get a major artist to do a window display would be very expensive, probably something in the six-figure range.'

I laughed. 'Good, you're immediately worried about the store budget. This will come out of special promotions, not your budget. Let's say we pay an artist a hundred grand or two to do the window, paint it, decorate it, whatever. What would it be worth in publicity?'

'Millions,' Pat said. 'It's a terrific investment. If you can do a window for a hundred thousand dollars that makes the news, the same coverage in terms of commercials or ads would cost you millions. More importantly, people actually watch news.'

'Exactly. So let's get an artist with a name. And when it's done, you can line up some out-of-work movie extras to stand around and gawk at the window, like paid mourners at a funeral. That'll draw a crowd. Hell, throw some has-been actor in the crowd, someone we can get cheap but who would be recognized. Pretty soon we'll need cops for crowd control.'

'The local stations love that sort of thing,' Pat said.

'Local stations, hell, I want the opening to go national. Get an artist who leans toward the risqué – quietly sexy, but definitely someone with modern tastes. And one of those *Baywatch* babes with a healthy chest. We'll put her in the window as a display piece, maybe clothed in nothing but diamond dust.'

Pat laughed. 'Bimbos on TV net more money every year than your store will gross. Remember, Win, sex came before diamonds.'

'Yeah, but diamonds stay warm when sex gets cold. Hey, something like that could be turned into a tag line for the promotion. Work on it,' I told Pat. 'Figure out a way to use it. Send me a memo on it.'

I turned Cameron loose to argue with the construction people putting in a plate-glass window and led Pat down Camden.

'Walk with me, I have a meeting at Dream Artists.'

The talent agency, located off Wilshire near Santa Monica Boulevard, was the hottest agency in town.

'Planning on becoming a movie star?'

'Considering what you say *Baywatch*-types get paid, maybe I'll try out for a part. From the looks of the newspaper ads I've seen around this town, if I don't have the right body parts at the moment, there are doctors here who can provide them at no small cost, everything from penile enlargements to breast augmentation, and not always for people born with the original equipment. But speaking of blondes who make millions, tell me what that bitch is pulling with my necklace.'

Shelly Lane was a major star, but as a woman pushing forty in a town that never forgave age in a woman, she found fewer and fewer roles. She had been a presenter at the Academy Awards and wore a diamond necklace from my New York store. Between Lane and other women, we had over a million dollars in gems at the Awards, and got millions in free publicity.

The jewels were loaners. And unlike my cousin Yvonne's method in Paris, where I learned the stunt, my gems were always real. Pastes didn't generate publicity, it had to be the real thing.

'Shelly refused to turn over the necklace to the messenger. Your New York manager spoke to her. She said she considered the necklace as payment for promoting your store.'

I chortled. 'If she doesn't give the necklace back, I'm going to garrote her with it. How much free publicity would that be worth?'

'Plenty. And you'd also get room and board until they fried you. Or gassed you, whatever is in vogue in our prisons. I tried calling Shelly, she won't return my calls.'

'I'll go by her house and get it.' I hadn't met Lane, but she had a reputation of being hard and tough.

'She has a couple hundred-pound dogs that eat intruders. And a bodyguard that eats anyone who survives the dogs.'

'Turn her over to the cops.'

'You'll get sued. Her claim that she's entitled to the necklace is bullshit, but it's still a claim. You're better off writing off the hundred grand.'

'I can't let her get away with it. It's not the money, it's the exposure. If she gets away with it, every star we drape a necklace on will insist on keeping it. When that happens, I'll have to drop the loaner program. It's a great promotional scheme. I need that necklace back to keep it going.'

'I don't know what to tell you.' She stopped in front of the parking garage where her car was parked. 'There's a charity banquet tonight, one of those things for cancer or diabetes or something that stars attend to make it look like they're raising money for a good cause when they're only there to be seen. I know Shelly's attending it and she might wear the necklace, since it's her new toy. From what I hear, she sleeps with it. And whoever else she has around.'

'Get me on the guest list.'

Katarina was the reason for my meeting at the talent agency. She had come out to Hollywood seven years before, financed by my Bugatti. She made some movies, good and some bad, but was usually in a supporting role because she didn't have that big star quality, that screen presence that some women and men had that permitted them to carry a movie and be 'bankable.'

She had a movie deal, this time a leading role as a woman in a concentration camp during the Holocaust. Some guy with a chain of car dealerships in the Midwest had come in as the financing angel, in return for getting the VIP-sucker-bucks treatment in Hollywood for a few weeks. The financing went south when he got busted for laundering drug money.

I was back hanging out with Katarina, but not as lovers. I deliberately avoided the bedroom scene because I didn't want to make any pillow-talk promises that I'd regret later – like financing a movie for her. She didn't push me, in bed or for financing, which was one of the reasons I wanted to help her. Katarina didn't have a greedy bone in her. When it came to money, she was more often the taken than the taker.

When she talked about making a movie and the financial woes, she piqued my interest. I hadn't said anything to her, but I was also interested in getting a movie made. However, I had a game plan that was different than what she had in mind.

Not that I wouldn't want to help Katarina out if I could. She was someone I liked, one of the few people in the world special to me. But Katarina was on one planet and I was on another. She was infected with movie fever. Once you got it, there was no place else in the world for you.

Even though I fit nicely into the town, Hollywood was a stopover for me. In a few months, after the new store was up and running smoothly, I was planning on heading west, across the Pacific, to check out Singapore, Tokyo and other points in Asia. I also wanted to drop in on Bangkok, which was becoming a major diamond-cutting center.

In the meantime, I'd do whatever I could to help Katarina. It just happened that what I had in mind would help us both.

68

Katarina was waiting in her agent's office. She gave me a kiss.

'Thanks for coming, Win.'

Harry Kidd, her agent, was a fast-talking, nervous energy, Type A+, pushy runt. He was one of those guys who you always wondered how they managed not to get their heads knocked in and asses kicked by the people they annoy with their motor mouths. My guess is that the Harry Kidds of this world simply moved too fast for anyone to catch and punch out.

He came around the desk, pumped my hand energetically, and asked what I wanted to drink.

I shook off a drink. 'Let's get the meeting over with. Are the production company people here?'

'Let's talk strategy before we—'

'Let's talk turkey with these people.'

'Did you read the script? Fabulous, isn't it? It'll make *Sophie's Choice* look like comic-book melodrama. Katarina would be a shoe-in for an Oscar. The movie would gross—'

'Can you turn off the bullshit and get the meeting going?'

Harry blinked. In this town, no one talked to a talent agent like that, at least not a Dream Artists agent. Except a guy with a checkbook.

'People don't talk to me like that,' he said.

'I'm sorry.' I grabbed his arm. 'I spent too much time in Angola where I had to kill someone once in a while to get my point across, so you'll have to excuse me if I act a little uncivilized. Maybe we can get started and my nerves will calm down.'

'Sure.' He gave Katarina a look as we followed him.

We took seats in the conference room where two representatives from the production company, a man and a woman, were waiting. I had already been told the woman was the decision maker.

When we were seated, Harry said, 'The script—'

'Is out,' I said. 'I can't wrap my head around it. If a simple guy like me can't understand it, no one else will. I'm not going to finance a movie that's going to play in art houses, get rave reviews, and doesn't earn back ten cents on the dollar.'

'Win, but – what—' Katarina said.

'I told you I'd front some money for a movie, but the Holocaust thing is not the movie, it's a work of art. I want a heist movie.'

'A heist movie?' The production company woman said. 'That's a tough sell nowadays. Who wrote the script?'

'There's no script – yet. You people can take care of that. And it's not going to be a fifty-million-dollar theatrical release that earns back its money in Asia if there's enough action in it. I want a two-hour television crime caper.'

'I don't understand this,' Harry the runt said. 'We're here to talk about a movie about the Holocaust that will be on the short list at Oscar time, not some TV crime drama.'

'You're here to get a movie made. I have a sponsor for a TV movie. The international diamond industry is reeling from all the bad publicity about blood diamonds. They're afraid diamonds will get the same sort of taint from human rights groups that animal rights people gave furs. Remember when people wearing fur coats risked having a can of red paint thrown on them when they showed up at restaurants and plays? The diamond industry is in a panic, that instead of being a girl's best friend, diamonds will be identified with atrocities and starvation in Africa.'

'The diamond industry is willing to sponsor a *heist* movie?' the production woman asked.

'It'll have a happy ending. And show how human and humanitarian people in the gem business are. I sold them on the idea of sponsoring an *entertaining* movie. A heist shows people just how valuable their own diamonds are.' That was a great bullshit concept I used during a meeting in Antwerp when I sold the concept of a TV movie to an international diamond association.

'I'll give you a list of points about diamonds that the script has to include. The title of the movie is *The Liberté Heist*. My new Beverly Hills store will be used as the prime set.'

'Ah, I see,' said the runt agent. 'In a two-hour TV movie, there is about an hour and a half of movie time, provided by advertisers who spend millions of dollars. Your firm is not going to be a sponsor, but the main star. Hell, do you know what an hour and a half of prime-time TV commercials would cost a sponsor – and you're getting it free?'

Yeah, I knew. But I said, 'Katarina's the star. I don't care if she's the thief, a customer caught in the robbery, the store manager, a cop, whatever you want, but she gets top billing. I'm sure she'll give an Emmy performance. And, of course, my store will be displayed throughout the movie.'

'Jesus,' the production woman said. 'I can't even imagine how that much prime television would cost if it were paid commercial time. And even if a company had that kind of money, half the people watching get up to hit the bathroom or kitchen while commercials are on. They won't do that if the commercial is part of the movie. What a hell of a deal for your store.'

I nodded modestly. 'It's rather a catchy title, don't you think? *The Liberté Heist.*'

'It sucks,' the production woman said. 'But,' she spread her fingers on the table, 'that doesn't mean we can't come up with something. How about *The Liberté Ice Heist?*'

'*The Great Liberté Diamond Robbery,*' the runt agent said. '*The Man Who Shot Liberté*—'

Katarina and I left them throwing titles across the table.

In the hallway she said, 'I've got to go back inside and make sure that I don't end up on the cutting-room floor.'

'Disappointed?' I asked.

'No, actually I think it's great. Really. They never would have let me play the lead in the Holocaust movie. What people say in this town, and what they mean and do, are not the same. Lying and bullshitting is considered part of doing business. They would have strung us along until it was time to shoot and then suddenly make a script change that they had planned from the beginning. I would have gotten a small supporting role and a woman with box-office clout would get the top billing. I knew that, but I would have been satisfied just playing a significant role. But this TV thing is great. It breaks me into TV and that's a better market for female roles.'

'They're not going to leave you on the cutting-room floor, I'll make sure of that.'

'Did you really kill people in Angola?'

I kissed her on the cheek. 'The CIA won't let me talk about it.'

69

As I walked down Wilshire, a car honked as it passed me and I flinched. It was just traffic talk – horns, shouted insults, and flipping the bird were the music of L.A. streets. But I was still cautious from an incident two days before when a car honked while I was walking. I looked over as the car went by. A woman in the front passenger seat stuck her head out the window and grinned.

It was Jonny, Simone's daughter.

It had been a long time since I had heard from my Lisbon friends, almost five years since I was almost killed in Paris, and three since Jonny spent the night with me in a Bel Air hotel room and Simone showed up the next morning. But I knew my duel with João over the Heart of the World wasn't over, that it was the quiet before the storm.

João had gone undercover for a while after the Paris fiasco. His Portuguese thugs left fingerprints in the limo that the Sûreté and Interpol traced back to his employees. Soon after that, the blood-diamond trade got hot after the wars in Angola and Sierra Leone heated up. But there were outcries about the sale of blood diamonds and an 'anonymous source' (the same one who turned my cousin Leo in to the feds) made sure that every humanitarian and police group in the world who were interested in the smuggling and sale of blood diamonds had João on their list. That kept João busy as he got eighty-sixed from diamond exchanges. Diamonds were a multibillion-dollar business, worldwide, but it was still a cottage industry in which everyone knew everyone else.

I kept ahead of João, always hopping from country to country and putting up stores, but when Jonny and Simone showed up at the same time three years ago, I knew I had to do something. And I knew what to do.

Going through the House of Liberté business files Bernie left behind, I found out that in all the dealings Bernie had with João, any money owed the Portuguese was sent to offshore accounts. In other words, João had the same philosophy about paying taxes that Leo had. Then I called Asher van Franck in Antwerp to find out what other deals João had been in. You couldn't swing a dead cat in the European diamond business without Franck knowing about it.

I supplied the information to the Portuguese taxing authority. The source was supposed to remain confidential, but I had no doubt João would realize who turned him in.

I heard rumors from diamond traders that João had serious medical problems, but I would have laid odds that it was his way of ducking the bullet when tax investigators showed up at his house.

Now Jonny was back in L.A., at the same time I was. It probably was a coincidence, she liked the town, and by now she had to be around nineteen or twenty, old enough to do what she wanted. Maybe she was going to school here.

Despite the logic, I still had a hollow, exposed feeling between my shoulder blades as I walked down the street. But I shook it off. I had something more urgent to do than worry about being murdered by João. I had to wrestle a movie star who had big claws.

Walking down the street, I gave Cross a call.

'Still interested in security work?' I asked, when he got on the phone.

'Hey, not in L.A. They shoot straighter here than Angola. And for less reason.'

'Grab your starlet friend. I'm going to a charity banquet and need some backup.'

'What kind of charity banquet do you need backup at? Something thrown by the Cripps and the Bloods – at the same time?'

'Worse, I'm taking on Shelly Lane. She ripped off a necklace from me and I have to rip it back – literally.'

'Kiss your ass good-bye if you plan to mess with that woman. I hear she has a full-metal-jacket heart and a cunt that's a revolving door. Megan was on location with her for a picture. The hotel staff claimed that when Lane called for room service, she really meant she wanted to be *serviced*. She likes a good fuck, but you fuck *with* her, you better start counting your balls.'

'Bring along Megan. Tell her I have the inside say on a part for her, a TV show that's already short-listed for an Emmy.'

'Shit, bubba, look at you, hardly been in town and you're already talking like one of those fuckin' guys who hang around Spago's and Le Dome, laying out lines of bullshit about how they're on the A list.'

I almost said at least I wasn't laying out lines of coke – which was more

285

than I could say for Cross. We made arrangements for me to pick them up in a limo later and hung up.

Cross worried me. He backed me up in Angola, I owed him. When the mine came in, I took care of the debt with money I'd promised. And I was still ready to help him out if he asked.

He walked out of the mine deal with a cool two million, most of which he stashed offshore so he wouldn't have to pay taxes. Every time I hit L.A., I looked him up. And every time he had put on more weight, ballooning up until he looked like a fat TV comic. And he had a runny nose from his sinuses rotting from the powder he sniffed. He was into drugs, big time. His apartment smelled like a dope den.

His girlfriend, Megan, was okay, she was worried about him, too. But she was too busy trying to make it as an actress to give him the support he needed. Not that he would have taken it if it was offered. Cross was a stubborn bastard. He didn't take well to criticism or anyone sticking their nose in his business. I made a crack once that he was sniffin' and smokin' all the money he earned in Angola and got growls in return.

I asked Cross and Megan to come to the banquet with me so I would have company. I didn't think there would be any real trouble with Shelly Lane. I'd just embarrass her into handing over the necklace. Her bodyguard would have to stay outside. Her reputation as a scrapper didn't bother me, either.

What could a hundred-and-twenty-pound woman do against a hundred-and-eighty-pound stud like me?

I should have remembered that old expression about hell having no fury like a woman scorned. It applied to diamonds as well as love.

70

We climbed out of the limo in front of the banquet hall on Avenue of the Stars in Century City. News cameras, paparazzi, tourists, and star-spotters

were lined up to see who got out. I heard the crowd immediately desig-
nate me as a nobody, Cross as a probable rap record producer, and a few
recognized Megan as the actress in a couple of movies and a *Friends*
episode.

We flowed inside with the other guests. The reception room, built
around a fountain with grinning stone dolphins spitting water, was
crowded with stylish people wearing designer clothes, pretending they
enjoyed drinking cheap champagne out of plastic champagne glasses. The
dinner room was up the stairways to the right, but I hoped I'd spot Shelly
Lane and be out of there without having to sit down for two hours of
boring dinner speeches.

I got separated from Cross and Megan when Megan spotted a producer
she wanted to cozy up to. The stairs leading to the dinner room would
make a good place to get a bird's-eye view of the people in the room, so I
started pushing my way through the crowd.

I had just reached the fountain when I spotted a woman at the top of
the stairs and a bolt of surprise hit me.

Marni.

I almost shouted her name.

She was with several other people, moving out of my sight, in the
direction of the dining room. She disappeared and that's when I read the
large banner hanging from the ceiling over the stairway: WORLD FOOD
EVENT.

I hadn't even bothered noting what charity the banquet was for.

I started pushing harder through the crowd. I bumped into a woman
who spun around, ready to throw a drink in my face.

'Watch where—'

She stopped and grinned. It was Shelly Lane.

'Well, if you're going to push me, pal, I'll tell you where my erogenous
zones are.'

'Shelly Lane, as I live and breathe.'

'The one and only,' she said.

She was wearing the diamond necklace. It looked stunning on her. She
also had had a few too many to drink. Her grin was a little lewd, a little
cockeyed. Everyone knew she was a lush, so she had probably started long
before the banquet.

'Now that you know my name, tell me yours.' She leaned forward,
breathing whiskey in my face. That wasn't champagne in her glass. 'Tell

me that you're not some fuckin' actor looking for a role, tell me that you're one of those billionaire dot-com nerds who are fuckin' stupid about everything but a computer and who'll finance a movie for a blowjob.'

'Right now, I'm in the repossession business.'

'Repossession? You mean like cars and refrigerators?'

'I mean like diamonds. I'm Win Liberte, and that's my necklace you're wearing.'

She felt the necklace. 'You're the guy who *gave* me the necklace?'

'I'm the guy you *stole* the necklace from. You can either give it back, or I'm going to embarrass you by taking it.'

'Embarrass me?' She shook with laughter. 'Why you poor stupid boob, you don't know what fuckin' embarrassment is.' She leaned in closer with ninety-proof breath. 'How's this for embarrassment?'

She threw her drink in my face.

'Fuckin' bitch!'

She hit me in the face with her glass and cocked back her fist to slug me. I caught her right cross as it came at me, twisting her around and lifting her up by her butt and threw her right into the fountain.

Just as she left my arms, going airborne, a paparazzi's hidden camera flashed.

Everyone in the place froze as Shelly Lane made a big splash.

Cross was suddenly at my side, grabbing my arm.

'Let's get the hell out of here.'

71

'I can't believe it was her after all these years.'

'You sure it was her?' Cross asked.

'It was Marni. It's also the organization she works for, that world food group.'

We were in the limo, heading downtown, which didn't mean the same thing as heading to 'downtown' New York or San Francisco or most other big cities where the action was. Unlike other metro areas, there was really no heart to this town. There was little in downtown L.A. except high-rise towers of law offices and accounting firms, government buildings, some convention hotels, and hovels for the poor. The only reason you went downtown was to appear in court or go to a meeting at your lawyer's office. And then it wasn't that pleasant, even in the daytime.

The homeless exercised some vague constitutional and moral right to camp out on the green area alongside the government buildings, stopping on their way to the soup kitchen to piss on the sidewalks and panhandle. Along with the homeless, the town was populated by a lot of hard-working poor people, mostly Latinos who lacked money and green cards, but busted their butts working jobs no one else would do. They lived on beans and tortillas, often sleeping on the floor, six to a room, so they could send a few dollars home each month.

We were on our way to the hottest new restaurant in town located in a warehouse in the almost abandoned downtown industrial area, the kind of neighborhood where you could plan on getting murdered if your car broke down. L.A. restaurants were like music groups – they popped up, hit the limelight if they were an in-place that people went to be seen . . . and then another one opened and the old one faded away. The highs and lows in the restaurant business weren't caused by the movement of great chefs from one establishment to another, but the movement of people in 'the industry.' No one gave a damn that they were eating mediocre food at an outrageous price. If a star frequented the restaurant, they wanted in. When the star moved on to another restaurant, so did the crowd.

For me, Cross's suggestion that we hit this place had the extra appeal of being a neighborhood where we wouldn't run the risk of running into Shelly Lane's bodyguard. Cross assured me she would send the guy out on a kill-or-cripple mission. We hadn't stayed around to fish Lane or the necklace out of the pond.

Cross, and a lot of other hip people, thought it was cool to go to a restaurant in the worst neighborhood in town, an area where you had to walk over blood, dogshit, and worse things on the sidewalk to get inside a converted warehouse with cement walls and floor and exposed plumbing and air vents.

I thought it was stupid. I wasn't impressed with L.A. restaurants, period. There was always something too parvenu, nouveau riche about them. In New York, waiters had an attitude, one that was often mouthy and pugilistic. In L.A., they didn't insult you or start a good argument. Instead, they acted like they weren't really waiters at all but a Somebody, that you were privileged to get waited on by them and they were only serving you while they waited for the next casting call.

But I didn't argue with Cross about his choice of restaurants. I owed him another one, he'd gotten me out of the banquet hall before Lane's bodyguard found me and ate me.

'Did Marni see you?' he asked.

'No, but by now she'll know who caused the splash at her fund-raiser.'

I called my PR person, Pat, the moment I was inside the limo. I instructed her to call Lane's PR person and have them concoct a story as to why I threw the star into the fountain. I didn't want a scandal about the necklace. Publicity was good, but a scandal could turn off future wearers and open the door for other jewelry firms. Her immediate reaction was a lover's quarrel. I told her, 'I don't care if you say we were fighting over our brands of lipstick, just keep the necklace out of it.'

When I hung up the phone, Cross asked, 'How come you never contacted her, all the times you've been in L.A.?'

'I didn't know she was here. In the back of my mind I imagined she'd be off in a jungle somewhere, handing out food to hungry people. Besides, she let me know in no uncertain terms that she didn't want to see me again.'

'Shit, I've tried that and you keep landing on my doorstep. Why don't you get off your high horse and contact the woman? I can tell from that wimpy sound that your voice gets when you mention her name, that you're hurting for this lady.'

He was right. I dialed Pat again.

'At the banquet, there was a woman named Marni Jones. She might have changed her name if she married, but there aren't that many Marnis in this world. Find out her address, where she works, if she's married.'

'That might be tough. If this woman isn't somebody with a capital S, you literally have to hire an investigator.'

'Whatever it takes, and I want the information yesterday.'

'Of course. And about the splash, at the banquet, the story being fed the press is that you and Shelly Lane were a number, she kicked you out of bed, and you went into a jealous rage. She's looking into a restraining order because you won't take no for an answer and have been parked outside her place for several nights in a row.'

'Jesus Christ, why didn't she just tell them I'm HIV positive, too?'

'Don't suggest it – and pray she doesn't think of it. By the way, she wants matching bracelets for the necklace. She says you owe it to her for all the publicity. You can bet that picture will make the front page of whatever tabloid that paparazzi works for.'

'Tell Shelly if she ever wants to leave the movie business, I know people in the Mafia who'd hire her as a negotiator. I'll have the bracelets messengered over.'

'Oh, and one more thing. She likes the way you manhandled her. She wants to see you again.' Pat's voice was coy.

'You know, I don't think Shelly Lane takes manhandling well, no matter what she says. What do you think the odds are that she'd have me chopped up for dog food if I actually showed up at her place?'

'First she'd fuck your pants off. Shelly isn't one to waste a good man.'

We signed off and I turned to Cross.

'I've been busy, too busy for the Marnis of this world, a woman who needs time and affection. That's the only excuse I have. But when I saw her, it felt like someone had kicked me in the balls. What does that sound like to you?'

'You're fucked, man, it's love, not lust. Lust is when it feels like she's licking your balls.'

Something else was bugging me. Earlier, when I picked him up at his place, Cross had come out of his apartment after Megan, giving her a few minutes to talk to me before he got in the limo. She told me that she was worried about him, that he was shooting everything up his nose. 'He's starting to sell things,' she told me.

I promised her I would help in any way I could. When a druggie starts to sell personal effects, you know everything's gone to hell. I wanted to do something for him, but dealing with him, trying to get him to take a helping hand, would be as easy as sticking your hands through the bars to pet a hungry tiger.

'You're wasted, sitting around on your ass,' I told him, as we neared the restaurant. 'Clipping coupons from your investments, that's no way for a real man to do it. Why don't you come back to work with me? You can start out as head of security at the Beverly Hills store. You like it and I'll make you national security director.'

291

'Do I look like I need a job, dick-head?'

I sighed. 'No, actually, you look like you need electrocompulsive shock treatment and a frontal lobotomy. And maybe a penile implant.'

72

A week later, I sat in my car across the street from a day-care center in Brentwood and re-read the investigator's report that sent me there.

Marni wasn't married, at least not presently. Whether she'd gotten married sometime overseas, the investigator didn't know. But she did have a child, a five-year-old girl. She dropped the child off each morning and picked her up in the afternoon. The tough schedule single moms and dads have to tow.

Her home address, make and model of car, unlisted phone number, social security number, credit history, employment history, all were in the packet. That stuff was easy to come by. Any good investigator had a contact at a credit-reporting agency who supplied credit reports for a price. Nowadays, of course, the provider of the information might be a computer hacker.

He also wasn't able to tell me if there was a man in her life or if she lived with someone. She lived in a 'security' apartment building and he couldn't get in and talk to neighbors but didn't see any man with her as she came and went.

One thing I knew – since she had a five-year-old kid, she hadn't waited long to get involved with some other guy after she walked out on me. My ego told me she went to someone else on the rebound.

What I didn't know was what my reception would be. What do I say to an ex-lover who I hadn't seen in over six years and who probably thought of me as someone who lied to her and betrayed her?

Add in the big splash I made at the charity banquet, and she probably thought I was a madman. Worse, she probably thought I lived in Los Angeles and wondered why I had never contacted her. She might have even read about me in the papers before the Shelly Lane fiasco.

She hadn't done badly for herself since dumping me. She was now a full, tenured professor at UCLA with a long string of published works about the socio-economic problems of the Third World. The titles alone looked intimidating. She had a UN award for her work and had attended a luncheon at the White House. I had an invitation to a White House luncheon, too, but it came with a string – a campaign donation. I passed on spending half a million on a plate of chicken salad.

I was pleased about Marni's progress. She had done something worth-while in the world. All I had done was make money. Reading Marni's accomplishments was the first time I questioned my own achievements. I could imagine her asking, 'And what have you done for the world lately, Win Liberte?' Well, I fucked a few broads and I even threw a movie star into a fountain.

I puzzled over my own feelings as I waited, surprised at the powerful emotions that seeing Marni had generated in me. It was as if I'd had everything bottled up inside and suddenly the cork popped. I'd had a dozen lovers since we parted in Angola, but none of them had stuck more than a few months. Part of it was because I was running too fast to build the business. But I now knew another part of it was that I still cared for Marni.

Why was I sitting outside the school waiting for her? What did I expect to gain? I wasn't ready for marriage, or even a relationship, if that was in the cards. So why didn't I just start the car and pull away before it was too late?

Analyzing my feelings got me nowhere. I just sat in the car, stewing over the situation, wavering back and forth about staying and going. The private investigator said Marni picked up her daughter on Fridays; on the other weekdays her housekeeper, Josie, picked her up.

I tensed as I saw a car approaching which matched the description in the report. It was her. She pulled up to the school and went inside.

I got out and crossed the street without giving it another thought.

A minute later she came out of the school, chatting and laughing with her little girl. I stood still and let her almost walk into me. When she saw me, I carefully watched her face, looking for a clue as to what her feelings might be. The only emotion I got was surprise.

'Win!'

'In the flesh.'

'I – I – what are you doing here?'

'I dropped by to meet your daughter.' I stuck out my hand to the little girl. 'Hi, I'm Win Liberte. Nice to meet you.'

The child looked up at Marni and Marni nodded her OK. 'It's OK, tell the gentleman your name.'

'Elena Jones,' she said shyly, shaking my hand.

'That's a beautiful name. Elena was my mother's name.'

'My mother's name is Marni.'

'Yes, I know.' I held out my hand to shake Marni's hand. When she took it, I didn't want to let go. 'It's been a long time.'

'Some people might say, not long enough. Have I thanked you for the lover's quarrel that made the front pages for the food program?'

'I can explain that. And I want to make a donation, to make up for it.'

'No explanation is needed, it was all in the papers, your pathetic efforts to get Shelly Lane to take you back. I hear you're going to be arrested for stalking her. I believe the tabloids described it as you going "postal" after having been kicked out of bed.'

'The papers like to exploit things—'

'But we'll take the donation, though I have to tell you that the publicity was wonderful for the program. You missed the best part. She took off her wet dress when she got out of the fountain and threw it aside. We're auctioning it off at the next banquet. You should attend. We can offer you as the booby prize.'

I got down on my hands and knees.

'What are you doing.'

'Making it easier for you to kick me.'

Two mothers coming out of the school building broke into laughter. 'If he's proposing and you don't want him, I'll take him,' one of them said.

'You wouldn't want him. Shelly Lane kicked him out of bed.'

Shrill laughter. 'Oh, God, is that *him*?'

Oh-God-my-ass. I got to my feet and took Elena's hand and led her off, to the jeers of the women. How humiliating.

'Where are you going with my daughter?'

'Elena and I are going to dinner. You can either join us or go home and cry in your milk.'

'How do you know there's not someone waiting for me at home?'

'I had you checked out by a private investigator. He said you are a lonely old maid who subscribes to lonely hearts' magazines and buys vibrators by the dozen.'

I didn't look back over my shoulder. Her telling me she had a husband or significant other would have stabbed me right between the shoulder blades.

73

I took Marni and Elena down to Gladstone's For Fish, a restaurant on the Pacific Coast Highway near where Sunset slid into the ocean. It wasn't one of my favorite spots – too crowded, too noisy – but it had the best location in town – right on the beach. Elena could run around in the sand while Marni and I talked and walked on the beach.

I sipped a bottle of Corona, no lime, no glass, and Marni licked salt on a margarita while we waited for a table and the kid threw sand back into the ocean.

'Great kid,' I said. 'She's beautiful, like her mother.'

'Give me a break, Win, stuff the compliments. You hate kids and you treated her mother like crap.'

'I don't hate kids, I don't know anything about them. I passed over being a kid myself, mostly I went to funerals as the people around me died. And I didn't treat you like crap. You walked out on me without giving me a chance to explain.'

'To explain what a bastard you are? That to squeeze a few more million when you already have a fortune, you supply guns to bloodthirsty criminals to use on innocent people?'

I undid my necktie. 'Here.'

'What's that for?'

'To hang me with. You want to lynch me, you're judge, jury, and executioner, you know everything and don't need any explanations. You walked out, left the country, and never heard my side of it.'

'All right. Explain.'

That shut me up. What was I going to tell her? That I ended up help-

ing Jomba get a load of weapons . . . for Savimbi? That the weapons were
used to keep a civil war going in Angola that was still going hot and heavy
today, without a pretense of a truce? That I had made a fortune in Angola,
digging the country's precious diamonds from the earth and had returned
nothing to it?

'Why don't I just shoot myself,' I said.

'That would be a good start.'

'Marni—'

'Win, it wasn't easy for me to walk away, I had never felt about anyone
like I felt about you. Now I don't want the wounds reopened.'

I nodded at the kid. 'You must have really been hurting bad, but it didn't
take you long to connect with someone and have Elena.'

She was about ready to throw the margarita in my face.

I held up my hands. 'The last woman who threw a drink in my face took
a bath. Please, let's just talk. I know you think I'm an unfeeling bastard, but
you're only half right. I do have feelings. I lied to you in Angola and I
regret it, but you have to give me a break about it. I had my back to the
wall and a gun to my head. Give me five minutes to tell you how Angola
came down. If you still think I'm dirt, you can leave and I won't try to
contact you again.'

I told her my story, from the time I first heard about Bernie's folly to
standing near a landing strip with a war going on. I gave her the truth, the
whole truth . . . and only left out a few details I didn't want her to hear. The
blood feud with João – and having screwed his wife and daughter – were a
couple subjects I censored. When I said we hit blue earth at the mine, I
added, 'And, I'm donating money for a hospital in the region.'

I made a mental note to have my secretary check out Angolan medical
donations with my tax lawyer. I hadn't actually lied. I had used the present
tense which meant I was in the process of doing it, not that it was a done
deal.

I had only one question for her: Was she currently involved with
anyone?

'Many men,' she said. 'Like Shelly Lane, I use and abuse them and kick
them out of bed when I tire of them. I have so much time, being a working single parent, that I go out every night to bars and pick up men.'

'Do you want me to turn around and bend over so you can kick me
some more? Or would you prefer I spread my legs so you can do it where
it hurts?'

She started laughing. That was a good sign, I thought.

During dinner, I complimented Marni on Elena's manners.

'She's a regular little adult,' I said.

'That's the problem with an only child. They spend most of their time talking to adult parents rather than squabbling with siblings and kids their own age.'

'Did her father help raise her?' It was an opening for her to tell me about the man she had become involved with so soon after she stormed out of my life. So far she had told me zero about her own life, except facetiously letting me know that there was no one current in her own life. Even though I hadn't seen her in nearly six years, I felt possessive and jealous that another man had fathered her child.

We had talked quietly, letting little of the conversation float across to where Elena was busy with crayons.

She took a sip of her margarita and gave me an ironic grin. 'Let's just say that he's as big a bastard as you. He didn't do a damn thing except provide the sperm and a little pleasure for himself.'

'Men are pricks,' I said. 'Most of them fuck and run. But the men in my family aren't that way. We have kids and die early.'

'Don't talk that way.'

I took her hand. 'I'm on a roll with the diamond business. I didn't realize how much it was in my blood, how much my father taught me stuck in me. But I really don't know what I'm going to do when I grow up. I want to become an astronaut. Or maybe I'll go to Angola and hand out food packs—'

I frowned at her. 'Why are you laughing.'

74

I went through the door of the offices we had set up on Canon close to the store, snapping orders at the receptionist as I came in. She pointed to a woman standing by the windows.

'You have a visitor.'

Simone turned around. She smiled. It had been three years since she had knocked on my Bel Air hotel room.

'Take a seat,' I told her as I ushered her into my offices. 'There's always a snake in paradise, isn't there?'

'Is that how you think of me? A repulsive reptile?'

'I think of you as a beautiful and dangerous woman, one I'd just as soon keep an ocean between.'

'You give me something not much bigger than an acorn, and I'll be out of your life forever. João had it, you know, before you were even born.'

'He stole it from my father.'

'He has a slightly different version of how the fire diamond came into his possession than you do.'

'He's a liar. He's also responsible for killing Bernie. I don't know how he did it, whether he sent a couple of his Lisbon thugs over to push Bernie out a window, sent you over to finesse Bernie out the window, or simply broke Bernie down so hard financially and emotionally, that Bernie crawled out the window. Whatever the scenario, he was responsible for Bernie's death. Go back and tell João that Bernie is paying him back.'

'Things have changed. João has had a hard time for years. We're not as rich as we used to be. He's had money problems, people won't do business with him, he's paid out millions in Portugal to keep from getting prosecuted. He blames you for his problems.'

'Blame Bernie's ghost. He's the one whispering in my ear.'

'Listen to me, Win, João is sick.'

'That breaks my heart.'

'He's dying.'

'I'm going to start crying.'

'He has nothing left to lose. He's going to kill you.'

'He can try.'

'He will. The only way to save yourself is to give him the diamond. He wants to hold it once more before he dies.'

'Tell him I'll put it in his cold, dead hand – as his soul is being shipped off to burn in hell. Look, let's knock off the bullshit. João will never see the diamond. And my will says it goes to the Smithsonian.' I lied. It occurred to me that I didn't even have a will. I probably needed one.

She stood up. 'I'm sorry it has to be this way.'

'No, you're not. You're sorry I don't roll over and play dead. If you had any human feelings, you'd feel sorry for Bernie.'

'I have enough trouble grieving the living – I don't have time for the dead.' She paused. 'You know Jonny's in town.'

'No, I didn't,' I lied. I'd seen her but not spoken to her.

'I'm surprised she hasn't contacted you. I think half the reason she came to L.A. was because she read you were here. She likes you, you know.'

'I like her, too. She's a great kid. Now, if you're finished . . .'

I took a cheap shot as she opened the door to leave. 'It's too bad you never had time for your daughter. She's a great kid who never had a chance because her father's a crook and her mother's a slut.'

I tensed. It looked like Simone was going to jump over the desk and rip out my throat. Her face turned several shades of purple before she got a grip on herself and walked away with calm deliberation.

As soon as she was gone, I called in my secretary.

'Call a detective agency. I want a bodyguard, twenty-four/seven. Someone with a gun. And someone who has experience using it. I don't want a guy who's going to fold in the clench.'

She gawked at me. 'You want me to ask for a murderer?'

'I want you to ask for an ex-cop or a soldier who's been in combat. For around-the-clock protection, they'll have to line up more than one man.' As she headed for the door I yelled another command. 'And call my lawyer. I need to make a will.'

I thought for a moment and then called Cross. 'You in the market to make some money? Big bucks?'

'Who do I have to kill?'

'João Carmona.'

There was silence on the line for a moment, then Cross grunted. 'Your boyfriend here or did he send over a hit team from Lisbon?'

'I'm not sure, maybe all of the above. For certain, Simone is here. She paid a visit to me, as good as told me that João was going to help me into an early grave and then piss on it. It's no longer about money or even the diamond, this is an old-fashioned blood feud. The only way out of this will be for one of us to die.'

'What are you gonna do? Call the cops?'

'You think the cops could help me?'

Cross gave an explosive laugh.

'My point exactly. I want to fight fire with fire, give João some of his own medicine. There are street gangs in this town that would scare the balls off a gorilla. I was wondering if you had any contacts.'

'Why? 'Cause I'm black? What do you think, you honky asshole, all blacks are into street violence?'

'You're only black on the outside, Cross, inside you're the color of dogshit. I'm asking you because you told me Megan had a cousin who was big in the gangs.'

'Oh, Latino gangs, yeah, those macho bastards will kill you because they don't like the color of your eyes, my people only kill for guns and money. What do you want, a meet?'

'That would be a starter.'

'What's in it for me? A piece of House of Liberté?'

'You think you're worth it?'

'What's your life worth?'

'Let's start with cash, and we'll see where we go from there. I'll pay you twenty-five thousand to set up a meet and hold my hand.'

After I hung up, I thought about Cross. I didn't trust him any more than I could pay him. He backed me up in Angola, but basically he went with the highest bidder. I wasn't going to make him rich again. I couldn't help but wonder what his attitude would be when he found that out.

75

Simone rolled down the window of the limo and lit a cigarette, blowing smoke out, as the limo pulled away from the passenger-loading curb at LAX. João's lungs had become sensitive to smoke. She hated being away from him for too long a period because it was always a shock to come back and see how much he appeared to age during her short absences. He wasn't really aging more when they were apart – it was a trick of her mind. She thought of João as vibrant and strong, even in his wheelchair, but when she saw him after being apart for a week she got a clearer picture. He was old and shriveling. *As I will be someday*, she thought, shuddering at the prospect of growing so old that her body began to self-destruct.

'What's going on with Juana?' he asked.

'I've only seen her briefly. She told me the only reason she even stays in contact with us is to make sure she gets her allowance on time. She's doing more partying than studying. I hired a tutor, but she bribed him with drugs and sex to do her schoolwork for her.'

'Has she been seeing that *bastardo*?'

Simone shrugged. 'I don't think so. When I asked her, she boasted she's sleeping with him. That makes me think that she's probably not telling the truth.'

'If she isn't now, she has been. My daughter spreading her legs for my enemy is just one of the many trespasses I have suffered from the *bastardo*.'

Simone met his eye without flinching. 'He said to tell you that he is paying you back for the murder of his uncle.'

'I should have killed his father forty years ago. I had the opportunity, now I am paying for a moment's hesitation I had when I was young.'

The limo pulled to a stop across the street from a day school in Brentwood.

A few minutes later, Simone and João watched as Elena ran to meet Marni.

'For sure, it's his daughter, you can see the *bastardo* in her face.'

'Yes,' Simone said. 'Yes, it's his child.'

João padded her leg. 'Good, you have done good. How did you find out?'

'From his friend. I found out the woman had a child and checked the birth records. Win is named as the father on the birth certificate.'

'And you don't think he knows?'

'I'm sure he doesn't. I talked to Cross.'

'Is it still for sale?'

'More than ever.'

João laughed. It wasn't a pleasant sound. 'That *bastardo* thinks he's tough, but he is pudding. I'm going to use his little girl to twist his balls.'

'João, I don't like this, she's just a child—'

He slapped her, hitting her hard enough to slam her back against the door. '*Puta*! I am in this mess because of you. Just hope I don't send him your ears, too.'

76

I picked up Cross and we headed east on Interstate 10, toward Palm Springs. Cross had set up a meet with a gangbanger there, Megan's cousin. We were in my Bugatti EB110GT, a two-seater with flip-up doors and 553 horses that went from zero to sixty in less than four seconds.

'Why Palm Springs?' I asked.

'That's where the man lives.'

'He runs a drug operation there?'

'He runs a drug operation everywhere – but he's not out hustling drugs on street corners. Roberto is Columbian, from an old family, good blood-line, no money. He got into the drug business because he likes the same toys you do – expensive cars and women. But he's strictly a manufacturer's rep rather than retail.'

'He sells drugs to gangs?'

'No, he sells drugs by the truckload to distributors. By the time it gets to the street-gang level, it's been through several hands.'

'That much coke ought to be good for about a thousand years in a federal pen if he gets caught.'

'The Robertos of this world never get caught,' Cross said, 'because they never get their hands dirty. When you read about some big bust, even the five-hundred-kilo kind, those people have had no dealings with guys like Roberto. The way drug busts work, the cops catch the small fry and try to get them to roll over on the next level up. They never get to Roberto because he's so far up the food chain, no one getting busted can lay anything on him. Cocaine comes across the border by eighteen-wheeler, airplane, and ship. Once it's here, Roberto's in charge of getting it warehoused and distributed, but he'd never see any of the stuff himself unless it's for personal use. Just think of him as the CEO in charge of American operations for a multibillion-dollar foreign company.' Cross shook his head. 'Maybe I've been in the wrong business all my life.'

'And maybe the life expectancy tables for the Robertos of this world aren't so great.'

'Yours don't look so hot, either.'

We cut off the small talk, each of us lost in our own thoughts. Earlier, I had brought up the subject again of Cross working for me and he bluntly told me to screw off, that he was clipping coupons each month from his investments.

He had changed since Angola. There was more bullshit to him now, more 'front' in the expensive way he dressed, the five-carat diamond on his pinkie, the gold Rolex watch.

Listening to him, I felt uncomfortable for the first time. I realized he lacked confidence, not in physical strength or guts, but in his own self-image. He made the killing he set out to get and blew it. From what Megan had told me, I gathered he made bad investments in stocks and real estate. Now, rather than shrugging it off and asking for a grubstake so he could tackle another fortune, he was hiding behind a façade of being successful.

The house crowned one of the desert hills along Highway 111 on the way to Palm Desert, east of Bob Hope's enormous mushroom-looking mansion. Spanish-style, surrounded by a high, white-washed earthen wall, the place had the look of a fortress as we drove up the narrow, single-lane road.

Once we reached the top, we pulled up to a tall wrought-iron gate with a callbox mounted nearby. Before I could call to announce our arrival, the gate started to open.

'Surveillance cameras,' Cross said. 'They've probably been tracking us since we turned off the highway.'

We pulled into the courtyard where an amiable older man, wearing a straw hat to protect his face from the desert sun, came out to meet us.

'That's fine, leave it there,' he said.

Cross was right about Roberto having a taste for fine cars – parked in the courtyard was a Corvette and a big Ford Expedition. As we passed by the open tailgate of the SUV, I saw scuba diving equipment.

'Good stuff,' I told Cross. 'I used to dive. This stuff is what Navy SEALS use.'

'Even ex-SEALS,' a voice behind me said. The man held out his hand. 'Welcome to *mi casa*, I'm Roberto Nunez.'

'How long were you in the SEALS?' I asked.

'One year. My father made me join. He said I was a worthless womanizing boozer who needed a lesson in life. The SEALS were the toughest thing he could think of. I survived the training but not the discipline. I don't make clandestine landings on beaches anymore, but I keep in practice at my place in Malibu and go down to Cozumel or pop over to the Great Barrier Reef for real dives.'

He talked as we followed him into the house. We were trailed by a man with ten-ply arms who Nunez didn't bother introducing. He didn't have to. He was obviously a bodyguard. He was packing a Baretta 9mm semiautomatic tucked in his belt at the small of his back.

Nunez was about thirty, slender but muscular. He led us into a white living room – white walls, white couches, sand-colored carpeting, and introduced me to his wife, Maribel, a dark-eyed beauty. A five- or six-year-old smaller version of lovely Maribel came running into the room who she introduced as Elena.

'Elena was my mother's name,' I said, 'and the name of my girlfriend's child.' On impulse, I pulled a small black velvet pouch out of my pocket. 'This is for Elena,' I told Maribel. I opened my palm and showed her a small, rough, pink stone.

'All right,' she laughed, 'what is it?'

I took out my loupe. 'If you give me a little light and a piece of white paper, I'll show you.'

'It's quite beautiful,' she said, examining it with the magnifying glass. 'Is it some sort of gem?'

'It's a pink diamond,' I said. 'In the rough.'

'A diamond in the rough.' She laughed again. 'Like Roberto, but he is not pink.'

I liked her. If Roberto hadn't looked like the type who would have killed me for breathing too close to his wife, I would have been sexually aroused. Hell, I was anyway.

'Colored diamonds are rarer and more valuable than most diamonds.' I was going to give the stone to Marni for her Elena, but decided on impulse that I might get myself in good with Roberto by sucking up to his kid.

'But it's so much smaller than this one.'

She showed me a rock on her hand that had to weigh in at over five carats. I didn't like big diamonds on rings for women. A quick glance told me that my much smaller pink, which was a carat, was worth many times more than her chunk. But I had to be careful, there was no doubt that it came from Roberto.

'That's a different kind of diamond,' I said, cautiously, 'very beautiful, it's a white diamond. Much better for an engagement ring than this pink.'

'Tell me the truth,' Roberto said. 'What's the comparative value of the two?'

'Let me look at it more closely.'

Maribel took off the ring and I examined it with the loupe. You don't get a complete picture examining a mounted diamond, but I could see the gem had flaws. I could imagine Roberto going into a jewelry store and slamming beaucoup bucks – twenty-dollar bills that would have sent a narc dog hitting the ceiling – paying several times what the gem was worth. He would not only have paid retail, but probably two or three times what the ring was worth. Jesus H. Christ, I had painted myself into a corner. I couldn't get out of it without lying and I was sure this guy had a built-in bullshit detector. With my back to the wall, I punted and tested the waters with a version of the truth.

'The diamond has good white color, with a little blue, not flawless, but it's okay, it has some minor inclusions.'

'Tell me in dollars and cents,' Roberto said.

'Yours, retail, less than ten thousand. My pink, three or four times as much.'

Nunez spun around to his shadow. 'Go into L.A. and kill the jeweler who sold me that diamond.'

He laughed at my expression. 'Just kidding.'

I wrote my store manager's name on my business card and gave it to Maribel. 'Call Cameron when you're ready. She'll arrange for you to select a cut and setting for the stone. I'd suggest a necklace, hopefully one Elena won't lose in a sandbox. By selecting a personalized cut, Elena will have a diamond that will be unique, like no other one in the world. Just like her.'

Maribel thanked me and excused herself. I could see she was awed by my gift. So was I – but my life was at stake. Besides, I didn't pay retail.

'What are you drinking?' Roberto asked.

'Corona, no glass, no lime,' I said.

Cross ordered the same. We sat on the couch to talk turkey. Roberto put his snakeskin cowboy boots up on the coffee table.

'Tell me what you want from me that is worth so valuable a diamond.'

'The diamond is worthless to me if I don't live to enjoy it.' I gave him a capsule version of the situation with João, sticking mostly to the truth. 'I'm certain he's in town and he wants me dead.'

'Amazing,' Roberto said. 'Lisbon, Africa, and now L.A.; I thought I led an adventurous existence.'

'It's been more nightmare than adventure,' I assured him.

'So, what do you want from me? You want this man killed? You came to the wrong person. I don't kill anyone—' He grinned. 'Except when it's family or personal.'

'I don't want him killed. I understand you deal with a variety of people. I want a name, someone I can contact, to let him know that I have friends who are annoyed at the fact he's planning to kill me.'

'Tell the police.'

'Give me a break.'

'Hire bodyguards.'

'I am. But I want to get a message to João. The kind he understands.'

Roberto shrugged. 'I will ask around, see if there is anyone who can frighten the *cojones* off this dude.' Roberto took a long swig of beer, eyeing me over the bottle as he did. 'It has occurred to me that diamonds might be a good investment. Do they hold their value?'

'They increase in value over time. Like oil, there're market forces that control supply and demand to keep prices stabilized.'

'Perhaps you and I should talk. I have some loose cash that needs to be invested. I think diamonds may be the best way to go.'

'Loose cash' translated into dirty money that needed washing. I had no intention of getting involved in money laundering – that kind of money came with prison stripes on it. But I just nodded and made a listening response.

We got off serious subjects and talked about fast cars and our scuba-diving experiences. After a couple Coronas and small talk, Roberto walked us to my Bugatti and checked it out. Like guys comparing the size of their dicks, I told Roberto my car could beat his car. No more was said about the situation with João. I got into the car and Cross suddenly said, 'Just a second.' He got out and went over to where Roberto was standing. They spoke outside my hearing and I could see Cross write something down.

'Got his phone number,' Cross said. 'I've got a few stones left over from Angola. Maybe I can sell them to him.'

Yeah, and maybe next year I'll go into selling pink elephants. I knew for a fact that Cross had no more Angolan stones. He called them his 'grubstake' when he came back to the States and had been selling them off to me almost from the day he landed. I bought the last one a couple years ago. But Cross had some knowledge of the diamond business and maybe even a few contacts, besides me. My suspicious mind told me that

Cross was getting desperate for money and was thinking in terms of playing with the kind of money that carries prison stripes.

'What'd you think of your meeting with Roberto?' Cross asked.

'I don't know, I have to think about it.' I wasn't sure what to think. I just dropped a stone in his lap that was worth plenty. I hoped he came through for me. He struck me as an honorable guy – as honorable as any international drug dealer could be.

Cross suddenly broke into my thoughts. 'Hey, bubba, if I need some diamonds on credit, you gonna let me have them?'

'Sure. But just remember, pal, that the feds have to be notified about large *cash* transactions . . . so make sure you pay by check when you settle up.' I wasn't going to get involved in money laundering.

'Hey, you know something, dickhead, I'll just take my business elsewhere.'

77

It was Thursday. Marni's housekeeper, Josie, picked up Elena at school. Fifty years old, Josie was a native of Mexico. She had come across the border illegally over three decades ago, brought across by 'coyotes' with twenty others in the back of a closed truck, frightened in the pitch-black sealed interior of the truck, nearly suffocating, and ingraining in her psyche a lifelong fear of the dark that caused her to sleep with a light on.

Her older sister, who came over before Josie, got her a job at subhuman wages working in an L.A. sweatshop that made cheap knockoff sports clothes of major brands. The woman who owned the shop spotted Josie's kind and gentle disposition and began using her to care for her children. Ultimately, she gained a green card and eventually citizenship through an amnesty for illegals. She never had any children of her own and found satisfaction in taking care of other people's children. Like most people of her culture, she was hardworking, honest, and loyal.

She came to work for Marni after a friend of hers who had cared for Elena during the child's first year had to return to Mexico to care for her mother.

Entering the apartment building with Elena, Josie smiled and said hello to Tony, the manager, who was exiting. 'I let the cable people in for you,' Tony said.

'Thank you,' Josie said. She didn't know why cable people needed access to their apartment. Marni hadn't said anything, but Josie was not particularly sophisticated when it came to anything electronic. She hoped that the TV was working – it was time for *Oprah*, her favorite show. Josie's English was still a little rusty. Even after a couple of decades in the country, she lacked that ability to parrot back words some people have, but Oprah wasn't difficult for her to understand, the woman's communications skills transcended mere language.

Two men wearing uniforms identifying themselves as cable TV employees were waiting in the living room when she walked in. They were not working with the television set, but were sitting in the living room drinking beer.

Josie frowned at them. 'Why you here? What wrong with TV?'

'Nothing,' one of them said.

He picked up something from the coffee table. It took a moment for Josie to realize he was pointing a gun at her.

78

I was going over sales figures for my Paris store when I heard a commotion in the other office and my door flew open. Marni came in looking haggard and in shock. I raised up out of my chair as she said, '*They have her.*' She spoke the words quietly, anguished. Her face was pale and drawn. My secretary came in behind her.

'I'm sorry, Win, she——' the secretary started.

'Get out.'

Marni stood in the middle of the room. I came around the desk and to her. Her words still hung in the air. 'What do you mean?' I asked, but for some reason, I knew the answer, I just didn't want to face it.

'*They have her.*'

'What are you talking about?'

'They have our daughter, they have Elena.'

'I – what?'

'You fucking bastard, they've taken her, they want the diamond. *Give it to me!*' She swung at me, wildly, her fists hitting my face and chest. I grabbed her wrists and held her, pulling her to me.

My secretary came running in. 'I've called security.'

'Get out of here!'

Marni sobbed against my chest. My heart was pounding. I spoke calmly, firmly. 'Tell me what happened.'

She sobbed and I shook her by the shoulders. 'Tell me exactly what happened.'

'I got home, Josie was tied up, taped up. She said two men took Elena. They want the fire diamond. They're supposed to call you. They'll send her back in a garbage bag in pieces if you don't give it to them.'

My cell phone rang. I froze for a second, then answered it.

'Listen carefully and don't say a word,' João told me. 'I hear anything in your voice I don't like and I cut off an ear – to start. And I'll keep cutting.'

I kept quiet.

'What?' Marni asked. 'What?'

She tried to take the phone and I brushed away her hand.

'I'm going to give you precise instructions,' João said. 'Pacific Coast Highway, there is a dirt road down to the beach exactly seven-point-seven miles from the last petrol station. Tonight, midnight exactly. Bring the diamond. If you want backup, bring your old friend from Africa. No one else. Tell the police – and you know what I will do.'

He hung up.

'Tell me!'

'It's arranged. I'll make the switch. I'll get Elena back.'

'*You sonofabitch.*'

'Stop, just stop it. I didn't know they'd go after her.' But even as I said the words, I knew that deep down João would figure out a way to hurt me. It had occurred to me that he could try to harm Marni, but I had eliminated the idea because I figured he wouldn't risk it. But I had underestimated him.

She refused a drink and I swallowed down three shots of Jack Daniels. My hands were shaking. *Elena was my daughter*. I had heard the words but there was too much shock for them to have any effect. I should have known it anyway. I was too busy and too stupid to see it.

'We have to call the police,' she said.

I shook my head. 'No, you don't know João, he's dying and he hates me. He wouldn't care if I showed up with the police, he'd kill Elena in front of me.'

'*Oh my God!*'

She started swaying and I pulled her over and let her bury her head against my shoulder as she cried.

It was four o'clock. The meet was set for midnight. I had a phone call to make. Maybe two. One was to Roberto Nunez. I needed some advice from a man who dealt with violence. He would know better than me how I should deal with João. I needed to know what to do. João could have the diamond, but I had a gut feeling he wouldn't be satisfied with just that. What would satisfy him would be to kill me. And maybe Elena because she would be a witness.

What was bothering me also was João saying the only person I could bring along was Cross. It left me between another rock and hard spot. If I took Cross with me, he might double-cross me. And if he was on João's take, he might be waiting with João when I got there.

Marni suddenly looked up at me. 'I saw them in Angola.'

'What do you mean?'

'The Joãos of this world – men capable of murdering or maiming children. He's not bluffing.'

I knew that, but I didn't say anything. I didn't know what to say.

79

João had chosen a lonely spot along Pacific Coast Highway north of Malibu for the swap. He would have a long view of cars approaching from either direction. I thought about his choice for the rendezvous and figured out something real quick. That deserted stretch of road would be to João's advantage by letting him monitor traffic in both directions – but it could also be a trap for him, because it limited his escape route if anything went wrong. João would be a fool to trap himself that way – and he was no fool.

'A boat,' I told Cross, as we drove along the dark highway on our way to the meet.

'Boat?'

'I'm thinking out loud. The spot João chose doesn't make sense.'

'It's deserted, isn't it?'

'Yeah, but there's only one escape route if João needs it – by water. Listen, Lisbon isn't just on the sea, the whole country borders it. It was once a great sea power, that's how they got Brazil and colonies around the world. Portuguese blood is half saltwater. João chose that spot because he can drive there – but as Bernie used to say, I'll bet a dollar to donuts that he plans to leave by boat. He just needs a boat waiting a hundred yards offshore and a dinghy to take him out.'

I had agonized whether to bring Cross along, whether he was friend or foe, and finally decided I had better take him. The fact that João had expressly said I could bring him had obviously sent my paranoia screaming. Why had João said it? To encourage me to bring him? Or knowing that it would make me suspicious of Cross so that I wouldn't have him backing me up?

I was unarmed, I didn't see what good a gun would do me, João wouldn't be alone. Cross was packing a 9mm semiautomatic pistol. I didn't encourage or discourage him from bringing a gun, but I didn't think it would help, either. Like I said, João was no fool.

I couldn't keep Marni out of the loop. I tried, but she wasn't buying it. Hell, she showed more courage in Angola than I had in a lifetime of racing cars and boats. Finally, I agreed she'd stand by in Malibu. If I didn't call her ten minutes after twelve and let her know I had Elena, she'd call 911 and at least get sheriff's deputies out. I figured that ten minutes ought to give João enough time to go through with the deal – or finish me off.

I was scared, for myself, for my daughter. *My daughter.* The words still had a strange ring to it. I tried to imagine Elena in my mind, to see myself in her features, but I could only see Marni because I couldn't imagine what I looked like. I never really planned on having kids. Too busy, I would have said, but maybe I was really too frightened. I experienced so much death so early I didn't want to expose a kid to it.

'Jesus Christ, slow down.'

I had been taking the narrow coast highway at top speed without thinking. I hit the brakes. João said twelve o'clock and he wouldn't want me showing up a minute earlier.

As we neared the rendezvous, the motion-picture camera in my mind went on as my long-term memory kicked in big time. I saw my mother lying cold and dead, my father watching carefully as I marked a diamond where it should be cut, eating a hamburger after school at a table with Uncle Bernie at the Diamond Club while Bernie kibitzed with his pals, playing one-upmanship in regaling about the big deals they handled that day, making love with Marni in Cape Town. Maybe it's not just drowning people who see their whole lives pass before their eyes – or maybe I was drowning and didn't know it.

There was nothing out on the highway, no cars, no lights. I would never have spotted the turnoff, but as I approached the spot, a man on the shoulder of the road waved me toward the dirt road with a flashlight. As I slowed to make the turn, the guy disappeared into the rocks and brush.

We were no more than a couple hundred feet from the water. There was a full moon and I could see something offshore, a boat with its running lights off. João's escape route. I should have told Marni to notify the Coast Guard. It was too late to make the call, I would be seen by João's men.

Sonofabitch.

I pulled the car to a stop ten feet off the highway and turned off the engine.

'Why you parking out here?' Cross asked.

'I wasn't told where to park, this is as good as any.' I parked my car so it would be seen if police patrol cars came flying down the highway.

'Vanity and greed,' I said, opening my car door.

'What?'

'That's what it's all about. It's a killer combination.' I felt the Heart of the World in the pouch in my breast pocket. 'What a fucking business. I should have gone into shoes.'

I subtly dropped my car key under the carriage of the car as I got out. I wanted to make it hard on João to have the car moved if I wasn't the one behind the wheel.

We walked toward the shore, our steps crunching on rock and sand, the only sound in the night waves slopping onto the beach. It was a warm night, little wind, calm seas, perfect for a moonlight sail. I almost laughed at the thought.

We moved around a mound of large boulders and saw João's limo first. As we slowly walked up, neither of us in a hurry, the man who had signaled us with the flashlight came out of the boulders behind us. He had a gun in his hand now.

'Keep moving,' he said in Portuguese. He was a knockoff of the thugs that tried for me in Paris. He might even have been one of them, for all I knew.

João was in his wheelchair, a blanket on his lap. An aluminum walker with big feet stood by the wheelchair. A large rubber dinghy was bellied on the beach. No doubt João meant to grab the walker and make a fast getaway to the dinghy. The driver's window was down. One of João's thugs stared impassively at me from the driver's seat. The tinted rear passenger window to the limo was also down and Simone watched me through it as I approached. She got out when I stopped about ten feet from João.

'Where's Elena?' I asked Simone.

'Out of harm's way. Jonny's taking her to Marni's, she should be there about now.'

'Jonny's in on this shit?'

'She knows nothing, she thinks she's doing a favor for you and Marni.'

'You fucking bastard,' João said.

'An amateur compared to a prick like you. I never made war on a kid.'

'I'd have cut the little *puta* up and had the pieces for you in a paper bag if my wife had not stolen her away from me.'

'He's gone *luoco*,' Simone said. The side of her face was blackened by a large bruise. 'You don't hurt children.'

'Give me the Heart,' João said.

I tossed him the pouch. He shook the diamond out of the pouch and held it in his hand. '*Sim, sim,* my baby has come back.' He looked up, nodding at the man behind us. 'Kill him.'

A gun exploded in my ear and blood splattered the side of my face. I staggered. Cross fell to the ground. I gaped down at him. The back of his head was blown off.

I turned my gape to João and he smiled. 'Repayment for Angola. I saved you for last because I am going to kill you slowly and painfully, slicing pieces off of you one by one.'

An explosion erupted off the coast. The boat João relied on for his escape blew up in a savage, fiery burst. It was João's turn to gape.

'Kill him!' he screamed.

As the gunman who had killed Cross turned to me, a burst of gunfire from the shoreline hit him, punching him, sending him backward. João pulled a gun out from under the blanket on his lap and raised it at me when Simone suddenly reached around from behind him and sliced his throat with a knife.

I stood dazed in the clearing as Simone jumped into the back of the limo and the car roared off, almost hitting me.

Roberto Nunez came walking in from the beach. He wore his SEALS wetsuit and carried an automatic weapon. He saluted me with the rifle.

'Not a bad night's work, eh, *amigo*? Just like the movies.'

When I called Roberto earlier and told him João had taken Elena, he told me he would come personally rather than give me a contact name. I heard the roar of cars coming from the road.

'My *compadres*,' Roberto said. 'We'll give you a ride.'

My cellular phone went off. It was Marni.

'Josie called. She says she has Elena. Are you all right?' Marni asked.

'Ask me after I finish shaking.'

80

Traveling with Marni and Elena put a crimp in my style. We took a flight to New York, after the wedding, and I had to sneak looks at the buxom flight attendant.

Coming into the passenger reception area at JFK was like déjà vu from the time Marni and I landed in Lisbon years ago.

There she was, waving a handkerchief with my name scribbled in lipstick on it.

'I don't believe it,' Marni said. 'The police of two continents should be looking for her.'

Marni didn't know I told the police I couldn't identify the woman who sliced João's throat.

'Don't go too far,' I told Marni. I was holding onto Elena's hand and I turned her over to Marni.

'Thanks,' I told Simone, as Marni and Elena moved away out of earshot.

'If it's any consolation, I didn't do it for you. João was turning crazy, I'm sure he would have ended up killing me, probably Jonny, too.' She shrugged. 'I honestly loved him once, but when a dog turns rabid, you have to put it down.'

Jesus, I hope I never foamed at the mouth in front of her.

She handed me a pouch. 'I came back to give you this.'

I squeezed the pouch and felt the Heart of the World.

'Why?'

'I've had a change of heart. I'm going into a convent, to become a nun.' She laughed at the look on my face.

'You're shitting me.' I didn't believe it for one minute.

'Of course. I tried to sell the damn thing, but no one would give me anything near what it was worth. The best offer I got was five million and I figured you'd give me that for a finder's fee. Saving your life is gratis.'

I shook my head. 'You are still a first-class bitch.' But my heart pounded and my palms sweated as I held the diamond. Vanity and greed – and I had a world-class dose of it in my hand.

'And you are a bastard. If your pretty new wife wasn't looking, you'd sneak me into the nearest closet and fuck me. You're never going to go to heaven, Win. Neither of us will. I'm not even sure the devil would want us.'

When I rejoined Marni, I reminded her that Simone had saved Elena's life.

'Sure, she rescued Elena, but threw her off a cliff first. Did she give you the fire diamond?'

'She gave me the fire diamond.'

'Why?'

'She got religious. She's going into a convent.'

'Bullshit.' She held out her hand. 'Give it to me.'

'Give you what?'

'Give me the diamond. It belongs in a museum, one that will pay plenty for it. Do you realize how much good we can do in Angola with the money? We can build a hospital or school or—'

I swept Elena into my arms and started walking. Marni had to do double-time to keep up. When she demanded the diamond, I felt like someone had squeezed my heart.

'Don't you want to do good in this world?' Marni asked.

'Yeah, for the three of us.'

'That diamond could cure so much misery—'

'What diamond?'

'You are a selfish bastard.'

'And you're going to a convent.'

Yeah, life's a bitch, but it's worth living when you have someone you love and who loves you in return. I knew exactly what I was going to do with the Heart of the World. It was going to my wife. She was a flawless gem and should only wear the most valuable jewel on Earth.